Robin Lee Hatcher

"Break out the tissues. I loved *The Forgiving Hour* and so will you. Robin Lee Hatcher shows God's grace and mercy in bringing healing into the most painful of circumstances. This book cuts through the darkness of betrayal and brings in the healing light of Jesus Christ."

FRANCINE RIVERS

BESTSELLING AUTHOR OF *REDEEMING LOVE* AND *LEOTA'S GARDEN*

"*Whispers from Yesterday* moved me to tears, again and again.... This remarkable love story glows with the light of truth and grace. Another winner from Robin Lee Hatcher. I loved it!"

LIZ CURTIS HIGGS

BESTSELLING AUTHOR OF *BOOKENDS* AND *BAD GIRLS OF THE BIBLE*

"[In *The Forgiving Hour*] Hatcher uses her well-honed skills to craft a compelling story of betrayal and forgiveness that will leave her readers both emotionally drained and spiritually satisfied."

LIBRARY JOURNAL

Angela Elwell Hunt

"[*The Immortal*] is a tale well-told by a talent that just keeps getting better. Rich in geographic and cultural detail, *The Immortal* is a powerful story of love, faith, destiny, and awakening spirituality."

JACK CAVANAUGH, NOVELIST

"*The Immortal* is wonderful!... Angela Hunt has given us the rare treat of a book that pleases and fascinates as it stretches our minds and enlarges our hearts."

GAYLE ROPER

AUTHOR OF *SPRING RAIN* AND *THE DECISION*

"Angela Hunt is brilliant, and her pen is sharper and more effective than any scalpel I've used. *The Immortal* is provocative and informative, with a theme that lives on long after the book is closed. This novel gets two thumbs up!"

Deborah Bedford

"[*A Child's Promise*] Deborah Bedford's characters shine like newly minted coins."

"[*Timberline*] The hope in Bedford's writing beckons like the sun over the Western mountains."

"[*Chickadee*] Well-crafted, powerful drama that is guaranteed to touch your heart...moving and eloquent."

The Story Jar

Robin Lee
HATCHER

Angela E.
HUNT

Deborah
BEDFORD

Multnomah®Publishers *Sisters, Oregon*

THE STORY JAR

© 2001 by Multnomah Publishers, Inc.
Published by Multnomah Publishers, Inc.

"The Hair Ribbons" © 2001 by Deborah Bedford

"Heart Rings" © 2001 by Robin Lee Hatcher
"Heart Rings" published in association with the literary agency of
Natasha Kern Agency, P. O. 2908, Portland, Oregon 97208

"The Yellow Sock" © 2001 by Angela Hunt Communications, Inc.

International Standard Book Number: 1-57673-699-7

Cover artwork by Gwen Babbitt

All Scripture quotations in "The Hair Ribbons" are taken from
The Holy Bible, New International Version (NIV) © 1973, 1984 by International Bible Society, used by permission of Zondervan Publishing House.
All Scripture quotations in "Heart Rings" are from, *New American Standard Bible* (NASB) © 1960, 1977, 1995 by the Lockman Foundation.
All Scripture quotations in "The Yellow Sock" are taken from *The Holy Bible,* New Living Translation (NLT) © 1996. Used by permission of Tyndale House Publishers, Inc. All rights reserved.

Multnomah is a trademark of Multnomah Publishers, Inc., and is registered at the U.S. Patent and Trademark office. The colophon is a trademark of Multnomah Publishers, Inc.

Printed in the United States of America

For information:
Multnomah Publishers, Inc.•Post Office Box 1720•Sisters, Oregon 97759
Library of Congress Cataloging–in–Publication Data
Bedford, Debbi.
  The story jar / by Deborah Bedford, Robin Lee Hatcher, Angela Elwell Hunt.   p.cm.
  Contents: The hair ribbons / Deborah Bedford—Heart rings / Robin Lee Hatcher—The yellow sock / Angela Elwell Hunt.   ISBN 1-57673-699-7   1. Mothers—Fiction. 2. Mother and child—Fiction. 3. Domestic fiction, American. 4. Christian fiction, American. 5. American fiction—Women authors. I. Hatcher, Robin Lee. II. Hunt, Angela Elwell, 1957– III. Title
PS648.M59 B43 2001   813'.0108'09051—dc21   00–01255

01 02 03 04 05—10 9 8 7 6 5 4 3 2 1 0

In memory of Katie Dunlap, beloved sister in Christ,
who danced so well before the Lord.
To my daughter, Avery Elizabeth.
To my mother, Tommie Catherine Pigg,
who reminds me as often as we talk what a gift it is to have a
mother who, above all things, loves the Father.

"Blessed are the pure in heart for they will see God."
Matthew 5:8
Deborah Bedford

To Jennifer Lee,
who taught me so much about looking
beneath the surface and into the heart.
Thanks for the creative license,
my beautiful sunshine girl.
Love, Mom

Robin Lee Hatcher

For Taryn and Tyler, who are and always will be my
"trees of life…."
Mom

Angela Hunt

With special thanks to Dr. Lisa Mallett, D.V.M., Seminole, Florida
Angela Hunt

Contents

INTRODUCTION

The Story behind the Story Jar

In September 1998, I received a story jar as a thank-you gift after speaking at a writers' conference in Nebraska. The small mason jar, the lid covered with a pretty handkerchief, was filled with many odds and ends—a Gerber baby spoon, an empty thread spindle, a colorful pen, several buttons, a tiny American flag, an earring, and more.

The idea behind this gift was a simple one. When a writer can't think of anything to write, she stares at one of the objects in the jar and lets her imagination play. Who owned that item? How old was she? What sort of person was she? What did the object represent in her life?

Writers love to play the "what if" game. It's how most stories come into being. Something piques their interest; they start asking questions, and a book is born.

A week after receiving my story jar, I attended a retreat with several writer friends of mine, Deborah Bedford included. On the flight home, I told Deborah about the jar. The next thing you know (after all, what better thing is there for writers to do on a plane than play "what if"?), we had begun brainstorming what would ultimately become the book you now hold, *The Story Jar.* We decided very quickly that we wanted this to be a book that celebrates motherhood in all its many facets, that encourages mothers, that recognizes how much they should be loved and honored and how much they've given us all.

Deborah and I were delighted when Angela Hunt agreed to write one of the novellas and were thrilled when Multnomah wanted to publish the book. When they asked about enhancing the book with true-life tributes to real mothers, we thought it was a great idea. And we were honored when so many people responded to our request for these tributes. What delight we've all found in remembering how precious our mothers are and all God has given us through them!

We hope you enjoy reading this book as much as we enjoyed creating it. We hope *The Story Jar* will touch and bless mothers of all ages and circumstances, reminding them what an amazing calling they've received, and letting them know how very much they are loved and appreciated.

For all of you who are mothers or mothers at heart, thank you! Thank for you for the part you've played in the lives of your children. May you find joy and blessings in these stories—and in the life work to which the Master has called you.

Robin Lee Hatcher

The Story Jar

The Story Jar

*B*eth Williams paused in the vestibule, ran her hand over the small wooden table against the wall, then crinkled her nose. The woman who'd called her had promised the job would be easy, no more than half a day's work. But a solid line of dust marked Beth's palm and fingertips, and the interior of the church probably wasn't in much better shape.

"'Just a light sprucing up for the new pastor,'" Beth mimicked, dropping her pail of supplies next to the table. "'Just a few hours' work. After all, how dirty can a church be?'"

Mrs. Vinci, chairman of the ladies' auxiliary, obviously hadn't spent much time cleaning her church. Beth regularly cleaned the Baptist facility on Main Street and the Methodist place on Fourth, and she knew how bubble gum tended to sprout from the underside of church pews. She knew that teenagers tended to hide their angst-filled notes among the pages of hymnals, and that every book in the back six rows would have to be lifted, dusted, and fanned to remove extracurricular reading material that might offend the sensibilities of a future worshiper.

Sighing, she pulled a clean dust cloth and a can of furniture polish from her pail. Better to start at the rear of the building and work forward, saving the easy work for last. Folks who sat up front tended to mind their manners more than people in the back—they were neater, at any rate.

She pushed through the double swinging doors and took in the sanctuary with one glance. This little church was brighter than most, with ivory-colored pews instead of the traditional dense mahogany. Sunlight streamed through wide windows, glinting off swirling dust motes in the slanted light. The faint scent of carnations hung in the air.

Up front, Beth noticed, an organ and piano faced off from opposites of a platform crowned by a small lectern that leaned slightly to the right. She felt one corner of her mouth lift in a wry smile. Someone here—either the pastor or his people—appreciated simplicity. There were no ornate carvings or wall hangings, no carved seats or tables, no elevated pulpit. Just two worn wing chairs on the platform and a leaning tower of preaching.

She shrugged. All the better; simple things were easier to dust.

She began at the back, pulling folded bulletins from hymnals and tucking them into the plastic garbage bag hanging from her belt. She hummed as she ran her dust cloth over the pews, thinking about the last time she'd taken her boys to church. They'd been small then, barely six and eight, but Tommy had pulled another kid's hair in the Sunday school class. When the teacher couldn't wait to tell Beth, she decided her kids didn't need scoldings on Sunday, too. She could barely manage to keep up with them Monday through Saturday, so if a Sunday school teacher couldn't make them mind, she'd just keep them at home.

She bent forward to pick up a forgotten card from a funeral service. She frowned as she read the date. Just yesterday. No wonder the place smelled like flowers.

A door opened behind her, and Beth glanced up to see a petite, white-haired lady enter the sanctuary. She came forward with a confident tread and nodded when she caught Beth's eye.

"Don't mind me," the woman said, gesturing toward the front. "I'm just going to sit a while, if you don't mind."

Beth nodded, though she felt a little foolish doing so. She certainly had no authority here; she didn't even attend this church. She'd have to clean around the woman when she reached the front, but that was certainly no big deal.

The lady slipped into the second pew and sat next to the aisle, her gaze lifting toward the simple pulpit. Beth caught herself glancing at the lectern, too, half expecting someone to miraculously appear behind it. What was the woman doing? Was she senile?

For twenty minutes Beth worked, and all that time the little lady sat without making a sound, her eyes fixed upon the platform, her mouth curved in a sweet smile. Finally, as Beth entered the row immediately behind the woman, she dared to speak: "Are you all right?"

The lady shook her head slightly, then threw Beth a guilty smile. "I'm fine. I was just…visiting. My husband was the pastor here, you see, until the Lord called him home."

Beth lowered her gaze. "I'm sorry."

The lady smiled again. "Don't be. John was eager for heaven, though I know he regretted leaving this church. And I know he regretted leaving...me."

The last word came out in a whisper. Beth strained to hear—and then she put the pieces together. After twelve years of faithful service at this church, yesterday Reverend John Halley had been memorialized and buried.

She looked at the woman. "You must be Mrs. Halley."

The woman inclined her head. "I am."

"I'm Beth. Beth Williams."

Suddenly at a loss for words, Beth sprayed the back of the pew with polish. What was she supposed to say next? She'd already used "I'm sorry." Did pastors and their wives have some sort of special arrangement in case one went to heaven before the other? Maybe pastors' wives filled their husbands' positions after they passed on, sort of like senators' wives often filled their husbands' seats until the next election. If so...should she be congratulating this lady?

She swiped at the wet spot with her dust cloth, her charm bracelet jingling in the silence. "What will you do now?" She risked a glance at the older woman. "Keep working in this church?"

Mrs. Halley turned, easing into a smile. "Heavens, no. That wouldn't be fair to the new pastor. People would feel torn if I stayed, so it's best I move on. That's why I'm sitting here—just soaking it all in before I go."

Beth moved a step to the right and sprayed again. "Where are you going?"

The lady's mouth curled in a one-sided smile. "Florida. Where else?"

Beth laughed softly and continued her polishing. "I have a grandmother in Florida. Lives in a condo in St. Petersburg. Eighty-nine and she still drives a car, though I hear she did pull out of the garage last year with the door still down."

Mrs. Halley chuckled. "I doubt I'll be doing much driving. I'll be staying with my daughter, and her kids are old enough to drive. I'm hoping they'll think it's cool to taxi grandma around."

Beth lifted a brow, but didn't respond. Her own boys, now seventeen and nineteen, would rather undergo oral surgery than drive an older person anywhere. They'd stopped wanting to be seen with her when they hit thirteen, and now she practically had to make an appointment to speak with them. They came and went at all hours, despite her fervent pleas for them to be home by midnight, and some of the young people they were hanging with weren't what she'd call bright-eyed examples of American youth....

Stuffing her dust cloth into her jeans pocket, Beth moved up to the platform. She'd come back to do the first two pews after Mrs. Halley left. It didn't seem respectful to dust around the lady, and despite that gentle smile, any woman with her husband just one day in the grave couldn't feel much like conversation.

She snorted softly as she climbed the two carpeted steps. Her own husband had been gone fifteen years, and only God knew where he was now. Probably New York or

California, some populated place where he could hide in a crowd and spin Cinderella talk to some unsuspecting woman who'd swallow his lies without a second thought…just like she had.

Kneeling, she brushed the padded seat of the wing chair with a whisk broom, then turned the cushion over and noticed that the fabric had faded. The regular church custodian obviously hadn't thought to turn the cushion on a regular basis.

"My, would you look at that."

Beth turned to see Mrs. Halley standing just before the platform, her eyes wide. "I never thought those chairs would fade."

"All fabrics fade, even if there's just a little sunlight in the room," Beth answered, shrugging. "It's only a matter of time."

The woman's smile held a hint of apology. "I should have seen to the chairs. They were new when we first came to this church, and I should have taken better care of them."

"Not your job," Beth said, running her whisk broom beneath the chair. "Whoever usually cleans this place should have—"

"Cleaning was my job." Mrs. Halley's brows flickered a little as her gaze ran over the furnishings of the platform. "John preached; I cleaned and taught Sunday school. We're a small church, you see."

Beth slowed her movements as she struggled to imagine this delicate, genteel woman scrubbing the foyer tile on her hands and knees. She didn't look strong.

"It's a big job for one person," Beth offered. "Most people don't realize how long it can take to clean a big space like this. You have to check the walls for fingerprints, vacuum, and clean out all those hymnals—"

"Those teenagers," Mrs. Halley interrupted, laughing. "They always wondered how I kept up with their little soap operas. I always knew who liked whom."

"I did find some interesting reading." Beth leaned forward to give the area under the chair one final sweep, then felt her broom encounter an object.

"What's this?" She squinted through the shadows. "There's something under this chair."

"Under the chair?" Mrs. Halley's voice rang with puzzlement. "Why, I can't imagine—"

"Just a minute." Lying flat on her stomach, Beth reached forward and felt the coolness of glass and metal. A moment later she pulled out a gallon-sized mason jar, its lid rusty with age.

"Oh!" Mrs. Halley's hand flew to her lips. "I thought we had lost it."

Beth sat up and pulled the jar into the light. Through the glass she glimpsed an odd assortment of objects—a length of blue ribbon, a silver earring, a tiny hospital identification bracelet, a Polaroid snapshot, a yellow sock that would only fit a baby or a doll. Slowly she turned the jar, the contents shifting and clinking against the glass. If this was some kind of religious object, she couldn't imagine how it was used.

She looked at the pastor's wife. Mrs. Halley was staring at the jar as if it contained a miracle.

"What is it?" Beth asked.

"The story jar." On wavering legs, Mrs. Halley climbed the steps, then sank into the wing chair and reached out for the jar. Beth gave it to her, then crossed her arms over her bent knees as the older woman turned the jar and smiled at the objects within.

"It's John's story jar," she whispered, setting the container on her lap. "Every year, beginning when we were first married, he would have the mothers of the church come forward on Mother's Day. Instead of honoring them with flowers and such, he asked them to honor God with some little memento, some small token of gratitude. As each woman placed her special item into the jar, she shared the story behind it with the congregation. Then, together with each mother, the body of Christ rejoiced... and sometimes sorrowed. But we all felt the power of the shared story. Every year, we could look at the story jar and see the evidence of God's hand at work in our lives."

Tilting her head, Beth studied the jar, now seeing other items—a theater ticket stub, a smooth pebble, a set of silver keys upon a simple chain.

"All these things—" Beth gestured toward the jar— "came from people in this church?"

"Not all." Mrs. Halley's voice had gone remote with memory. "Some came from churches we pastored years ago. Everywhere we went, we took the story jar with us because we wanted people to know that God is still working miracles in His people's lives. Not all the stories of His works are found in the Bible. Some are found—" her hand twisted the rusty lid—"in here."

And then, as Beth watched, the woman's frail hand reached into the jar and pulled out a winding length of blue ribbon.

"This belonged to Heidi McKinnis," she said, draping the silken strand over her uplifted hand. Beth could see where the lustrous decoration had frayed at the edges and had wrinkled from its many times of being tied into someone's hair.

"Heidi and her family were traveling through, on their way to a conference where Heidi's mother was a featured speaker. She said she was so excited about the warm weather after living in all that snow! It was only a couple of years ago, I believe, and summer had come early that year. I know it's sometimes hard for a teenager to stand up and tell how a mother has influenced her faith. It took a long time for her to gather her courage to bring this to the altar. It was so hot the walls were sweating. But nobody was thinking about the weather by the time that young girl finished telling her story."

"What was it?" Beth couldn't stop the question. She hugged her knees to her chest and managed a nonchalant laugh. "I'm the mother of two teenage boys, you see, and—well, I could use a little encouragement these days."

Mrs. Halley smiled, her blue eyes shimmering with light from the wide windows. "It all began," she said, running the satin strand between her fingers, "with the annual Christmas production of the Nutcracker...."

The Hair Ribbons

Deborah Bedford

Prologue

September 1964

Theia Harkin hadn't gotten a wink of sleep all night. She'd tossed and turned so much that the covers had wound themselves around and around her legs until she felt like she was a sea creature in a shell.

She lay in bed and pretended she was a butterfly, wrapped in a cocoon, in desperate need of breaking out.

She stared at the three-quarter moon, which beamed in through her window, and pretended she could see the man there smiling and frowning, smiling and frowning, moving his face.

Tomorrow, when the sun came up, maybe she'd be too old for pretending anymore.

When morning came, her mother shook her shoulder. "Theia." She said her name soft and melodic, like a song. "Time to wake up."

Theia sat up so fast she got dizzy. She swung her feet to the floor. She could smell bacon frying. Her mother sat beside her, wearing her red polka-dot apron and wielding a spatula, which meant pancakes.

Mother and daughter gave each other a little sideways hug.

"Ready for your first day of first grade?"

Theia nodded. "Yep."

"Breakfast is almost ready. Come downstairs in ten minutes. I've made something that's just right for sending you off into the world."

Theia didn't want to get dressed too early; she didn't want to get syrup on her new clothes. Her new dress from Lester's waited on a hanger at the front of her closet. Two new Mary Jane shoes sat buckle-to-buckle on the floor beside the bureau, one white bobby sock rolled up inside each toe.

She padded barefoot down the hallway, brushed her hair in the mirror, washed her face, and donned her pink quilted robe. Downstairs, after she slid into her place at the kitchen table, her mother set before her a feast of bacon, a tower of pancakes, and a glass of orange juice as tall and beaming as the sun.

Her mother switched on the AM radio beside the sink as she washed up the dishes. Petula Clark came on singing "Downtown!" Theia giggled as her mother sang right along beside Petula, spreading sudsy circles in rhythm with a sponge. Once the song had ended, the disc jockey announced, "Played that on purpose this morning for all you kids out there who are getting up and getting ready! Moms, rest assured that the buses are running on schedule. And remember, kids, you can always tell your parents that you are sick and climb *right back in bed.*"

The bad feeling started right then in the pit of Theia's belly. She couldn't eat anymore. She swigged some of the orange juice, then carried the plate, with most of the bacon and pancakes still on it, to the counter.

"You didn't eat very much."

"I'm not hungry."

"You'd better go get ready. Bus will be here in twenty minutes."

Theia padded to the bathroom, stood on the toilet beside her father, and brushed her teeth. She loved looking at their faces together in the mirror.

"Better hurry up," her daddy said, giving Theia a love pat on the small of her back. "Bus will be here in fifteen minutes."

She pulled on her socks and carefully turned the tops down, buckled her shoes, and checked her reflection again. She decided to braid her hair; it made her look more grown up. Her mother handed her a brown paper sack, and she peeked inside. It contained a cheese sandwich, an apple, a package of chocolate Hostess cupcakes, and milk money.

"Thanks, Mama."

"Can you see the road? Is the bus here yet?"

"Nope. Not yet."

"You got everything in your satchel? You've got your new ruler and your scissors? The paste? The box of crayons?"

"I've got everything."

"Well, that's it then. Nothing to do but wait."

The awful feeling grew bigger and bigger in the pit of Theia's stomach. She felt like something was growling down there, whispering frightening things. *What if I have to sit by Larry Wells? What if I get on the wrong bus coming home? What if my new teacher doesn't like me?* Finally, she admitted the truth out loud.

"Mama, I'm scared."

"You are?"

"Yes."

Her mother winked at her as if she knew the answer to some secret. "I'll tell you what." Mama went to pull her sewing box from behind the old tattered easy chair. She flipped open the cover, rummaged through pin cushions and an assortment of thimbles and a jumble of threads. "Ah, here it is!" She pulled out a curl of blue, satin ribbon. Next came a pair of pinking shears, and Mama snipped off two perfectly matching lengths.

Theia wrinkled her nose. "What's that?"

"You just wait and see. Come here."

Theia stepped dutifully across the room and stood still while Mama tied a ribbon on first one braid, and then the other.

Mama straightened each bow with a flourish. "From now on, these are your magic hair ribbons. Whenever you feel afraid of something, we'll tie them into your hair. Every time you've got these on, let them remind you that I am praying for you. That my heart is right beside you. That God is right beside you. And when God's right beside you, you never have to worry about a thing."

"Look, Mama! Here comes the bus. I gotta go."

"Okay. You go. Have a good day. Be careful crossing the street!"

"I will. I promise."

"Love you!"

Theia climbed on the bus, and she didn't have to sit by Larry Wells. She got a seat beside Barbie Middlebrook and Cindy Peterson instead. The whole time, they compared tissue boxes and names of crayon colors and how the handles on left-handed scissors were different from the handles on right-handed scissors.

When the bus driver let them off at Colter Elementary, Theia heard a car honk. She turned around. There was Mama's beige Chevrolet Impala. She'd followed the bus all the way to school.

Theia waved.

Mama waved back.

Theia walked through the glass front doors of Colter School thinking she'd never have to be afraid of anything again.

One

Thirty-five Years Later

*I*n the basement of the Pink Garter Plaza, the day finally arrived—as it arrived every year—for the Nutcracker rehearsals to begin.

Party-scene dancers and clowns crowded into dressing rooms, giggling and jamming on ballet slippers that had grown two sizes tight over the summer. Angels and mice played boisterous tag, weaving in and out among everyone's legs, around the furniture, under the rest room doors. Little girls all, with their hair finger-combed into haphazard buns, wearing tights with knees that hadn't come quite as clean as they ought, running amok the way little girls run in every hallway in every dance studio in every town.

Behind them came their mothers, lugging younger siblings, toting coats and backpacks, handing off crumpled lunch bags that smelled of bologna and greasy potato chips and sharp cheese.

"Angels in studio one."

"Pick up a schedule on your way out."

"Mice over here."

Nobody could hear over the music, shouts, laughter, and

voices in every key. Mothers chattered and waved hello to friends. They dodged one another and hugged in the hallway. Several stopped to watch their daughters warm up through the one-way mirror.

"We need volunteers!" Mary Levy, a dance teacher, dangled a tape measure in the air. "This may be the only time we have them together in one place. Can somebody take measurements? We've got to see if the ears are going to fit."

A small group of mothers got the tape and went about measuring heads. They jotted numbers, recounting as they did so the joys and hassles of other dance performances in other years. But after the hoopla had died down, after the confusion had ended and the dancing had begun, only one mother was left waiting outside the one-way mirror. Only one mother stood alone, savoring her daughter's every glissade, every pirouette and plié, watching as if she couldn't stand to take her eyes away.

It wasn't a difficult dance, this dance of the angels. Theia Harkin McKinnis knew each of the delicate, careful movements by heart. Heidi, her daughter, had danced the role of angel last year. And the year before. And the year before that.

A door opened across the way, and out came Julie Stevens, the Nutcracker director of performance. "Sorry to keep you waiting. I've been on the telephone. You know what it's like when you get stuck talking."

Muted from behind the glass, Tchaikovsky's music swelled to its elegant climax before it ebbed away and began again. "Oh no. I'm not worried about the time." Theia checked the clock above the studio door.

"Come in my office. We'll talk."

Theia took a seat inside. She folded her arms across her chest as if she needed to protect herself from something. She realized at that moment exactly why she'd come. In this one place, she needed to regain control.

"I'm here to talk about Heidi's dancing."

"Her dancing in the Nutcracker? She's been cast in the role of an angel."

"She's danced as an angel for three years."

"Do you see that as a problem?"

In this small town, in another week it would be impossible for anybody not to have heard about Theia's cancer.

"Of course there is time," Dr. Sugden had told her in his office when he'd given them the results of the biopsy. "You have plenty of time to seek out a second opinion, if you'd like. I could even recommend somebody. You have plenty of time to educate your-self. You have plenty of time to develop a survival plan."

Even in the dance studio, Theia had to fight to keep the panic out of her voice, just thinking about it. *A survival plan.* "Heidi wants to dance something different this year. She wants to do something more difficult, something that shows she's growing up."

The dance director picked up a roll of breath mints and ran her fingernail around one mint, popping it loose before she peeled the foil. "Surely you realize that we can't jostle everyone around once the girls have been cast."

"I know it might be difficult, but—"

"We can't give every child the part that she dreams of, Mrs. McKinnis. If we did that, we'd have thirty girls dancing the part of the Sugar Plum Fairy and thirty more dancing the role of Marie. Heidi is perfect as our lead angel. Heidi *looks* like an angel."

"She's the oldest one, in the easiest dance."

"She knows the part so well that the younger girls can follow her. That's why we always put her in the front the way we do."

"It is small consolation, standing on the front row in a place where you don't want to be."

"Mrs. McKinnis." Julie Stevens crunched up her breath mint and reached for another. "I promise that I will make note of this. I promise that I will cast your daughter in a different role next year."

There isn't any guarantee that I will be here next year.

Heidi didn't even fit into the angel costume anymore. Every year, some volunteer mom let out and lengthened the burgundy dress with its hoop skirt, its tinsel halo, and its gossamer wings.

Theia laced her fingers together, her hands a perfect plait in her lap that belied the anger rising in her midsection. The only problem was, she didn't know exactly who to be angry with. With herself, for letting time slip past without stopping to notice? With Julie Stevens, for holding Heidi back and not letting her blossom?

With God, for letting cancer slip into her life when she least expected it?

Theia stood from the chair and didn't smile. A crazy motto from some deodorant commercial played in her mind: 'Never let them see you sweat.' She clutched her purse in front of her and gave a sad little shake of her head. "Miss Stevens, someday you will realize that a child's heart is more important than the quality of some annual performance."

The teenagers in Jackson Hole, the ones still too young to drive, had gotten their freedom this past summer: a paved bike path that ribboned past meadows and neighborhoods, past the middle school and the new post office, clear up to the northern outskirts of town. Kate McKinnis and her best friend, Jaycee, leaned their Rocket Jazz mountain bikes against the side of the house, hurried inside to get sodas, and tromped upstairs to Kate's room. Jaycee sorted through CDs while Kate put one of her favorites in the disc player.

'N Sync belted out their newest number one hit.

"Turn it up." Jaycee flopped on the bed and buttressed her chin against a plush rabbit that happened to be in her way. "I love that song."

"I can't. Today's Saturday. Dad works on his sermons on Saturdays. I have to keep it quiet."

"That reeks."

"On Saturdays, he waits to hear from the Lord. He doesn't want to hear 'N Sync instead." Kate picked a bottle of chartreuse nail polish and handed it to Jaycee. "I'll do your right hand if you'll do my left."

"Only if I can put it on my toes, too."

"I'm kind of worried about my mom. She hasn't been smiling much lately. And neither has Dad."

"My parents do the same thing. Maybe they had a fight. Can I use purple? Do you think it would look stupid if I used both colors?"

"If it does, you can always take it off."

They bent over each other's splayed fingers and toes, accompanied by the constant murmur of the music. Jaycee finished with the purple and screwed on the lid. "Did you hear about Megan Spence? Her parents are letting her drive the car already. She gets her learner's permit now that she's fourteen."

"I want to drive, too. Just imagine what it'll be like, Jaycee. We can go anywhere we want."

"Megan's getting her hardship license or something."

"Not fair." Kate waved her nails in the air to dry them and then pulled her hair back with one hand.

"Let me do that. You'll get smudges." Jaycee grabbed the brush, made a quick ponytail in her friend's hair, and clipped it with a hair claw so it sprang from Kate's head like a rhododendron. "There."

"How do I look?" Kate surveyed both her hair and her upheld green fingernails in the mirror.

"Like a hottie. Same as me." Jaycee surveyed her reflection, too. "I bet your parents will be okay. Just wait a few days."

"Do you think Sam Hastings is cute?"

"He rocks. But he's got a girlfriend."

"Well, you know, I just like him as a *friend.*"

"When I get my license, I'm going to get in the car and just start driving. Just take any road I think looks good." Jaycee started brushing her own hair, too. "Maybe I'll drive all the way to Canada. Or Alaska. Or Mars."

"You can't drive to Mars, silly. There aren't any roads."

"I'll make my own roads. Really, I'll just start out somewhere and take any road I want, without a map or anything. Just to drive forever and see where I'd end up."

"You'd end up lost."

"You can't end up lost, can you, if you don't need to know where you're going?"

It occurred to Joe McKinnis, as he watched the blanket flutter to the grass, that perhaps he hadn't chosen the best spot for a picnic.

Theia stood at the edge of Flat Creek, protective arms crossed over her bosom, counting swallows as they swooped and dipped under the bridge and over the water. Her hair, the same color as the cured autumn grasses in the meadow, had gone webby and golden in the sunlight. As she stood at water's edge, she belonged to the countryside around her, the standing pines, the weeds, the wind.

I wonder if chemo's going to make her lose her hair?

As soon as he asked himself that question, he wished he could take it back. *This isn't what she needs from you, Joe. She needs you to stand beside her. She needs you to tell her to believe in miracles. She needs you to counsel her the way you counsel every parishioner who comes to your office seeking answers.*

But this was his own wife he was talking about. For her, he could give no answers.

Joe settled on his knees. "Theia? You ready for lunch?"

"Not quite." She didn't turn when she answered him. "It's such a beautiful place."

"It *is* pretty, isn't it?"

When she started toward him, her steps rustled like crinoline in the grass. "Thank you. A picnic was a good idea."

"We needed to talk."

Theia stopped beside a little makeshift cross resting against a pile of rocks. Kate and Heidi had made it last year, lashing together sticks with string to mark their dog's grave. Even now he heard the girls' voices, their sad pointed questions:

"Do you think dogs go to heaven when they die, Daddy?"

"Maybe dogs don't have to ask Jesus in their heart because they aren't people."

"This was a good place to bury Maggie," Theia said now. "She loved it here."

"Maybe not such a good place to come today." He began to set out their food. Two sandwiches with ham and mustard. Apples. The clear plastic container of brownies.

Theia knelt beside him, unwrapped a sandwich. "Why? Why wouldn't it be a good place?"

"Because this is where we buried the dog."

She took her first bite, but after a moment her chewing slowed. "I guess we should pray," she said, her mouth full. But they didn't. She kept right on eating. Joe chomped into his apple, as crisp as the air.

For two people who had so much to say to each other, it seemed strange—all the silence between them.

At last when they spoke, they spoke together.

He said, "Kate knows something is wrong."

And she said, "Heidi's going to be an angel again."

"Theodore? What are we going to do?"

His pet name for her. Theodore. Always when he said it, she laughed and poked him in the ribs and said, "Joe, this isn't *Alvin and the Chipmunks.*"

But not today. Today she said, "We're going to do what the doctors tell us to do, I guess."

Joe picked a piece of grass and threaded it between his two thumbs. When he blew to make it whistle, nothing happened.

"Of course, this is your chance, Joe. If you ever wanted a different woman—" He looked up, horrified, before he realized what she meant. "I could get big bosoms. Have them remade any size. And I could change my hair."

"You're nuts."

"I could get a brunette wig or even go platinum; no more of this boring, dishwater blonde. We could put me back together exactly the way you want me to be."

"I don't want you any other way except the way that you are right now."

"Well." Her eyes measured his with great care. "That's one choice that you *don't* have."

"You know what I meant. I meant it the nice way. That I

wouldn't change anything if I didn't have to."

"I know what you meant. I do."

A Saran wrapper scudded away in the breeze. Neither of them made a move to grab it. "We're going to have to tell the girls. And your father."

"I don't think I can tell my dad, Joe. After everything that happened with Mama, this is going to be harder on him than on anybody else." She started to pack picnic items back into the basket. The jar of pickles. What was left of the brownies. "Maybe you could be the one to talk to him. You're so good at saying the right things to people."

"Not about this. It doesn't come so easy when you're talking about your own life."

For all the things he might be afraid of, he feared this worse than he feared cancer or even losing her: He felt like he was losing his faith.

Two

The best way to tell the girls about Theia's cancer, they decided, was to take them someplace they liked, to spend one special family day together, before Theia broke the difficult news. They signed the girls out of school on a Tuesday, the day before Theia's surgery, and drove to Rock Springs for a spree at the mall.

As they traveled the countryside, leaves rattled across the road in front of the car. Fields of ripe barley rippled in the breeze. A herd of antelope grazed beside the roadside. Combines waited to harvest, parked atop the rolling hills like guards against the sky.

After an hour or so, the farmland gave way to subdivisions. Traffic began to pass them at speeds that made Theia dizzy. "Can we go to the pet store first?" Heidi glanced up from the game of hangman she and Kate were playing in the backseat.

"I want the music store first." Kate drew an arm on Heidi's hanging body.

Joe readjusted the rearview mirror so he could see the girls. "Guess you two are going to have to take turns."

Once they'd gotten to Grand Teton Mall, the girls were anxious to go their own ways. "*Please*. I'll meet you at the pet store in fifteen minutes," Kate pleaded. "All I want to do is look at the new releases."

Heidi pulled them in the opposite direction. "There's ferrets in the window. They're so cute. Can we go in and look at them?"

"We aren't getting a ferret, Heidi."

"I know. But that doesn't mean I can't hold one." She disappeared into Pet City.

So much for their family togetherness, Theia thought. "Maybe we shouldn't have done it this way, Joe. Maybe we've ruined one of their favorite things for them. Every time they come shopping from now on, they'll remember today."

"There isn't any 'best way' to do this." Joe wrapped an arm around her shoulders. "Any way we do it, it's going to be awful."

After everyone had spent time in the shops of their choice, they ate lunch at Garcia's. The four of them piled into a half-moon booth with paper flowers in jugs behind them and a bright piñata dangling overhead. The waitress served a basket of chips, bowls of salsa, and brought them each a Dr. Pepper.

Joe took Theia's hand and started. "We brought you here because your mother and I needed a good place to talk to you."

Chips paused in midair. "What?"

Theia had practiced the words many times, but her voice froze now. *What do I say? How do I tell them?* She forced the words from her mouth. "I'm going into the hospital tomorrow for surgery."

Kate dipped her chip and munched it with feigned nonchalance. "What kind of surgery?"

"I won't be in there very long. Just two or three days if everything goes well."

Heidi peeled the paper meticulously off her straw and left it lying beside her glass. "Can we come visit you?"

"I'd like that very much. And after I get home, I'll need to take treatments. I'll need you both to help me before this is all over."

"Treatments for what, Mom?" Kate laid the chips on her plate and stared at her mother. "What do you have?"

Theia glanced at Joe, willing strength into all of them. "I have breast cancer."

Silence engulfed the table. The waitress came and placed steaming hot plates in front of them. No one ate. No one said a word. Until Heidi said what they were all thinking, with a hint of a cry in her voice. "But some people *die* from breast cancer."

"Yes, I know that. But others don't."

"You're not going to die, are you?"

"I don't know, Heidi."

How could she attempt to reassure them when she had no idea what lay ahead?

"Well, I know what's going to happen," Heidi said with sudden aplomb. "Nothing's going to happen to you. It can't. Jesus heals people who are sick."

"Sometimes."

"When they believe enough, He does. It happened to everybody in the Bible."

"We just have to trust that He's doing this because it works for our good."

How can something like this work for good? They're my daughters. They need me.

Lip service, all of it. When it came to trusting God right now, Theia knew that neither she nor Joe stood a chance. Ever since her diagnosis, she'd awakened every night, doubts assailing her, loneliness cutting into her, fear calling out to her from the dark corners of her bedroom.

A Scripture came to her from out of nowhere: "He who doubts is like a wave of the sea, blown and tossed by the wind. He is a double-minded man, unstable in all he does."

I don't want to doubt, Father. I don't want to be double minded. But I can't be something that I'm not.

They didn't discuss cancer again during the meal. The waitress came to check on them. "Is your food okay?" she asked.

"It's fine," Theia said.

What began as a festive occasion had degenerated to a hushed clanking of forks. The waitress came back and took their plates away, still half full.

Kate didn't often allow her little sister to hang out in her room. "Private Property of Kate McKinnis," read a sign that she'd made in art class and hung on the door. "Do not knock. Do not enter."

Heidi knocked.

"Come in."

Heidi opened the door and stood still for a moment, not sure how she should behave being allowed into such a hallowed place.

"I don't want to go to school tomorrow."

"I told Mom that, too. I want to be at the hospital."

"You worried?"

"Sort of. Yeah, I am. Are you?"

"Yeah."

Kate opened a desk drawer and began to organize it. Pens. Lip gloss. A seashell she'd brought home from a trip to Olympic National Park. "Do you think Mom's scared?"

Heidi had to think about that. "No. Moms are never scared about anything."

"I'll bet she is."

"She didn't act like it."

"That's the way mothers are. They act like they're scared over things when they aren't. They don't act like they're scared when they are."

"When has Mom ever acted like she was scared when she wasn't?"

"Remember that time on our vacation when Dad put the pinecone in the bed? And Mom started screaming because she thought it was a frog?"

"Oh yeah."

"She isn't afraid of frogs. She isn't afraid of pinecones. So why did she go screaming and jumping around all over the motel room?"

"I don't know. It was fun."

"The whole time she was acting scared, she had just as much fun as we were. She did it because she's a mom. So Dad could laugh and we would have a good time."

Heidi surveyed her Winnie the Pooh watch that her mom and dad had given her for Christmas. "Do you think we'll ever know how to do all this stuff? How to laugh? How to know when it's not right to laugh at all?"

"It's hard thinking about that, isn't it? I hope it won't be as hard as it looks, learning to be somebody's mom."

Heidi nodded. And waited. And hoped.

To hug your sister when you're a teenager is a disreputable thing. So Kate maneuvered Heidi into a playful headlock instead. She knuckle-rubbed her sister's head before they fell, giggling and tussling, on the carpet. In the end, Heidi had to beg to be let go.

Theia entered the hospital through the wide panel of glass doors at the same time a young mother was being wheeled out, her arms full of balloons and teddy bears and new baby. Once she'd gotten to the surgery center, she folded her clothes into the white plastic bag printed with bold blue letters. "Property of _____."

Did anyone ever take the time to actually write their names on those things?

Theia donned a threadbare gown, thick socks, and a green paper cap. The girls and Joe, their arms already full of presents, waved good-bye. The orderly pushing the gurney took Theia down one hall, up another, through double doors. The last thing she remembered was bright light.

When she woke up, she felt as if hours had passed. Voices surrounded her, voices she didn't know. "There we go. We've got her. That's good."

A blood pressure cuff tightened, released, tightened, released on her arm. Theia wanted it off. If she could scratch around and find it, she'd throw the thing across the room.

She needed to wake up and she knew it. The girls and Joe were waiting for her. Heidi would be so tired of sitting around she'd have at least ten get-well cards cut out and glued together by now. And Kate would be wandering the halls, begging another soda off Joe, dealing with this on teenager terms, silently, not talking until things were better, when she didn't have to show that she was afraid.

Theia didn't cry until she saw Joe. They'd led him into the recovery room, and here he came, looking handsome, his hands covering hers, the rhythm of the heart monitor beeping overhead, the IV threaded into her arm, oxygen tubes jabbing her nose.

"Hey, Theodore." How she loved the sound of his voice. "They're having a hard time bringing you around, I hear." He held her head and stroked her hair.

There were so many things she wanted to tell him. "Joe—"

"Shhhh. Don't talk now. Just rest."

She tried to raise her head; it flopped back of its own accord. "Are the girls tired of waiting for me?"

"The girls are in your room. They've got it all set up and ready. Heidi's got plenty of pictures drawn. And Kate's watching some game show."

"Tell them I love them."

"I will."

For long moments, she closed her eyes, slipped in and out of consciousness. Her hand, taped and tethered with IV tubes, began roving. She searched for the bandages by feel; when she found them, she touched her bosom.

"Did they have to take all of it? Or did they leave a little bit?"

No matter how woozy the drugs made her, Theia could see the answer in Joe's eyes. He'd been dreading this moment. Perhaps, like she'd done yesterday, he'd been practicing in his head, over and over again, what he should say.

"They had to take everything, Theia."

"It's gone? All of it?"

He nodded. "There was a lymph node involved. Dr. Waterhouse did what he had to do."

Fresh tears came and rolled down the sides of her face.

"I know, honey. I'm sorry." He kept stroking her hair. "It's going to be okay." They both realized, as he repeated himself for what seemed like the hundredth time, that the words were feeble and empty. "We're going to get through this."

"It isn't fair that my father has to do this twice."

"It was different with your mother, Theia. Everything has changed so much since then."

"No, not everything. So many things are still the same."

A tube led from her underarm, draining fluid into a bottle pinned to her hospital gown. She watched as it filled with peach-colored liquid. Everything ached. It hurt just keeping her eyes open. From behind them, an unnamed nurse began to work. One by one, she disconnected various wires and tubes. "We're taking you to your room now." She hooked the IV bag to a rack where it could ride shotgun on the gurney. "They keep delivering flowers and balloons with your name on them. It's like a birthday down there."

The girls met them halfway out in the hall. Both of them acted exuberant and happy. "That took forever, Mom."

"Mrs. Clark and Mrs. Ballinger came by and sat with us for a little while."

"Everybody from the church is taking food over to the house. Only we told Rhonda Stuart not to make chicken tetrazzini because Dad hates mushrooms."

"Do you feel better, Mom?"

"No, silly. She feels worse. She just had her operation."

"Like the game. OPERATION! Did they take out your funny bone, Mom? I always make the buzzer go off."

The girls think it's over, don't they? They think I'm safe.

"No." Joe knotted his knuckle on Heidi's head. "I told the doctors to leave your mother's funny bone in."

"Very f-funny."

"Is the cancer gone? Did they get it out, Mom?"

Theia reached for Joe's hand, but he wasn't standing close enough for her to grasp onto. "We don't know, sweetie."

Harry Harkin plunged his spade deep into the soil, freeing the root-bound English ivy from its terra-cotta confines. He shook the roots free of old dirt, gingerly checking to make certain that the plant didn't have rot or nematodes, before he settled it with care into the soft new loam of a larger pot.

It always made him feel like praying, fiddling in the dirt. Nothing like repotting plants to make one think about the Father, he thought, humming as he tamped down new soil around the ivy stems. Every so often, a man got root bound. God had to pick

him up and shake the soil out of his innards and transplant him
to a larger pot.

Usually, he'd been thankful for the transplant.

Sometimes, he hadn't been.

Harry rattled through his array of tubs and tins that fit
together in size like the nesting soldiers he'd once played with as a
boy. He glanced up and, through the wavery greenhouse glass in
the waning light, saw his son-in-law drive into the driveway and
his two granddaughters jump out of the car.

Where had everybody been all day? Place had been way too
quiet with the whole brood away.

Harry figured he had the best of both worlds, living in the
father-in-law apartment the church elders had added onto the
parsonage, being close to the grandkids, having his separate life
and his life with his family, as well. More often than not, he knew
the entire McKinnis clan's daily schedules and procedures, but for
the past few weeks, everyone had been racing around so fast that
he'd lost track. Dance rehearsals. Girl Scout meetings. Swim team
competitions.

It was enough to make an old man's head spin.

Now that he'd finished transplanting the ivy, he moved on to
other things. The church bazaar would come faster than he knew
it, and everyone expected his annual offering of forced paperwhites, just in time for the holidays. He'd just pulled out a burlap
bag full of bulbs, sprouts already burgeoning from beneath oniony
skin, when a knock sounded on the greenhouse screen door.

He walked over and opened it, a stack of planters in his hand.
"Come in, come in," he said to Joe. Something in his son-in-law's
face made him wary. "It's about time we ran into each other somewhere."

"I'm sorry, Dad. I have some difficult news to tell you."

There had been some discussion among the congregation last year that he ought to root his paperwhites in pebbles and not in dirt. He made his final decision and chose dirt. He turned on the garden spigot and ran water. "Out with it then. No need to drag it out."

"Theia has breast cancer. She's had a mastectomy today."

Harry's hands faltered as they moved in the soil. "Today?" A pause. "Come help me mix this, Joe. Make yourself useful."

They stood side by side, old man and younger one, making mud pies. "I'm sorry, Dad."

"You might have told me a little sooner than this. I could have been at the hospital today." Anger and fear caught like stones in his throat. Anger at Joe for not saying something until now. Fear that Theia might have to walk a path he'd never wanted to travel with anyone again.

"We didn't want you to be worrying."

"I wouldn't have been worrying. I would have been praying."

"You know why we waited, Dad. It's because of everything that happened to Edna. Theia thought this would be harder on you than on anybody else."

Harry said it again, for emphasis. "I would have been *praying,* not worrying." But maybe Theia was right. After what had happened to his wife, he ought to be terrified. He turned from Joe and fiddled with the burlap bag, his only means of escape. He handed three bulbs from the sack to Joe, each of them plump and succulent. "You plant these. It's nice when they've got tops on them like this. That way you know which end is up."

Lord, surely you wouldn't take two women away from the same old man.

He had to hand it to Joe. His son-in-law looked a whole lot more comfortable standing behind a pulpit than he did planting bulbs into buckets, but Joe was doing as he'd told him, burying the paperwhites deep and then sprinkling them with Harry's massive watering can. For long moments, they listened together to the *glub-glub-glub* as moisture sank into the soil, the pleasant sound of something drinking.

You moving me from one pot to a bigger one, Lord? You out to show me something about my roots, that I've been sinking them too deep in the wrong places?

It occurred to him that the man who stood beside him had every bit as strong a reason to feel as mad and lost as he did. He turned to Joe. Paying no heed to his dirt-encrusted fingers, he wrapped his arms around the man who, through marriage, had become his son. "You're working mighty hard to hold back your sorrow, aren't you, Joe?"

Joe hugged him back, hard. Harry felt Joe's warm moist breath against his ear. "You're right. I don't know what to do now, Dad. I don't know what to say to people. I don't know what to believe."

"I'm here for you, Joe. There's not much good about me, other than the fact that I've already been through this once. Maybe the good Lord can make some use of that."

Harry hoped so. He truly hoped so. Perhaps some good could come out of this, and not just sorrow.

He'd had enough sorrow to last a lifetime.

Three

During the past few days, Joe had canceled at least five counseling appointments at his office.

He had neither the time nor the inclination to listen to other people's problems.

Perception, he always told everyone during the sessions. It's a matter of perception. When you see something as being hopeless, it will be.

He leaned back in his office chair and stared out the window onto the church lawn. He'd left the hospital this afternoon because he couldn't stand to be near the antiseptic smell any longer. He felt like he'd been wandering the halls of St. John's for days, thanking people for bringing flowers and food, being useless.

He'd been touched by his father-in-law's response to news of Theia's illness. Where Harry might have railed at the injustice of Theia's cancer, he'd responded to Joe's pain instead.

Is that what You do, Lord? Use men who've been broken and emptied to minister, so everyone will see that it's You?

It occurred to him that this was the first time since they'd diagnosed his wife that he'd spoken directly to his Heavenly Father.

Isn't there some other, easier way?

He'd gotten so tired of putting on the charade. Theia needed him to be strong, and he was nothing but a fraud.

His secretary, Sarah Hodges, buzzed him on his intercom. "Joe? The church decorating committee is here. They're meeting in the adult Sunday school room. Can you come?"

He'd procrastinated with church business for as long as humanly possible. He'd already instructed Sarah to keep all of his appointments on the books today. "Tell them I'll be there in a few minutes."

When he walked in the room, he was accosted by five different churchwomen, all with varying opinions about the upcoming holiday decorating.

"I think it's a shame we don't put a tree at the front of the church," announced Mary Cathcart. "We used to do that when we were in the small sanctuary, and it was beautiful."

"I don't like the idea of a tree beside the altar. It puts too much emphasis on secular Christmas celebrations."

"We made Christian decorations for it one year. Cut them out of those white trays that they use for the meat at Albertson's and outlined them with glitter. Jesus fish and crosses."

"People like getting married that time of year because they can have the tree."

"I think we ought to put the manger scene on the chancel. That's what we need to emphasize."

"We need to have a Saturday potluck where everyone comes prepared to decorate. A churchwide hanging-of-the-greens ceremony."

"The Presbyterians always do a hanging-of-the-greens. They'll think we're copying them."

"Well, aren't we?"

They quieted down. It became obvious as they eyed him that

they were waiting for Joe to tell them who was right and who was wrong.

"We shouldn't copy the Presbyterians," was all he could think to say.

Next on Joe's agenda came a meeting with his choir director, Ray Johnson.

"The youth worship team feels that the Lord is leading them to do a song this Sunday called 'Love to the Highest Power.'"

"It sounds like a good song with a good message."

"It's rock, Joe. I think it might scare some people."

Joe scrubbed his forehead with his fingers. What to do with this? "Can you convince them to wait a week or two? We'll call it youth Sunday or something. That way nobody will be offended."

After Ray left, Joe straightened his shirt. He puffed out his cheeks and let the air go out of them. When Dr. Waterhouse had come to the room to see Theia early this morning, he'd told them everything they didn't want to hear. "Your tumor did not have a distinct boundary, Mrs. McKinnis. We are reasonably certain that we got it all. Not positive, but reasonably certain."

"When can you be more than reasonably certain? When can we be positive?"

"After her treatments are over, if there are no new recurrences in five years—then we can be positive."

"Five years? She's going to have to live with this for five years?"

The surgeon made notes on his clipboard. "We hope so, Mr. McKinnis."

His last appointment of the day. Joe was ashamed, but he'd been dreading it the most. He walked into the front office and gave Winston Taylor a hearty handshake. He knew what they'd be talking about. He'd been counseling this man for well over a year.

"Thanks for making the time for me, Joe." Winston toted his

Bible with him, tucked beneath one elbow of his sheepskin coat.

"Come on back, Win."

He shut the door behind him, and they were alone. He settled Winston in one of the portly chairs arranged in a conversational grouping and settled himself in the chair opposite. He crossed his legs and cleared his throat, waiting for the other man to begin.

"You're going to be surprised at what I came here to talk about." Winston uncrossed his own legs and leaned forward.

"I will?" *Good luck.*

"I came here to talk about you and your wife."

Joe was instantly taken aback. "Theia and I are fine, Win. There's no need worrying yourself about that."

"That's not what the Lord's been telling me, Pastor Joe. Every time I start out trying to pray for something else, *bam!* There I am praying for you two instead."

"That's amazing."

"Seems to me there must be some sort of a battle going on. And it isn't about what's going on in Theia's body. It's about what's going on in your heart."

Joe laughed. It was the only way he knew to cover the pain welling in his own soul, the grief welling in his spirit. "I thought I was supposed to be the pastor here."

"I got a sermon to give you, so you just sit back and listen."

"Okay." Joe repositioned himself in his chair.

"As I see it, Joe McKinnis, God's looking for something specific from you. He wants you to step away from all the trappings of being religious. He wants you to figure out what it is from Him that you're expecting."

"Expecting?"

"Think about it. How did everybody feel when the soldiers crucified Jesus? How did they feel when Jesus died?"

"That doesn't have anything to do with this situation."

"It has *everything* to do with it.

"I don't see that."

"Think what Christ's followers *expected* on His crucifixion day. Then consider that they *got,* instead. A thousandfold more. But Christ had to die first as they stood there waiting for miracles to happen."

Joe slowly began to nod.

"Those folks had to go through the experience from top to bottom. They got all of the anguish, and then they got all of the restoration. The impossible happened. The moment Christ died on the cross, life as they knew it was over. Nothing looked the way they'd expected it to look. Then, an empty tomb. Mary Magdalene in the garden. Some of them so sure He was gone that when they saw Him walking around, they didn't even *recognize* Him."

"It's an amazing story, isn't it?"

"I'll tell you this much, Pastor Joe. What's going to happen with Theia is going to happen, whether you let yourself expect it or not. If you don't get anything else from me, get this: What you *expect* from Theia's situation is going to influence the way you *see* it."

Should he listen to this man, this parishioner who so often had come to Joe for help before? He didn't know. Just because he was a pastor, did it mean he was the only one who had authority to teach in Jesus' name? The Gospel of Matthew said, "You have hidden these things from the wise, and revealed them to little children." After Winston left his office, Joe stared at Theia's picture.

What do I expect, Lord?

This hurt so much. If only he, instead of his wife, could fight this battle.

Theia had had a chance once to be a dancer. She'd gotten a dance scholarship to Utah State. She'd married him instead. She'd fed him and nurtured him through seminary. She had mothered the girls. She'd put up with 3 A.M. phone calls during church crises. She had welcomed her father into their fold, being just as loving a daughter as she was a mother.

Do I expect peace? Assurance that You will heal her? That she could go through all of this and not have to be afraid?

He buried his face in his hands.

EXPECT ME, BELOVED.

But it was as though Joe couldn't hear. His grief overpowered everything else, and he focused on that rather than the phone's constant ringing in the office, the Mothers of Preschoolers meeting in the Fellowship Hall.

And the insistent, gentle voice calling, giving him the very answer that he sought.

"It's okay, Grandpa." Kate clutched Harry Harkin's hand as she poked her nose inside the hospital room. "If Mom's sleeping, we can wake her up. She wants to see you."

At the sound of her daughter's voice, Theia rolled her head sideways on the pillow. "Hey you." She shot Kate a little sad smile. "What's up?"

"Just checking on you. Grandpa's been driving me all around town in his old car."

"Grandpa's here? Daddy?" Theia pushed herself against the mattress and did her best to sit higher. She winced.

Harry came to the foot of the bed, a pot of pink geraniums in his hand. "Since Joe came to tell me what was going on, thought I'd better stop on over for a visit."

"Those are beautiful."

"They ought to be, coming from my greenhouse."

Kate took the flowers from him and set them, exuberant and lacy bright, in the hospital window.

"Thought getting that old Ford Fairlane out of the meadow would be a good excuse." He doffed his tweed hat. "Thought I'd best come over here and let you know that I know."

She could guess at the things he wanted to say to her. She knew he wanted to offer simple reassurances, but he couldn't. "I'm so sorry, Daddy."

I never wanted this to happen to you, he might have said.

I never wanted you to go through this a second time, she might have said.

But they wouldn't delve into the past or the future with Kate standing there.

They changed the subject and talked about the Ford instead.

"You got that old car started. With the weather this cold, too."

"Had to drive to Shervin's and get a new battery. Once it turned over, though, that was it. Purred like a kitten ever since."

Kate plucked one yellow leaf from the geraniums in the window. She walked across the room and threw it away. "Grandpa says I can have that old car when I start driving, Mom. He thinks it'll be the perfect car for a teenager."

It was clear Harry hadn't wanted Kate to announce it like that. He had the grace to appear a little sheepish. "Thought that might take everybody's mind off other things."

Theia's lunch came rattling in on a metal cart. The candy striper moved a basket of daisies, a box of tissues, and situated the tray.

"You want something to eat, Kate? You can get a hamburger in the cafeteria. There's money in my bag."

"I've got money." Harry plopped his hat on Theia's feet and fished out his wallet. He unfolded his money and counted out three one-dollar bills. He was getting so slow, Theia thought. If she hadn't been sick, she'd have taken money from her purse and whisked Kate out the door before he'd ever had the chance to pitch in. Those hands. Hands that had held her as a baby. She hadn't noticed they were growing so feeble.

"Thanks, Grandpa." Kate took the proffered bills. "I'll probably just get a hamburger. Nothing much. You want me to bring you anything?"

He shook his head. "I ate already."

Kate headed out the door, and the moment she did, the mood between Theia and her father changed. He seemed to sag. He lowered himself into the plastic chair beside the bed. "Joe came over and told me everything last night."

"Of all people, I hated for you to hear this news."

"You'd better eat your lunch. It's going to get cold."

"Jell-O is already cold. I won't do much harm to it by waiting."

"You need to do everything the doctors tell you to do."

"I will. I promise, Daddy."

"You get plenty of rest. You've got to do everything that they know to do to fight this thing."

"I'm thinking it will be different for me. They found my lump so much earlier than they found Mama's. Treatments are much more advanced now than they were then."

"You take care of yourself. And take care of Joe. I told him last night, I may not be good for much, but maybe I can steer him the right direction some."

"He needs that. Everybody depends on him. It's hard to start depending on people when you're used to them depending on you."

Harry rose from the chair and fiddled with the window blinds. "You know what I was thinking going off to sleep last night? About those times when your mother and I used to tuck you in bed."

"Oh no." Theia smiled in spite of everything. "Not this."

Kate walked back in with her hamburger.

"The 'Purple People Eater' song."

"Dad. No. It hurts too much to laugh."

Kate started unwrapping her burger. "What's the 'Purple People Eater' song?"

"You want to hear it?" Harry grabbed his hat again and held out one arm, vaudeville style.

"Dad, don't." But Theia was already laughing. She grabbed a pillow and hugged it, giggling against it. And that made her feel just fine.

Harry began to sing. "It was a long-haired, long-eared flying Purple People Eater."

"Don't!" Oh, how her chest hurt when she laughed. But it didn't matter. Laughter felt wonderful. "You aren't even singing the right words!"

"Yeah, but I've got the tune down exactly."

"Mama hated when you did that. You always made me scream and act silly right at bedtime."

"I've never heard of that song." Kate bit into her hamburger and spoke with her mouth full. "It sounds way goofy."

"Mama always got stuck with the job of calming me down. She'd bring me hot cocoa and let me sip it in bed. Then she'd pray with me and tuck me in and tell me I didn't have to worry about Dad's crazy songs because I wasn't purple."

Father and daughter shared a smile. It seemed an odd, nice time to be enjoying a memory.

"Your mother was always finding ways to settle you down."

"You know what *I* was thinking about the other day?" Theia asked.

Kate gave a grimace of distaste and pulled a pickle from inside the bun. "What?"

"Something I haven't thought about in a long time. Mama gave me hair ribbons once. She got them out of her sewing box and tied them in my braids on the first day of first grade."

"So?"

"They were just for me. I was scared to ride the school bus and go in to meet my new teacher. And—" she grinned at her dad again—"she wanted me to stretch my wings and go through those things on my own. But she followed the bus in her car. I saw her in the parking lot! She waved at me and then drove off."

"Is that how come you followed me and Heidi in your car on the first day of school, too?"

Theia nodded. "Yep."

Kate threw away the burger wrappings and shrugged into her sweatshirt. "I don't see what hair ribbons have to do with anything."

"For a long time, I wore them whenever I was afraid. Larry Wells told me he was going to steal my lunch once, but I wore my ribbons, and I wouldn't let him have it. Told him I was going to kick him where it counted if he stole my bologna sandwich."

Harry and Kate both spoke at the same time.

"Mom!"

"Theia!"

"I wore them every Friday when I had spelling tests. I wore them in the third grade choir concert when I had to sing 'Fifty-Nifty' on stage by myself. I wore them on the day I had to give away all my kittens and on the day I had to get stitches in my chin. When I got too big to wear them in my hair, I wore them tied to my sneakers."

Harry put his hat on his head and took his granddaughter's arm. "We'd better get home and let you get some rest."

"I wonder where those ribbons went...." Theia settled back down in her pillows, feeling a hundred times better than she'd felt when Harry and Kate first arrived. "I'd like to find them. I'm sure they're hidden away in a drawer somewhere. I haven't seen them for years."

"We'll help you look, Mom." Kate waved as she ducked out the door. "I'd like to see them, too."

Four

When the phone began ringing, Heidi raced through the kitchen, slipping on the linoleum in her socks, doing her best to beat her sister.

"I don't know why you're in such a hurry to answer the phone." Kate perched beside the sink, nonchalantly crisscrossing a new Delia's ribbon shoelace into her Sketchers. "It's just somebody else calling to see if Mom's home from the hospital. Or else it's for me."

"No, it's for me." Heidi rounded the kitchen counter and grabbed the receiver.

"It isn't for you. It's never for you. If it isn't about Mom, it's for me. Everybody wants to talk about the car Grandpa Harkin's giving me."

"Hello?" Heidi almost couldn't answer, she was panting so hard. "McKinnis residence."

"I'd like to speak with Heidi McKinnis, please."

Heidi poked out her chin and grinned at her sister, a blatant gesture of victory. "This is Heidi."

"This is Julie Stevens from Dancers' Workshop. Do you have a minute? I'd like to talk to you."

"I-I have a minute." At the sound of such astonishment in Heidi's voice, even Kate stopped to listen.

"Good." A hesitation. "Well, you see, it's this. I'm making a change or two in the Nutcracker performance."

"Oh, I'm so sorry I missed practice last Saturday. My mom was in the hospital. I promise I'll be there next week."

"I know all about that. Missing practice every once in a while is nothing to be concerned about. But I do want to talk to you about your role as an angel."

"You do?"

"As you know, Heidi, the angels are an audience favorite. Gauzy wings, hoop skirts, the tiniest floating steps, the youngest most angelic girls we can find."

"My mom tells me that every year."

"I hope you don't mind that I'm having to change things."

"Change things?" Heidi gripped the receiver. "What do you mean?"

"I'd like to change your part, Heidi, if you don't mind."

"I don't mind."

"I'm having trouble with the clowns this year. I didn't cast as many for some reason, and for the choreography to come off the way I want it to, I've got to bring in another girl."

"Oh!"

"Do you think you might be interested?"

"I'm interested, all right! I *love* the clowns. That's always been my favorite part, seeing everyone come out from under Mother Ginger's skirt."

"Of course, this doesn't give you long to learn the part. They've already been dancing it for several weeks. But I'll bet you can pull it off."

"I can. I know I can."

"As part of the choreography, you'll have to turn a cartwheel. Do you know how to turn a cartwheel?"

For the first time during the conversation, Heidi faltered. "No. I don't."

"Do you think you could learn? Is there someone who can teach you?"

"My mother can show me how."

"That's it, then. We're all set. Rehearsal time is the same. Only you'll be dancing in studio three instead of studio one."

"I'll be there. I promise I'll be there."

"Someone will measure you Saturday so we can fit you with a costume."

"Thank you. I'll be a good clown. You'll see."

"Perfect. We'll see you on Saturday."

Kate knocked on Heidi's door. Heidi's door didn't have any signs that said "Private Property." It didn't have any signs that read, "Do not knock. Do not enter."

When Heidi opened the door and saw her sister come to visit, she gestured with a wide-eyed expression. She might as well have been entertaining royalty.

Kate parted the dangling, blue door beads and entered.

"You can sit at my desk if you want."

"Thanks."

Kate sat down and turned around in the wooden chair, gripping the back. Above them both, glow-in-the-dark stars dotted the ceiling. A jumble of stuffed animals filled up an entire corner.

"How many animals do you have, Heidi?"

"Forty-three."

"You counted them?"

"Yep. But those don't count the ones that are in the garage."

A lull came. "I just wanted to tell you something."

"What?"

"That I think your dancing's really cool."

"Huh?"

"I think it's sweet that you've moved up and you're dancing the part of a clown."

Heidi stared at her sister. "How come you say that?"

"Well, I couldn't get up and dance like that in front of everybody. I was thinking about it, going off to sleep last night, and I thought I should tell you. It's bad enough dancing something that you *know*. But getting up in front of the town and dancing something that's different, I think that's really cool."

"Are you trying to scare me about this?"

"No. I just wanted you to know how I felt."

"Well, thanks."

"You're welcome."

Kate stared at the stars on the ceiling. "Do those glow all night long after you've turned out the lights?"

"Not all night. They go dark about three or four in the morning."

"You lay here and watch them that long?"

"No. But sometimes I wake up."

Kate scrubbed the toe of her Sketcher against the carpet. "I woke up last night. Do you ever wonder what it will be like when we grow up and get to be moms?"

"Yeah."

"We'll have kids."

"Yeah."

"I decided I'm going to keep a journal."

"You are?"

"Yeah. I'm going to write down everything I think about being the mother of a teenager. And then when I'm the mother of somebody that's as old as me, I can open up my journal and take my own advice."

"What if your own advice is wrong?"

"I don't know. Guess I'll figure that out. I'll pray about it the way Mom does. The way Grandma did."

"I think that will be fun, too."

"You know how you feel about dancing? All proud and everything? That's the way I think I'll feel about having kids and stuff."

"Do you think Mom feels that way about us?"

Kate thought for a moment. "Yes, I think she does."

The Sunday before church, it snowed.

A brisk tinge in the air came first and then the flakes, tiny flakes at sunrise, then larger ones, a confetti celebration outside the windows.

Snow blanketed the grass and etched a scalloped edge along the picket fence. At the morning service, excitement from outside carried into the sanctuary. A vast jumble of coats, from ski parkas to furs, hung on pegs in the front vestibule. Snow boots lay in disarray, no two together the same. Folks shivered and laughed and tucked their gloves away, talking about the mountain, when the runs would open for skiing, if the new snow had brought elk down into the refuge out of the hills.

Theia found her place along the pew and tried her best to concentrate on God.

She couldn't think about the church service at hand. She couldn't think about the snow outside. Even though she'd laughed miraculously with her father's singing, she could only think about breast cancer today. Her mind drifted. Worried. Wondered.

Had the cancer spread to other parts of her body?

If it hadn't yet, would it still?

As music began to fill the place of worship, Kate and Jaycee sidled into the seats beside them. "Where's your sister?" Theia asked.

"Oh, she'll get here. She's probably back in the Sunday school room helping the little kids clean up."

"She's probably back in the Sunday school room trying to get extra candy from Mrs. Taggart. They played some game in there with chocolate chips."

One by one, the women sitting near Theia began to rub her on the shoulder or nod their heads at her or wish her well: *We were worried about you. We've been praying. Are you okay? Is there anything we can do to help? We know how you must feel.*

She gave the same response, the same answers to each of them. *Thank you for praying. No need to worry. Everything's fine. You know how it is.*

Lord, please. I don't want to be here. I shouldn't have come to church today. It's too soon. I'm not ready for this.

Theia felt as if she were drowning in the deep, thrashing about, exhausted, trying to keep her head where she could breathe.

Why did they all have to be so sympathetic? Why couldn't they talk about something else? Why couldn't they share their own problems or something fun that was going on?

Why couldn't they pretend that none of this was happening?

Theia glanced down to see a little boy she'd taught in vacation Bible school at her knees. He threw his arms around her legs and hugged her. He gazed up at her with dark eyes so wide and pure, she wanted to cry out.

"Hello, Landon." Despite her missing oblique muscle, her tight tendons, she managed to lift him cautiously into her arms. It felt so odd, hugging him this way. Just holding a small child's body against her wounded chest brought forth a sense of loss that overwhelmed her. She ached to be whole again. The little boy planted a wet kiss on her lips. "I love you," he whispered.

"I love you, too, Landon." She couldn't keep the tears from coming to her eyes.

Lord, I'm the pastor's wife. I'm a mother to two girls of my own. I can't tell anybody that I'm afraid. I have no right.

Everyone around her kept offering advice:

"You ought to meet Jo Beth Mason. She's a cancer survivor. She's doing really well."

"I have a miracle book you can read. All about the herbal things you can do."

"We know you can do this, Theia." This one was always said with a careful I-know-you-can-do-it smile.

Landon's mother came to take him away, and when the next person tapped her on the shoulder, she turned again, expecting another embrace.

Instead she came face-to-face with Sue Masterson.

Mrs. Masterson did not reach out in love and offer pleasantries. Instead, she pointed out the front window and jabbed her finger as she enunciated each word. "Do you have any idea what your daughter is doing?"

She'd forgotten all about Heidi. Theia glanced about, expecting to find her daughter standing with some friend in the service. But Heidi wasn't in the sanctuary. Mrs. Taggart, her Sunday school teacher, had already come into the room and had situated herself with her family. Theia gave a half-guilty shrug. "Well, no. I guess I don't."

"You'd better go find out." Sue planted her hands on her hips and gave a righteous toss of her hair. "She's outside in the parking lot terrorizing little children with snowballs."

"Oh, that's ridiculous."

Theia knew this about herself: Above all else she would fight for the honor of her family. She'd done the exact thing when she'd gone to speak with Julie Stevens about Heidi's dancing. "I'll bet those kids are all having fun in the snow."

In her velvet skirt. In the forty-dollar clogs I bought her from Broadway Toys-n-Togs.

"You ought to see what she's done to Dillon. He's drenched from head to toe. I'm embarrassed to bring him into the service. Water is running from his hair. He's out there *crying.*"

"He's crying? Because he got a little wet?"

"He's crying because your daughter shoveled snow down his pants."

Oh, dear. For the first time since her father had sung 'Purple People Eater,' Theia found something comical. She felt like doubled-over, stitches-in-her-side, bellyache laughter. Glorious. Splendid. But Sue Masterson had to go and spoil it all. "For heaven's sake, Theia. Your kids are the preacher's kids. They're supposed to act better than everyone else, aren't they?"

I can't do this, Lord. I cannot do this.

Without telling Joe where she was headed, she laid her Bible in the chair and ducked out. She hurried to the front vestibule to find her coat. There she found poor Dillon Masterson, his hair plastered flat to his head and a dark patch of wet spreading down to the knee of his cargo pants.

BELOVED.

A Savior's calling, in the midst of a mother's mile-a-minute day. Theia had come to the end of herself. But she kept going anyway, not heeding the gentle summons in her spirit. She tilted her head at Dillon. "You okay?"

He nodded.

"So Heidi did this to you?"

He nodded again.

She rumpled his wet hair with her one operable arm. At least *some* good had come of his snowball fight. His face was cleaner than she'd seen it in weeks. "You go on in there with your mother."

"But I'm wet."

"The Lord doesn't care if you're wet. Only mothers care about something like that." She gave him a little pat-shove in the proper direction.

Theia found a troupe of fifth graders outside, acting like they owned the world, bellowing and running and smearing each other with snowballs. She got there just in time to see Heidi get walloped in the head.

Heidi wasted no time in retaliating. She scooped up snow, packed it hard between her hands, and let it fly. "Take *that,* you slimeball!"

The sphere hit its target, Trey Martin's backside, and exploded into icy particles. "Heidi Louise McKinnis!" Theia shouted. "You come here this instant!"

Amazing how silence could fall on a group of fifth graders. "Hi, Mom."

"You want to tell me what's going on out here?"

"Snowball fights. We're killing each other."

"Do you think this is the proper place to be, out in the parking lot calling your classmates 'slimeball' while there's a worship service going on inside?"

"But it's *snowing.*"

"I know, and if I were ten years old, I'd feel the same way. But I'm not. I'm your mother. And Dillon Masterson is inside with a major problem."

"Am I in trouble?"

"That depends."

"On what?"

"Do you think you owe Dillon an apology?"

"No."

Theia stood in the snow, waiting, using the silent, stern approach, hoping her daughter would recant. But Heidi did no such thing.

"You won't apologize?"

"No."

"You'd better examine your heart, young lady."

"You should have heard what he said at school on Friday, Mom. He told Miss Vickers that the only reason I got moved up from angel to clown is because you've got cancer, and everybody found out, and they got worried if they didn't let me dance some other part this year that you'd never get to see it."

The force of Dillon's words almost knocked Theia to her knees. She felt like she'd been booted in the gut.

"I told him you were going to see me dance plenty. I told him he was stupid."

"Well, good for you. That's exactly what you needed to say."

"Dillon says I dance like a *chicken.*"

"That is a cruel thing to say." The words pushed Theia to the brink. Her words blazed with passion. "*Listen* to me. You are a beautiful dancer. A *wonderful* dancer. You dance like a princess." Oh, how she wanted to say more. Oh, how she wanted to tell Heidi that she'd gotten the part because Julie Stevens must have noticed how she'd improved, or how she'd learned new steps, or how hard she'd tried. Theia cupped her daughter's cheeks inside her own two cold hands. "Do you hear me? Don't you ever let *anybody* tell you that you can't do something you want to do."

I can't do this, Father. I can't tell her Dillon's wrong about me. What if this is the last time I see Heidi dance?

Heidi grinned, her face innocent and open. "Mom, I know he isn't right. Don't you listen to Dillon either. That's why I shoved snow down his pants."

"Let's go inside."

"I like it out here. Let's have another snowball fight."

"Your father will be disappointed if we miss his sermon." Mother wrapped one arm around daughter, and they sauntered hip to hip toward the door. "You know how he always likes us to tell him that it was good."

"Yeah, Mama. I know."

But Theia wondered, as they entered the front vestibule, whether she'd ever be able to know again that God and faith were good.

Five

Theia spent all Sunday afternoon digging in her cedar chest, looking for her hair ribbons.

They had to be here somewhere.

She found a pink plastic toy telephone, three of her own baby sleepers, and a tulip quilt that had been hand stitched by Joe's great-grandmother. She found a little purse made of white rabbit fur, a pair of gloves, and a box of silkworms someone had sent Edna from China.

But no hair ribbons.

If they weren't in the cedar chest, she didn't know where she might have put them. Maybe they had gotten put away with some of the girl's baby things. Maybe they were still attached to some ancient pair of shoes. Maybe she'd accidentally stuck them in the pocket of some old dress, something she'd dropped off at Browse and Buy.

Theia tried to remember when she had last seen them. She poked her head further into the chest and kept digging.

"What are you looking for?" Kate flipped off the light to the bathroom and came out.

Theia spoke from beneath a pile of wool blankets. "Those hair ribbons I was telling you about."

"Here. I'll help."

"I'm almost to the bottom. I don't think they're here."

"What's this?" Kate held up one of the sleepers.

Theia glanced up and kept digging. "That was mine. Isn't it pretty?"

"Yes."

"I've saved your sleepers, too. I've got them put away in a box in the attic."

"I like it when you save things."

"Good. Be sure and tell your father that next time he's in the mood to clean out the garage." Theia pulled out her head and brushed off her hands. "I wish I could find those. I really wanted to get them out before I start chemotherapy tomorrow."

"I've got to go, Mom. I promised Jaycee I'd help her with her English project."

"That's okay."

"But I promised I would help you find them."

"I haven't seen those ribbons in years, Kate," Theia said, her face flush with disappointment. "I'm afraid they're gone for good."

Joe and Theia lay side by side in the bed, Joe with his big study Bible propped open on his chest, Theia with the pillow plumped up beneath her neck as if she'd fallen asleep.

He knew from her breathing that she hadn't.

Joe turned a page in his Bible, looked at it, turned back. He had no idea what he'd just read. "You want me to go with you tomorrow?"

"Go with me where?"

"To chemo."

"There isn't any need for you to. They say I won't feel bad until I've had several sessions. The effects are cumulative."

"I'd still like to be there."

Theia readjusted the pillow beneath her head and snuggled down deeper. "I don't want you to come, Joe."

When she pushed him away like this, it made Joe feel more helpless than ever. "I want to support you, Theia. I want to be there for you."

"I was asleep. You woke me up."

"No, you weren't."

She sighed, but didn't disagree with him.

"Was the sermon okay today?"

"It was good."

"I'm not so sure."

"It was."

"Frank Martin looked bored. And Sue Masterson couldn't stop drying off Dillon with Kleenex the entire time."

"Hmm."

She answered with brusque, short sentences, his cue that she wanted him to be quiet. He shut the Bible with a crack and laid it on his bedside table. Then he waited, watching, hoping his wife would turn to him, only she didn't.

"Theodore?"

"Hmm?"

"How long do we have to wait before…" He couldn't figure out exactly how to say it. "Well, you know."

He heard her voice catch. "We don't have to wait if we don't want to."

But she didn't move toward him. She didn't move at all.

"Or we can."

"Yes."

A good five minutes of silence passed between them.

Outside the parsonage a hay truck rattled past, carrying its two-ton limit, on its way to deliver a load to one of the local ranches. The lampshade rattled. They could feel the truck's wheels rumbling up through the floor. Joe stared at the ceiling above them; Theia stared at the wall on her side of the bed.

He thought of what he would do, loving her the way he did, if he ever had to go through one day without her.

She thought of what it might feel like to be gone from this earth, to be looking down upon them from heaven. She wondered what would happen to the girls if she died, and who would take care of Joe. So much she'd miss. All their silly jokes. Sewing those maddening patches onto Heidi's Girl Scout vest.

Sorting Joe's socks.

The weight of everything they carried together tonight felt like the truck outside with its huge load of hay, running across their hearts, crushing them both.

"Theia." This time, Joe couldn't keep himself from reaching out to her. He turned back the covers and placed his hand in the crook of her shoulder, bunching her nightgown in a way that had always given him pleasure. Beneath the cool sheer of the fabric, she felt the way a wife should feel to her husband: warm, compliant, soft, everything he needed. The slightest bit of pressure now, and she would roll toward him, loop her arms around his neck.

"My b-b-breasts aren't there anymore," she sobbed up at him as she wrapped her forearms around the nape of his neck. "You sh-shouldn't expect me to be b-b-beautiful anymore. I'm all c-cut away."

He wanted so badly to reassure her, but his words rang hollow in his own ears. "That doesn't matter to me."

"It does matter. You'll have to help me change the dressing soon, and then you'll see it. It's awful."

"But you are still *you* inside. You'll still be beautiful, Theia."

"My body looks like someone tried to sew up the corners of a cushion."

"None of that makes any difference to me."

"It *will*. I hate cancer. It isn't fair."

"You know what makes you beautiful to me? I've watched you give birth to my babies. That's what makes you beautiful."

"Why would God make this happen to me when he also made it happen to my *mother?*"

He didn't know why he made the next mistake. He'd stopped thinking perhaps. He was enjoying winning her over, saying all the right things. "I know how goofy you acted when we were young. That's what makes you beautiful to me. Because I was with you the time you stood up on the roller coaster at Lagoon. That makes you beautiful. Because I know you're going to be all snaggle-toothed and funny-looking when we both get old together. That's what makes you—"

It took Joe a full ten seconds to realize the horrible, wrong thing he'd said. He froze. For a moment she just lay there, staring up at him like she hadn't heard him right. As realization hit, her countenance crumpled. Her chin began to quiver. Her mouth contorted. Her eyes welled with tears.

"Theodore, I'm sorry. I'm so sorry."

She shoved him off, cast the rest of the blankets aside, and jumped out of bed. "How could you say that? *How could you talk about growing old?*"

"I didn't mean to. I wasn't thinking. I'm sorry."

She pulled on a sweatshirt over her nightgown. She stepped into her snow boots and shoved her arms into her coat.

"Where are you going?"

"I don't know. I'm just *going*."

He was up and beside her. "I'm coming, too."

"No, you aren't. I want to be alone."

"It's the middle of the night. You can't go out there by yourself. It's cold."

She screamed the words at him. "I'm a big girl, Joe. I go out walking, at all times of day and night, *by myself*. Just because you've said something stupid doesn't give you the right to come along with me!"

He couldn't stop himself. He'd borne his own burdens too long. "How can you act like this is just about you? If something happens to you, Theia, it happens to both of us. If you die—" He stood in the middle of the room, amid blankets that had fallen to the floor in angry knots, his hands balled into incapable fists at his side. "If you die, everything for me ends, too. You have to think about us together, not just you."

Theia walked away and didn't look back. She shut the door soundly behind her. Joe sank to the side of the bed, feeling totally cut off from his wife, wondering what had happened to the woman he'd been able to share everything with. "Please, God," he whispered aloud. "Please, God."

But that was as far as he could go. When he tried to find words to speak his heart, he found he wasn't able.

Theia's hurt hammered with every beat of her heart, a rhythmic throb of grief. She pulled her coat tighter as she stumbled across the unbroken snow, her boots stamping waffle patterns behind her.

When she looked over her shoulder, she could just make out the shape of the church and the parsonage and her dad's green-house, pink-washed in the moonlight. Theia stared up at stars, pinpricks in the night sky. She listened, heard only unerring silence, only the rustle of breeze in the trees. She stood in the midst of the snowfield, her lanky shadow lengthening in the moonlight, her own steps solitary behind her, and cried. "I c-can't do this. I can't be strong for everybody else. I can't even be strong for m-me."

So many things she needed.... to be held close and rocked, to hear the affirmations that everyone around her could no longer give. To hold her children close and know that she would be alive to enjoy their growing.

"You've got so much food here," Laura Jones had said last week when she'd brought over lasagna. "You aren't going to have to cook for a *year.*"

She cried because Joe said she'd be beautiful when she was old. She cried because Laura Jones had taken stock of her refrigerator.

You won't have to cook for a year.

Did it occur to anybody that she might *want* to cook? That she might hold dear a hundred different chores because nothing guaranteed that she'd be around for those chores in another year.

I didn't want Joe to see me, to touch me. And maybe that's one less time for him to touch me in the time that we have left.

"Nobody understands, Lord! Nobody understands."

How she yearned for her father's arms. Not the feeble, aged way he held her lately, but the strong, big way he'd hugged her when she'd been a little girl. When he'd lifted her to the mirror so she could match her face to his. When he'd picked her up and carried her upstairs to sing "Purple People Eater." "I c-can't do this." Her nose ran, and tears rolled down her jaw to soak the collar of her coat. She did nothing to stop them. "I'm *mad* at You! Mad. How could You *do* this?"

She'd never been so afraid in all her life.

She'd never been so *angry*.

"Why would I have to drag my own two children through this?"

Clearly, as clearly as if a friend touched her on the shoulder and said, "Look and see," Theia saw her eighth birthday. A truck from Preston Lumber had turned into the alley, with a crane on it so big she thought it might knock the neighbor's fence down. The crane lifted her new playhouse, its wood fragrant and stark, into the corner beside the patio.

Her daddy hugged her.

Her mama carried out boxes of doll furniture.

"Here are curtains." Her mother handed her a box. "You want to hang them up?"

"She's going to have to wait fifteen minutes or so, Edna." Harry waggled a screwdriver in the air. "I don't have the curtain rods hung yet."

She ran from one window to the other and peered in. "Can I bring my dolls out here, Mama?"

"Of course you can. That's what it's for. A place they can live." Her mother held out something flat in her palm. "Here's something else."

There in her hand lay a doll-sized embroidery framed in a hoop, carefully signed and dated: *Jesus Loves Me, This I Know.* Mama kissed Theia on the forehead. "Now it will feel like home."

That had been a long, long time ago.

No dolls anymore, but real daughters.

No tiny wooden furniture, but a living room of Thomasville instead.

Jesus Loves Me....

Do You? Do You really? Because if You do, why would You take Mama away? Why would You let it happen to her, and then to me, too?

The childhood images faded away, replaced by cold, stone reality. Dr. Sugden, aligning the charts and the diagram flat on his desk for her to see. Class IIA cancer. Upper right quadrant of the right breast.

"Not the sort of cancer that goes away without a fight," he said. "The sort that, if you live, you live with. The sort of cancer that if you survive it makes you certain that you are a survivor."

Where are You in this, Father? I can't find You, no matter how hard I try.

If He loved you, if He cared about you, none of this would have happened. A God who loves His children wouldn't let anything like this come into your life.

I HAVE DRAWN YOU WITH LOVING-KINDNESS. I HAVE LOVED YOU WITH AN EVERLASTING LOVE.

That means He isn't there at all, don't you see? If He were there, you wouldn't feel like He wasn't. You wouldn't have this awful emptiness inside. He'd be beside you, every step of the way. It's easy to tell that He isn't.

WHO SHALL SEPARATE YOU FROM THE LOVE OF CHRIST? SHALL TROUBLE OR HARDSHIP OR PERSECUTION…?

Fool. How could you believe such a ridiculous thing after what happened to your mother?

The lurid, dreadful voice in her head drowned out every other sound, every other thought, as she stood alone in the snow.

Her cheeks were wet from crying. She turned back toward the house and toward the bedroom where her husband would keep his back toward her, pretending to sleep. Her breath came as mere wisps of frost.

And her heart broke in the icy darkness.

Six

*H*arry Harkin lay wide-awake in his bed for the third night in a row.

Why can't I stop thinking, Lord? Why won't my mind shut down for a while?

He couldn't look at his daughter, at all those gauze bandages he knew were wrapped around her chest and her heart like armor, without thinking of Edna, of Edna's bandages, Edna's faith.

Harry didn't have to reach for the clock. When he woke up like this, he always knew the time: 3 A.M. Right on the money.

Last night when he'd been jolted out of sleep, he'd been stupid enough to punch the button. The clock spoke aloud, a woman's tinny, electronic voice from this clock he'd bought at K-Mart because he was getting old and he couldn't see in the dark without finding his spectacles.

"The time is three-oh-three A.M."

This morning, he didn't ask the confounded thing again.

He knew.

For six weeks after Edna died, Harry wouldn't touch her things. He'd left her belongings right where she'd arranged them, small cherished altars that kept him feeling close to his wife even after she'd gone. The small blue jar of Vick's VapoRub on her nightstand. A basket of Betsy McCall paper dolls. The crumpled hanky that still smelled of Emeraude. Her favorite pearl earbobs. As if she'd come back for them tomorrow, poke them in her pocketbook, laugh at him for thinking she might not need them anymore.

Then had come the day when he couldn't bear her things sitting around any longer. He'd swept through the house like a drill sergeant, his anger so tangible and hard that he'd taken no prisoners. *Sweep,* into the box everything went. Family photos that she'd loved. Notes from the children. The grocery list he'd kept like a shrine on the counter, the last one she had scribbled in her own hand: "Don't forget laundry detergent, ground beef, toilet paper."

Gone.

The Vicks and the bottle of Emeraude. Purses and hankies and even her favorite red polka-dot apron.

Gone.

He scrounged through the laundry room shelves, searching for packing tape. When he couldn't find anything better, he sealed the box shut with black electrical tape instead. He wanted this sealed. Finished.

Over and done with.

Lord, why the urge to see what's inside the box now? Why, after all these years?

He'd endured. He'd made precarious peace with his heavenly Father, if only to bring himself to a place of somewhat baffled acceptance of Edna's death.

Wouldn't digging through Edna's personal effects open wounds again, Father? Can't I keep those old hurts sealed in the recesses of my heart? I know myself. If I let myself relive that now, I stand to lose the hope I still have for my daughter.

He reached toward the nightstand and thumped the button on the clock.

"The time is three-oh-two A.M."

A shadow flitted past his window. Harry sat up and fumbled for his bifocals. He saw Theia trudging through the snow toward the parsonage. He watched as she backhanded her nose with a mitten. She'd been crying.

The time is now, his heart pulsed to him in its underlying, faultless rhythm. *The time is now.*

None of us can go on like this, Father. What is it that You want me to do?

That afternoon so long ago, he'd backed the Fairlane out of the garage, propped up the ladder, and stowed Edna's things as far back as he could get them into the corner. He'd moved that box with him three times. After all these years, he'd neither unfastened it nor looked inside.

No sense in mistaking an old man's folly for the Spirit of the Lord.

He asked the question aloud in the darkness, his forehead still pressed up against the cold windowpane. "You want me to open all that up again, Lord? Sure don't see what good it'll do anybody."

Silence.

No reassuring voice in the darkness.

Only the dull aching of his heart, the memory of the day when he'd swept through room after room, fighting to purge every painful recollection, every broken promise, from his household and his life with his little girl.

Theia decided the hair ribbons had to be in the buffet.

Digging for hair ribbons seemed as good a therapy as any after her sleepless angry night.

She wasn't due at St. John's for her chemo treatment for several hours. She had the entire morning to herself. She got down on her hands and knees and, piece by piece, began to bring out the tiers of plates that made up her wedding china. First came the Gorham Rondelle saucers, then the dessert plates, then the bread and butters. Even though she was a preacher's wife, she was a preacher's wife in Wyoming. She hadn't set a table with these fancy dishes in ages.

Just to make sure, she checked the stacks of linen napkins and the basket she used when she served dinner rolls. She checked inside the plastic sack where she kept Christmas candles, wrapped in tissue.

She sat back on her heels.

There wasn't anything here.

"You know what I wish for?" she said aloud to nobody there. "Maybe some pictures. Something to put around the house that would remind me of...*me*."

Even as she said her wish aloud, she realized how she could make it happen.

Beneath the maple lamp stand in the front room sat a row of thick photo albums, dating back to the days when the girls had worn diapers.

Theia piled the Gorham back into the buffet and then sat cross-legged on the floor beside the lamp stand. She unshelved each album and thumbed through it, occasionally slipping a picture out from behind the plastic, reading the back, checking its date. Some she put back where they belonged. Others she kept on the floor beside her.

An hour passed, and she'd only gotten halfway through the albums. An array of photos lay strewn in a circle from her right ankle to her left knee.

A snapshot of Joe holding a large Mackinaw trout.

A backside view of Kate as she stood, topless and toddling, trying to reach a watermelon bigger than she was in the refrigerator.

A black-and-white picture of Theia's best friend, Bobbie Galden, riding a horse.

The girls with their Easter baskets, squinting into the sun.

Then, her favorite, one she'd kept forever and hadn't looked at for years: the litter of kittens she hadn't wanted to part with when she'd been ten. In this photo, she wore her two blue hair ribbons, tied at jaunty angles, one on each pigtail.

She would just have to be satisfied with a picture.

She couldn't come up with those hair ribbons any other way.

If Theia hurried, she had just enough time to take these to Big Horn Photo on the way to St. John's. She would buy pretty frames at Global Exchange and arrange them according to size on the table behind the sofa. She would display a few on the mantel. She would scatter some beside lamps and along windowsills.

Forget the expensive decorator prints and the watercolor she and Joe had bought each other for their tenth wedding anniversary and the pencil etching of a moose by the pond that they'd won top bid in a church auction.

Unnecessary adornments would come down from her walls. She would fill this house with life. Her life.

Joe fanned out the pages of his sermon across his desk and tried to make sense of them. He scrubbed his eyes with his palms, picked up his pen and made a note. Then he stared at what he'd written for a full fifteen seconds before he shook his head, drew a line through the entire thing, and pitched the pen across his desk.

The backbone of his Sunday message. Gibberish. He'd worked

on this for hours, and now it made no sense at all.

I'm a failure at being a husband for her, Lord. I don't know what to say to give her strength. I don't know what to say to let her know how much I love her. Even when I do think I know what to say, I open my mouth and the wrong words come out.

Stupid words. Hurtful words.

WHAT GOOD ARE YOU, HUSBAND, IF YOU HAVE FORGOTTEN TO RELY ON THE ONE WHO SEEKS YOU FOR HIS BRIDE?

Joe picked up the pages of his sermon one by one, scanned them, crumpled them into wads, and flung them against the wall.

Who am I to think I can teach anybody about You? Who am I, that I've taken responsibility for shepherding Your flock?

Joe stood in the middle of the office where he'd counseled close to hundreds, waiting, his breath coming in short laborious wheezes, his own heart an empty cavern.

He raised his fist to the ceiling and shook it. "Show me, Father. Show me who I am!"

The room felt as empty, as cavernous, as the portions of his own self that he'd finally opened up and laid out upon the winds of the heavens. Joe knew this to be true: Nothing about him was worthy or good enough or strong enough for the task that had been laid before him.

Joe lowered his arm.

He closed his eyes.

When he did, the picture came. Not so much a picture, maybe, but a living depiction. Moving figures. Wailing women gathering frightened children and herding them away. A trail of dirty, jeering Roman soldiers as they followed a bent man heaving a cross along through the dust up the hill of Golgotha.

Behind the cross stumbled this Jesus, this man they called the Christ, and Joe, standing alone in his office, saw the human man as he'd never been able to see Him before.

Their voices shrieked at Him as He staggered onward up the hill.

"Hail, king of the Jews!"

Again and again they struck Him on the head with a staff. One of them ran ahead, fell on his knees, paid mocking homage to Jesus as He passed.

"Hail, king of the Jews! Oh, mighty savior of the world. If You could only save Yourself now!"

Spittle coursed down His face from where they spat on Him.

Joe watched, horrified, as the soldiers lifted the cross from the shoulders of another man and began to erect it. This, then, was as far as he needed to see. But even though Joe's eyes were closed, the scene remained.

He knew what would come next.

They would put thorns on Jesus' head that would dig into His scalp and rip out His hair.

They would pluck the beard from His chin until there was scarcely anything left of His face.

With a cat-o'-nine-tails, they would scourge Him until his innards hung out of His body and His skin was shredded into tatters.

They would pierce what was left of Him with a spear, and His blood would begin to pour out onto the ground.

His followers would desert Him. His friends would betray Him. Even His own Father God would have to turn away from Him.

"No," Joe whispered. "No."

They kicked Jesus and put a bag over His head and shouted taunts. And when the bag was ripped off, this human man turned and fixed His eyes on Joe with an expression that took Joe's breath away.

THIS IS WHO YOU ARE, JOE MCKINNIS.

This then, he saw, was love. Love with no ulterior motive, unadulterated and true. The very definition of love, not in a dictionary, but on the cross.

"Lord!" Joe cried out as this man Jesus climbed past him, onward, to His crucifixion. "Lord!"

COME UNTO ME.

This is how God showed His love among us: He sent His one and only Son into the world that we might live through Him. This love: not that we loved God, but that He loved us and sent His Son as an atoning sacrifice for our sins.

At that moment, the room filled with a quiet gentle presence, a peace that vibrated to the very core of the pastor's soul.

"Lord?"

It had been so long.

So long.

COME THAT I MIGHT BEAR ALL YOUR BURDENS. COME THAT I MIGHT SHEPHERD YOUR FLOCK, EVEN AS YOU AGREED TO SHEPHERD MINE.

Joe fell to his knees, his kneecaps making a huge, hollow thud on the floor. He didn't care. His entire body shook. The trembling wouldn't stop, and he didn't want it to. He bowed before his Holy God, his tears pouring forth from the very headwaters of his soul. "I'm s-s-sorry. Oh, Lord, I'm so sorry. Oh, I'm sorry." He cried out like an orphaned child. "I've tried so hard to do the r-right things. And I've b-b-been so wrong."

He cried out the same way that the apostle Paul had cried out after he'd served thirty years in the ministry. "I want to know You, Lord. I've been looking at myself, not at You. Help me to stop imitating You, Lord." He lifted his eyes to the heavens. "I'm so t-tired of trying to live that way. All I want is to seek You, Father. You working through me, not me trying to do the right things anymore."

Help me with Theia, Father. I don't even know where to start. She's shutting me out.

And then, he knew.

Oh, Lord. I'm sorry for being afraid. I'm sorry for being selfish. I'm sorry for counting the cost for myself when I ought to have been thinking of her instead. Oh, Father.

A knock came at his door.

Joe stumbled to his feet. He didn't take the time to straighten his shirt, fix his hair, or attend to his face. He turned the knob and yanked the door open.

There stood Sarah Hodges, his secretary, with a cup of coffee strong enough to jump-start a Studebaker in her hands. She offered it to him. "I was just cleaning out the pot."

He'd thought she'd stare at him, only she didn't. Sarah was too busy taking stock of the wadded-up pages of sermon that had landed in various corners of the room. She finally met his eyes. Her brows furrowed. "You working on your Sunday message?"

"I am, oh, I *am*." He said it with such vigor, he splashed coffee dregs onto the carpet. It seemed years since he'd had this much joy, this much hope. He grinned and booted a wadded page of sermon out of his way. "Do we have any Coffee-mate for this, Sarah? It's going to make my hair stand on end."

Seven

Number nineteen, the regular Teton County middle-school bus, crept past the McKinnis's house at the exact same time every afternoon. Today, as the bus took the corner and made its way up Ten Sleep Drive, Kate had a minute to lean across Jaycee and scrub everyone's foggy breath off one window.

"See, you guys—" she pointed to the Fairlane where it sat waiting in the side yard—"I *told* you Grandpa was giving me his car. There it is."

"Whoopeee." Paul Jacobs pulled his Game Boy out of his backpack and started punching buttons. "That drools. What a piece of junk."

"It isn't junk. My grandpa's been driving it for twenty-seven years. He put a new battery in it and everything."

Paul won some sort of victory on the Game Boy, and it exploded into a mass crescendo of electronic sound. He rolled his eyes. "Like I said..."

"It rocks, Kate." Jaycee snuck her a red Twizzler, being especially careful because they weren't supposed to share anything to eat on the bus. "Paul is just jealous."

"It's a Ford."

"*F-O-R-D* stands for Found on Road Dead."

"When I get my permit, he said he'll take me out to the elk refuge so I can practice."

"I'll bet that car hasn't gone anywhere in ten years. It's buried in snow up past its hubcaps."

"That's because it just snowed this weekend, stupid. He drove it to the hospital last week."

The school bus hissed to a halt, the red stop sign folded out like an oar, and the huge yellow door accordioned open. "Stupid," Paul mimicked as Kate zipped up her Columbia jacket.

Jaycee waved. "See you later."

"Come over if you aren't doing anything."

"I will."

Kate hadn't thought to actually dig the car out of the snow until she saw the snow shovel propped beside the shed. *Hm-mmm.* If she cleared off the hood, her friends could see it better. Then annoying people on the bus couldn't make any more comments about the Fairlane not going anywhere for ten years. "Mom! I'm home." She left her backpack on the floor where she wasn't supposed to leave it, and went to the pantry to find a snack.

Her mother had left a note on the kitchen counter. "Gone to doctor's. There all afternoon. Heidi @ dancing after that. Love, Mom."

Oh yeah. It was Tuesday. The day of her mother's first chemo session. Kate jammed her mouth full of Doritos, found the broom, and hurried outside to begin laboring.

First, Kate used the broom to sweep snow from the Fairlane's windows. Next she pushed snow off the car's roof. After that she brushed snow from each fender.

She stepped back to survey her work.

She'd left huge piles behind the wheels and in front of the headlights. This was going to be a lot harder than it looked.

Kate yanked the shovel out of the snow and started digging. She hadn't scooped more than a dozen shovelsful before her back began to ache and her thumbs began to throb. She kept shoveling anyway, slicing into the ice with the shovel blade, pitching the load off to one side until she had the beginnings of a path.

Just let Paul Jacobs try to say this car won't go anywhere!

Slice. Pitch. Slice. Pitch.

I could get in and turn it on and drive all the way to Colorado if I wanted to!

That thought kept her going a long time. She had no idea how long she'd been digging when Jaycee came walking up the street toward her house. "Oh my gosh. Kate! You're really digging out the car. Is your grandfather going to let you drive it somewhere?"

"Sure." Kate hesitated. "Sure he will. He might even let me take it on the highway if I'm careful."

"No way!"

She didn't know why it seemed important to one-up Jaycee, but just now, it did. "He said he would," she lied. "That's why I'm doing all this." Kate jabbed the shovel hard into the snow so it stood unaided in the middle of the path.

"You're so lucky."

Kate dusted the snow off her mittens, satisfied.

Jaycee pulled her stocking cap down further over her ears in frustration. "It's so boring riding bikes when everybody else is getting cars."

"It's your turn to spend the night here Friday night. You want to?"

A long moment passed. Jaycee didn't answer right away. She slumped against the fender of the Fairlane and stared off into oblivion, looking guilty about something. At last she said, "I don't think I can."

"Why not?"

"You know." She shrugged easily, but Kate could tell something wasn't right. "There's always a whole lot going on."

"There's nothing going on. I'll ask Mom. She'll say it's fine. You'll see."

"I can't come over, Kate. Don't bother her about it."

Kate grew silent as she stored the shovel back in the shed, and the two girls walked together back toward the house. Suspicion niggled at her heart. Jaycee had never turned down a sleepover before. She asked with great caution, "You want to come inside?"

"That sounds good."

It was the right time of day to play music; her father was still working in his office at church. Kate grabbed the Doritos bag and the bean dip from the fridge.

"Paul Jacobs was being a total jerk today on the bus." Jaycee followed Kate upstairs. She paused, and then spoke the next few words with entirely too much emphasis. "There are a lot of people being jerks right now."

"Including you."

"I can't help it."

Kate shrugged, trying to push the pain away, but she couldn't do it. "Did you take notes in Miss Rainey's class today? On 'To Build a Fire'?" They'd been reading a Jack London story in English. "Tiffany kept passing me notes, and I never wrote anything down."

"I wrote down some stuff."

"If you came over Friday night, we could study for the test."

"Kate, I've already said I can't come."

"Whatever." Kate's lips contracted into a tight line of hurt. "Sorry I asked."

Jaycee turned away and fiddled with the row of first place blue ribbons that Kate had mounted on her bulletin board with push-pins. She'd won them all at the Teton County Fair, entering art projects. Jaycee sniffed and her shoulders heaved. It took Kate about five seconds to figure out that her best friend was trying not to cry.

"You want to tell me what's going on?"

Jaycee shook her head, still toying with the ribbons. "I promised that I wouldn't. It stinks."

Kate thought of her grandfather's car again, the Fairlane, out sitting in the snow, ready to cruise. Whenever things got bad, she thought of the car, and it made her feel better. But even that didn't help much now. "Fine then. I wouldn't want you to break any promises."

"I told you that everybody was being a jerk. Well, that means more than Paul Jacobs."

"Who does it mean?"

Jaycee turned around, drew a line with a finger beneath each eye to clear away tears without smudging mascara. "Tiffany Haas. She's having her birthday party Friday night, and she isn't inviting you."

Kate looked stunned. "She isn't? We're good friends. I had her to my birthday this year."

"I know."

"She kept passing me all those notes in Miss Rainey's class today."

"She's invited six people, and she's made us all promise that you don't find out."

It devastated Kate, everyone knowing the secret but her, being left out and alone. Her fair skin turned an angry red. "How come she doesn't want me?"

Jaycee didn't answer the question. "We're driving to Riverton. Her mother's gotten us a room at the Holiday Inn, and we're going to spend the night and swim. We're going shopping at the mall the next day."

Kate asked the same question again. "How come she doesn't want me?"

"If you ask her to her face, she'll have an excuse."

"Which is—?"

"That there isn't room in her mom's Suburban for anybody else."

Kate tried her best not to get upset. In her head, she listed the names of Tiffany's other friends, girls Kate liked and would have wanted to shop with. It would have been so much fun to be a part of the crowd. "Maybe that's a good-enough excuse."

"It's a fine excuse. Only it isn't why."

"It isn't?"

"It's because of your mother, Kate. Because she has cancer. Tiffany didn't invite you because she was worried you might talk about your mother's cancer. Her mom agreed with her, too. She thought it wouldn't be fair, asking you to have fun when there was something so sad happening to your family. Tiffany's mother said she wouldn't know what to say."

To cry in front of your best friend is a disreputable thing. So Kate didn't cry in front of Jaycee now. The muscles of her throat moved in a convulsive swallow. Why did stupid people always worry about saying the right thing?

It wasn't fair. None of it.

Kate picked up the phone book and searched through it for Tiffany Haas's number.

Theia pushed herself up off the couch in the waiting area and watched Heidi through the one-way mirror in studio three. Heidi did her best to keep up with the other clowns, but it would take weeks for her to grasp this complicated dance. Even so, she bounded around the room to the strains of Tchaikovsky as if she'd been given a gift, springing forward in the circle and catching hands, grinning when she made a misstep, catching hands, trying it over.

At one point when she made a mistake, Heidi gestured with wild animation toward her teacher. The instructor nodded. Theia watched as everyone took hands again, circled once, broke the circle, and then whipped into it backwards. The teacher pursed her lips and tilted her chin, then began slowly nodding again. "That's great—" Theia could read her words through the glass— "Let's add it to the dance."

Theia stood in the hallway the way she'd stood so many times before, her hand barely resting on the temporary cotton prosthesis beneath her blouse. Somewhere deep in her belly, the queasiness and the exhaustion that the doctor had predicted had begun.

No one could tell her exactly how her body would respond to chemo or what to expect. Dr. Sugden had given her two IV drips, the first something supposed to quell nausea, and the second a liquid similar to red Kool-Aid that made her entire body hum like a guitar. They sent her home with a list of printed instructions. She was to call the nurse if she developed fever over 101, started bleeding or bruising, or if the nausea didn't go away.

Other people had been in the waiting room with friends, but Theia had brought no one.

Why couldn't I tell Joe that I was afraid?

The door had opened upstairs. Four or five little dancers came trampling down the wooden steps, their snow-booted feet clattering as they came. Inside the studio, the instructor started the clowns on their cartwheels. Even though Heidi couldn't hear, Theia whispered the same instructions her own mother had given her once, out in a grassy yard, somewhere long ago.

"Hand. Hand. Foot. Foot."

Come on, Heidi. You can do it.

"Hand. Hand. Foot. Foot."

Heidi moved across the floor like a gigantic broken turtle, shaking her head and laughing, trying to get her hands on the floor and her feet in the air.

At her side, Theia's fingers closed and then opened again.

I should have been able to teach her. I should have been able to take her out in the front yard and tumble across the grass with her.

At that moment, she felt like cancer had devastated her. Cancer had kept her from helping her daughter grow.

It certainly hadn't taken much time, calling the girls from Miss Rainey's class and having them all over. "I know about your birthday, Tiffany." Kate planted her hands on her hips and flipped her hair over her shoulder in defiance. "Next time your mother doesn't want me to come to something, you can just tell me. You don't have to talk to everybody else in school first."

Tiffany tilted her head toward Jaycee. "You've got a big mouth, you know that?"

"I can't help it. Kate's my best friend."

"I trusted you."

"If you didn't want me to tell Kate, you shouldn't have invited me in the first place."

Tiffany squared her hands on her hips, too. "Well, maybe I'm sorry that I did."

After all of the hurt and disappointment, Kate did her best to be the peacemaker. "It's okay, Tiffany. I made her tell me. I bugged her and bugged her until she'd say what was going on."

Jaycee didn't back off. "I'm going to stay here Friday night and spend the night with Kate."

"Fine. You do whatever you want to do. The rest of us are going where we can have fun. Nothing fun ever happens around this place."

Megan Spence, who had been flipping through CDs in the corner, gave out a little laugh. "Tiffany. This reeks. Of course there's fun stuff to do here. Kate has her own car."

"Yeah," Jaycee echoed.

"So what?" Tiffany was gathering up her things to go. "She can't drive it yet."

"Yeah. But *I* can."

All three girls stared at Megan.

She waved her billfold in the air. "I've got my hardship license right here."

Kate's heart froze.

"So." Tiffany slid her arms into her coat. "Why are we all sitting around here? Let's go somewhere."

"We can't do that."

"Why not? It's your car, isn't it?"

"Yes, but I haven't—"

"You've been bragging about it for days."

"I know, but it's not the way I've made it sound."

"Where can we go?"

"The library?"

"We can't make any noise at the library."

"I could get a book for my book report though."

"We could drive up and down Elk Refuge Road and listen to KMTN."

"We could go to Dairy Queen."

By the time they'd all chimed in, Kate could not say no. Only

Jaycee glanced back at her with some hint of remorse as they went outside, glanced in every direction to make sure that nobody was watching them, and Megan started up the car.

"Where's your grandpa?" Jaycee asked as Megan backed out.

"I don't know."

Kate fingered the door handle. A piece of silver peeled off beneath her nail. The inside of the precious Fairlane smelled musty and old.

It wasn't supposed to be like this. It was supposed to be something special that Grandpa and I did together.

"Where's your dad?"

"In his office. He's got counseling appointments and stuff."

They stopped at the sign on the corner of Ten Sleep and made a right onto the highway. "Turn on the radio!"

"It's cold back here. Can you turn on the heater?"

"Just a minute! I have to figure out how to turn everything on." Megan turned on the radio, but it took a few seconds to warm up and start playing. "Kate, this car is really old."

"I know that."

They passed the turnoff to High School Road where the middle school and the high school sat side by side. They passed McDonald's, the Wyoming Inn, the pawnshop, and the Sagebrush Motel.

"I hate that song. Can you change it?"

"Where are we going?"

"Did anyone bring any money?"

They ended up at Dairy Queen. They pooled all their change and had enough to buy one Blizzard. They doubled back and drove halfway to Moose-Wilson Road. They honked at two different carloads of friends. They waved at the Teton County school bus bringing the Jackson Bronc JV football team home from a game. They hung a U-turn and started back toward the town square, heading for Elk Refuge Road.

That's when Megan glanced back over her shoulder at Kate and grinned. "It's your turn. You want to try?"

"Me?"

"It's your car, isn't it?"

Tiffany laughed nervously. "She can't drive, Megan. You're being crazy."

Jaycee sat beside Kate, her fists clenched at her sides, not saying a word.

Kate stared at her friend, her pulse drumming in her throat. She squirmed in her seat. They were all looking at her.

I can handle everything everybody's throwing at me. I can. "Well, it isn't a big deal." She said it mostly to Jaycee. "If Megan can do it, so can I."

"You can?"

"Sure."

Megan turned around again and eyed her from the front seat. "Kate, you're such a goody-goody. A preacher's kid. You know you don't really want to drive this thing."

"I do."

For what seemed an eternity, nobody moved. Tiffany finally flipped down the sun visor, opened her little pot of Carmex, and smeared some across her mouth. "It's not that big a deal. Everybody's tried it by now," she said with nonchalance. "Cheri Fraser walked home one day when her mom had gone to Dubois and drove us up to Yellowstone. We were gone all day."

"Driving ought to be easy," Jaycee said.

"You really want to try?" Megan's eyes met hers in the rearview mirror.

"Yes."

Kate had thought her positive answer would send them running from the car screaming, but it didn't. They sat right where they were, except for Megan, who pulled the car to the side of the road, got out, and gestured for Kate to scoot in behind the steering wheel. "Go ahead. I'll teach you."

Kate climbed out of the backseat, came around, and slid inside. She put her hands on the steering wheel. In her mind, the car grew ten times bigger. Kate leaned against the bench seat and felt the ancient upholstery crackle beneath her. She checked the rearview mirror, but all she could see were her own eyebrows, her own pale forehead.

"I don't think I want to do this."

"Just turn it on. Put the car in gear, and it'll go forward. That's all there is to it."

From where Kate sat, she could see Tiffany stretching her arm along the door beside the window, flicking her nails against the grid where the heat flowed.

Tiffany, who hadn't wanted Kate at her overnight party because having her might spoil the fun.

At this one moment, driving this car became a declaration of liberty for her, a way to show the whole world—God and her parents included—that she could handle growing up.

I don't need my mother! I can do things on my own.

Kate turned the key. The engine roared to life at first try.

It felt incredible sitting here, a powerful engine throbbing beneath the hood, as if Kate controlled the whole world.

"Put your foot on the brake first. Then you put it in drive."

Which one was drive? Kate manhandled the shift and moved the red line to R, which she decided must stand for "regular." They rolled backwards, bumping up over the curb.

"No. No! That's reverse," three girls hollered to her all at once.

"Put it on the *D*. That's drive. That makes you go forward."

She pulled the stick down, felt a clunk beneath her.

"You're doing fine. Fine. Now press down on the accelerator. That other pedal down there."

"There's another pedal?" Almost as fast as she asked the question, she found it with her foot. The Fairlane lurched forward. Jaycee grabbed the door handle. Megan screamed.

Just try to take my mother away, God. Do what You want to do, but You can't scare me!

She thought she was laughing, but then she realized she was choking on her tears. Her chest heaved, expanding for the air it wasn't getting.

"You're driving in the bike lane."

She yanked the wheel and went too far, jerking the car left, across the yellow line into the turn lane.

"Put the car in park, Kate. Put it on the *P!*"

A pickup truck loomed in the turn lane, coming right at them. They all three screamed at her, "Move over! Kate!"

She craned her neck over her right shoulder to check the lane. A Suburban roared past. "I can't."

Brakes squealed. For precious seconds, Kate sought the brakes in the Fairlane and found only air.

Bumpers came together in a terrifying crunch of metal. The girls pitched forward. Gravel flew.

When the car stopped, Kate moved the red line to *P.*

She ignored the tears of frustration and defeat as they coursed down her cheeks. Instead, she switched the key off like an expert and sat taller.

Eight

arry had never been one for tearing up good boxes.
He retrieved a table knife from the drawer in his little
kitchenette, made one clean slice through the right
end of the box, then the left. He cut across the center seam in the
box, making a clean dissection. He laid the knife beside him on
the carpet and steeled his heart against what he knew he would
find inside.

He expected to throw open the panels of cardboard and have
the scent, the very essence of Edna, come pouring out at him. But
it didn't. Instead, when he bent back the lid, everything inside
smelled bitter and brittle, decayed with age.

He recoiled.

How fresh and painful these treasures once had been. How
old and lost they seemed to him now.

He sat high on his old haunches, allowing himself, for the
briefest of moments, to feel cheated. For this he could blame no
one but himself.

There could be no hurrying the grieving process.

Sealing this box had been his one desperate attempt to contain
an unbearable, devastating hurt. A hurt that had proven impossible to escape. Harry had journeyed in its shadow for a lifetime.

Would that he had not locked away these memories, these

precious belongings of the woman who'd slept beside him and held him and nursed him and encouraged him for thirty-one years.

Would that he had touched these and cherished them while they still bore the fresh scent of her, the recent grip of her hand, the rare allusion of her presence.

Harry edged close again and, with a sense of desperation, peered inside.

Lord, will You show me? What is it that You intend for me to find here?

With one tentative hand, he began to remove items from the box.

Edna's favorite polka-dot apron. A tiny bowl she'd kept on the kitchen windowsill where she laid her wedding rings when she took them off to wash the dishes. Her darning thimble, kept in the wooden sewing basket beside her feet, worn so thin where she'd used it that daylight shone through the tin. The monogrammed mint green towel he'd found in the bathroom the day of her funeral, right where she'd left it, folded and lopped over the side of the tub. He lifted it high, let it fall open, seeking Edna.

He found only dust.

Harry refolded the towel and laid it aside with her other things. He reached in again. Touched leather. And knew.

Edna had always loved the feel of this Bible. He'd watched her when it was new, balancing it in one hand and running a palm over it with her other, enjoying the limber weight of it, the gold foiled pages, the way, when she dropped it open, it fell right to a place in the middle of Psalms.

He held it in both hands and stared at it.

It's only her Bible, after all. This is no surprise. I've known it was here ever since I closed that box.

Harry couldn't put it down. He remembered how she read

every page of this book as if it were a treasure, lifting the page from the bottom right-hand corner, turning it slowly, smoothing the center of the leather-bound volume with the flat of her hand.

Father, what do You want from this?

As if to answer him, the Bible plopped open.

When he glanced down, expecting Psalms, he found something more. A vaguely familiar onionskin envelope with pink rosebuds and scalloped edges, like lace...

What *was* this? Harry was afraid to touch.

Edna had such stationery once. He remembered her writing notes on it.

He picked up the envelope and turned it over. What he saw made chills run up his spine.

"To Theia," it read in Edna's bold, slanted script.

In his own mind, Harry began to play devil's advocate, thinking of all the reasons this letter might not be what it seemed. Perhaps it had already been opened. Perhaps it was something Theia had already read, something day-to-day and childlike, not significant at all.

Harry flipped the envelope over again and checked the flap.

Still sealed.

Harry's chest went tight with anticipation. He understood the full truth. Theia had not read this letter.

She might never have seen it, if not for his digging in the box.

Emotion clogged his nostrils, misted his eyes. Harry closed the Bible, leaving the letter exactly as he'd found it so his daughter could discover the envelope the way he had discovered it, the way Edna had intended it to be discovered all along.

He laid his wife's Bible with great care on the floor beside him.

Then he rocked back on his heels and whispered words of praise and gratefulness up to the sky.

Theia had just slammed the car door, opened the hatch of the Taurus, and lugged groceries to the kitchen counter when Joe came crashing in through the garage door. "Theia, did you hear from Kate this afternoon? Did she leave you a note or anything?"

Theia moved several grocery bags and checked the kitchen table, where they always left notes for each other if need be. "Nope. Nothing here. Where is she, Joe? Is something wrong?"

"Yes. She's been in an accident. A car accident."

"Oh, Joe, is she hurt?"

"Apparently not. Who was she with? Why didn't she leave a note to tell you she was going somewhere?" Joe gestured toward the car. They climbed in, and Joe backed out of the driveway, bumping over the wedge of snow that the plow left every time it cleared the road.

Theia buckled her seat belt. "I have no idea. She's always so good about that."

"She was with some friend. Jaycee maybe? I don't know who else would have come over after school."

"Joe, I—" Theia leaned her head back against the seat. The nausea she'd been battling all afternoon came upon her full bore. Her stomach roiled. "Joe, I'm going to be sick."

He pulled over for her at the corner of Ten Sleep Drive, yanked the door open, leaned over her, and held her head while she gave in to the effects of chemotherapy. She retched onto the graveled shoulder, gasping for air. "We've got to get there."

"We're okay, Theia." This time, his words didn't sound empty at all. He meant them. "She's waited for us already. She can wait a little bit longer." Joe searched the car for something so she could wipe her face. He found a pack of wet wipes in the glove compartment.

When Theia sat up and leaned against the headrest, he folded one of them to make a cool compress. He pressed it against her forehead, her temple, her other temple.

"Thanks," she whispered, shooting him a weak smile. "That's been coming on all afternoon."

"Are you okay to go?"

She closed her eyes and nodded. "Yeah."

They drove another three blocks, his knuckles white knobs as he clenched the wheel. Then in one abrupt motion, he steered them off to the right again and pushed the emergency brake on.

She stared at him. "Joe? What are you doing?"

For a long moment, he stared at his hands. Then he turned to her, spoke aloud to her the things he had given over to his Holy Father earlier. "Theia, I'm so sorry for so many things."

When she spoke, he heard hurt edging into her voice. "I don't think this is exactly the time to be discussing this."

"Perhaps it isn't, but we must discuss it soon." He took her hands. "Right now, there's something else more important."

She lifted her eyes to his. "What is that?"

"We have to pray. Together."

He saw her jaw go tight, saw the line of her lips begin to stiffen and then to tremble.

"I know." He touched her face, touched all the pain that he knew she still carried. "I know," he whispered, as he took her hands in his. He pulled them to him, entwined his fingers with hers, held them there.

"I can't pray."

He didn't let her go. "You want to tell me about it?"

She shook her head. "He wouldn't want to listen to me."

"He would. He *does*."

"I don't think God cares about me, Joe. How could a God who

cares about His children let cancer come into their lives?"

"I've seen it, Theia. I've felt it. He's made me to understand His love better than I've ever understood it before."

"I can't see it. I can't feel it."

"What He feels about His children having cancer, He took to the cross."

"If He died on the cross, He died for my sins, Joe, not for my cancer."

"All I know is this, Theodore. On that cross, He rendered evil ineffective. He took it upon Himself, and then He crushed it. Disease, sin, bad things, they haven't ceased to exist, but their power over His children has been broken. Your cancer has not been abolished, but it has been overthrown."

Her fingers curled into the safety of his hand. She stared at them there, and he followed suit. His fingers covering hers, their fingers wrought together like sinews of rope.

At last she spoke. "I was so wrong not to let you come with me today."

"I'll come the next time. And the next and the next. I am your husband. I want to be there."

Her two words, only a slight whisper. "Thank you."

"Will you pray with me for Kate, Theia?"

She nodded, tears in her eyes. "Yes, I will."

For the first time since she'd been diagnosed with breast cancer, they bent heads side by side, rearranged their clasped hands. "Holy God," Joe whispered, speaking aloud while Theia joined her heart with his. "Protect our daughter, Father. Keep her from harm. We can't do it, Lord, but we know You can. Surround her with Your angels. And give us renewed wisdom. Help us to know what to say, where to turn, when we see her. Amen."

"Amen," Theia said, too.

And thus for the first time in many months, husband and wife, mother and father, prayed together as one voice.

Nine

The fluorescent bulb glared overhead, bathing the sergeant's metal desk in sterile, harsh light. Theia watched her daughter sit in a wooden chair in one corner, rocking even though the chair was stationary, her hands trapped between her knees.

"Sergeant Ray Howard," his nametag read.

"Which one of you—" Joe wrapped one arm around Theia and held her next to him—"is going to tell us what's going on?"

Kate stared at her knees.

Sergeant Howard flipped a felt tip pen and caught it midair. "That ought to be up to your daughter, Pastor McKinnis. It seems she has a few important details that she needs to pass along."

"And the details are—?" Joe stared at their daughter.

The sergeant flipped his pen again. "We couldn't find any insurance information in the glove compartment, for one thing."

Theia spoke to her daughter in a gentle, urging voice, the same way a child might urge a kitten down out of a tree. Even as she did, she realized that she and Kate had not talked, really talked, for weeks. "Kate, will you tell us what happened?"

Joe addressed the officer behind the desk. "What do you mean, you couldn't find any insurance information in the glove compartment? *What* glove compartment?"

"The glove compartment of that antique contraption your daughter calls a car."

"Our insurance ought not to be responsible. Whoever was *driving* ought to be responsible. Whoever owns the *car* ought to be responsible."

Sergeant Howard gave an exasperated little chuff of breath, and as if to say *It's in your court now, girl,* he shrugged at Kate.

"I was driving, Dad." Kate said it so softly that they almost couldn't hear her.

Stunned silence filled the room. Then, "What? What were you driving?"

"Grandpa's car."

Neither Joe nor Theia had the wherewithal to figure out how they had not noticed that the old Fairlane was gone. It sat in plain sight at the side of the house, where anyone walking past could see it.

Theia closed her eyes. *I've distanced myself from my family, Lord. I've been so focused on having cancer that I'm living my life as if I've lost everything already.*

Joe raked one hand through his hair. "Grandpa Harkin was going to *teach* you, Kate. He wanted to use the experience to help you grow up and become a responsible person. How could you just throw such a gift away? From someone who loves you like that?"

She shook her head, and Theia's heart broke as the tears pooled in her daughter's eyes. "I don't know, Dad. I really don't."

"*Is* the car insured, Pastor McKinnis?"

"I don't know. I'll have to talk to my father-in-law about that."

Theia left Joe's side and sank to the floor beside Kate, laying a hand of reassurance on her daughter's flank. "He doesn't have insurance on that old car, honey," she said to Joe. She turned to the officer. "It isn't a roadworthy vehicle. He had it out once, about ten days ago. But he didn't insure it. I'm sure he planned to take care of it before he gave his granddaughter driving lessons."

Sergeant Howard scribbled a note on the report. Then another. "The registration isn't up to date either. We found that out when we ran the license plate number. It hasn't been renewed in the state of Wyoming since 1989."

"Where is the car right now?" Joe asked.

"We've got it out in the impound lot. We towed it in with damage to the left front fender. And here's a copy of the police report filed by the driver of the other vehicle." He yanked a copy out of the clipboard and handed it over.

Joe took the papers but didn't read them.

Sergeant Howard ran his forehead back and forth in the flat of his hand. "So let's go over the charges, shall we? First, driving an uninsured vehicle. Second, driving a vehicle with expired tags. Third, failure to signal a lane change. Fourth, driving without a license. Usually in cases like these, where the driver has borrowed a vehicle from a member of the family, the family elects not to press charges of vehicle theft. But, I—"

"She's our fourteen-year-old daughter, Officer Howard. I doubt very much that her grandfather will want to prosecute."

"I'll need to talk to Mr. Harkin about that, I'm afraid. Although he hasn't phoned us to report the car missing at present time."

"He doesn't even know it's missing. None of us knew."

"Maybe if you kept a closer eye on your children, Pastor, these things wouldn't come as such a surprise."

Joe's anger exploded. "How *dare* you accuse me of not watching over my own daughter?" He rose from the chair and advanced on the officer's desk. "If you had any *clue* what this family's been facing, you'd keep your comments to yourself."

"Honey—" Theia reached out to him—"Joe." *Lord, I don't want to distance myself from my own life any longer. I don't want to be distant from my children, from my husband, from You.*

Sergeant Howard slapped the clipboard on his desk the same way a judge would clap down a gavel. "She'll be scheduled to appear in Juvenile District Court two weeks from today, in front of Judge Terry Rogers. You are welcome to hire a lawyer or let Kate plead her case on her own. It makes no difference really. The outcome is generally the same."

Theia waited outside Kate's bedroom, her hand on the doorknob, her forehead leaning against the wooden door. Faint pop music played inside her daughter's room.

At last she gave a timid knock, once, twice, not knowing if Kate would invite her to enter or not.

"Hm-m-mm?" came a sleepy voice.

"Kate? It's Mom."

"Come in."

Kate was curled up in her single bed, propped up by pillows, reading a paperback novel.

"How are you doing in here?"

"Okay." Kate flipped a page of her book and kept reading.

Theia shoved her arms inside the big pockets of her bathrobe, touched one toe of her slipper to the other. "I just came to say good night. To tuck you in if you wanted me to."

Another page turned. "You haven't tucked me in since I was eleven years old."

"I know that. I thought maybe it was time to start it again."

On Kate's stereo, the CD player made a whirring sound and a click before it started playing another song. "I don't want to talk about today, Mom."

"It's okay." Theia didn't move toward her daughter. She stood in the middle of the room, feeling stranded. "I don't think I want to talk about it either."

Outside, gauze clouds stretched thin across the stars, and the moon shone transparent against the sky as though someone had tried to erase it. Theia's sense of loss settled someplace deep inside her ribcage, growing hard and heavy and cold there.

"I need to apologize to you, Kate."

"No, you don't."

"I've been a pretty crummy mom for the past few weeks."

Kate laid the book upside down, the pages forming a tent on her belly. "You haven't been. You've been fine."

"Even though I've been in this house with you, I've been far away."

"I can understand it, really. You've had some pretty crummy things happening to you lately."

Theia moved toward her daughter and sat on the edge of the mattress. The mattress creaked as it bore her weight. "There's no reason that you and your sister and your father should have to live through crummy things right along with me."

"Yes, there is." Kate rustled around in all the pillows and blankets until she could sit straight up beside her mother. "We're your family."

Another minute of silence passed. Kate pitched her book on the floor and flopped back three layers of covers. She patted the bed beside her. "Would you get all the way in bed with me, the way you used to do, Mom? Back in the days when we used to read stories?"

Theia touched her daughter's cheek and swallowed so hugely that they both heard it. "I don't know if there's room for both of us anymore. I haven't done this since you were—"

"Eleven years old." Kate smiled.

"We're both bigger than we used to be."

"That doesn't make any difference."

Theia crawled into bed with her daughter, turned on her side so they fit together like spoons. The Creator had cut them from the same family cloth. Their hips fit. Their bellies and their backs curved like instruments at the same places. Their shoulder bones jutted at the same angle, shadow images like limbs of the same tree, one alongside the other.

Kate moved over to give her mother more room. Theia scrunched around until she got the comforter adjusted. The bed felt wonderful. At last she could give in to the weariness that sapped her strength.

"Knock-knock," Kate whispered into the darkness.

"Who's there?"

"Little old lady."

"Little old lady who?"

"That's funny. I didn't know you could yodel."

Theia shook her head at her daughter.

"Didn't you get it? Little old lady who."

"I got it."

"I have another one."

"I'm almost afraid to ask."

"What did Snow White say when she took her film in to be developed?"

Theia couldn't help herself. She started to giggle. "I don't know. What did Snow White say?"

"She said, 'Someday my *prints* will come.' Get it? My *prints*."

That was all it took; they both dissolved in laughter.

They laughed until it hurt, pressing their faces into the pillows to keep from waking everybody else. They laughed until they cried. When they finally flopped over backwards, their bellies sore and their hearts lighter than they'd been in weeks, Theia rested her fingers on top of Kate's head.

She experienced at that moment an almost excruciating sense of the beauty, the texture, of life. She combed through silky strands of Kate's hair, reveling in the blend of its colors together, chicory brown and golden, sheening like water. She smelled her daughter's fragrance, sweet and fresh, like field clover tossed by a breeze. Even the bed linens exploded onto her senses, the entwining of the cotton threads, crisp and soft at the same time, a gift.

She thought of Heidi dancing in the studio, skipping across wooden honey floors, laughing at her missteps, her hair tucked behind one ear, her body pirouetting with joyful abandon before the mirrors.

The girls were each so beautiful and young and talented and…and *blessed.*

The world and all of heaven awaited her daughters.

How dearly she loved the two of them. She loved them fiercely, completely, to a depth that proved unbearable.

I HAVE LOVED YOU WITH AN EVERLASTING LOVE, THEIA. I HAVE DRAWN YOU WITH LOVING-KINDNESS.

Her entire body quickened. Here, in this quiet place, lying in bed with her daughter, she could hear without distraction or debate. No other voices plagued her. Only the gentle, quiet declaration that delved deep, winnowed her spirit to its very core.

BELOVED.

He came to her, an audible voice out of the stars and the darkness and the breeze outside the window. She rose up in response to the waves of warm certainty and love that enveloped her spirit.

Lord? Lord, is that You?

Her heart waited, poised for an answer. It didn't come in the form she'd expected. It came as the seed of something deep and new, a jewel of wisdom, embedded securely in her soul.

All at once she understood something about herself that she hadn't understood before. All at once she held in her hand a freeing truth.

In the midst of her struggle with cancer, she'd spent the last weeks methodically counting the cost in her life. The time had come now to take the same careful account of every blessing.

Theia wound a strand of Kate's hair around her pointer finger, unwound it, and rewound it again.

I'm afraid, Lord.

LET GO.

Father, it scares me to let go.

MY ARMS WILL CATCH YOU. MY ARMS WILL HOLD YOU. DON'T YOU KNOW?

I know, but I don't know. Sometimes it seems so hard to believe.

There are times when the most eloquent prayers to the Father are the ones that contain no words. Theia took a deep breath, reveling as the air rushed into her lungs. Surely, she wasn't alone. None of this had to be faced alone. She didn't have to figure it out or understand it. She curled up in the bed beside Kate and gave herself up, gave up all the burdens of her heart, her shame, her terror, her anger, her faithlessness, to the heavenly Father who already knew her heart to its very center.

And as she did, she knew something else. She knew her Lord's love. She felt Him holding her. She grasped the knowledge for the thousandth time and for the first time. She tasted how wide and how long and how high and deep was His love for her. He loved her, cared for her, more than her husband or her own daughters. All those earthly blessings were only a reflection of the love that He wanted her to know from the depths and the heights of heaven.

The love for her that He had carried to the cross.

After a long while she whispered, "Kate, I'm so glad to be your mother."

Kate nestled even closer against her in the single bed. "I'm glad you're my mom, too." A long pause, and then, "I know why I drove Grandpa's car today. I drove it to show you how independent I could be. I drove it to show that no matter what happens with you, I can manage on my own."

"Your dad and I both know you're growing up." But this went much deeper than just recognizing that Kate was maturing, and Theia knew it. "I'm here for you, sweetie. You can talk about all this stuff with me."

"I get really scared, Mom, when I think that something might happen to you."

It was what Theia had expected all along. *Put the right words in my mouth, Father. Please. I don't know what to say to her about this.*

Magically, miraculously, the words began almost to speak themselves. "Growing up doesn't mean that you have to grow independent, Kate. God wants you to rely on Him, no matter what happens. He wants you to know that, no matter how difficult things become, you'll never have to manage on your own."

Goose bumps raised on Theia's arms. She had no idea where any of this was coming from. *It's what You want me to learn, too, isn't it, Father?*

"I want to do that, Mom. I want to trust that much in the Lord."

"Oh, Kate, so do I."

It's so hard to let go, Father. Show me how. Saying something and doing something are two such different things.

Again her heart waited, poised, listening. Again the Father answered Theia in a different way than she'd expected. In the midst of her asking to be shown, the heavenly Father was already showing her.

He was using her to teach the lesson to someone else.

Ten

It was Thanksgiving morning, and the living room at the McKinnis household had been transformed into a room for a family feast.

While overzealous, overdressed television stars gave viewers a blow-by-blow description of the floats in the Macy's Thanksgiving Day parade, Joe added both leaves to their huge country oak table. He found his wife in the kitchen in her bathrobe, wrestling with the turkey and getting it ready to go into the pan.

He kissed the back of her neck, almost liking the idea that he no longer had to move her mantle of hair to do so. Since her hair had fallen out, first in strands and then in clumps, Joe had fallen in love with new parts of his wife that he hadn't seen before, the hollow at the base of her skull that perfectly fit the shape of his thumb, the swan arch of her spine that made her seem so beautiful and strong. He loved the way she wore gypsy-colored scarves knotted to look like flowers on her head. He enjoyed noticing her vast array of earrings. And for Christmas, he had already decided to give her diamonds.

"Hey," she said. He could feel her smiling even though he couldn't see her expression. "You want to open the oven door for this bird?"

He'd forgotten until he saw Theia struggle with the heavy roaster that her pectoral muscle didn't work so well these days.

"Here. Let me get that. You're trying to do too much."

"No, I'm not. Everybody's helping."

Indeed, they were. The girls would be up in no time and clamoring to get started on the pumpkin cake. Everyone that they'd invited to share in this day had insisted on bringing something: cranberry salad, mashed potatoes and gravy, fresh green beans, sweet potato pie. Even though everyone had offered to help, Theia could not be persuaded to give up cooking the McKinnis family turkey.

"Theodore. Promise me you'll lie down today and rest if you need to."

"I promise." She pecked him on the nose. "Thank you for agreeing to let me do this crazy thing."

"Not many people give huge holiday parties while they're battling cancer."

"I know that. But I want to see everyone."

"It's going to be a wonderful Thanksgiving."

"More wonderful—" a jangle of earrings punctuated her joy— "because I realize how much we have to be thankful for."

Because so many had insisted on helping Theia with the food, she'd been left free to arrange her table as she pleased. She'd sent her mother's antique-lace tablecloth off to Blue Spruce cleaners to be pressed. This morning she unfolded it and arranged the lace just as she wanted across the dark grain of the wood. At each place she set an index card with goofy turkey and pilgrim stickers. On each card at each place she'd written a different Scripture.

"Therefore, since we are receiving a kingdom that cannot be shaken, let us be thankful, and so worship God acceptably with reverence and awe." (Hebrews 12:28)

"Give thanks to the LORD, call on his name; make known among the nations what he has done." (1 Chronicles 16:8)

"Enter his gates with thanksgiving and his courts with praise; give thanks to him and praise his name. For the LORD is good and his love endures forever; his faithfulness continues through all generations." (Psalm 100:4–5)

She stepped back and inspected her handiwork. The goblets stood polished and gleaming, ready for iced tea. The candlesticks stood tall and proud, a Mr. and Mrs. Pilgrim bedecked in Early American finery, a gift from Joe's mother one November.

Theia came to her own chair, the seat closest to the kitchen where she could jump up and retrieve condiments and refills when necessary. She set the card beside her goblet and read her verse for the umpteenth, glorious time.

"Let your gentleness be evident to all. The LORD is near. Do not be anxious about anything, but in everything, by prayer and petition, with thanksgiving, present your requests to God. And the peace of God, which transcends all understanding, will guard your hearts and your minds in Christ Jesus." (Philippians 4:5–7)

On the television the parade ended and football began. Kate and Heidi stood at the kitchen counter, arguing over who got to lick cream cheese frosting off the beaters. The doorbell rang. Theia's father arrived carrying a huge basket of chrysanthemums to sit beside the hearth, an assortment of breads from The Bunnery, and a gift, wrapped the way he always swathed his packages, in ancient tissue paper tied with string.

Before Theia had the chance to ask him about it, Sarah Hodges drove up with her family. Next came Winston Taylor, who shook Joe's hand roundly and hugged both of the girls. Jaycee appeared at the door with her parents, Lois and Tom Maxwell, and her two little brothers. "Happy Thanksgiving!" Joe welcomed them and took their coats at the door.

"Oh, Theia. What a beautiful table. Look at the Bible verses."

"Everything's so pretty."

"We made the cake." Kate held up a beater just to prove it.

"And everything smells so good!"

Not one person walked through the door without bearing a dish of something wonderful. Cakes and pies and casseroles vied for position on the buffet, then overflowed onto the coffee table. The very sight of so much food, the aromas, the ingredients, the hearts and hands that had prepared the meal, set Theia's senses reeling. She'd been having a difficult time eating since chemotherapy started. Even when the nausea subsided, she battled with a metallic tang that stayed in her mouth for days. She lowered herself into a chair in the dining room, gripping the back of it for support.

Lord, help me to be open and aware today. In the midst of my thankfulness, help me to be vulnerable and real. That's what You want from me, and I know it.

Eleanor Taggart sat beside her and touched her knee. "What can I do for you today, Theia?"

On her lips were the words, "Nothing. Everything's taken care of." But Theia realized that wasn't what she was meant to say at all. She thought for a moment and came up with something. "When the timer buzzes, will you take the dressing out of the turkey for me? Before Joe carves."

"I can do that."

"Thanks, Eleanor. For the time being, just sit and talk while I get my bearings, okay? All this food…well, I could use a little conversation."

"Yes. I will." A light, gentle smile. "How have you been?"

Theia had begun to understand, during these past weeks, that this was the way she needed to be talked to. She needed to be asked easy questions, questions that let her choose between answering, "I've been driving so many dance carpools that I feel like a taxi driver," and "I had a rough chemo session this week, and my eyebrows fell out."

She understood that she needed to choose, more often than not, to feel cared for when people bumbled conversations around her and said the wrong thing.

With each passing day, the Father was helping her to know her own self and to trust Him more.

She chose truthful words for Eleanor now. "This week has been a good one, but there've been bad ones, too. I've been scared, and I've been discouraged. And I've spent the past days rejoicing that, for however long it lasts, I'm so lucky to be Joe's wife and Kate and Heidi's mother."

"It's tough going sometimes, isn't it?"

"You see this pottery?" Theia reached for a casserole filled with sweet potatoes. "It had to be formed and fired, painted and refired, for it to turn out as beautiful and colorful and *useful* as it is now. There are days when I feel like that's where I am, Eleanor. In the fire, burning up. That's when I have to remind myself that I'm in the kiln, being handmade into some useful new vessel for the Lord."

Eleanor squeezed her hand. "Your friends are here for you, to help you walk through this. We may not do it right, but we want you to let us try."

"Thank you." Theia hugged her. "I need to let you do that. For so long I've tried not to let anybody know that I was afraid. And I've been so alone."

The buzzer on the stove went off. Joe came into the kitchen with a troop full of men who brandished knives and planned to carve the turkey.

"Now that's a scary sight, all those men in the kitchen with knives."

"Out, out, all of you!" Theia grinned at Eleanor, rose from the chair, and shooed the men out of the kitchen with her apron like she'd shoo a flock of geese. "Eleanor has to take care of the stuffing first. Then we'll call you."

"We can just cut into it, can't we? The stuffing will fall out."

"Women have a way that they like to do things, and that isn't it."

Between the two genders, the great crowd of people managed to get everything uncovered and cut to serve, ice in glasses, tea poured, dressing in a bowl with a silver serving spoon, and a mountain of turkey sliced to perfection. Everyone oohed and aahed when Joe set the huge platter of meat on the table before them.

Winston Taylor volunteered to eat one of the legs whole.

Jaycee's little brothers began to shout at top volume for the wishbone.

Theia joined hands with Eleanor on her right and Sarah on her left. From across the way, her husband winked at her and then mouthed, "I love you." They had prayed together and had decided on the order of things just this morning.

Joe began. "Before we thank the Lord for the meal, Theia has something she wants to say to everybody here."

Lord, even while I walk through the valley of death, shine Your light through me.

"We invited you all here because we love you. Because the Lord loves you, too, and He's put you in our lives now, at a time when we need you the most." Her voice faltered. "We have not been easy to stand beside these past few months, but you have done it anyway. On this day of all days, when we offer up thanksgiving to our Father, we want to tell you that we thank God for you."

Down the table, Jaycee's mother, Lois, picked up the index card that had been propped beside her goblet. Jaycee had told her mother about the Lord and had invited her several times to come to church, but so far she hadn't. "Can I read this?" the woman asked, her voice almost as shaky as Theia's. "I don't read the Bible much, but I'd like to read it today."

Theia nodded. "Oh, Lois. Please do."

"'Come, let us sing for joy to the LORD; let us shout aloud to the Rock of our salvation. Let us come before him with thanksgiving and extol him with music and song.'"

Lois's gentle, hope-filled voice encircled the table even as they all encircled it with their hands.

Joe prayed after that, and everyone started passing the feast.

Theia hadn't been able to get back into her own kitchen all afternoon.

Kate, Heidi, and Jaycee had made quick work of the dishes. Others had served coffee and wrapped up the leftovers and left plates out with goodies for everyone to nibble while they watched football. Theia had even taken a nap.

It wasn't until almost dusk, after everyone had gone home and she went in to make a pot of tea, that she found the package wrapped in ancient tissue paper and tied with twine.

"What's this?" she asked anyone within earshot.

"Something your dad brought over when he came this morning. I don't know."

She untied the string, tore open the paper.

When she recognized it, her hands started to tremble. She couldn't swallow past the lump in her throat.

"Joe, this is my mother's Bible."

"How can that be?"

"I don't know. Dad must have found it somewhere."

Theia set her teacup down in the precise center of the saucer. She lifted the huge, leather book from its wrappings, and the pages fell open. Pencil notes, gleaned from her mother's favorite sermons and studies, lined the margins. In almost every chapter, verses had been underlined and some of them even dated.

"All of her notes are here. All of the things she was learning when she—"

Joe came up behind her and captured her shoulders. "When she got cancer?"

Theia nodded. "And before."

Her hands drifted to the brittle yellowed pages, fingering them as if they were gold. Out the window she could see the light in her father's greenhouse, his dark silhouette stooped over the gardener's bench.

"I've got to talk to him."

Joe nodded, and she saw in his eyes that he understood. Love for her husband, for all they were becoming together, overwhelmed her.

She rose and went to find the other man in her life who loved her above all else.

Her father glanced up when she knocked on the screen. "Anybody home?"

He raised a trowel in her direction and gestured for her to enter. "That was a fine meal today, Theia. A fine meal." The light from the bulb above him seemed to catch in his eyes and gleam there.

She went inside, taking a deep draught of the smells of her father, of old fabric and of loose, dark soil in the greenhouse, of potash and bone meal and nitrogen and of new warm things growing outdoors. She held up the Bible in her hands.

"I found it, Daddy. Thank you."

He drove the trowel deep into the dirt. "Thought you could put that to good use right about now."

"I thought her Bible had gotten thrown out with the rest of her things. It's been missing for years."

He told her the story of how he'd sealed it away in the box.

"The more I kept praying for you, Theia, the more I kept thinking about that box. I swept your mother's life away before I'd scarcely even given you the chance to grieve for her. It was the wrong thing to do."

Theia laid her head against the rough flannel of her father's work shirt. It became difficult, at the moment, to discern who was holding whom for comfort. Her own father seemed so much smaller, so much more feeble, than she'd ever noticed before. As if he were withering away somehow. As if she'd become the parent and he, the child. "It's okay. You didn't know."

"Should have learned a long time ago. When you push aside the bad things, you also push aside God's power to heal and reconstruct."

"Maybe that's what God's doing now. Giving us both a second chance to heal."

Now that he'd dug all the dirt out of the pot, her dad selected a begonia from a plastic flat, turned it upside down, and emptied the squared soil and root into his gnarled old hands. "There's more inside that Bible than you've found."

"What do you mean?"

"Just look."

She began to thumb through the pages.

"There's notes all in here. And a church bulletin from some service back in 1979."

"Keep going."

At first Theia didn't see the envelope. But the page fell open, and she recognized the scalloped edge, the tiny pink roses, the paper as thin as an autumn-cured leaf. She picked it up. "What's this?"

"Maybe you can tell me."

She flipped the envelope over and saw her name written there in her mother's strong, slanted script.

Theia ran her fingernail under the flap and with the greatest of care opened a letter from her mother that had been sealed away for twenty-two years.

Dearest Theia,

If you are reading this letter now, it means that I have gone home to be with the Father, and you are looking through my Bible.

It is the most difficult thing I have ever done, thinking of leaving you and your father behind. But leave you behind, I must. I have faith in God and I have faith in the two of you. I know that, after I leave, you and your father will make it just fine. But you're going to have to help him a little bit. He's going to be lonely for a while, until he gets used to being without me.

I remind you now, and someday you will know, that healing is more than what some people think it is. To be healed is to be made whole. And I have been made whole, even though my body is against me, because cancer has made me realize that Jesus is here with me, loving me, telling me about myself, holding my heart. This has been, because of that new discovery, a most glorious time.

You, my precious daughter, are the one who has prayed the most for me. As I go, I stand firm on the belief that God does not cause cancer in this world. We humans mess up all of the time, but God never fails. Prayer must be, in the end, as in everything else, the perfect act of trusting God. Isn't relinquishment of everything to God very much the same as acceptance that God is in everything?

You have grown up so fast. You haven't worn these ribbons in your hair in a long time. I found them on the shelf beside my hairbrush today and thought you might enjoy having them to remember our mornings by. Being your mama is the joy of my life. You are a beauty, dear heart, inside and out, and I am so proud of you.

Mama

Two blue satin hair ribbons fell out of the folds of the letter, making two perfect curls in the flat of Theia's hand.

Theia held the strands of blue satin ribbon high for her father to see. They represented so much to her. A childhood that she'd almost let herself lose because parts of it were painful to remember. A loving mother who had done her best to teach her to grow and walk in courage and in freedom, despite the obstacle of disease.

Her father hoisted his latest potted begonia high upon the shelf. "Anything in that letter that an old man might get to hear about?"

"Plenty." Theia laid her head in a careful place, against the broad of his back where he still seemed powerful and young, where she could feel the strength of his heart beating. "She had faith in us, Dad. She knew we'd be okay."

Her father's voice was choked with emotion. "A good woman, my Edna." He turned and gave his daughter a sad, wise smile. "Guess it's time I stopped thinking about her dying. Guess it's time I started thinking about her living instead."

"Yes."

"She lived for us, Theia. She lived for us, and she lived for her Lord. Just the way you're doing now with your husband and your little ones."

For a moment, Theia stared at the ribbons, winding them between her fingers the same way she had wound Kate's hair not so long ago. She reached behind her nape and, with no further ado, looped them around her neck. She tied them into a double bow at the base of her throat. There would be no more ponytails or plaits for a while, not until her hair grew back.

"I always felt so special wearing these. I went through the whole day reminding myself that Mom had put those ribbons in my hair."

The same way she'd learned to get through each day with cancer, reminding herself of God's presence in her life.

Her dad took another tin bucket off the shelf and drove a nail in the bottom with one easy *thwack*. He turned it right side up and started to place rocks inside. "Remember how your mother used to stuff her Thanksgiving turkeys? Remember how she used to stand it upside down in the sink and wiggle its legs and tell us it was doing the tango so it wouldn't go down the drain?"

Theia tucked her mother's letter back inside the Bible, ready to carry it inside. "Oh, Daddy." She kissed him on the sandpapery cheek. "How could I ever forget?"

Opening night of the Nutcracker performance, and pandemonium reigned backstage at The Pink Garter Theater.

"My wing is torn." One of the littlest angels tugged on Theia's sweater. "Can you sew it for me?"

"I can't find my leotard." A reindeer jingled her bell harness for attention.

"The Sugar Plum Fairy can't find her crown."

Theia stood there, a corral mom helping out backstage, trying to figure out how to clean the grape juice out of Jake Mason's jabot before he had to dance in the party scene, dabbing circles of Shangri-La Ruby lipstick on each reindeer's nose, and making certain that no one chewed gum when she lined up to take the stage.

Ten minutes before the show began, Julie Stevens came behind the curtain and crouched close to her dancers. They gathered around her as she gave them last minute encouragement and suggestions. "We've got a full house out there tonight, so be sure to dance your best. Angels, when you make the arch with your scepters, remember to make a slow big motion, big enough to carry to the last row of the theater."

Eight angels nodded, their halos bobbing.

"Mice, when you throw the cannonballs, remember that they are heavy. *Heavy.* You are not throwing plastic balls around. You are battling, iron against iron."

One mouse flexed her forearm and proudly showed everyone some muscle.

"Reindeer. I don't care what else happens out there, do *not* get too far ahead of the sleigh."

"We won't," they all shrieked while jingling the bells on their harnesses one more time.

"Sh-h-hhh."

"This is it. What we've been working toward for months. I'm on my way to the sound booth."

The dance students cheered.

Just as Julie Stevens headed downstage, she and Heidi almost collided. "Have a good time out there tonight, Heidi. You've worked really hard, and I'm proud of you." Theia's gaze locked with Julie's over Heidi's head. "I'm glad you're here tonight, Mrs. McKinnis."

Theia inclined her jaw. "I am, too." That's all that needed to be said.

In the theater the overture swelled, and on stage the spotlights faded from twilight to black. They came up again in lavish colors, blue, green, red, yellow, bathing the set, a Christmas tree, an English Victorian parlor decorated for a party, in radiant light. Partygoers, young and old alike, began dancing their way up the aisles toward the stage.

"Are you going out in the audience to see me dance?" Heidi whispered.

Theia nodded. "I wouldn't miss it. They said I could sneak out and sit on the stairs to watch."

"Where are Grandpa and Dad and Kate?"

Theia opened the side of the curtain just an inch. "Over there." She pointed. "See. On the fourth row."

There they sat, all three of them, already enthralled by the performance, their faces captured in the vivid lighting. Theia closed the curtain. Heidi nodded at the double bow that Theia had pinned to the chest of her sweater. "You wear those ribbons Grandma gave you all the time now, don't you?"

"Yes, I do. I brought them along for a special reason tonight though. Just in case you thought you might want to borrow them."

Heidi checked her braids, pinned with what felt like six hundred bobby pins and sprayed with hair lacquer so they wouldn't give way during the cartwheels. "There isn't anyplace to put them."

"If you wanted, we could always come up with something."

"What if I mess up the cartwheels after I've practiced them so many times?"

"Remember what I taught you. It's all in the rhythm. Hand. Hand. Foot. Foot."

"Can you tie a ribbon on my arm, Mom? That way I'll know it's there, but no one else can see it."

"Ah. There you go. Perfect idea." She unpinned the ribbons from her sweater and made a lovely bow on her daughter's arm with a flourish. "I'll be praying that every cartwheel lands right."

Heidi pulled her sleeve down over the little bow.

"Clowns. Three minutes! Line up."

"That's you." Theia gave her a little swat on the behind. "You're on."

Heidi took a deep breath, smoothed her pantaloons, and lifted her chin. "I'm ready."

Theia kissed her good-bye, snuck past the curtain, and found a place on the steps so she could watch. Minutes passed. The stage stayed bright. Suddenly music surged again through the theater. Mother Ginger clumped across the stage on her stilts, hid a giggle behind her gloved hand and lifted her swaying skirts.

Out cartwheeled five clowns.

Hand. Hand. Foot. Foot.

Each cartwheeling clown landed perfectly.

Heidi tilted her beaming face up toward the lights and began to dance. In her heart, Theia danced alongside her daughter. And perhaps in heaven, Edna Harkin danced, too, spinning, laughing, landing a cartwheel or two, delighting in the heavenly Father who had brought forth from three generations—daughters, mother, grandmother—His finest legacy of love.

Tributes to Our Mothers

Heavenly Cloth

Not all mothers are cut from the same cloth, but I believe *all* the cloth is made in heaven.

My mom never baked cookies or acted like a TV mom—or like anyone else's mom for that matter. Unable to find a Mother's Day card that really fit her, I modified one a year or so ago of a mom in a dress and apron holding a big bouquet of flowers, obviously homegrown. I cut out a man's cap from a woodworker's catalog, along with some tools, which I inserted in the bouquet—paintbrushes, pliers, pruning sheers, etc. I hung a sander from her apron. Now *that* looked more like her—although I should have done away with the dress for a pair of jeans and one of those tunic type aprons with lots of pockets for her tools. Just try to find a card with a mom dressed like that!

I didn't get home-baked cookies or have the luxury of having her there when I got off school, much less help with homework, but I learned how to tackle home projects and business projects without intimidation. She's been there for every one I've ever undertaken, usually commandeering the crew. She taught me to be independent, to think for myself, and that nothing is impossible with God on my side.

She is not just my mother. She is my best friend and mentor. I have her to thank for who I am and what I am—for teaching me to dare to dream.

LINDA WINDSOR

MOTHER AND NOVELIST, *MAIRE* and *NOT EXACTLY EDEN*

I Love My Mama...

I love my Mama because...

She always helps me clean my room.

She makes good food for me to eat.

She stands up for me.

She gives me *great* hugs and kisses.

She is not only my mom, but one of my best friends.

She went through lots of pain just to have me.

She always finds time to be with me.

She tries to act like a teenager to make me like her more.

She makes me tea when I get a sore throat.

She always gives me her true, honest answer.

I love my MOM.

AVERY BEDFORD, AGE 11, DAUGHTER OF DEBORAH BEDFORD

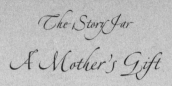

The Story Jar

A Mother's Gift

My mother, Frieda King, was a devoted woman of letters and journals. From the time I was a little girl, I remember her sitting at a small, brown, painted desk with three drawers on each side and with the top covered with horrendous green vinyl. There she wrote letters to family and friends on stationery, and observations of the day in a spiral notebook. She always used the same beige fountain pen, which she guarded as though it were made of solid gold and set with diamonds.

When we went on family vacations, Mom would sit in the front seat with a steno pad and write descriptions of the scenes, finishing the entries during the evening hours as we camped. During the early years, it was tent camping and writing by firelight. Later, it was camping by small—then larger—travel trailers and writing by blue butane. My mother was the first to encourage me to write.

Mom had beautiful penmanship—consistently elegant, plain, round, slanting letters. As an adult with a home and family of my own, I always knew how Mom was feeling physically and emotionally—not by the words in her letters, but by her handwriting. Her penmanship was a barometer on the storms of her life: my brother's capture by the North Vietnamese, my father's heart condition and liver cancer, and finally, the dwindling of her physical strength as she lived with breast cancer.

As Mom calmly faced death, she asked me what I wanted from the house. I asked for her journals. If I couldn't have her, I wanted her work so that I could spend time with her even after she had gone to be with the Lord. I consider her worn steno pads and spiral notebooks my most precious inheritance. It wasn't until after

The Story Jar

Mom died and I found some short stories and a full-length novel, as well as letters from a roommate from her nurses' training days, that I learned my mother had dreamed of being a professional writer.

Instead of pursuing her dream, she set it aside and became the wind beneath my wings.

FRANCINE RIVERS

MOTHER AND AUTHOR, *REDEEMING LOVE* AND *RAHAB*

A Celebration Heart

There are a million memories I have of my mother. She's filled so many roles: pastor's wife, mother, teacher's aide, camp cook, craft instructor, referee (between my brothers and me), encourager, discipliner, and the anchor of our family.

She taught me the value of celebration. She's always had a true celebration heart—a heart that makes every event in life something special. Holidays, birthdays, events of every shape and kind were treated equally, with great enthusiasm and delight. And laughter. Lots of laughter.

Valentine's Day saw the table set with everything red, from the plates and napkins to the food and drink. St. Patrick's Day was a festival of green. Whatever the celebration, we always found little gifts at our places at the table, just to remind us how special we were. Easter was a masterpiece of specially prepared eggs and baskets hidden to perfection.

Christmas was a month-long festival, complete with singing and decorations and cookies and special food, and "shopping night," where mom took each of us, my two brothers and me, out for shopping and dinner at the restaurant of our choice. (I can still taste those milkshakes from Newberrys, which tasted that much better because we got to sit at the counter and drink them.)

Now, anytime my brothers and parents and I are together, the rooms ring with laughter as we remember those times. To this day, whenever a holiday or special event approaches, I find myself growing giddy with anticipation. When I was living two thousand miles away from my family, I decided to pass on my mom's legacy of a celebration heart. I invited friends from our Bible study and work over for special Valentine's dinners, all set up just as Mom had set them up for us as kids. It was a delight to see our friends' eyes light up, to watch them enter into the spirit, and know I was, at least in part, sharing my mother with them.

One of those friends, after years of listening to me go on and on about my parents and my childhood, went with me to Oregon on vacation. I didn't know it, but she was convinced my memories had been exaggerated over the years. No one, she later told me, could be as great as I'd painted my mom and dad.

Within a day of being at my folks' house, this friend came up to me, eyes wide, head shaking. "They really are the way you said."

At her wondering words, I grinned. "Yup, they are."

As a child, I never would have understood my friend's amazement. I thought my mom was just like anyone else's mom. I looked forward to the end of each school day, for that was when I raced home to perch on the counter, regaling my mother with the day's events as she fixed dinner. She listened and laughed with me; she exclaimed over my latest poem or story or masterpiece of artwork; she disciplined when necessary, but always with a strong dose of love mixed in; she played innumerable games with us, never letting us win, but never minding when we did. She showed us, every day, the reality of a life dedicated to God, a heart submitted to His leading; a Christian who treated faith as a verb, not as some idealistic theory.

Now, as an adult, I know just how rare my mother was—and is. To this day, she is one of my closest friends, the one I want to share my day with, the one whose smiles and hugs and laughter bless and encourage me. When I see her looking at me, those green eyes—so like mine—shining with love, I know how abundantly I've been blessed.

I don't deserve her. I never could. But I'll ever and always be grateful to the Father for letting me have her. I've heard others say their mother is the best in the world, and I just hold my tongue. Because Mom always taught me to respect others' ideas and opinions, even when they're wrong. And they *must* be wrong, because I *know* who the best mom in the world really is: Paula Ann Sapp, woman of God, servant, wife, mother. A woman of laughter and wonder and delight. A woman who blesses the lives she touches.

My mom.

My special gift from God.

KAREN BALL

EDITOR AND AUTHOR, *WILDERNESS* AND
THREE WEDDINGS AND A GIGGLE

A Mother's Miracle

Thursday, May 28, 1998, was just like any other day at my Florida home. The weather had not really warmed up yet, but Brooke, my seven-year-old daughter, and her best friend wanted to go swimming. I baby-sit infants during the day, so I knew I wouldn't be able to swim with them, but both of the older girls are good swimmers.

My three-year-old, Lacey, wanted to swim, too. I was reluctant at first but thought she'd be okay with her big sister. As I cared for the babies, I pulled up all the blinds at the window so I could keep an eye on the older children.

In the midst of their fun, Lacey decided to take off her flotation device. She went down the slide without it and sank straight to the bottom. Brooke and Julia were on the other side of the pool and didn't see Lacey on the bottom. No one knows how long she was underwater, but when Brooke *did* see her, she swam over right away. Lacey was unconscious and too heavy for the older girls to lift. Finally, in an adrenaline rush, Brooke pulled Lacey out by both arms and started screaming.

Inside the house, I heard the noise and realized something was terribly wrong. I ran out as fast as I could and saw Lacey on the ground, blue and lifeless. For a moment I couldn't move. I looked at Brooke, then she ran into the house to dial 911.

I thank God that I had undergone CPR training in preparation for my childcare business. Lacey was so blue that I didn't think I'd be successful. I kept pushing and breathing, pushing and breathing, until the emergency medical technicians arrived.

While I was working and waiting for help, I cried out to God. *Please, help me! God, please help!* That's when I heard a faint groan.

I looked down at my daughter, then heard the sound of the ambulance and the EMTs.

They worked on her, too, pumping and breathing life into a dying child, but nothing they did made her wake up. I heard one of them say, "We've got to get her out of here now!" While I watched in horror, they took my baby and put her in the back of the ambulance. My husband, Mike, pulled up just then and asked what had happened. They told him there had been a drowning…and then he looked into the back of the vehicle and saw our little girl on the stretcher. Mike's knees buckled, and he fell in the road.

I couldn't leave the house because of the babies in my care, but I went into my room and picked out a dress for Lacey, thinking it would be her last. Out in the ambulance, one of the technicians radioed the hospital that they were coming in with a drowning victim, DOA.

But before the ambulance had gone half a block, Lacey awakened! One of the medics opened the back door and yelled to my husband, telling him to meet them at the hospital.

In the emergency room, they ran brain scans and lung tests on Lacey, and every test came back normal. When our little girl woke up the next morning in ICU and asked me to fix her hair, I knew the Lord had put His hand on her and saved her.

God worked at least three miracles that day: He brought Lacey back to life. A seven-year-old saved her sister. And, oddly enough, when the ambulance arrived at our house, the front door was locked. One of the EMTs ran to the truck to get an ax, but when he returned to the door, it stood open. No one—no one human—could have opened it. The only people in the house were my day-care babies.

I used to take the word *miracle* for granted. A baby's birth, that was a miracle. The growth of a child from a baby to maturity was another kind of miracle. But now that word has an entirely new meaning, and I will never say it again without knowing that God has power to work real miracles every day.

I know that God is sovereign, and He doesn't always work in the way we would like Him to. But now that I've seen Him work this way, I know I can trust Him in all things.

DANA ELWELL LAWHON, MOTHER

Mom's Old Bible

Late one night when I was a teenager, I took a good look at my mother's old Bible. The crumbling cover and dog-eared pages brought back memories of bedtime prayers. I thought of Mom when she was Mommy.

An inscription from Dad dates the Bible from before my birth. Mom's maiden name was barely readable on the cover. Two references were penned onto the dirty first page. One—John 3:5—is unmistakably written by my oldest brother, Jim. The backward scrawl reminded me of those years when the old Bible was passed around, carried to church, and claimed as "mine" by three different boys. Mom didn't often get to carry the Bible herself while we were growing up, but we frequently found her reading it at home when we came in from paper routes or baseball games.

The other reference on that first page was Psalm 37:4 in Mom's handwriting. I turned to the chapter and saw that Mom had underscored the verbs in the first five verses. They admonish: "Fret not thyself because of evildoers.... Trust in the LORD, and do good.... Delight thyself also in the LORD.... Commit thy way unto the LORD; trust also in Him; and He shall bring it to pass" (KJV).

But apparently her favorite verse was "Delight thyself also in the LORD; and He shall give thee the desires of thine heart."

On the next page is the inscription from Dad: "To Bonnie, in loving remembrance of October 21, 1942. Your devoted Red. Matthew 19:6." He'd been nearly nineteen, she sixteen, when they were engaged. World War II and his thirty-two months in the Pacific delayed their marriage until December 1945.

I turned the next page. "Hello everybody." Jim's writing again, probably kindling someone's indignation, but the words were never scratched out, and they remain as a child's warm welcome for anyone who cares to open Mom's old Bible.

On the next page Jim wrote "The Way of Salvation" with a verse for each of five steps. Despite the inconsistent strokes of the preteen writer, the guidelines are still there for men of all ages who want, as Jim pointed out in step three, a "way of escape."

Scanning the page, I noted several of Mom's markings, countless underlinings of promises and passages that look to heaven. The penciled markings had faded, and the inked jottings had bled through to other pages. But the evidence remained of well-listened-to sermons and cherished hours alone in the Word.

In the back, after the concordance, the guides, and the maps, Mom listed several references to crown of joy, righteousness, life, and glory. Looking up 1 Thessalonians 2:19 showed me again that Mom loved to rejoice in the thought of Christ's return.

On the last page of Mom's Bible, she again wrote "Psalm 37:4." That last inscription is framed by the doodling of youthful hands. One of the desires of Mom's heart was that her little boys would grow up and do something more profitable with those once-small hands. Mom's first desire, she told us, was that her four boys would make decisions to trust Christ. We have all done that.

Mom still delights herself in the Lord, which is a continual encouragement for me to do something constructive with the hands that scribbled in her Bible so many years ago.

Mom's old Bible reminds me of her hands. Hands that held, spanked, mended, and wiped tears; hands that produced a magic knot in the shoelaces on my three-year-old feet.

Mom's hands turned the pages of her old Bible for me until I learned to read it myself.

JERRY B. JENKINS
AUTHOR, THE LEFT BEHIND SERIES

World's Greatest Mom

When my mom asked my sister and me if we would like to write a little piece on motherhood, I promptly said "Yes! No problem." Yet all I have done since is ponder. Deadline is coming up....

"Is it done yet?"

"I'm working on it, Mom," I said with a sigh.

I could happily reminiscence for hours about my mother, especially memories from my childhood days, but none of them could possibly describe how great my mother has always been at just that: being a great mom.

So each time I found myself at my keyboard, all I could do was stare at a blank screen. How can I describe my mom for what she is worth to me?

Last night as I tucked my son into bed, kissed his cheek and whispered, "Sweet dreams," I remembered something very prominent—I could hear from recent years, since my boy was born, when I have been given the ultimate compliment: "What a great mom you are." I realized then that I am the best proof of what a perfect mom my mother was and is. I accomplished this by following in her footsteps, continuing the tradition that my grandmother's grandmother started and embarked on the road to becoming someone else's memories of…

The World's Greatest Mom.

JENNIFER LEE WHITT
DAUGHTER OF ROBIN LEE HATCHER

The Story Jar

*B*y the time Mrs. Halley finished telling Theia's story and returned the blue ribbon to the jar, Beth had an enormous lump in her throat, and her eyes were swimming with tears.

"My goodness," the pastor's widow said. "I didn't mean to go on so long. I've interrupted your work. You must think me a bother." She started to rise.

"No!" Beth said quickly. "Please don't go yet. I-I don't have that much more to do."

"Well, if you're sure you don't mind, I'm in no hurry to leave. This church has been a part of my life for twelve years. It's difficult to say farewell." She sat back in the chair again. "Enough about me. Why don't you tell me about you and your boys? You said you have two sons?"

"Yes. Tommy's nineteen, and Mark is seventeen. Nearly grown. But if they keep going in the direction they're headed now, I don't know what will…" With a shake of her head, Beth let the sentence fade into silence.

She was at her wit's end, completely out of answers…still, she didn't think she wanted to air her concerns to a stranger, no matter how kind Mrs. Halley was.

The older woman seemed to understand. "It's always a

challenge, being a parent. Every stage of their lives brings new dilemmas with it. But children *are* a blessing from the Lord. Of that I'm sure."

Did teenagers count as children? Beth wondered. Or did they count as alien beings?

Mrs. Halley held out the gallon jar. "Could I trouble you to use your glass cleaner on this? The dust is rather thick."

"Sure." Beth took the jar and set it on the floor, then pulled a cloth from her back pocket and a spray bottle from the pail of cleaning supplies.

"I wonder what John would want me to do with it."

"Take it to Florida, I imagine. Sounds like you're the only one who'd know all the stories that go with the things inside." After wiping the mouth of the jar clean, she reached inside and pulled out a delicate silver earring, admiring its simple elegance. "How pretty…" She glanced at Mrs. Halley. "What about this one? Do you know its story?"

"Oh, my, yes. Leah Carpenter was a visitor to our congregation. She came forward on a very special Mother's Day to drop that item into the story jar and share her joy. Hmm. I guess that must have been about eight years ago now. The nose ring you're holding belonged to Leah's daughter, Shoshanna."

"It's a *nose* ring?" Beth's eyes widened as she looked at the silver hoop again. She knew the type of people who wore body jewelry. She'd seen them hanging around the high school whenever she'd had to visit the principal regarding one of her boys. Hoodlums and troublemakers, the lot of them.

How could something like this possibly represent one of God's miracles?

Mrs. Halley seemed to read her thoughts. "You never know what the good Lord will use to draw a person unto Himself. He works in mysterious ways, His wonders to perform. Leah and Shoshanna were certainly evidence of that."

"I think I'd like to hear this story," Beth said, doubtful but curious.

"And I'd love to share it with you." Mrs. Halley chuckled softly as she settled deeper into the wing chair. "It all began when Shoshanna was sixteen years old...."

Heart Rings

Robin Lee Hatcher

"God sees not as man sees
for man looks at the outward appearance,
but the LORD *looks at the heart."*

1 SAMUEL 16:7B

One

March 1986

Seated at the head table overlooking the banquet hall, Leah Carpenter fought to keep her anger in check.

"Relax, honey," Wes whispered near her ear. "Give her some time. Traffic's bad out there tonight. Shoshanna will be here. She promised."

Leah glanced at the empty chair below the podium, then at her husband. "She's doing this to spite me."

He shook his head, and there was sadness in his eyes.

She was thankful he didn't argue with her. Not tonight. Not this night of all nights.

How many other women had been honored by the town of Beaker Heights as Citizen of the Year? None. Leah Carpenter was the first.

She'd been selected for this honor because of Together We Can, a nonprofit organization that helped homeless women, especially single mothers, get on their feet and back into the workforce. In the years since it was founded, Together We Can—Leah's brainchild—had become a model for similar community programs around the country.

Leah had given countless hours to make certain her labor of love succeeded. She had poured herself into it, giving 110 percent. There had been times, especially in the beginning, when others on the nonprofit corporation's board of directors had wanted to give up, but she hadn't let them.

Tonight the people of Beaker Heights were recognizing her accomplishments.

And her daughter wasn't there to see it.

Why am I surprised? I should have known she'd do this.

She'd had a horrible argument with Shoshanna last night. Her sixteen-year-old daughter had announced she wanted to get her nose pierced, like her friend Krissie Tombs. Leah had exploded at the very suggestion. She had grounded Shoshanna for a week and forbidden her to see Krissie.

A pierced nose? No child of Leah Carpenter's was going to do such a thing. Leah had her position in the community to consider. What would people think if she allowed her daughter to parade around town with a ring in her nose? She wouldn't be able to hold her head up in church for the utter shame. No daughter of hers was going to do such a thing.

It hadn't helped Leah's humor any when Wes suggested she was overreacting.

"She's sixteen, for crying out loud," he'd said after Shoshanna fled the room in tears. "She's *supposed* to make outrageous suggestions. It's part of growing up and pulling away."

He's always been too easy on her, Leah thought now, her resentment increasing. *I have to play the heavy, and he gets to be the favorite adult. It isn't fair.*

She picked up her fork and moved the food around on her plate without taking a bite. Reluctantly she admitted she wasn't being fair to Wes, her husband of three years. Wes had entered her life and filled a place in her heart that she'd thought could never be filled after twelve years as a widow. He was good to her in countless ways, and he loved Shoshanna as if she were his own daughter. The feeling was mutual, too—so much so that Shoshanna had legally changed her name to Carpenter last year.

Leah glanced at Wes. When their gazes met, she gave him a tiny smile. In return, he squeezed her hand beneath the table.

Maybe I did overreact. Maybe forbidding Shoshanna to see Krissie was a bit harsh.

Wes's grip on her hand tightened. "Look who's here."

She turned and saw Shoshanna being escorted to her table. She felt a rush of relief. Thank goodness she was here. Tonight meant so much to Leah, and if her daughter hadn't come to share it with—

Her thoughts died abruptly as the small silver ring in Shoshanna's left nostril glittered in the light of the crystal chandeliers.

Something twisted in Leah's chest.

Something painful.

Her baby. Her beautiful, loving, sunshine girl. Her precious child—who for the better part of her sixteen years had brought her nothing but joy—had defied Leah's wishes and had her nose pierced.

No matter what happened next, the evening was ruined.

"How could you do it?" Leah stood in the doorway to Shoshanna's basement bedroom. "How could you embarrass me in front of all those people? Did you see the way they were looking at you?"

"There's no reason for you to be embarrassed, Mom. *I'm* the one with the nose ring. Besides, it's no big deal."

"It's a big deal to me. Good heavens! Don't you realize how you look? Don't you know what people think of kids who mutilate their bodies like this?"

Shoshanna flicked a stray strand of long blond hair over her shoulder. "You know what your problem is, Mom? You're always worried about what other people might think. What about what *I* think? Doesn't that count for anything in this family? I think this ring is cool. I like it. Besides, it isn't really any different than an earring, you know."

"It *is* different, and you will remove that hideous piece of metal from your face. I won't allow a daughter of mine to have a pierced nose!"

"It's my face. I can do what I want with it."

"That's what you think, young lady. I'm still your mother."

"I wish you *weren't!*"

Leah was left momentarily speechless.

"Why can't you be cool like Krissie's mom?" Shoshanna flicked tears from her cheeks with her fingertips. "All you care about is your dumb job. You don't care about me at all. You don't care if I'm happy."

The accusations stung. They weren't true—nothing was more important to Leah than her daughter—but they stung nonetheless.

Shoshanna's tactics changed abruptly. In a wheedling tone, she said, "Please, Mom, can't I keep—"

"*No!*" Leah clenched her hands into tight fists at her side. Her voice rose sharply. "When I see you in the morning, Shoshanna Marie Carpenter, that...that *thing*...will be gone from your nose. We'll discuss your punishment then. And mark my words, you *will* be punished." She turned quickly and strode from the room.

"I hate you!"

Leah winced but didn't look back.

Shoshanna slammed her door closed.

Wes was waiting in their second story bedroom. "How'd it go?"

As if he hadn't heard with the two of them shouting like a couple of fishwives. Leah gave her head a slight shake, then went into the walk-in closet and began to disrobe.

Her husband appeared in the doorway. "Leah?"

"You heard her. She hates me."

"No, she doesn't. She's angry, but she doesn't hate you."

"She thinks she does." Leah draped her tailored suit jacket over a padded hanger. After releasing a deep sigh, she answered his unspoken question. "I told her she had to remove that ugly thing from her face. I told her we would discuss punishment in the morning."

Wes was silent for a few moments before saying, "She loves you, honey. Try to remember that."

"Well, this is a fine way to show it." With her back toward him, she closed her eyes against an unwelcome urge to cry.

"Didn't you ever rebel as a teen?"

"You'll do no such thing." Her mother's voice was as clear in Leah's mind as if Frances Anderson were actually in this closet, speaking those words now instead of over two decades before. *"No daughter of mine will appear in public unless properly groomed. Certainly never in an outfit like that. It may be good enough for other girls, but not for you. Understood?"*

"No," Leah answered her husband. "I never rebelled." She swallowed the lump in her throat. "How can you defend her, Wes? If it were up to you, I suppose she could do anything she pleased."

His hand alighted on her shoulder, and he gently turned her

to face him. "I'm not saying what she did was right or that she shouldn't receive appropriate punishment. I'm just asking you to think carefully about what you do or say next."

Unable to reply, she pressed her forehead against his chest. Anger, disappointment, frustration, and a host of indefinable emotions roiled inside her.

When does it get easier?

Surely she'd had enough trouble and turmoil in her life. She'd been widowed while still in her twenties. She'd raised her daughter alone. She'd scrimped and saved and struggled to get by and given up many things so Shoshanna wouldn't feel deprived. Why did her once-perfect child have to suddenly turn against her? After all she'd done. After all she'd given.

It wasn't fair.

Wes stroked her hair. It felt nice. If only she could let him handle this. She was tired of always being strong. If only she could.

But she couldn't. Shoshanna was her daughter and her responsibility. She would have to decide on the punishment and then see it through.

"She's a good kid," Wes said softly. "You've raised her right. She'll come through this. What's the Bible say? 'Raise up a child in the way she should go, and when she's grown, she won't depart from it.'"

"Oh, Wes." She stepped out of his embrace. "That's no help. Not now. I need *real* answers."

He shrugged. "Some folks think God's Word *is* a real answer, Leah."

She sighed, turning away to unzip her skirt. The tension in her shoulders made her want to scream. She knew Wes wanted to say something more, but finally she heard him leave the walk-in, his thoughts still unspoken.

She felt a sting of guilt. It wasn't that she didn't believe the Bible was God's Word, although she knew that was how it had sounded to Wes. At one time she'd found comfort when reading the Scriptures—something she hadn't had time for in ages....

She shook off the thought and her guilt. Right now she needed to find a solution to her problems. God helped those who helped themselves, and that's what she meant to do. She had to have an answer tonight.

But by morning, none of it mattered.

Leah had a white-knuckled grip on the telephone receiver as she listened to Krissie Tombs on the other end of the line.

"I'm sorry, Mrs. Carpenter. I can't tell you where Sho went."

"Can't? Or won't?"

"I don't *know* where. She didn't tell me. All she said was she was leaving town."

Leah sank onto the kitchen barstool. "Please, Krissie," she whispered, fighting tears of panic. "If you know anything—"

"I don't. Honest."

Her gaze met Wes's across the room, and she shook her head slowly.

"I gotta hang up now, Mrs. Carpenter. 'Bye."

The dial tone buzzed in Leah's ear, but she couldn't seem to move. It was Wes who came to her rescue, taking the receiver from her hand and setting it back in its cradle.

"We'll find her," he said as he gathered her into his arms. "She can't have gone far."

"I hate you!"

Those had been her daughter's last words to her, and they cut into her heart like a dagger.

"I hate you!"

Leah had known Shoshanna was angry, but they'd always been able to iron out their difficulties and disagreements in the past. It hadn't occurred to her that Shoshanna might run away from home.

"Where would she go, Wes?" She pressed her face against his chest. "How will she get by?"

"I don't know."

"She doesn't have much money." Her stomach clenched as she gazed up at her husband. "She wouldn't be foolish enough to hitchhike, would she?"

He didn't answer. What could he say? Both of them knew that hitchhiking was the most likely mode of transportation for a runaway teenager.

"I hate you!"

The pain in Leah's heart was too great to be borne. She was suffocating beneath it. She wanted to wail in grief. She wanted to strike out, wanted to do anything that might stop the hurt. She wanted to take back her ultimatums and her threats of punishment. She wanted to erase the past forty-eight hours. She wanted a chance to do them over.

"I hate you!"

The tears came then, like a flood.

"Oh, Shoshanna." She pressed her face against Wes's chest again, gripping his arms, holding on lest the storm sweep her away. "Oh, my baby girl. Don't do this. Don't do this. Please don't do this."

Two

Two years later

Cindy Markowitz leaned through the open doorway of Leah's office. "Did you hear the news? Dwayne's wife had her baby last night. A little girl. Everybody's doing fine."

"Oh, that's wonderful." Leah forced a smile, ignoring the sudden ache in her chest. "They did so want a daughter this time."

"A bunch of us are going over to the hospital at noon. Want to come along?"

"Sorry. I can't today. I've got a lunch date with Wes. But give Patricia my love and tell her I'll come to see her soon."

"I'll do it. Say hi to Wes for me." Cindy disappeared from view.

Pressing her lips together, Leah rose from her chair, walked to the door, and closed it.

She could have told Dwayne and Patricia Jones that they might very well be sorry some day, that they might wish they'd stopped having children after the birth of their third son, that a daughter could bring them more joy and more sorrow than they'd ever imagined possible.

When does the pain go away?

She leaned her back against the door and closed her eyes, fighting tears. *If only I knew where she is. If only I knew if she's okay, if she's safe, if she's got food to eat.*

Leah had received two phone calls from Shoshanna, both within the first six months after she ran away from home. Both calls had ended badly, with Leah saying things she later regretted and Shoshanna hanging up in anger.

"Oh, baby girl," Leah whispered. "I'm so sorry. I'm so very sorry."

Drawing a deep breath, she straightened her shoulders and returned to her desk. She wasn't going to sink into maudlin spirits again. She'd done far too much of that in the past two years. She recognized all the symptoms. She also knew it had far more to do with the recent passing of Shoshanna's birthday than with the arrival of the Jones baby.

She's eighteen now. A knot formed in Leah's belly. *If she's alive.*

A shudder ran through her, as it always did when that horrendous possibility sprang to mind. *Please, God, let her be alive. Even if I never see or hear from her again—*

The phone rang, startling Leah from her grim ruminations.

"Hi, hon," Wes said when she answered. "About lunch—"

"Don't tell me it's noon already." She glanced at the wall clock.

"No," he answered. "I need to cancel our date. I have to meet with…someone from out of town. Noon seems to be the only time available. Can we reschedule for tomorrow?"

She was disappointed, but it was probably for the best. Wes would know the moment he saw her that she was having one of her blue days. She knew it made him feel helpless when she got like this. He wanted to fix it, make it better, and he couldn't.

"That okay, hon?" he asked.

"Sure. Tomorrow's good for me. It's better if I stay in the office today anyway. You should see the stack of papers on my desk, and I've got a newspaper reporter coming for an interview at three this afternoon. I haven't begun to prepare for that yet."

"Want me to bring home Chinese for supper? Fried rice? Sweet-and-sour pork? Egg rolls?"

"My hero," she said with a sigh, meaning it.

He chuckled. "I take it that means all of the above."

"Yes, please."

"Leah?"

"Hmm?"

"I love you."

"I love you, too."

"See you around five-thirty."

"Okay. 'Bye."

"'Bye."

She placed the handset in its cradle, wondering as she stared at the phone how she would have made it through the past two years without Wes to lean on.

The answer was simple: She wouldn't have.

It was pouring down rain by the time Leah left the Together We Can offices on Main Street. Visibility was low, and traffic was snarled throughout the Beaker Heights business district. Leah muttered more than one uncharitable word at other motorists as she inched her way out of the downtown core. It seemed an eternity before she reached the freeway.

When she arrived home forty minutes later, she was surprised to discover Wes's 1965 Ford Mustang already parked in the garage. She couldn't imagine how he'd managed to pick up dinner and beat her home. Not with traffic as bad as it was tonight.

She pulled into her space in the garage, cut the engine, then reached for her purse and leather briefcase. As she got out of the car, her stomach growled, reminding her that she'd worked through lunch. Chinese take-out was sounding better and better.

Maybe they should eat by candlelight in the family room. She could light a fire in the fireplace and put on one of Wes's favorite soundtracks. A romantic evening with her husband might be just the ticket to lift her out of the doldrums. Besides, it wouldn't hurt to remind Wes how much she loved and appreciated him.

She opened the door into the house. "I'm home." She sniffed the air experimentally. Not even a whiff of sweet-and-sour pork. "Wes?"

He appeared in the kitchen doorway. "I was starting to get worried." He glanced over his shoulder, then back at Leah. "I tried to call you at the office, but you'd already left."

"Traffic was a bear. How did you miss it?"

"I…ah…well, the truth is I didn't go back to the office this afternoon."

She looked at him more closely. He had something serious to tell her; she could see it in his eyes. "Why not?"

"Maybe you ought to sit down."

"I don't want to sit down." A shiver of alarm swept through her. "Tell me what it is."

From the kitchen came a soft reply, "It's me, Mom."

Leah did sit then. Not by choice, but because her knees buckled beneath her. She sank onto the edge of the sofa, barely keeping from sliding off onto the floor.

"Sho?" she formed the word, but no sound came out of her mouth.

Wes strode forward, his expression anxious. He knelt on one knee in front of Leah and took both of her hands between his, squeezing gently. For a moment he seemed to be pleading with her with his eyes. Then a movement at the edge of her vision drew Leah's gaze from her husband toward the kitchen doorway.

It was Shoshanna—a very different Shoshanna from the daughter in the photographs Leah had stared at every day for the past two years. She looked taller and thinner than when she'd left home. Her face had matured, as had her figure. She wore tight-fitting, faded jeans with a hole in one knee, a bulky blue sweater, a leather jacket, and what looked like army boots. She also wore a small ring in her nose.

But it wasn't her clothes or even that offensive piece of jewelry that stopped Leah's breathing. It was something worse.

Shoshanna was nearly bald. All her beautiful blond hair, gone…her scalp covered by little more than peach fuzz. She resembled the photos of people on chemotherapy.

Oh, please, no!

"Hi, Mom."

Pressing a fist to the base of her throat, Leah rose to her feet. "You were Wes's meeting?"

"Yeah. I…I didn't know if you'd want to see me after the things I said to you the night I left. I thought I'd better check with Dad first."

"Oh, Sho. How could you believe I wouldn't want to see you? Even for a moment? I've been so worried. All this time without a word…" She let her words fade into silence, at the same time steeling herself for the bad news. "Tell me what's wrong with you."

"Wrong?" Shoshanna glanced toward her stepfather, then back at Leah. "Nothing's wrong. In fact, everything's great now. That's why I came back, 'cause I finally got my head together and I wanted—"

"You needn't pretend for my sake." Leah blinked away her

tears. "I want the truth, Sho. What's the prognosis? What have the doctors told you?"

"What doctors?"

"Beaker Heights has one of the best research hospitals in the country. I'm sure they—"

"Mom, what're you talking about? I don't need a hospital or any doctors." Shoshanna smiled broadly. "I'm fine. Never felt better. Honest."

"But...but your hair. It's gone. I thought...I was afraid..." She let her words fade into silence.

Her daughter's eyes widened a fraction—and then she laughed. "I'm not sick, Mom. I shaved my head."

"Whatever for?"

"Well—" Shoshanna's amused smile vanished, and she exchanged a quick look with Wes—"I guess now's as good a time as any." She drew a deep breath before turning her head, offering Leah a profile. "I shaved it so people could see my tattoo better."

Her tattoo?

Wes placed his arm around Leah's shoulders. Perhaps he feared she would pass out.

Maybe she would.

Through the quarter-inch-long—if that—pale, gold hair that covered Shoshanna's scalp, Leah could see what appeared to be a large blue and gold star, streaking across the right side of her daughter's head.

She couldn't think of anything to say. Not one single word. Her mind was a complete blank.

"It started out as a joke," Shoshanna said softly, turning to face her mother again.

"A...joke?" Leah whispered.

Her daughter nodded. "And you might as well know. I've got another one."

"Another one?"

"Uh-huh." Shoshanna touched her right shoulder blade with her left hand. "Back here. Of the earth."

How was Leah supposed to respond? She didn't know what was expected of her, what was the right thing to say, the right way to react. If she said the wrong thing, Shoshanna might leave again, and Leah couldn't bear that. She couldn't. She couldn't bear the not knowing, the loneliness, the overwhelming need to hold her child—a need that couldn't be fulfilled—the unnamable fears that struck in the middle of the night.

But a tattoo?

Two of them?

"Mom…"

Leah felt as if something were crushing her heart.

"Mom, I need to tell you I'm sorry."

She met her daughter's gaze.

"I'm sorry I ran away and caused you to worry about me all this time. I'm sorry I didn't let you know I was okay. I should've let you know I loved you. I *didn't* hate you, even when I said it. I was angry and hurt, but I always loved you. I'm sorry. I missed you something awful while I was gone. I'm sorry I disobeyed you so much when I *was* here. I know now how defiant I was." Tears slipped down Shoshanna's cheeks. "I'd like to come home, for at least a while, if you'll let me. I'd understand if you didn't. Really I would. But I hope you'll be able to forgive me and let me come home. I'd like to see if we can't make things right between us."

Wes gave Leah a light squeeze of encouragement.

"Things'll be different than before, Mom. I promise."

Tearfully, Leah gathered her daughter into her arms, still unable to speak for the lump in her throat.

Please, God, let it all be different than before.

Three

Still sleepless at four in the morning, Leah rose from the bed, slipped on her robe, and knotted the belt around her waist. On her way to the kitchen, she paused in the hall to bump up the thermostat. A short while later, the coffee was perking, and the furnace was pouring heat through the vents.

Not that Leah noticed. She stood before the sliding glass door, staring into the darkness beyond, her arms crossed over her chest.

"What did I do that was so wrong?" she whispered.

She'd been a good mother. She'd given Shoshanna everything she could. Whatever her daughter had been interested in, she'd involved herself in, too. When Shoshanna wanted to be a Girl Scout, Leah had become a Girl Scout leader. When Shoshanna wanted to be a ballerina, Leah had watched her practice and attended every performance. She had read to her daughter and held her when she hurt and explained the facts of life in gentle but clear terms. She had laughed with Shoshanna and cried with Shoshanna. Right up until Shoshanna's sixteenth year, they'd been close. Closer than most mothers and daughters were. Certainly closer than Leah had been with her mother, despite how hard she'd tried.

"Stop slouching, Leah Nadine. Honestly, I wonder sometimes if they didn't switch babies at the hospital and send the wrong one home with

us. How can you possibly be my daughter? You have positively no social
skills, no style whatsoever. I despair for you, child."

"Mom?"

With a soft gasp of surprise, Leah turned from the window.

Shoshanna stood in the kitchen doorway wearing a ratty old
bathrobe that surely had come from the Salvation Army or
Goodwill. She ran the fingers of one hand through her short-
cropped hair while squinting at Leah with sleepy eyes. "What're
you doing up at this hour?"

"Making coffee," Leah answered, avoiding the real question.
"It's ready. Do you want some?"

"Sure. I guess." Shoshanna yawned, then shuffled toward the
kitchen table. "It's still raining. Never let up all night. I could hear
it running through the gutters."

Leah crossed the kitchen and took two large mugs from the
cupboard. She filled them with coffee from the carafe, then carried
them to the table, setting one in front of Shoshanna.

"Got any cream, Mom? If not, milk'll do fine."

Strange, the way Shoshanna's request upset Leah. A mother
should know that her daughter preferred cream in her coffee.

Shoshanna didn't wait for a reply. She rose from her chair and
walked to the refrigerator. "I didn't know there *was* a 4:00 A.M."
With her head hidden from view as she looked inside, she asked,
"Do you always get up this early?"

"No."

"I was wondering." Shoshanna straightened, milk carton in
hand, and met her mother's gaze. "Do you have to go to work
today? We really need to talk about what happened to me while I
was away."

"Well…" Leah wasn't sure she wanted to talk about that. She
didn't think she wanted to hear what had happened to her daugh-

ter for the past two years. Maybe it was better to live in blissful ignorance. Or was it better to know all, no matter how painful it might be?

"Can't you skip work for one day, Mom?"

"Yes," she relented. "I can stay home with you."

"Thanks." Shoshanna returned to the table. After she was seated again, she poured a generous portion of milk into her mug and stirred it with a spoon before taking a sip. "Mmm. This is really good."

"You didn't drink coffee before you left."

"I was too young. You wouldn't let me. Remember?"

Leah lowered her gaze, staring into her mug, which was clenched between her two hands. She didn't want to talk about it, yet she couldn't seem to stop herself from asking, "Where did you go, Sho? How did you manage to live?"

"I was in Portland, Oregon, most of the time."

"Portland."

"I lived with friends and got a job working at a used bookstore."

Were you scared? Did anyone hurt you? Did you—?

"It was a guy at the bookstore who led me to Christ."

Leah straightened, and her gaze darted toward her daughter.

Shoshanna smiled. "I was born again a few months ago. I'm a Christian now."

"What on earth are you talking about? You've been a Christian since you were a little girl."

Her smile vanished. "No, Mom. I wasn't."

"Don't be absurd. I remember the day you were confirmed as clearly as if it were only yesterday."

Shoshanna got up from the table and went to the sliding glass door, staring outside as Leah had done earlier. "I knew all about

Jesus from Sunday school, and I knew all the right things to say and what I was *supposed* to believe. But I never knew *Him*. Not personally. I never made Him my Lord and Savior. I never had the joy of the Lord." Leah's daughter turned. She was smiling again, a twinkle in her eyes. "My friend Greg calls me a turbo Christian." She laughed softly. "You know, like a big souped-up engine, all revved and ready to go. I want to share Jesus with *everybody!*"

"You're not going to start preaching on street corners, I hope."

"Would it be easier for you if I was talking about sex and drugs?" There was a note of confusion in Shoshanna's voice.

Leah's mouth tasted as dry as sawdust. She hadn't meant to sound sarcastic, but neither could she take back her bitter retort.

"I did a lot of dumb things in those two years I was gone." Shoshanna took two steps toward the table. "But by the grace of God, I wasn't hurt. I had friends who weren't as lucky. They'll never get a second chance. One girl got really messed up on drugs. She'll never think straight again. Another girl was killed by her boyfriend. It could just as easily have been me. I don't know why it wasn't, except for God's mercy."

In an instant, Leah's mind replayed all her secret fears. Even now, with Shoshanna safely home, they loomed large and terrifying, too real to contemplate.

"I came home because God's Word says I'm to honor my mother and father, and I needed to make things right with you again. I don't know how I'm supposed to do that. I'm going to need your help." She sat on the chair, then leaned toward Leah across the table. "But most of all, I want to share with you the joy I've found in knowing Jesus as my Lord."

Leah pressed her lips together, biting back another sharp retort. How dare Shoshanna sit there, with that ring in her nose and those horrid tattoos marring her body, and talk about God and Jesus? As if she knew something Leah didn't. Honor her mother? Make things right?

"Mom…"

"If you really wanted to make things right with me," she snapped, "you'd take that ugly thing out of your nose."

Shoshanna leaned forward, lifting a hand, palm up, as if pleading for understanding. But she didn't say a word. Instead, she lowered her hand and sat back in the chair. "Okay. If it'll make you feel better, I won't wear it when I'm with you."

"Well, it's hard to take anything you say seriously when I'm forced to look at it." Leah felt like a petulant child, which only added fuel to her bad temper. "Too bad you can't get rid of those tattoos as easily."

"I wish you'd try to see the inside of the cup."

"What on earth is that supposed to mean?"

"It's something from the Bible. It's about—"

"The Bible?"

Shoshanna shook her head. "Never mind, Mom." She stood once again. "We've probably said all we should for now." She turned and walked toward the kitchen doorway. Once there, she paused and glanced over her shoulder. "I love you, you know." Then she was gone from view.

The furnace blower shut off. Rain pelted the windows and rushed through the gutters. The coffeepot gurgled and sputtered.

"I wish you'd try to see the inside of the cup."

What *had* Shoshanna meant by that? Leah covered her face with her hands. "I only want what's best," she insisted to the empty room. "That's all. One day she'll thank me."

"Inside of the cup…"

"O God, help me."

Four

*L*eah swore to herself that she wouldn't mention either the nose ring or the tattoos again. Even if she had to bite off the tip of her own tongue, she wasn't going to say another word about them. As far as she was concerned, they didn't exist. They weren't there.

Denial wasn't *always* a bad thing. Right?

Her daughter's wardrobe, however, was another matter. Leah didn't know what young folks called their style of dress these days—funky, hippie, whatever—but she called it atrocious.

Shoshanna—sans nose ring—appeared at the breakfast table that morning attired in what had to be Salvation Army giveaways. No one could have asked for money for clothes like this!

The crushed-velvet patchwork overalls were at least three sizes too big. Every six-by-six-inch square was a different color, from palest pink to fluorescent orange. Beneath the bibbed front, Shoshanna wore a ragged, purple T-shirt. Her black shoes appeared to be men's loafers, complete with tassels.

She looks hideous! Leah barely kept from saying so aloud.

Shoshanna poured a generous helping of maple syrup on her waffles. "I thought I'd start job hunting next week."

Leah nearly choked on her orange juice.

"I'll need to get a bus schedule and check out the want ads."

"I've taken the day off," Leah said. "Let's go to the mall this morning. We can buy you some new clothes. My treat. You'll want to look your best for those interviews."

"Thanks, Mom, but that isn't necessary. I've got plenty of things to wear."

"But I *want* to do it, dear. There's nothing like a new outfit or two to make a woman feel better about herself."

Leah's gaze flicked momentarily to Shoshanna's hair, then dropped away. Who was going to hire a girl with a nearly shaved head and a tattoo peeking through?

"Maybe there's something for me to do at Together We Can. I've learned a thing or two about living on the streets with homeless people. I'd like to help others get through the tough times. The same way you have."

Several emotions warred within Leah—dread at the thought of her coworkers seeing Shoshanna's tattoos; pride that her daughter wanted to emulate the work that meant so much to her; horror at the confirmation that Shoshanna had lived on the streets under God alone knew what kind of conditions.

"Sounds like a good idea," Wes interjected from his side of the table. "You're always saying you could use more help at the office."

"That's true." Leah met Shoshanna's gaze. "But we can't pay much. We're mostly a volunteer organization, and our goal has always been for 90 percent of our fund-raising to go directly to the people in need rather than to administrative costs."

Her daughter shrugged. "It isn't the money that's important. I just want to do something useful. I didn't come home so I could bum off you guys."

"It's settled then." Leah smiled. "We'll go shopping for some appropriate office attire for you. Then Monday you can talk to

Carlotta in personnel. She'll have to make the final decision."

"Don't worry, honey," Wes said to Shoshanna as he placed an arm around his stepdaughter's shoulders. "I'll put in a good word for you with the boss." He punctuated his remark with a conspiratorial wink for Leah and a hug for Shoshanna.

Judging by the number of cars in the mall parking lot, Beaker Heights Towne Square was the place to be on a rainy Friday morning. Leah pulled her Mazda into an open spot, then pushed the button to unlock the doors.

"I brought an umbrella for you," she said as she reached into the backseat.

"It's okay." Shoshanna opened her car door. "A little bit of rain won't cause me to melt, and it sure won't hurt this hairdo of mine."

Leah didn't want to talk about her daughter's hair—or lack thereof. Being reminded defeated her new policy of complete denial.

Let it pass. Don't say a thing.

She got out of the car, opened her umbrella, and hurriedly followed Shoshanna toward the mall's main entrance. Once inside, she tried to steer them in the direction of her favorite upscale department store.

Her daughter had another destination in mind.

Leah had never been in Retrospect before. To tell the truth, she wasn't sure she'd noticed its existence. Raucous music blared from speakers in the back of the shop. Shoshanna didn't seem to mind the noise, however. She headed directly for a rack of long, bright-colored skirts and began poking through them.

"How do you like this one?" Shoshanna asked.

"Well…" Leah knew she sounded skeptical.

"If I put it with a vest—"

"Wouldn't you like to see what's available at Nordstrom's? I'm sure they've got a great selection for young people."

"Nordie's isn't my style, Mom. This is." Shoshanna raised an eyebrow. "It'd be okay at your office, wouldn't it?"

Leah had to admit there wasn't anything wrong with the skirt or the vests on the neighboring rack. It simply wasn't what she'd had in mind. Her thinking had been more along the lines of a nice linen suit with a silk blouse. Light blue to go with Shoshanna's eyes, and silver jewelry to accessorize.

Before Leah could form a reply, a clerk appeared on the other side of the rack from Shoshanna.

"Would you like to try that on?" the young woman asked.

Shoshanna glanced at Leah, and after a moment's hesitation, Leah nodded.

"Yes," her daughter said, facing the clerk with a smile. "In a little while. But I want to look around a bit more."

"There are some great blouses over there you might want to try." The clerk pointed.

"Thanks." Shoshanna began rifling through the skirts again.

"I've gotta tell you. I love your haircut. Wish I could wear mine that short, but it just doesn't look good on me. My cheeks are too fat or something." The young woman leaned forward. "Hey, is that a tattoo on your scalp?"

Leah wanted the floor to open up and swallow her.

Shoshanna laughed. "Yeah, it is."

"Cool."

Another customer, a girl about the same age as Shoshanna, moved closer to Leah, attempting to appear disinterested but obviously wanting a better look.

The clerk asked, "Did it hurt?"

"A little when he was doing the spot near my nape. But mostly it just sort of reverberated."

That's because there's nothing between your ears, Leah thought, wishing the clerk would shut up and go away.

But she didn't go away. Instead she said, "I've been wanting a tattoo forever. Maybe a little one on my ankle. Everybody's getting them these days."

"Not in my house," Leah muttered to herself.

The other customer turned wide, brown eyes in Leah's direction. "Like, I got grounded when I got my ears double pierced," she said softly. "My parents would, like, *die* if I got a tattoo."

Like, I know just how they'd feel.

Shoshanna looked toward her mother again. She must have guessed what Leah was thinking, for her smile disappeared.

Pricked by her conscience, Leah glanced down at the rack of clothes in front of her. She held up the first thing her hand fell upon, paying no attention to what it was. "What about this one?"

"I don't think so, Mom." There was a note of hurt in Shoshanna's voice. "I'm gonna try on what I've got here."

Leah looked up in time to see her daughter working her way through the racks toward the dressing rooms.

I didn't mean to hurt her. But am I so wrong to feel the way I do?

Maybe she didn't want to know the answer to her silent question.

Five

*I*t's a real miracle, isn't it?" Rebekah Borders, the pastor's wife, said as she shook Leah's hand following Sunday's service. "Praise God for bringing Shoshanna safely home."

"Yes."

"There's such joy in her eyes. It's the first thing I noticed about her."

Leah looked across the narthex to where Shoshanna was standing with Josh Borders, Eugene and Rebekah's oldest son.

"It can only be the joy of the Lord," the pastor's wife continued. "One day I hope she'll share her story with us. I'm sure we would all be blessed by it."

"Perhaps someday," Leah replied softly before moving on.

She exchanged a few perfunctory good mornings with other members of the congregation as she made her way toward the front doors of the church, shook a few more hands, agreed with those who said how wonderful it was that her daughter had returned.

But in Leah's heart there was only disquiet, and she couldn't for the life of her say why.

Rebekah Borders was right about the joy on Shoshanna's face. Leah had observed it throughout the service, particularly during the worship time. While singing, Shoshanna had turned her face toward heaven, totally unaware of those around her. It was as if she'd been transported to another dimension.

Leah tried to remember if she'd ever experienced the same sort of total abandon during a church service. The answer, of course, was no, she never had. For one thing, it wouldn't have been dignified. Church was a place for sober reflection and to receive instructions on how to live.

"The Andersons are leaders in our community, Leah Nadine. Never forget that. God expects us to set a good example. Remember your dignity. Others will be watching."

Shoshanna had called herself a "turbo Christian." Quite the descriptive phrase. It sounded courageous and enthusiastic, and she supposed such an attitude was fine for the young. But faith without works was dead. Being a Christian meant sacrifice and service. It meant setting an example for others to follow, just as Frances Anderson had taught Leah, and as Shoshanna would learn someday, too.

Leah stepped outside. Bright sunshine beat down upon the front steps of the church, its warmth muted by a crisp March wind.

The door opened behind her. "Hey, Mom."

She glanced over her shoulder.

"Would you care very much if I didn't go out with you and Dad to eat?"

"Well, I—"

"I've been invited to go with the youth group to help at the soup kitchen this afternoon. I'd really like to. I'll get a ride home from somebody."

Leah was struck in that instant with a difficult truth: Shoshanna was never going to be her little girl again. They couldn't return to a simpler, more innocent time, before body piercing and tattoos and outright rebellion. Shoshanna was a young woman, not a child, and although she had returned home, Leah couldn't hold her there. She couldn't mold her into her own image. She couldn't make a miniature Leah Carpenter out of her.

Is that what I've tried to do to her?

She recalled her own mother again, remembering how Frances had so carefully directed every detail of Leah's life. Her mother would never have considered Shoshanna's request, let alone approved of it. Charity work, yes. But a soup kitchen? Never.

But why not? she puzzled.

"It's all right, isn't it?" Shoshanna asked again. "You don't mind?"

Leah realized her daughter could have wanted to spend the day hanging out at the mall or doing a hundred things much worse than that. Instead, she wanted to help those less fortunate than herself.

Perhaps Leah hadn't completely failed as a mother.

The next morning, Shoshanna appeared at the breakfast table wearing one of the new outfits from Retrospect. The ankle-length floral skirt was brightly colored. The hot pink blouse had peasant sleeves and a drawstring neckline, and the purple vest had tassels in front and back. Except for her short, short hair, she looked like a folksinger from the sixties.

Leah started humming "Monday, Monday" as she served breakfast.

Wes grinned as he met her gaze across the table. "Exactly what I was thinking."

The two of them broke into song, making up new lyrics when

they couldn't remember the real ones. Finally, unable to continue, they collapsed into helpless laughter.

"You guys are weird," Shoshanna pronounced when the room was silent again.

"*We're* weird?" Leah arched her eyebrows, pretending to be insulted. Seeing Wes's expression, she burst into laughter a second time.

Half an hour later as they left the house, Wes pulled Leah into his embrace and kissed her with delicious tenderness. Then, with his mouth near her ear, he said, "It's good to see you smiling."

Have I done it so little? she wondered as she met his gaze again.

Yes, she answered herself. *You have.*

Wes gave her another quick kiss, then said, "You'd better go. You'll get caught in the worst of morning traffic if you don't." He looked beyond Leah toward the Mazda. "Good luck with the interview," he called to Shoshanna. "Be nice to the boss, maybe bring her a cup of coffee, and I think you've got a good chance at landing a job. She's a bit weird, sings really old tunes, but I bet you can handle her okay."

Leah playfully punched him in the stomach.

He grunted, then grinned. "Have a great day, honey."

"I intend to."

"Want that Chinese take-out tonight?"

"Sounds good to me. Any excuse not to cook."

The heels of her spectator pumps clicked against the sidewalk as she strode to her car. Opening the rear driver's side door, she placed her leather briefcase on the floor. Moments later, seated behind the steering wheel, she started the engine and backed out of the drive.

Once they were out of the subdivision and into the flow of traffic headed toward the city, Leah cast a furtive glance in her daughter's direction. She wondered if Shoshanna was nervous about this morning's interview with the personnel manager. If she was, she didn't show it.

I would have been terrified at her age, she thought as she returned her gaze to the road ahead. *I would have counted off all the things that were wrong with me, all the reasons I wouldn't get the job.*

"I can't get over how much Beaker Heights has grown in just a couple years," Shoshanna said, breaking the silence. "Those are all new subdivisions over there."

"Yes, we've enjoyed all the growth that comes with a strong economy." Leah flipped on her turn signal and changed lanes. "And all the problems that go with it, too. So many homeless and hungry. So many women living in poverty. So many fatherless children. The need for more social programs in this city is great."

"I know all that's important, Mom, but we can offer the needy a whole lot more than just some social program. We can share our hope in Christ."

Leah glanced at her daughter again.

"'For it is for this we labor and strive,'" Shoshanna said softly, looking out the window to her right, "'because we have fixed our hope on the living God, who is the Savior of all men, especially of believers.'"

Leah felt a twinge of guilt. Had she *ever* offered her faith to someone as a reason for hope? Or had she depended only upon good food and better clothing and education to make the difference for the people whom Together We Can served?

What kind of Christian am I? When was the last time I prayed and asked God for help or guidance or anything?

Those were not questions that brought comfort, so she shoved them aside. Besides, God helped those who helped themselves, right? Leah and TWC gave others the tools with which to improve

their circumstances, and that was important. More than important. It was critical.

"Give a man a fish, and he has food for a day. Teach a man to fish, and he can feed himself forever." Everyone recognized the truth of that maxim.

"Does Ms. Rodriguez know I'm coming in this morning?" Shoshanna asked, again pulling Leah from her musings.

"Yes. And remember, Carlotta won't hire you unless she thinks you can really do the job. That's why she's in charge of personnel."

"Well, if I don't get hired to work in the office, I can still volunteer to help at one of the shelters. Right?"

"Of course. We never have enough volunteers."

"That's good. It's working with people I really want to do anyway. I mean, I know paperwork's important and all, but it isn't what makes the real difference." She sighed. "You know, Mom, if nobody'd reached down into the mire I was living in and showed me a better way, if Greg hadn't shared the good news about how much Jesus loves me, I'd probably be dead by now."

Leah gasped.

Shoshanna's voice softened to a near whisper. "Someday, Mom, I hope you'll let me share what happened while I was away. I know you're not ready to hear all of it yet. But someday I hope you will be."

I won't. Leah's lips pressed together. *I won't ever be ready. I don't want to be ready to hear about it.*

Six

eah opened the large glass door to the mauve-and-teal decorated lobby of Together We Can. The receptionist looked up and smiled.

"Morning, Mrs. Carpenter."

"Good morning, Barbara."

Behind her, Shoshanna released a soft whistle. "Fancy new digs, Mom. I thought you said most of the money raised didn't go to overhead."

Leah smiled as she glanced over her shoulder. "It doesn't. These offices are generously provided by the owners of the building. They're a group of attorneys who believe in what TWC is doing for the community."

Even if she'd tried, she couldn't have kept the note of pride out of her voice. After all, donated or not, she had spent a great deal of time and energy designing and decorating these offices. She'd chosen soft colors, wanting to make the place seem comforting and inviting. She'd also wanted to make a statement of success, something she'd found helped bring in more and bigger contributions from corporate sponsors.

"If you want to be successful, Leah Nadine, you must look successful."

"Of course, I'm sure the tax write-off doesn't do them any harm either," Leah added.

"Right."

Looking at the receptionist again, she said, "Barbara, this is my daughter, Shoshanna. She has an appointment with Ms. Rodriguez at eight-thirty. When she's ready, please have Carlotta buzz my office."

"I'll tell her, Mrs. Carpenter."

"Follow me, Sho." Leah moved through the lobby, headed for her office at the end of a long hallway. She gave a running commentary along the way. "That room is used for training classes. We instruct women who've never been in the job market on how to conduct themselves during an interview." She motioned with her hand. "At the other end of the building we've got a computer lab where we teach basic computing and office skills. And this room is where we help women find the right clothes to wear." She stopped and opened the door, revealing a large room with racks and racks of clothing. "We give every woman who finishes our course a nice suit or an appropriate dress to wear on her job hunts. The clothes aren't new, but they look it. You'd be amazed at what some people give away."

"Aren't the women you help a bit intimidated by this fancy office?"

"Some are at first, but most get over it quickly." She continued down the hall. "Our largest women's shelter is only two blocks away. We offer childcare so the mothers can come here to attend their classes."

"How long after they get jobs can they stay in the shelters?"

Leah opened the door to her office. "Up to a year, if needed."

"Good. There was a similar organization to TWC in Portland that only lets women stay for two months after they've found employment. That's not long enough from what I've seen."

"No, it isn't."

Sudden, bitter sorrow for the innocence that had been lost squeezed Leah's heart. *Shoshanna's only eighteen. She shouldn't know so much about the destitute and downtrodden. She should be finishing her high school education and preparing for college in the fall. I wanted so many things for her. I had so many dreams for my daughter. Why did they all go so wrong?*

Arriving at her desk, Leah stepped behind it, then turned.

Shoshanna had stopped at the bookcase near a large, plate-glass window. Morning sunlight gilded her short-cropped hair and revealed a thoughtful crease in her forehead as she perused the titles on the eye-level shelf.

"This is quite a collection, Mom." She tapped her chin with her index finger. "Maybe I can borrow some to read. I couldn't bring any of my collection with me when I came back. Too heavy and too many."

Leah almost said that the particular books she was looking at would be too advanced for a high school dropout.

"Did I tell you I hope to be a social worker someday?"

Leah tasted defeat. Didn't Shoshanna realize all that she'd thrown away when she ran away from home? Didn't she realize that businesses rarely hired people with nose rings and tattoos? As for social work, it required a college degree. Didn't she realize that—

"I got my GED while I was in Portland," Shoshanna said, as if reading her mother's thoughts. "Greg helped me. In fact, we were filling out forms to apply to the university when I realized I needed to come home first."

"Who exactly is this Greg? What was he to you?"

"I told you. I worked with him at the bookstore. He was my friend."

"Did you live with him?" The implied question was understood: *Was he your lover?*

Shoshanna didn't reply immediately. She simply stared back at her mother, disappointment in her eyes. At last she answered, "No, Mom."

Leah might have made matters worse, but she was saved from herself by the buzzing of the phone. She jabbed the intercom button. "Yes?"

"It's Carlotta. Is Shoshanna ready to meet with me now?"

"She's ready." Leah punched the button again. To her daughter she said, "Down the hall to your right. Fourth office. Her name is on the door."

Shoshanna opened her mouth to say something. Then, apparently thinking better of it, she nodded, turned, and left the room.

"Good luck," Leah said, seconds too late, the door already closed behind her daughter.

About half an hour later, Leah stood at the window, staring sightlessly at the street below, when the door opened again.

"Mind if I come in?" Carlotta asked.

"No." She turned around. "How did it go?"

Carlotta Rodriguez, an attractive woman in her midthirties, steered her motorized wheelchair into the room. "I was impressed," she answered once she stopped opposite Leah's desk. "Shoshanna's bright and articulate. I think she'll be an asset to the organization."

"So you offered her a position?"

"I did."

Leah looked toward the door. "Is she waiting outside?"

"No. She asked me to tell you she'd be back before lunch. She wanted to go over to the shelter on Elm and meet some of the women and children."

"I see." Leah released a deep sigh.

"Want to tell me what's bothering you?"

"I blew it with Sho. Again." She sank onto her desk chair. "I always seem to say the wrong things to her. I hurt her feelings every time I turn around. I don't mean to, but I keep right on doing it." She shook her head. "Carlotta, I'm angry and I'm scared and I wonder what she did while she was gone and if she's going to be okay and I fear for her future and—"

"Don't you think you should say all this to her instead of me?"

"I'm afraid to."

"Why?"

"You know why. We see the reasons every day. We know what happens to girls who live on the streets." Leah blinked, fighting to keep tears from falling. Then, in a whisper, she continued, "I don't think I could bear knowing if any of those horrible things happened to her."

"But every time you look at that tattoo, you wonder. Don't you?"

Leah nodded.

Carlotta's gaze was full of wisdom and sympathy. "You know, my friend, it could be that God can make better use of Shoshanna with the way she looks and who she is than He ever did with you or me. We're so conventional, so conservative." She chuckled. "Shoshanna isn't."

"No, she certainly isn't."

"Maybe it's all part of some grand design. God is turning the mistakes of her past into good."

"Sounds like something Sho would say."

"I get the feeling she's wise beyond her years. And her faith in God is great. She shared a little bit with me about that. How thankful you must be to know she's embraced the truth."

Leah rose a second time, returning to the window. She remembered the way Shoshanna had looked during worship the previous morning. She thought about the expression of joy and wonder on her face.

What's lacking in me? Why don't I feel what Sho feels?

Not only didn't she feel that joy, that wonder, that peace, Leah realized, she also didn't understand it.

Why not, God? Aren't I good enough?

For as long as she could remember, Leah had sought to please God with the way she lived, the work she did. She believed in Christ. She'd been no more than seven or eight when a kindly, white-haired Sunday school teacher asked her if she'd like Jesus to live in her heart, and Leah had said, "Yes."

She'd always gone to church, first with her mother, then as an adult. She'd made faithful Sunday attendance a priority in her life. She prayed. Not as often as she should, she supposed, but she did pray. She read the Bible whenever she found time. It was hard when she had a husband and a home and a business to run and people who were dependent upon her.

God had to understand how busy she was. And not reading the Bible or praying didn't make her any less of a Christian.

Did it?

But Shoshanna seemed to have found something…more. Something Leah didn't have.

I'm envious.

The realization stunned her—and left her more than a little unsettled.

Seven

Rosalyn Donner slid a check across the glass surface of Leah's desk. "I do wish the women's auxiliary had raised more for the shelter's reading program, but the board has pledged to redouble our efforts next year."

"We appreciate every gift. This is a generous sum and will help a great deal."

"I'm sure I've told you, Mrs. Carpenter, but I've always admired your work here." She fingered the tiny rhinestone pin on the collar of her cashmere sweater as she stood. "By the way, I met your daughter in the lobby. We had quite a chat while I waited to see you."

Apprehension turned Leah's mouth as dry as sawdust.

"You must be very proud of that girl."

Those weren't the exact words Leah had expected to hear. "Y-yes," she stammered, rising from her chair as her guest had moments before.

"She's obviously bright and most articulate. Not like so many young people today. Can't string three intelligent words together, most of them. And Shoshanna is passionate about what she's doing and her dreams of the future. That's a gift." Rosalyn patted her silver-gray hair. "Wouldn't I love to give up my weekly visits to the beauty parlor? I could if I had hair like hers." She chuckled softly. "If I were her age, believe me, I'd do it."

Leah couldn't think of anything to say. She settled for a nod.

"You be sure to keep that third Saturday next month free to attend our auction." Rosalyn headed for the office door.

"Yes. I will." Leah hurried to reach it first so she could open it.

"Bring your daughter to the auction. I'd love to introduce her to my grandson. She's just the kind of girl he needs to know."

"I…I'll ask her."

Rosalyn stopped, took hold of Leah's hand, and shook it. "I look forward to seeing you both again soon. Good day, Mrs. Carpenter."

"Good day, Mrs. Donner. And…and thanks again."

Leah watched the older woman walk down the hall, still not sure she'd heard right. Rosalyn Donner—the grande dame of Beaker Heights society—wanted to set up her grandson with Shoshanna! What on earth had Shoshanna said to her?

Wanting some answers, she looked for Shoshanna in the file room, then in the computer room, and finally in the break room, but she was nowhere to be found.

"She finished the work I had for her," Cindy Markowitz said in answer to Leah's query, "so she went over to the Family Center." The secretary smiled. "That's where her heart is, you know."

"Yes, I know. She's told me so more than once this past week."

"Would you like me to call the shelter? Have them send her back?"

"No thanks. I'll walk over. It's a nice day, and it wouldn't hurt me to stretch my legs a bit." Leah turned. "Have a nice weekend, Cindy."

"You do the same."

Downtown Beaker Heights was a pleasant blend of the old and the new. Restored sandstone buildings—including some on the

Historical Registry—resided beside new high-rises of glass, steel, and brick. Even here, in the core of the city, trees lifted leafy branches toward the blue, cloudless sky. Daffodils and tulips in large clay pots brightened the sidewalks.

Stepping out of the back door, Leah drew in a deep breath of spring air, then turned in the direction of the TWC women's shelter. A soft breeze tugged at her hair and the hem of her skirt as she followed the sidewalk, glancing occasionally at the displays in the shop windows.

It had been a good week, she mused, silently admitting she hadn't expected it to go so well. She'd anticipated problems that never developed. Look what happened with Rosalyn Donner. And that wasn't the only time either. Whenever she'd introduced her daughter to someone new, she'd expected to see a look of disdain or censure. But if anyone had been surprised by or disapproving of Shoshanna, they hadn't let on to Leah.

Of course, those people were her friends and business associates. They would do their best to hide their true feelings. The rest of the world wouldn't be as kind. Leah knew that.

Worrying her lower lip between her teeth, she turned the corner onto Elm Avenue. One block away, she saw Shoshanna—her short-cropped hair made her easy to identify at a distance—sitting on the front stoop of one of the turn-of-the-century brownstones that housed the TWC Family Center. She wasn't alone. Someone was seated beside her. The two were deeply engrossed in conversation. As Leah drew closer, she could see the other person was female and pregnant. She was dressed all in black, from her skintight leggings to the sweater stretched over her enlarged stomach.

Leah's footsteps on the sidewalk alerted them to her arrival. Shoshanna turned to look over her shoulder. The other girl—who looked even younger than Shoshanna—leaned forward.

Leah slowed, then stopped.

The pregnant girl had metallic purple hair, worn heavily gelled and spiked. There were two silver rings in her nose and a pewter one in her left eyebrow. A dog collar circled her throat. She wore black eye shadow and black lipstick. The effect was ghoulish.

"Mom." Shoshanna stood. "Do you remember Annie Layton?"

"Layton?"

"We used to live next door to them when I was at Lincoln Elementary. Remember?"

Councilman Layton's daughter?

Howard Layton was one of Together We Can's biggest supporters; more than once he had praised TWC in the press. He spoke often regarding the importance of programs that helped strengthen the family unit.

And this is his daughter?

Annie rose awkwardly from the step, then placed both hands on her abdomen. "Hi, Mrs. Carpenter. Sho told me you got married again. Congratulations."

"Thank you, Annie." Leah tried to reconcile this counterculture teen with the sweet child she'd once known—and the man who was her father—but she failed.

"Did you need me back at the office?" Shoshanna asked. "I was hoping to show Annie around the shelter, if you don't mind." With her eyes, she seemed to add, *Please, Mom.*

Leah nodded. "Go ahead. I'll meet you here when you're through."

"Thanks." Shoshanna slipped her hand into the crook of Annie's arm. "Come on. I'll give you the grand tour."

After they'd disappeared inside, Leah sat on a bench in the shade of an ancient elm tree.

Why had Annie Layton come to see Shoshanna? As far as Leah knew, the two girls hadn't seen each other since elementary school. Had they met by chance? Would Shoshanna renew an old friendship with this obviously troubled girl?

With a shudder, Leah closed her eyes. Was Annie the sort of person her daughter had befriended in Portland?

O God, how do I keep Sho safe from bad influences?

Half an hour later, Shoshanna came out the front door of the shelter. She was alone.

Leah rose from the bench and waited for her daughter to join her on the sidewalk. "Where's Annie?"

"They gave her a room. She's staying."

Leah's mouth went dry. She hadn't considered the possibility that Annie Layton had come to the shelter looking for a place to live. She should have realized it, of course. That's why most women came here.

But Annie was young, rebellious, pregnant—and the daughter of one of the city's most prominent politicians.

"Tell me what happened," Leah said, trying to focus her thoughts.

"She lost her job and couldn't pay the rent. Nobody'll hire her because she's pregnant."

Not to mention because of the way she looks, Leah added mentally before asking, "How old is Annie?"

"Seventeen next week." Shoshanna turned and started walking.

Leah fell in beside her. "Is she taking illegal drugs?"

"I don't think so. She seems to care about the baby she's carrying." She glanced at her mother. "Not everybody who looks like her uses drugs, you know."

Leah ignored that comment. "Is she married to the baby's father?"

"No, and they aren't together anymore either. She said he left town. She doesn't know where he went. He took off one day and didn't come back."

"I'll have to notify the Laytons that Annie's at the shelter."

"She doesn't want her father to know where she is. Besides, it doesn't sound to me like he'll care."

A heaviness pressed on Leah's heart. "Is that what you thought about me when you were gone? That I didn't care?" The questions came out of nowhere, surprising her. She didn't have the courage to look at Shoshanna to see if she were equally surprised. Softly, Leah continued, "Because I did care. I cared desperately."

There was a lengthy silence, then, "This is different, Mom. Annie's dad *really* doesn't care."

"How can you be sure?"

"Because he told her he didn't."

"Howard Layton? I can't believe that's true. He's a very well-respected member of this community. Everyone thinks highly of him."

"People aren't always what they seem."

Leah sent a sidelong glance at her daughter. "It's possible Annie misunderstood what he said, isn't it?"

"I don't think so."

As if it were yesterday, Leah recalled the night before Shoshanna ran away. They'd exchanged heated words, but Leah hadn't suspected the argument would cause her daughter to leave home.

Annie's father must be worried sick about his wayward child. It was doubtful he would come looking for her at the TWC Family Center; it wasn't the sort of place where kids like Annie usually took refuge.

Another thought sprang to mind, causing Leah to mutter to herself, "And wouldn't the press have a heyday with this?"

Shoshanna came to an abrupt halt. "Is that what you're worried about? The *press?*" She made the word sound dirty.

"I have to be concerned about what—"

"Mom, Annie's in trouble. She might look tough, but she's just a kid. She needs help. That's what's important here. Not what the papers say."

Leah placed a hand on Shoshanna's shoulder. "I'm very aware of that. I also know Annie's a minor, and that her father is a powerful member of our city government. The press could use this against him if they chose. If they do, that could hurt the work we do. We're dependent upon fund-raising and the benevolence of donors. We have to stay above reproach. If we get bad press, the support could dry up overnight."

Her daughter made a noise of frustration.

"Like it or not, I must let Councilman Layton know where Annie is. I'll have to call him tomorrow." She paused a moment, then added, "This is in Annie's best interests, too."

Eight

ate on Saturday morning, Leah was shown into Howard and Donita Layton's formal living room by a housemaid in uniform.

"Make yourself comfortable, Ms. Carpenter," the young woman said. "I'll tell Mr. Layton you're here." She slipped from the room, all sounds of departure muted by the thick carpeting underfoot.

The Layton home—an impressive, two-story, glass-and-brick structure—sat on a bluff overlooking the swift flowing Juniper River. Ceiling to floor windows formed the south side of the living room, affording an awe-inspiring view of Beaker Heights and the valley beyond.

Leah hesitated beside an off-white, overstuffed chair, then crossed to the window instead of sitting down. She stared at the sun-sparkled river below, thinking how pleasant it must be to lounge on the deck beside the swimming pool on a summer's evening and look over the valley.

"Leah Carpenter," Howard said from behind her. "Great to see you. It's been too long."

Leah turned as he entered the room.

The councilman was a large bear of a man, at least six foot four and well over two hundred pounds. In his fifties, he had thick, salt-and-pepper hair that was stylishly cut and a smile that had won him thousands of votes over the years.

"Good morning, Councilman," Leah said as she shook his proffered hand. "Thanks for seeing me on such short notice."

He motioned toward a chair. "Please, have a seat. I've asked Nancy to bring us some coffee."

"That wasn't necessary. I—"

He waved off her words. "I assume my secretary informed you Donita is out of town."

Leah didn't reply, understanding it was a rhetorical question.

"My wife goes to New York every spring to shop for a new wardrobe." He flashed one of his most charming smiles. "It's especially important in an election year."

"I'm sure it is." She returned his smile but felt oddly uncomfortable.

"Ah, here's our coffee now." He pointed at the cherry wood table in front of him. "Just put the tray there, Nancy. We'll pour for ourselves."

"Yes, sir," the maid replied.

As soon as she was gone, Howard asked, "Cream or sugar?" while filling a delicate china cup with coffee from the sterling silver pot.

"No, thank you. Black is fine."

He grinned as he passed the cup and saucer to her. "It's strong, but you strike me as the sort of woman who'd like it that way. Am I right?"

Her discomfort increased. She'd never noticed before how *smooth* he seemed.

"Now tell me—" Howard leaned back in his chair—"what brings you to my home? I assume this has something to do with Together We Can. How can I help?"

"You're partially right, Councilman." Leah set the cup down, the coffee untouched. "It does have something to do with Together We Can."

He gave her one of those enigmatic looks peculiar to politicians—one that seemed to express both curiosity and patience at the same time.

"Your daughter is at one of our shelters."

A strange, hard look flashed in his eyes, then disappeared an instant later. "My daughter?"

"Annie."

"What's she doing there?"

"She said she had nowhere else to go."

"Oh no." He rose from the chair and strode toward the windows. Squinting against the bright sunlight, he said, "I warned her this could happen if she went to live with that no-good boyfriend of hers. I told her he'd get tired of her and throw her out. But she wouldn't listen to my advice."

Leah clenched her hands in her lap. "Are you aware that she's expecting a baby?"

"Sadly, yes. I am aware of it." He sighed deeply. "Kids today. But we never thought our family would have to go through this sort of thing. Annie was always such a sweet, obedient child. We thought…Well, never mind. You didn't come here to listen to a father's broken heart."

Leah felt a rush of relief. She'd known Shoshanna had to be wrong about Howard Layton. He *was* concerned about Annie. He *did* care.

"I understand what you're feeling, Councilman, and I suspected you didn't know she was at the shelter. That's why I came. Of course, since we aren't set up to meet the needs of unwed teenage mothers, I thought—"

"Say no more, Mrs. Carpenter." He put up a hand for emphasis. "I have no intention of leaving Annie there. Her mother and I want her home with us where she belongs. We want to make certain she gets the best prenatal care and gets sound counseling to help her through her troubles."

Leah rose from her chair. "I'm sure she'll be delighted to know how you feel."

"I'd rather you didn't tell her we're coming to get her," he said quickly. "I don't want to risk her disappearing again."

"I understand." She offered her hand. "I won't say a word."

He smiled at her as they walked toward the entry hall. In the living room doorway, he stopped. "If you'll excuse me, I'll let Nancy show you out. I have some important calls to make."

"Of course. Good day, Councilman."

He nodded, still smiling, then turned around and crossed the living room toward another doorway.

Leah glanced at her watch. It wasn't quite noon. There was plenty of time to stop at the mall. Wes was doing some volunteer work for the church and wouldn't be home until suppertime.

She looked at Nancy. "Could I trouble you for the use of a bathroom before I go?"

The maid nodded. "Of course. Right this way." She led Leah into a small hallway off the entry. "Right in there," she said, pointing.

"Thank you." Leah entered the guest bath, which was as beautifully appointed as every other room in this house.

She was just about to unbutton her slacks when she heard Howard Layton's voice as clearly as if he were standing in the bathroom with her.

"I don't want excuses!"

Leah jumped and whirled around, but the bathroom door was closed.

"You find a way to quietly get her out of that blasted shelter and out of Beaker Heights."

Leah turned again, this time spying the intercom on the wall. A part of her brain realized the councilman had no idea his phone conversation was being broadcast to another room, perhaps throughout every room in the house, but the rest of her brain was riveted by his words.

"You've got to be careful about this. You've got to convince her this is her idea so she can't deny it later." He cursed. "This is a minefield. Do you realize what it would *do* to me politically if her picture got in the paper? I'd be finished."

Leah leaned her back against the bathroom door.

"Is it too late for one of those partial birth abortions? That would be the best route.... Of course I know they're controversial, but if it was done out of the country, we could keep it a secret."

Leah placed a hand over her mouth, staring at the intercom as if it were a snake.

"Well, then, see what you can do. Just keep me informed."

Leah turned, grasped the knob, and opened the door as quietly as possible. She wanted out. She needed air. She had to escape this house.

How could I have not realized what he's really like?

Leah drove aimlessly, her thoughts and stomach churning.

How could I have been so fooled by his charm and charisma?

She gripped the steering wheel with force.

And what about Annie? How do I help her? She's only sixteen. A child. And her father...her father wants to destroy her.

This was all Leah's fault. If she hadn't taken it into her own hands to go see the councilman, he wouldn't know where Annie was. All he cared about was how this baby would affect his career.

Of course Annie wouldn't make a suitable parent. She *should* give the baby up for adoption. She was sixteen, unwed, a high school dropout. And then there was the matter of her purple hair and hideous makeup. No, the wise thing would be to help her get into Beaker Memorial, a home for unwed mothers. They would see to her medical needs and give her counseling and continue her education. And they would see that the baby was placed in a good home.

Yes, Leah would help her get into Beaker Memorial. Leah had no legal rights, of course, but neither could she sit idly by while someone tried to force Annie to have an abortion, especially a late term one.

If only I hadn't been deceived by Howard Layton, but he's always seemed so—

A blaring horn jerked Leah from her thoughts just in time to avoid hitting another car. She slammed on her brakes, turned the wheel hard, and came to a stop on the side of the road. The other car's driver shouted at her and made a rude gesture before driving on.

Leah sat there and shook, but she suspected her reaction had more to do with her troubled thoughts than the near accident.

Leah arrived at the TWC Family Center half an hour later. She greeted the receptionist at the front desk, then asked what room Annie had been assigned.

"Twenty-seven, Ms. Carpenter. Your daughter's up there now."

"Shoshanna's here?"

"Yes, ma'am. Arrived about fifteen minutes ago. Maybe half an hour."

"Thanks." She turned and headed for the staircase. She recognized Shoshanna's voice as she neared room twenty-seven.

"At the foot of the cross. That's the only place to go for real help, Annie. To the foot of the cross."

At the foot of the cross. The words echoed in Leah's heart. *That's the only place to go for real help. To the foot of the cross.*

Leah stopped before reaching the doorway, holding still and listening.

"I can't tell you that turning your life over to Christ will make any difference with your dad," Shoshanna continued, her voice low but clear. "I *can* promise it'll make all the difference in you."

Annie replied, "I tried going back to church once. It wasn't for me. You know how your mom looked at me yesterday?"

Leah winced.

"That's the way they looked at me in that church I went to. I don't fit in anymore."

Shoshanna laughed softly. "Jesus spent all His time with the people who didn't fit in. The outcasts. The poor. The tax collectors. The lepers. The prostitutes. The people society didn't care for. The ones who couldn't measure up. He loved them the way they were, but He didn't leave them that way."

"I've had enough of hypocrites." Annie's voice rose, tinged with bitterness. "Dad only goes to church 'cause he thinks it's good for votes. He doesn't believe in any religion far as I can tell. Bet there are plenty like him in those places."

"You're right, Annie. The church has its share of hypocrites, but nobody ever said Christians were perfect. People are people. They'll disappoint you all the time. Even the ones who love you most are going to fail you, the same way you'll fail them, even when you don't mean to. But Christ won't ever fail you. Not ever."

Leah could hear the calm assurance in Shoshanna's words. She could envision the patient smile on her daughter's face.

"Jesus doesn't expect you to be perfect the way some people do. He won't judge you if you look different, the way your dad does. He won't ever send you away if you make a mistake. God isn't sitting up there in heaven waiting to smack you down when you mess up. He wants to help you become everything He wants you to be. He wants to love you and to have you love Him. That's where true Christianity starts. With love."

Her daughter's words cut straight to Leah's heart. She felt suddenly lost and alone.

"You can't earn your way to heaven," Shoshanna continued, "no matter how many good things you do. Not even if you twist yourself inside out. Not even if you manage to please your dad 100 percent of the time."

For some reason, Leah knew she couldn't face Annie or Shoshanna right now. With tears in her eyes, she turned and walked away.

A full moon bathed the neighborhood in a white glow, casting long, inky shadows behind objects, both large and small. March-bare tree limbs waved their arms in a ghostly dance while the wind whistled around eaves and down chimneys.

Leah observed the night scene through the bedroom window, her arms hugged tightly over her chest.

"I wish you'd try to see the inside of the cup."

She'd found the verse in the book of Matthew. Now she wished she hadn't. The words seemed to scream at her, accusing her.

"Woe to you, scribes and Pharisees, hypocrites! For you clean the outside of the cup and of the dish, but inside they are full of robbery and

self-indulgence. You blind Pharisee, first clean the inside of the cup and of the dish, so that the outside of it may become clean also."

"Care to tell me what's troubling you?" Wes asked softly from the opposite side of the room.

Without looking at her husband, she shook her head.

"It's after midnight." He got out of bed and came to stand behind her. "Honey?" He placed a hand on her shoulder.

"Am I a hypocrite?"

"What?"

"Am I a hypocrite?"

He moved his hand from her shoulder to her hair, stroking it gently. "No. Why do you ask?"

"I think maybe I am."

Wes turned her to face him. "Come on. Tell me what's eating at you. You've been moody ever since you got home. Is this about Councilman Layton?"

"No." She shook her head again. "Not really."

"Shoshanna?"

A lump in her throat kept her from answering.

Wes drew her close, pressing the side of her face to his chest, his other hand against the center of her back. "I'm here. Just know that. If you need me, I'm here for you."

She wished she could talk to him, tell him everything. She wanted to. She knew she could trust him. But she couldn't put her thoughts or feelings into words. Not yet. They were all a jumble, part of her overall confusion. She felt raw and exposed, and verbalizing what little she understood would only make that worse.

Hypocrite! Pharisee!

The accusing thoughts tore at her, bringing a renewed flow of tears as she buried her face in Wes's solid chest. As his arms circled her and tightened, she wished she could stay there forever. But for all the haven her husband provided her, Leah knew he couldn't be a shelter against her greatest foe of all.

Herself.

Nine

Leah felt better than she had in more than a week. Nothing like redecorating to restore a woman's spirits, she thought, especially when it was a surprise for her daughter.

Standing in the center of Shoshanna's bedroom, Leah looked around with pleasure. The new furniture—bookcase headboard, bedside table, large desk, and five-drawer dresser—was made of light oak in a contemporary design. It went well with the matching royal blue-and-yellow-flowered comforter, bed skirt, and curtains. A lamp with a yellow shade sat on the bedside table; its twin had been placed on the corner of the desk.

"I should find a print for the wall above the bed," Leah said to herself with a nod.

She knew the perfect store to find what she wanted, too. That art gallery at the corner of Swan Falls and Eighth Street. Maybe tomorrow on her lunch hour she could—

"Mom, what're you doing?"

"Sho!" She spun toward the door. "You aren't supposed to be home this afternoon."

"Neither are you." Her daughter stepped into the room. "What have you done with my things?"

"I wanted it to be a surprise. Do you like it?"

Shoshanna met her gaze for a moment, then glanced around the room. "It's pretty," she finally answered, her voice soft, almost inaudible. "Very tasteful."

The response was lackluster at best, and it stung Leah, stealing her pleasure.

"Why'd you do it, Mom?"

Leah's disappointment turned to anger. "Well, for crying out loud. Don't bother to be grateful or anything. I was just trying to make things nice for you."

"I know that's what you think you were doing. But look at it. This is *you*. Not me. Don't you see that? This is *your* taste, not mine." Shoshanna pinioned her with a hard gaze. "Is it because you can't change me, so you had to change my room instead?"

"Of course not!" Leah protested. "Of all the stupid, psycho-babble kind of things to say."

Shoshanna's eyes widened slightly.

"I don't know why I bother to do anything nice for you, Sho. Put your old things back if you want. I don't care." She stormed out of the room.

Her daughter followed. "We need to talk this through."

"I don't want to talk about it."

"You've got to let me be who I am, Mom."

She spun around at the top of the stairs. "I'm not trying to keep you from being who you are. All I want to do is to—"

"Change me."

"Why are you fighting with me? Why can't you say thank you and let it go at that?"

"Because you're not going to stop until I'm a carbon copy of you, and I can't be you."

"Am I that bad?"

Shoshanna reached out with one hand. "You're not bad at all.

You're just not me." She moved up one step. "I didn't mean to hurt your feelings. Really I didn't. It was nice what you tried to do. I just think—"

"I already *know* what you think. You think you're so smart and know so much more than your mother. Well, I've got news for you, kiddo. You don't know much about anything. You may not want to conform to what our society thinks is acceptable, but you'll have to if you want to succeed, if you're going to make anything of yourself in this world."

Her voice rose by degrees as she continued. "Life is going to knock you down, Sho. It'll knock you down again and again. You're only eighteen. You haven't been there, but I have. I've been around the block a few more times than you and I know how hard it can be. I was widowed young and forced into the job market when I wasn't prepared for it. I've missed promotions because I didn't have the right degree or because I was a woman or because I was too young and then too old." She raised her hands in a gesture of frustration. "Can't you see I only want to protect you, to make your way a little bit easier?"

Shoshanna's shoulders slumped as she took a step downward on the stairs. "Maybe easier isn't the way it's supposed to be for me. Maybe I've got a different kind of path to follow."

Leah experienced a horrible, out-of-body moment—she saw herself, saw her behavior, heard what she'd said as if listening to another…and she was ashamed. Her shame only increased when she saw the tears slip from her daughter's eyes, leaving twin tracks down her cheeks.

"I wish you'd try to see the inside of the cup."

Leah winced. Then another voice from the past intruded on her thoughts.

"You'll never amount to anything, Leah Nadine. Despite everything

I've done for you, you'll never be what I want you to be. I wash my hands of you. You're hopeless."

Leah had tried to be the perfect daughter. From as early as she could remember, she'd done everything she could to please her mother. Yet they'd never been close. The harder Leah had tried, the more of a disappointment she'd seemed to be. Until this moment, she hadn't realized how much that had colored her view of the world, how it had infiltrated so many aspects of her life and affected her relationships with others.

Had she passed on that legacy to Shoshanna? Would her daughter believe she was a failure in Leah's eyes? Had the sins of the mother been visited upon the child, like an Old Testament curse?

"O God," she whispered beneath her breath, the only prayer she could manage.

Shoshanna flicked away tears with her fingertips.

"Forgive me, Sho."

"It's okay."

"No." She shook her head. "It isn't okay. But I want it to be."

The church was cool and dim, the only light filtering through the stained-glass windows at the front and rear of the sanctuary.

Leah slipped into a back pew. She sat with her hands folded tightly in her lap, staring all the while at the large cross above the altar.

She remembered when they'd hung it there against a backdrop of purple fabric. That was the year after Eugene Borders had come to pastor their church. Leah hadn't cared for him much at the time. He'd made too many changes too quickly. Not that they'd been bad changes really, but Leah liked things to be familiar, to hold true to tradition. She liked to maintain the status quo whenever possible. She liked to know what every day was going to bring with it so she could plan and prepare.

She had desperately tried to control her own life. What a joke.

Closing her eyes, she let the silence of the sanctuary envelope her. Slowly, the turmoil in her mind and in her heart began to still. After a long while, she opened her eyes again.

The afternoon sun had moved in those minutes of silent reflection, and now the light streamed through the stained-glass balcony window from a new angle, casting tiny rainbows against the royal-colored cloth, causing a halo effect around the cross.

"Have You the answers for me?"

She didn't hear the voice of God in reply.

"Have I ever heard You? I don't remember. Was there a time when I knew You the way others seem to?" She paused, then added, "The way Sho does?"

She closed her eyes again and lowered her chin toward her chest.

I forced her away once before, God. I don't want to do it again. I don't want to make her feel like I'm always judging her…but maybe I am always judging her. Maybe I am trying to make her like me. I only want what's best for her. I'm trying the only way I know how to guide her and do what's best for her.

In her mind, she heard Shoshanna's soft laughter, heard her saying to Annie, "Jesus spent all His time with the people who didn't fit in. The outcasts…"

That's true, and it's all well and good. But things are different now than they were when Jesus walked the earth. We don't live in the same kind of world. We have to care what others think about us if we're to make a difference. If I hadn't cared what others thought, how much would I have been able to accomplish in this community? People give their money to Together We Can because they know they can trust me and my organization. They know it because they can see who I am. So we do need to care about appearances. Right?

She looked at the cross again.

"Well, aren't I right?" she challenged aloud.

Leah thought of Councilman Layton. He was someone who also coveted the approval of others, who knew the importance of the public image.

The thought left an unpleasant taste in her mouth.

But I'm not like him. Look at Together We Can. Look at how it helps people. I'm not doing this for personal glory or to get votes or to make a lot of money. I'm doing it because it's a good thing to help others who are less fortunate. That's the Christian thing to do. That's the essence of the Christian creed. Right? To help others.

She had to be right. She'd dedicated her life to helping others: the downtrodden, the hurting, the homeless, the poor.

BUT DO YOU HELP THEM BECAUSE YOU LOVE THEM?

Love them? Well…

DO YOU HELP THEM BECAUSE YOU LOVE ME, LEAH?

She held her breath.

BELOVED, DO YOU HELP THEM BECAUSE YOU KNOW I LOVE YOU?

Leah called home from a payphone outside the convenience store two blocks from the church. Shoshanna didn't answer; Leah got the answering machine instead.

She dropped another coin into the slot and dialed the office. As soon as she heard the receptionist's greeting, she said, "Barbara, it's Leah Carpenter. I need to talk to my daughter."

"Sorry, Ms. Carpenter," Barbara replied. "Shoshanna won't be back in this afternoon. She said something about helping a friend move."

Leah thoughtfully bit her lower lip.

"I think it was somebody over at the shelter," the young woman added.

"Did she say who?"

"Sorry. No."

"Okay, thanks." Leah replaced the handset in the cradle, then returned to her car.

A friend at the shelter meant Annie Layton. Leah was sure of that.

She started the engine and drove out of the parking lot, headed into the downtown area just as the rush to leave the city began. She didn't know what she would say to Shoshanna. She simply knew she couldn't put it off.

But she had one very important stop to make first.

Ten

When Leah turned onto Elm Avenue, she saw Shoshanna carrying a box down the front steps of the shelter. By the time Leah parked her car behind a dented, paint-faded Chevy van, Shoshanna had already set the box inside it. Then she stood beside the vehicle and watched as her mother got out of the car.

Shoshanna's expression was inscrutable.

"Would you like some help?" Leah asked as she stepped onto the curb.

"That's all there is."

"Annie?"

"Yeah."

"Does Beaker Memorial have an opening for her?"

"No, but she didn't want to go there anyway."

Leah looked toward the front stoop of the shelter. "Is she going home then? To her parents?" She wished she could believe the councilman had come to his senses, but she didn't.

"No. I found her a place to stay with a couple from church. Maybe you know them? The Stuarts. They've got a little studio apartment in their basement they're going to let Annie use. If she decides to keep the baby, they're going to help her whatever way they can. But I think she's realized the best thing for her child is to put it up for adoption."

Leah nodded, relieved but recognizing the decision hadn't been an easy one, even for a sixteen-year-old.

"I've been talking to Annie about returning to school. I think she will."

"You've been a good friend to her."

"I've tried."

Leah was silent a few moments, then asked, "Can you spare me a few minutes? Maybe after you take Annie to the Stuarts?"

Shoshanna shrugged. "Sure. But now's fine if you want. Annie's already over there. I just borrowed the van to get her things for her." She motioned toward the bench beneath the shade tree. "This okay?"

Leah nodded her assent, and the two of them sat down.

Silence stretched between them.

At last, Leah drew a deep breath, met her daughter's gaze, and began, "I've been doing a lot of thinking since I saw you earlier this afternoon. I...I think you're right about my reasons for redecorating your room." She sighed, looked down at her hands clenched tightly in her lap. "But it went beyond that. I think I was running away from an even greater truth." A lump formed in her throat, making it difficult to continue. When she did, she spoke barely above a whisper. "I've been guilty of the sin of pride." Tears flooded her eyes, blurring her vision. "And it's separated me from God for years. Pride made my first love grow cold."

"Oh, Mom, you—"

"No." She held up a hand to stop Shoshanna's protest. "It's true. I've spent most of my Christian life looking at appearances and making judgments and decisions based upon those appearances. I've expected others to do the same. I've expected them to be impressed by the good works that I've done. Why shouldn't they be? Haven't I won awards and been honored by the community? Haven't I been the good Samaritan, saving people from poverty, changing lives? I even expected God to be impressed by all I've achieved." She glanced at her daughter. "It took you coming home for me to take a good hard look at myself and my relationships. With you. With Wes. With the people at work. And most of all, my relationship with Christ."

Shoshanna took hold of Leah's left hand and gently squeezed it. Forgiveness flowed through the gesture. It flowed straight into Leah's heart, releasing a beautiful peace.

"I…I have something for you." Leah reached into her suit coat pocket and removed the small package. She looked at it for a moment, then passed it to her daughter.

Shoshanna accepted it, lifted a questioning gaze toward her mother, then opened the mouth of the plain white sack. She removed a tiny wad of tissue paper and slowly unwrapped the gift. When she saw what it was, she looked at Leah once again, her eyes wide with surprise and glittering with unshed tears.

Leah laughed nervously. "Never expected something like that from me, did you?"

"No." Shoshanna lifted the small silver hoop from the folds of the tissue paper.

"I don't want you to be me, Sho," Leah whispered. "I want you to be the wonderful person God made you to be. The unique and special individual He formed in my womb."

Leah reached out, placing both of her hands around her daughter's hand, the one that held the silver nose ring. That simple piece of body jewelry was a symbol of the changes that had taken place inside Leah's heart, a symbol only the two of them and God would ever truly understand.

"Thanks for helping me see the inside of the cup, Sho. I love you."

Eleven

May 1993

Leah had the door open before the taxi rolled to a stop in front of the hospital. She grabbed her carry-on bag with one hand while shoving two twenty-dollar bills at the driver.

"Keep the change," she said as she half-slid, half-stepped from the rear of the cab.

She bypassed the automatic door, knowing it would move too slowly. Once inside, she raced to the information desk.

"May I help you?" a volunteer in a pink pinstriped dress asked.

"My daughter's here. She's having a baby."

"Her name?"

"Shoshanna Borders."

The volunteer glanced down at a computer screen while tapping a few keys. "There's nothing in the system yet. You'll need to check at the desk in delivery. Take the elevator to the second floor, turn right when you come out of the elevator, and go down the hall. You'll be able to see the desk."

"Thanks." She hurried off, gripping her bag and purse and wishing she could be rid of them both.

Lord, please let everything go okay. Please protect Sho and her baby. Let it be a safe and normal delivery.

It was the same type of prayer she'd been lifting to heaven for the past several hours, ever since she'd received the call from her son-in-law.

"Shoshanna's in labor," Josh had said without even a hello.

"Labor?" Leah had exclaimed. "But she isn't due for another three weeks. Are you sure it isn't false labor?"

"We're sure. We're at the hospital now."

"I'll catch the first flight out. I'll be there as soon as I can. Tell Sho I'm coming."

Amazing, she thought now, how long a relatively short flight could seem when a person was in a hurry.

The elevator doors opened. Leah looked up—and there stood Josh, as if he'd been waiting for her. She knew in an instant that all was well. Judging by the humongous grin on his face, she also surmised that she was too late to personally witness her grandchild's introduction to the world.

"Hi, Mom," he greeted her.

"Hi."

She stepped out of the elevator and into his embrace.

"Glad you got here okay. Wes coming?"

"No, he couldn't leave today. He'll fly in tomorrow." She drew back from him. "Well? Don't you have something to tell me?"

"Shoshanna's fine."

"And the baby?"

"You have a beautiful granddaughter."

"A girl." Joy welled in Leah's chest. "A granddaughter."

Josh put his arm around her shoulders. "Come on. I'll take you to them." He guided her down the hall, his stride shortened to accommodate hers.

Thank You, Father-God, for giving Sho a wonderful man who loves her just the way she is, a man whom she loves in return. Thank You for putting these two unlikely people together. I never would have seen it coming, but You knew before either of them were born. Just as You know what lies ahead for their new baby.

Josh steered Leah into a room decorated with soft yellow wallpaper. Shoshanna was lying in the bed, a small bundle held in her arms.

"Hi, Mom," she said, sounding both tired and happy. "You made it okay."

Shoshanna wore her hair long now because Josh liked it that way. But it was no longer blond. She'd started dying it a royal shade of blue more than a year ago.

A perfect complement to her lovely blue eyes, Leah thought, then grinned.

"Yes, I made it okay." She moved toward the bed, her gaze glued to the tiny knitted cap on the baby's head. "But I plan to have a long talk with your husband about moving you away from Beaker Heights."

"He already knows. But we have to go—"

"—where the Lord calls," Leah finished for her.

Shoshanna pulled down the receiving blanket with two fingers, revealing the baby's face. "Grandma Leah, meet Chloe Leanne Borders."

Two hours later, Leah sat in the corner of the hospital room, her granddaughter cradled in her arms. The room was enveloped in silence. Shoshanna was sleeping. Josh had gone to the church where he was a part-time youth pastor; he'd promised to return in a couple of hours.

Leah smiled as her gaze drifted to her blue-haired daughter. Shoshanna slept on her side, the tattoo on her right shoulder blade peeking over the top of her nightgown.

"Not exactly the picture of a pastor's wife, huh, Chloe?" she whispered as she looked down at the newborn. "But what a heart for God she has."

Leah's thoughts wandered back through time, to the fateful night of the Beaker Heights' Citizen of the Year banquet. She remembered that sick feeling in her stomach when she'd seen her daughter with the tiny silver ring in the side of her nostril. She remembered her anger as she'd argued with Shoshanna later that evening.

"It hurt to look at her." She shook her head, her fingertips lightly stroking the downy softness of the baby's head while she pondered her memories. "Imagine that, Chloe. A silly little ring in her nose was like a pain in my heart that built a wall between us."

Funny how unimportant the tattoos and body jewelry—and blue hair!—seemed to Leah today. They were mere cosmetics in the overall scheme of things. It was the person underneath who counted. It was the condition of a heart that mattered.

The inside of the cup.

And what a beautiful cup the Lord had made of Shoshanna.

Smiling, the new grandmother closed her eyes, leaned her head against the back of the chair, and reveled in the never-ending flow of grace that had been poured out for her.

Tributes to Our Mothers

My Mom

One of my favorite memories is of an event that proved to me that my mother was always on my side.

I was about eleven years old and attending a new school for the first time since kindergarten. I had never attended a school that I could walk to. My only experience had been riding a school bus several miles back and forth every day.

One lunch hour at my new school, one of the girls invited several of us to come to her house for lunch. Her house could be seen from the playground, but a very tall fence stood in the way of the shortest route there. Being active sixth graders, we just climbed over it. We went to her house, ate some lunch, played around for a while, and then went back to school.

Of course, we had to go back over the fence, but this time, waiting on the other side, were the principal and another teacher. We were in trouble. Leaving the school grounds was against the rules. I hadn't known this, and had actually walked home during lunch before when I'd forgotten something.

But this time we were considered truant, and our parents had to be called. I had never been in trouble before, and I was scared and confused about what we'd done wrong. My mother came and picked me up. I told her what had happened and that the principal had threatened to spank all of us for it. That made my mom mad. She told me that before he could lay a hand on me he'd have to go through her first.

That's when I first knew my mom would always be there for me, and she always has been.

MICHAELYN J. HATCHER-SMITH
DAUGHTER OF ROBIN LEE HATCHER

And to All a Good Night

After Christmas many years ago, three elementary-school-aged boys played with their new toys until they were tired of them—three days or so later.

Their mother brought an empty cardboard box into the dining room, sat the boys down, and told them of underprivileged boys at a local orphanage who each got a piece of fruit, a candy bar, a comb, and a cheap toy in a standard package.

"Merry Christmas," one of the brothers said with sarcasm.

Their mother nodded, brows arched. "How about we give some of those guys a Christmas they won't forget?"

They sat silent. She continued. "Let's fill this box with toys that will make Christmas special. We'll do what Jesus would do."

One of the brothers had an idea. "With all my new stuff, I don't need all my old stuff!" He ran to get armloads full of dingy, dilapidated toys, but when he returned, his mother's look stopped him.

"Is that what Jesus would do?"

He pursed his lips and shrugged. "You want us to give our new stuff?"

"It's just a suggestion."

"All of it?"

"I didn't have in mind all of it. Just whatever toys you think."

"I'll give this car," one said, placing it in the box.

"If you don't want it," another said, "I'll take it."

"I'm not givin' it to you; I'm givin' it to the orphans."

"I'm done with this bow and arrow set," another said.

"I'll take that," another chimed in. "I'll trade you these pens for that model."

"No deal, but I'll take the pens and that cap gun."

The boys hardly noticed their mother leave the room. The box sat there, empty and glaring. The boys idly slipped away and played on the floor. But there was none of the usual laughing, arguing, roughhousing. Each played with his favorite toys with renewed vigor.

One by one the boys visited the kitchen. It was a small house, and that was the only place their mother could be.

Each found her sitting at the table, her coat and hat and gloves on. Her face had that fighting tears look. No words were exchanged.

The boys got the picture. She wasn't going to browbeat her sons into filling that box. No guilt trips, no pressure. It had been just a suggestion. Each returned to play quietly, as if in farewell to certain toys. And to selfishness.

A few minutes later, their mother came for the box. The eldest had carefully and resolutely placed almost all his new toys in it. The others selected more carefully but chose the best for the box.

Their mother took the box to the car without a word, an expression, or a gesture. She never reported on the reception of the orphans, and she was never asked.

Several years of childhood remained, but childishness had been dealt a blow.

JERRY B. JENKINS

AUTHOR, THE LEFT BEHIND SERIES

A Grandmother Remembers Mama

Maurine, who was age four when I was born, begged Mother to name me Dolly Dimples, for the famous paper doll. Mother wrote this name in the family Bible and later changed it to Dolly Beatrice, persuading Maurine that I would not always be little, and later I would not want the name of Dimples. Before I was old enough to go to school, I persuaded Mother to let me change my name from Dolly to Dorothy. So Mother let me enroll in school with a new grown-up name: Dorothy Beatrice.

In my most recent memories of my mother, I see her as she was at almost eighty-seven years. She was living alone in our great old family home, still strong and courageous and, of course, always loving. Yet in my most precious memories of her, I see her just as she was when she was our very young, beautiful mother. She sang to us, songs like "The Old Armchair," as she sat working, her fingers worn thin with sewing at night after all the ironing and the dishes were done for the day, sewing clothes for the six children and shirts for Dad. And shirts for the good doctor, too, to apply on the ever-present bill.

I have a clear picture of all of us, her children, standing in the front yard on the snowy morning of Valentine's Day. We stood waiting just as she told us to as we watched her open the gate of the picket fence and walk a short way down the road to the big mailbox. She had always loved red, and on this day she wore the bright red coat she had sewn for herself. Slim and beautiful, with black wavy hair pinned in a thick bun, she hurried along to the mailbox, then turned to wave at us. That picture—a flash of scarlet in the snow—will always stay with me. As she opened the gate, returning quickly, we saw in her hands a stack of valentines, one for every one of her six children! We were happy and wondered who sent them! We were too young to notice that the Valentine's cards had no postmarks or stamps.

One Monday, Great-Aunt Laura came to our house, shocked to find wash day going on as usual. It had been widely predicted that, on this particular day, the world was coming to an end. So our Aunt Laura wouldn't dream of washing that day!

"Why, Lula," she said to Mother, "You shouldn't be washing clothes when the Lord comes." Mother said nothing and went on scrubbing on that old rub board.

My mother was interested in the news and what went on in the government. She took no public lead, but she listened and learned and had a mind of her own. Many years ago, when the news reached Georgetown by wire that women had been granted the right to vote, word spread quickly around the town square. When the big old clock in the courthouse tolled twelve bells for noon, Dad hurried home to tell Mother the exciting news. He was so happy! He always loved politics, and after various elections, when the returns came in, he rejoiced. "I won three of my votes," or "I just lost one vote," or however it was at the time.

On that special day, Dad came in from town, striding to the kitchen where Mother was rolling out biscuits for dinner. I was sitting there cutting out the paper doll from its special page in *The Delineator*. Nothing very much distracted me from this once-a-month pleasure, but I looked up—and my scissors stopped when

Dad said: "It has been passed! Women can vote."

My mother stopped rolling her dough, wiped her hands on her calico apron and looked at Dad, astonished.

"Oh, this is good," he said. "I will have *two* votes now."

Mother looked at him, a very still, long, long look. I put down my scissors and my paper doll page.

"That's what you think." Very softly, she said it. "I will choose the one I vote for."

DOROTHY SHELL BUNTING
GRANDMOTHER OF DEBORAH BEDFORD

The Best Times of Your Life

I love babies and big families and always wanted that for myself. The book and movie I loved was *I Remember Mama*. I decided I wanted a dozen children, too. If my husband didn't agree to twelve, then eight—but no fewer.

My feelings about family came from my mother, Connie Adler. She was the oldest of eight children in a second family. (Her mother was a widow with five children when she married my grandfather, Florian Zimmerman.) For me this meant lots of cousins and a large extended family. During the baby boom years following World War II, there were five of us Adler cousins, all born within a few months of one another. In fact, I owe my entire writing career to my brother and two of my cousins who copied my diary and sold it to the boys in my eighth grade class. It was my first best-seller!

Eighteen months after Wayne and I married, our first daughter arrived. Jody was my parents' first grandchild and the apple of their eye. My mother came for two weeks and helped me adjust to motherhood. The following year when Jenny arrived, my mother came again, as she did when I delivered Ted and Dale, who followed in quick succession. After four babies in five years, Wayne and I knew we'd reached our emotional and financial limit.

Shortly after Dale was born (my last), I was both emotionally and physically worn out. I don't know what I would have done without Mom there to help me through this recovery time. All four of the children used to sit in the rocking chair my father built, and I'd rock them back and forth. Jody and Jenny were on my legs while the two boys shared my lap. My mother told me about her mother rocking seven children all at one time.

Then she looked at me with such joy and said, "Treasure these days, Debbie. These will be the happiest years of your life."

Happiest of my life? I hadn't slept a full night through in two or three years. I remember looking at my mom and asking, "You mean it gets worse?"

Mom laughed and suggested I wait and see. Now that I'm a grandmother myself, I can appreciate my mother's wisdom. Those were the easy times, when I could cuddle my children close, protect them from the temptations of the world, share with them the wonder of God's love. As I look back upon those days, draining as they were, I realize how right she was.

Thanks, Mom, for pointing me toward the future and reminding me to savor what I have right this moment.

DEBBIE MACOMBER, MOTHER AND AUTHOR

Dear Mom

Dear Mom,

It's been thirty-three years now since you went to be with the Lord. How joyful your new life must be!

I was a young woman when you left us that rainy morning in May, so we never really got to have a woman-to-woman talk like so many moms and daughters enjoy. I was barely able to comprehend the meaning of life, let alone know the hole your passing would leave in my heart. Today, having raised three children of my own, I know a little more about a mother's love.

Those last few hours you opened your eyes and chanted the soft litany, "I love you, I love you, I love you." Well, Mom, I loved you, too. And I didn't tell you nearly enough. I know that I didn't thank you sufficiently for the multitude of ways that you expressed your love for me. Remember that special doll we argued over? A childish extravagance that I thought I'd die if I didn't get. You bought the doll, knowing that you would have to skimp on necessities the following week. You skimped often for your children. Thank you.

Thank you for giving me unconditional love during times when I was unlovable. For taking me to Sunday school and church every Sunday and teaching me that the Lord is the Way, the Truth, and the Life. The knowledge has made my life a lot richer.

Thank you for working a night shift at a paper cup factory to provide me with clothes and food and a roof over my head. For the long walks home at two o'clock in the morning, in pelting rain and blowing snowstorms, because the car wouldn't climb the rutted county hill leading to our house. Those treks must have been scary and lonely, and I thank you, Mom.

You were only fifteen when you married Dad. Your childhood wasn't the best and you wanted to make sure that your children's were better. Well, you and Dad met your goal. Your little chicks have grown into responsible adults: no one's been in jail yet (a little humor there, Mom). I know you appreciate humor because after thirty-three years what I remember most about you was your friendly smile. You gave it to everyone.

Thanks for circuses, movies on Saturday afternoons, and for that mouthwatering cocoa fudge you made every Sunday night. I can taste it to this day: creamy, warm chocolate, rich black walnuts, with a generous dollop of butter. Real butter. We don't eat that way these days, Mom. Cholesterol's a naughty word. I can still see you standing at the stove and stirring the candy to a boil, and then testing it in a cup of cold water until it formed a perfect soft ball.

Thanks for leaving the porch light on until I was safely home.

I really miss you, Mom, and having grown older, I realize the importance of having a mother at any age. Cancer is still an ugly blight upon this earth, and hopefully someday the disease will be eradicated.

Mother's Day is coming around again. We buried you on Mother's Day. Still, every May I honor you in my heart and know that today you are walking with God. How could I wish anything more for my special mom?

This Mother's Day I wanted to share a few thoughts that I had forgotten to voice while you were still with me. And to say thanks, Josephine Alice Smart, for giving me life and for teaching me that each new day is a gift from God, a wondrous bequest to be treasured. I'll see you one day soon, Mom. Keep the porch light on.

Your loving daughter, Lori

LORI COPELAND, MOTHER AND AUTHOR, *FAITH AND HOPE*

A Life That Mattered

My mom grew up poor in everything but faith, love, and laughter—those she knew in abundance and shared freely. She had polio when she was young and a lung condition exacerbated by growing up in poverty in the depression and dust bowl.

My mother did nothing particularly heroic in her life, yet every day of her life took heroic effort. Diagnosed with rheumatoid arthritis in her twenties, she did not let it defeat her. She lived in pain almost every day of her last fifty years, but that did not stop her. She was a den mother, a friend, a confidant, a working woman, and a volunteer for everything from band fund-raisers to comforting ICU patients' families. She ran her own business for a while and, when widowed in her early fifties, became a single parent. She lost six babies, but that did not make her bitter, it just made those of us who survived more precious. Her fibrosis of the lungs (which her smoking did not help) plagued her always and she had frequent bouts of life-threatening pneumonia.

In her later years, she broke both her hips, had them replaced, and was up weeks before the doctors thought she would be (some thought she would never walk again). Despite the fact that she had most of the joints in her hands replaced—her disease had maimed them into tiny claws—she still reached out to others. Since she loved us, Mom was always on our side no matter how stupid, stubborn, misguided, or selfish we were being. She might not condone our actions, and she'd let us know when she disapproved, but she loved us anyway, and we never doubted it.

In her last days in the hospital, she was surrounded by three generations of women, all touched by her spirit in their own lives and called to come one last time to say good-bye. We were determined she would not go alone, and yet the mother in her would not surrender to the racking struggle for every breath and the swelling of her brain (from a massive stroke) as long as one of her children stood by, looking on. More than once she stopped breathing, but when she heard her child's voice, she rallied, literally from the brink of death to stay with us as she had promised: "I will always be here for you."

To the end she was the best kind of mother, one who would endure anything within her power to spare her children heartache. And so she held on until the night we all slipped away to eat and a cousin came to sit with her. My cousin held her tight, then sat beside the bed singing hymns softly until Mom just stopped breathing. Later, my cousin wondered if her singing had finally done Mom in, and we all laughed—we laughed a lot in those days, despite our tears.

There is so much more to tell about my mom—her wisdom, her humor, her fairness. But I think, perhaps, the best thing to say is what I told her on her last day: Her life mattered. Too many of us muddle through our lives, self-involved, petty, unhappy, and alone. She did none of those things, and in the end, the very fact that she rose above the human tendency to feel sorry for herself, to be mean when life is hard, to surrender to ugliness and despair in the face of unfairness and suffering, made the difference.

I am better for having known her, having seen her faith in action, and having been loved by her gentle spirit, and in turn the people my life touches will be better for what she instilled in me. That is her testament. Her love survives.

ANNIE JONES

MOTHER AND AUTHOR, *SAVING GRACE* AND *THE SNOWBIRDS*

The Story Jar

So you see," Mrs. Halley said as she returned the nose ring to the jar, her gaze kind upon Beth's face, "God can use any of us. No matter our backgrounds. No matter our flaws. No matter our appearance. All He needs is a willing heart, and He is able to work miracles."

Beth found herself teary eyed for the second time, more moved by the widow's words than she cared to admit. She reminded herself she was nothing like the mothers in Mrs. Halley's stories. Besides, she was more accustomed to cleaning churches than to sitting in one on a Sunday morning. Not exactly the kind of person God listened to.

"Nothing is impossible with the Lord, my dear," Mrs. Halley said, once again reading Beth's thoughts.

Beth rose from the floor, her muscles complaining over the length of time she'd been sitting there.

Nothing is impossible with the Lord.

She reached for her cleaning bucket. As she did so, her charm bracelet slipped forward with a faint jingle.

The boys had given the bracelet to her for Christmas five years ago. It wasn't anything fancy, but she prized it above every piece of jewelry she owned. Tommy and Mark had been so proud when she opened that package and exclaimed over their gift. They'd saved their allowance for weeks in order to buy it, then had talked the next-door neighbor into taking them to the mall.

She smiled at the memory, even as tears flooded her eyes once more.

"Is there something I can do for you, my dear?" Mrs. Halley asked softly.

It seemed a strange request, coming from a woman who'd recently buried her husband. Yet Beth was certain it was asked with genuine concern. She didn't intend to reply. She knew there was nothing the elderly widow could do to help her. But then, suddenly, the words were there, echoing in the sanctuary.

"Sometimes I feel like such a failure as a mother." Beth stared at the various items in her pail of cleaning products and rags. "Such a complete failure. Maybe I was never meant to be a mother in the first place."

"Mrs. Williams?"

There was something about the way Mrs. Halley said her name that caused Beth to turn and meet the other woman's gaze.

"Could you spare me a little more of your time?" The elderly woman held a tiny yellow sock in one hand. "I'd like to share one more story with you. Perhaps, when I'm finished, you'll feel differently than you do now."

If only she could…

"Please," Mrs. Halley repeated, motioning for Beth to join her once again.

What choice had she but to comply? Beth set aside her pail, then sank onto the floor near the other woman's feet.

"I suppose I should begin about six years ago." Mrs. Halley stared at the yellow sock. "Yes; it was at least six years ago now…"

The Yellow Sock

Angela Elwell Hunt

One

rs. Leber?" Megan Wingfield looked up from the medical chart in her hand and smiled at the petite woman sitting on the edge of a chair in the examination room. "I've got some interesting news for you. Princess is not sick or overweight—she's pregnant. Carrying five puppies, to be exact, and due in about a week."

"Pregnant?" The older woman's face went pale. "Impossible. Princess stays in the house with me except when I go to work, and then she's in a fenced backyard. She hasn't been around any other dogs."

Megan lifted a brow. "Any holes under your fence? Any loose boards? You'd be surprised how easy it is for a determined dog to, er, visit."

The woman shook her head decisively. "It's a chain-link fence, and I keep my yard locked up tight as a drum. No way Princess has had a visitor."

Megan folded her arms. "Well, she's definitely pregnant, so there's a daddy dog somewhere in your neighborhood. You might begin by asking your neighbors if their male dogs have been neutered."

"Oh, my." If possible, Mrs. Leber's face went a shade paler. "My precious purebred…"

"Great Danes are wonderful dogs," Megan said, trying to soften the blow, "so even if the puppies are mixed, they are sure to inherit many of Princess's fine qualities."

"You don't understand." The red line of Mrs. Leber's mouth thinned for a moment. "That annoying boy who lives behind me—he has a male dog. A Chihuahua. A yappy, irritating, pesky little runt that is always yipping at Princess through the fence...."

In spite of herself, Megan grinned. A Chihuahua could easily slip beneath a chain-link fence, but she couldn't imagine what sort of pups would result from a union between a giant, docile Dane and a high-strung toy breed.

"We'll have to see what the puppies are like when they are born." Megan moved toward the door. "Now, if you'll excuse me a moment, I'll go get Princess. The doctor will be in to discuss the delivery with you."

"Five puppies," Mrs. Leber murmured, her gaze drifting toward the wall. "What am I supposed to do with five bizarre little mutts?"

After closing the door behind her, Megan walked back to the X-ray room, where Dr. Bob Duncan and Tom, another technician, were easing the huge Harlequin Dane off the examination table. Princess was a sweet animal, though in her present condition she seemed all legs and belly.

"Mrs. Leber thinks the pups might have been fathered by a Chihuahua," Megan told the doctor, trying her best not to giggle.

"Egads." Dr. Duncan's genial face split into a grin. "Won't that be an interesting combination?"

The black-and-white Dane lumbered over to Megan and sniffed at her fingers.

"You want a treat?" Megan pulled the bottle of canine vitamins from her pocket and opened it. "You're a lucky girl. You get two—

one for you and one for the pups."

"Is she going to be all right?" Dr. Duncan asked, turning toward the door.

Megan flashed him a wry smile. "Mrs. Leber or Princess?"

The doctor laughed. "I know the dog will be fine. I'm worried about the owner."

"I think she'll be okay once she gets over the shock," Megan said, slipping her hand beneath the huge dog's collar. "But we might have to help her find homes for those puppies."

"Hmmm." The doctor made a polite sound as he took the dog's chart and scribbled a note. "Ought to insist upon spay/neuters for the pups, too, as soon as possible. I don't think I'd want to encourage the breeding of Great Chihuahuas."

"No, sir."

Following the doctor, Megan led the pregnant Princess to the examination room and paused as the doctor pasted on a straight face. After giving her a "here goes nothing" look, he opened the door and called out in a cheery voice, "Mrs. Leber! I hear you're about to become the grandmother of five!"

Megan lowered her head to hide her expression as she led the Great Dane into the exam room. The huge, spotted dog had never found it easy to maneuver in the room designed more for cats and small breeds, so it took Megan a full five minutes to pull the heavily expectant animal into the open space between the patient door and the exam table.

As the doctor tried to explain why Mrs. Leber should build a whelping box no matter what breed had fathered the puppies, Megan urged Princess to sit. The gentle giant was eager to comply and dropped to the cool tiles with a long sigh. Megan sat beside her on the floor. As she stroked the dog's neck, she felt her own thoughts drifting away.

Life. Birth. Death. Every day she saw the cycle repeated in this office where animals were born, grew through the stages of development, and finally died in their weeping owners' arms. Her love of life and animals had brought her to this veterinary hospital, and she'd willingly stay forever if not for her own desire to experience the cycle of life.

She wanted a baby. And, if God was merciful, she might have one on the way.

She lowered her head to gaze into the Dane's beautiful brown eyes.

"When did you know?" she whispered, fondling the dog's silky ears. "Did you know right away, or did you have to wait until you felt the puppies moving?"

Princess didn't answer, but when she lifted her head, Megan could have sworn the dog was smiling.

Most teachers had summers off, but Dave had chosen to spend his July teaching a summer school class for Alta Vista high school students who'd flunked American history. Often he remained late to tutor kids who were having difficulty in the intensive class, but his car stood in the driveway when Megan arrived home. She snatched her keys out of the ignition, sailed through the front door, and found her handsome husband on the deck, a plate of raw hamburger patties in his hand.

"Hi, Chef Wingfield." She gave him a quick kiss, then stood back and nodded appreciatively at the flaming grill. "Mmm, those burgers look good. But be sure they're done in the middle, okay?" She almost added that eating raw meat was bad for pregnant women, but then thought better of it.

"Have I ever fed you a raw hamburger?" Dave's blue eyes

twinkled over his shoulder as she moved to a deck chair. "They don't call me Chef-Boy-ar-Dave for nothing."

"Yeah, right." She sank into the seat and propped her feet on the edge of the vacant chair behind her husband. Though the sun had begun to lower toward the Virginia mountains in the west, the air was still warm and muggy.

She pushed her bangs off her damp forehead and smiled up at him. "Have a good day?"

"The kids were fine, no problems." Dave dropped the patties onto the grill, where they immediately began to sizzle. "Dr. Comfort called to talk to me about next year. Seems she's thinking about making it her *last* year. She wants to retire."

Megan stared at him, a tingle of excitement beginning to flow through her veins. Dr. Stella Comfort was Dave's boss at Valley View Elementary School, where he worked during the regular school year. "If she's retiring—"

"Yep, she wants me to take her place. She says she'll recommend me to the school board even though I'd be the youngest principal in the county."

"That's *wonderful* news, honey." Megan beamed at him as she fanned her face with her hand. "I always knew you were the best, but this proves it."

Dave shrugged. "It means Dr. Comfort likes my work. I'd still have to convince the school board I could handle the job, and there are other assistant principals who'd kill to have that spot."

"But you've been at that school four years. The teachers know and respect you, and the parents have never had a bad word to say—"

"All the same, it's up to the school board." Turning, he winked at her. "But thanks for the vote of confidence."

"You're welcome." Megan crossed her legs at the ankle, wondering if the fluttering in her stomach was the result of hunger or something else. "I might have some other good news."

His brow lifted. "Not another pet, I hope."

"No, two cats are enough." She looked down at her hands as a sudden feeling of awkwardness overtook her. How many times had they replayed this conversation?

"I'm two days late."

His voice softened. "You've been late before."

"Yeah, but today, around lunchtime, I felt really queasy. Laurie says that's how she felt in the first month. She said she couldn't even stand the *sight* of food."

"Maybe you ate something you shouldn't have."

"I didn't eat. I skipped lunch."

When Dave didn't answer, she hurried to fill the silence. "And there are other signs, too. Breast tenderness. And I'm tired, really tired. So on the way home I stopped to pick up another test kit."

His eyes, when she looked up, were soft with sympathy. "I'd wait a day or two," he whispered, keeping his gaze on her while he absently patted the burgers with a pancake turner. "Save your money."

Megan's eyes filled with tears as he turned his attention back to the grill. Why couldn't he be optimistic? They'd been through so much together—twenty-two long months of the struggle to conceive a baby. Everyone said they just needed to relax, to trust in God's timing, to let themselves settle into married life. Well, they'd been married and settled for three years and still there was no baby. No pregnancy. Nothing but hope after hope, month after month, an endless roller coaster of rising optimism and falling dreams....

Megan's stomach gurgled as the scent of sizzling fat reached her nostrils. She placed a protective hand over her belly, then pulled herself out of the deep chair. "Yell at me when the burgers are done," she called as she left the porch. "I'm going in to cool off."

Once inside the house, she locked herself in the bathroom. A moment later she discovered that Dave had been right—she *should* have saved her money and not bought the pregnancy kit. This would be another month without a baby.

After dashing tears from her eyes, she opened the cupboard beneath the sink and fumbled for the box of tampons. She tried to tell herself it was no big deal, just another minor setback, but her pep talk did nothing to stem the hot tears stinging her eyes.

Dave pressed the flat blade of the metal pancake turner to the mound of ground beef on the grill and blinked as steam rose from the dripping fat. He'd heard the note of resentment in Megan's voice, and he knew his wife was nearing the limits of her endurance. She'd been remarkably patient in the face of frustration, but soon she'd be looking at him again with mute appeal in her blue eyes.

They both wanted a child, but Megan had been far more active than he in the pursuit of their goal. After their first anniversary, Megan brought up the topic of children, and he agreed—they had been blessed with a home, their marriage was stable, and they were mature enough to pursue parenthood. So they stopped using birth control and waited for God to bless them with a baby.

Now, two years later, they were still waiting.

To her credit, Megan didn't become anxious right away. The books she read assured them that no couple should consider themselves infertile until they'd been unable to conceive for an entire year, so she waited six months before taking the matter up with her gynecologist. At her annual physical, the doctor did a cursory examination and said everything looked normal. To appease her doubts, he sent Megan home with charts and instructions on how to determine the time of her ovulation—prime time for conception. For three months, Megan began the day with a thermometer in her mouth, then recorded her waking temperature. On the days that the thermometer dipped a degree, she told Dave that they'd reached the *appointed time*.

Dave had never minded the act of intimacy between a husband and his wife, but Megan's no-nonsense tone on those days was anything but romantic. Still, if her efforts and record keeping resulted in a baby, he figured it would all be worthwhile.

After a year of temperature taking, Megan tossed out her tattered charts and turned her eagle eye on Dave. A man's fertility, she told him, could depend upon what type of underwear he wore, so he had to switch from briefs to boxers. Dave grumbled a bit at this, but the concession seemed small when he considered what she had endured with her thermometers and charts.

After six months of boxer shorts, Megan's gaze narrowed even further. "You need to see a urologist," she told him in a flat voice. "There's no sense in me taking drugs if…"

The problem lies with you.

Megan had left her sentence unfinished, but Dave could hear the note of accusation in her tone.

Trouble was, a visit to the urologist was at the bottom of his list of enjoyable pursuits. The appointment was certain to be inconvenient, uncomfortable, and embarrassing. He'd never been to a urologist before, and he wasn't eager to establish a relationship with any doctor who worked…down there.

But as he carried the steaming burgers into the kitchen, he saw Megan's watery eyes and knew they'd failed again. Those eyes lifted to him in a silent plea, and he found himself whispering, "Okay, honey. I'll make an appointment."

One week later, amid the yipping and yapping of a litter of miniature Doberman puppies in the waiting room, Megan paused behind the reception desk and glanced at the clock. Dave's appointment with the doctor had been scheduled for nine o'clock that morning, and at lunch he'd called to say that the doctor would have results by three. He'd be back in the classroom by that time, but if Megan wanted to call and check on things...

She forced herself to concentrate on the woman behind the counter. Her Persian cat, an aloof creature named King Midas, had just had his teeth cleaned, and was definitely unhappy with the situation.

"Here's the doctor's report," she said, handing a copy of the kitty health report to the cat's solicitous owner. "King Midas should be fine, but he'll need to have those teeth cleaned at least once a year."

As the woman moved away, Midas scowled at Megan, who scowled back, then shifted her gaze to the clock above the desk. One o'clock. Two more hours before she would know anything.

"Laurie," she said, turning her back on the waiting patients, "I'm going to the back for a minute."

Craving a moment of silence and privacy, she moved into the rest room, then locked the door and leaned against it. The afternoon had crept by, each moment longer than the one preceding it. The morning had begun like all the others, but at the breakfast table she had opened her book of daily devotions and read an unusual challenge. "What is the thing you want most from God right now?" the writer had asked. "Are you willing to surrender that desire so God can work His will in your life?"

She had stared at the page in silence, feeling oddly betrayed. Someone had been reading her mind; the author obviously knew her deepest secret. The thing she wanted most in life was to become pregnant, and no, she wasn't willing to abandon that desire…not while there was even a slight chance that her dream might become a reality.

Did God ask such things of His children? She'd grown up believing that if you followed the principles of the Bible, God would grant the desires of your heart. And He knew her heart's desire was a baby.

She exhaled slowly, then lifted her chin and stared in the small bathroom mirror, bracing herself to face the waiting patients and their owners. If she kept busy, this afternoon would pass quickly.

She counted the minutes between one and two, her eyes gravitating to the clock between patients. At one-thirty she'd prayed that Dave's test results would be good; at two o'clock she amended her prayer. "Please, Father," she prayed in the quiet X-ray room. "Let Your will be done, but please end this uncertainty. I'd rather know there was absolutely no chance for us to have children than continue this emotional roller-coaster ride."

No matter how bad the news might be, Megan found comfort in the thought that their waiting might soon end. By some miracle of modern medicine, perhaps this doctor could provide an answer…and a baby. But even if all he could give was a clear reason why they had failed, at least the months of disappointment would end.

She made a face as she glanced at the calendar. Dr. Comfort, Dave's boss at Valley View Elementary, was coming to the house tonight. Dave felt that she wanted to discuss his future away from the school, so Megan had planned a nice dinner—cranberry chicken, tossed salad, and her famous yeast rolls. Maybe, if she had time after work, she'd whip up a chocolate chess pie for dessert.

Two-thirty found her at the desk, explaining the doctor's instructions to Mrs. Wilt, whose dainty Pekinese had developed a urinary tract infection. After Mrs. Wilt pocketed the prescription, Megan offered a flavored vitamin to the petite Peke, who accepted it with delicate pleasure. "Take care now," Megan said, smiling them out the door. "The doctor will call in a few days to see how she's doing."

Three o'clock found Megan at the desk again, her hands on the counter, her attention a million miles away from her job. When the minute hand of the large clock over the desk shifted and creaked past the straight vertical position, she picked up the phone and punched in the number she'd scrawled on an appointment card.

After being passed from the receptionist to the doctor's private office, Megan waited on hold for about five minutes, then heard a male voice.

"Mrs. Wingfield?"

"Yes?"

As the doctor proceeded to speak in a flat monotone, Megan stared at the image of a sad-eyed bassett pup on the desk calendar. When he finished, she thanked him and hung up.

So that settled the matter. Her prayer had been completely answered in an instant. God didn't even want to negotiate.

She blinked as the image of the puppy began to waver. "Laurie," she said, turning toward the receptionist sitting behind her, "would you tell Dr. Duncan that I needed to leave early? It's sort of a family crisis."

Laurie opened her mouth as if to ask for details, then nodded wordlessly when she saw Megan's face.

Megan moved through the waiting room toward the door, a little amazed that her arms and legs and hands could still function. How could they open doors and walk and unlock the car when her brain was numb and her heart breaking?

Two

An hour later, Megan lay on her bed, the pillow damp beneath her cheeks. The sense of numbness had carried her home, but the dam broke when she crossed the threshold of their bedroom. After the tears, dry sobs wracked her body for a brief interval, then faded away.

The tears did nothing to ease the pain. She had thought she'd feel better after a good cry, but this burden was far too heavy to be wept away in an hour.

Lying there, she listened to the steady click of the cuckoo clock in the hall and waited for the sound of Dave's key in the lock. He'd be home at any moment, then she could share this heaviness.

She closed her eyes as she heard the soft sound of the opening door followed by the squeak of his shoes on the foyer tiles. "Megan?"

"In here." The pillow muffled her voice, but he had no trouble finding her. When she sat up to greet him, the look on his face told her he knew. Obviously, he'd called the doctor, too.

She stood and held out her arms, and they moved together, holding each other in a soundless embrace. Closing her eyes, she pressed her hand to the back of his head.

"I'm so sorry, honey," he whispered, his breath stirring the hair by her ear. "It's all my fault."

"Shhh." Pulling back, she pressed a finger to his lips even as fresh tears threatened to erupt. She shook her head. "You can't say that."

"But I had a feeling, and I didn't want to face it."

"Hush." She lowered her forehead to his chest, not willing to watch him take the blame. This would have to be a shared problem, not his or hers, but *theirs*. If the situation were allowed to come between them, it could separate them forever.

"We have to decide—" she took his hands in hers—"what we're going to do next. We can try to conceive with a doctor's help, and there's always artificial insemination. Or we could adopt."

"I don't know what we should do." Holding her hands, he sat on the edge of the bed and pulled her down next to him. "But we'll pray about it and see how we feel—"

"I can't pray any more." She gulped hard, tears slipping down her cheeks. "I've been praying for so long. I can't pray another month. I've been praying for a sign, and this is it. Now we have to decide what we're going to do."

She turned to face him. "Honey, this afternoon I asked God to make our path clear. I told Him I'd rather have no chance for a baby than only a little chance, and I'm afraid that's what we'd be facing if we went to the doctor and investigated experimental procedures. We'd be signing on for more waiting, and struggle, and lab reports, and tests. The frustration and uncertainty, not to mention the expense, might drain us."

He absorbed this news in silence, then lifted his chin. "So you want to adopt?"

She drew a deep breath. "I've been thinking about it. We both love children, and we know there are thousands of kids who need parents. We could be parents to one of them—if we can't have our own. But I think we should check out all the options. Maybe there is medical hope for us. Maybe I was wrong to pray that prayer this afternoon. Maybe I was testing God. I don't know. I just know I want a baby."

Watching her husband, Megan saw a look pass across his face, a look she recognized. She'd worn the same expression half an hour ago—when she had realized she might have to surrender her dream of a biological baby and move on.

Dave's hand reached up and touched her jaw, then her hair. "I was hoping for a daughter like you," he said, his voice husky.

Megan touched his cheek, and felt his tears burn her fingertips like hot wax. "A son like you would be wonderful," she whispered, "but we'll have to see what God has planned."

And then, because she had an important guest coming for dinner, Megan pushed her sorrows down, clamped a smile over them, and went out to the kitchen to begin making dinner.

Megan toyed with a wilting lettuce leaf on her plate as Dr. Comfort—Stella, in this casual environment—laughed with Dave about the child who'd brought his pet tarantula to school and turned it loose in the kindergarten classroom. "I'll never forget Miss Pritchard's face," Dave said, leaning back in his chair. "I don't think she'll ever promote Pet Day again!"

"I couldn't get over the fact that the boy couldn't understand why we reacted so strongly." Stella laughed softly. "After all, he pretty much let the spider run free in his bedroom."

Dave shook his head. "I remember that boy—Ricky Feldon. I taught him the next year, in first grade. He and his family must have been cut from a different bolt of cloth—they were all creative and bright, but they definitely marched to the beat of a different drummer."

"Remember his sister, Moonglow?" Stella's blond brows arched mischievously. "She was three years ahead of Ricky. One day she brought a book to show and tell, then proceeded to read the poems of a love-struck seventeen-year-old."

Dave frowned. "A library book?"

"Her older sister's diary!"

Megan reflexively joined in the laughter, but her thoughts were drifting far from the current conversation. She looked at Dave—six foot three, handsome, and as appealing on the inside as he was attractive on the outside. All of her girlfriends at the community college had thought him a great catch—but would any of them willingly trade places with her now?

Of all the young men she had dated in high school and college, why had God led her to marry Dave? She'd been in love with several of the guys she dated, and any one of them might have made a fine husband. But God had led her to Dave Wingfield, and as a result, He had brought her face to face with infertility.

She dropped her fork to the table and picked up her iced tea glass. Of all the physical problems Dave could have had, why did he have to have one that prevented them from having biological children? He could have been born with one leg shorter than the other…or without a sense of smell. He could have developed allergies or diabetes or epilepsy, and none of those things would have prevented him from being a father. But God had allowed Dave, a man with a unique love for children, to face a future without any kids to call his own.

She lowered her gaze as tears stung her eyes. She had to rein in her thoughts, turn them toward something useful. God had led her to Dave, and she had vowed to love him in good times and bad, in sickness and in health. And this problem wasn't his alone; it belonged to both of them. Since God had called her to this marriage—and she truly believed He had—then infertility had to be part of God's will and plan for her life as well as Dave's.

But why?

She'd lived her entire life by the rules: don't smoke, don't drink, don't have sex before marriage. Do go to church, do study hard, do get a job, do maintain a good reputation. Her name was on the dean's list at college and listed in two volumes of *Who's Who in American Universities*. She'd grown up with God, and no one could say she hadn't been at least a dutiful example of what a Christian young woman should be. She wasn't perfect, no one was, but she'd always done her best to make good choices. She'd waited for Mr. Right, and she'd been delighted to find Dave and learn that he was planning to spend his life teaching young children. He was the most giving person she had ever met, and she'd been convinced they would make a great team.

So why was God sabotaging her plans?

*The Lord knows what He is doing. He has promised to be with you in every difficulty, and He will not allow you to suffer beyond the limits of your endurance….*The words echoed in her mind, a lesson learned from Sunday school classes and Bible studies of years gone by. She believed those words in her head, but that belief, springing from her rational brain, did nothing to assuage the clawing pain that ripped at her heart.

She wanted to be pregnant; she wanted a baby; she wanted to raise a baby who would be flesh of her flesh and bone of her bones. And she did not want to wait. They had been married for three years and waiting for two.

Surely they had waited long enough….

"Honey?"

She looked up. Both Dave and Stella were staring at her.

"Stella was just saying she has to leave soon. Would you like to serve the dessert now?"

Megan felt her lips twitch in an automatic smile. "Sure. I made chocolate pie." She pushed back her chair and kept talking as she walked to the kitchen counter. "It's an old recipe, from a friend. Sometimes the cocoa doesn't dissolve; that's why you'll see these little sprinkles on top, but it should still taste okay...."

She stopped her mindless babbling when she heard the creak of a chair. She turned and saw Dave standing behind her, and something in his forlorn expression broke her heart.

Unable to speak, she burst into tears.

With his sobbing wife in his arms, Dave looked at his boss. "I'm sorry, Stella," he said, softening his voice. "We got a bit of bad news today. Apparently...well, it looks like we're not going to have children in the usual way."

The older woman's eyes closed for a moment, then she nodded slowly. "I didn't know you were trying, but I should have guessed. After all, you've been married for a while now, and I know you both love children...."

Her voice trailed off as Dave pressed his hand to the back of Megan's head. He had never felt more helpless in his life.

"I'm okay," Megan said, sniffing. She lifted her head and wiped away tears. "I'm so sorry. I didn't mean to blubber in the middle of dinner."

Stella stood, then reached out and placed a hand on both Dave's and Megan's shoulders. "My friends," she said, her voice breaking with huskiness, "you two are precious people. I know

God has something special in store for you. But nothing worthwhile is easy. If it were, we wouldn't appreciate it like we should."

Her gaze drifted toward the window. "I'd like to share a proverb with you: 'Hope deferred makes the heart sick; but when the desire comes, it is a tree of life.'" She smiled, her eyes shining with beautiful candor as she looked at Megan. "Not *if* the desire comes, but *when*. This is God's promise for you. Trust Him."

She gave Megan a quick hug. "The pie looks delicious, my dear, but I ought to be going. I think you and Dave need some time alone."

Dave stepped forward to see her to the door, but she waved at him over her shoulder as she picked up her purse. "Never mind me, I'll see myself out. Thank you for the dinner, Megan. Thank you both for the fellowship…and the trust." She gave Dave a confident smile. "I'll be praying for your future—concerning your child and your job. I know you'd make an excellent principal, Dave. I'm curious to see how the Lord will work things out."

Dave waited until he heard the click of the front door, then he turned to Megan, who stood at the kitchen counter, her woebegone gaze fastened to the speckled chocolate pie.

"I want to show you something, honey." He pulled a photograph from his wallet. "Do you remember this day?"

He gave her the picture and waited while she studied it. He had taken the photo nearly six years before, just after they began to date. Megan had come to see him at the school where he taught, and during a lunch break she'd spent some time reading picture books to the first graders. One little girl—a blond, blue-eyed waif called Daniella—had stolen Megan's heart. They'd made such a pretty pair, Daniella with her blond hair and Megan with her brunette, that Dave had snapped a picture of the girl sitting on Megan's lap. Later, when he explained that Daniella was a foster child, Megan's eyes had filled with tears. And at that moment, he decided to marry Megan Myers.

Her eyes were flowing again as she stared at the snapshot.

"I fell in love with you that day," he whispered, leaning against the counter, "because I knew any woman who loved kids as much as I did would be a wonderful wife and mother. Nothing has changed, Meg. You're still the same girl, and you'll still make a wonderful mother."

Her lower lip trembled, but she didn't speak.

"Daniella needed a home...and though I don't know what happened to her, I know there are thousands like her in foster care. We can be parents, Meg. I think we can find a child fairly quickly if we're willing to accept one as old as Daniella."

Megan bit her lip as she traced the little girl's image with her fingernail. "I'd forgotten her name," she said, her voice wavering. "But I could never forget her."

Reaching out, Dave drew his wife into the circle of his arms. "We will have a child," he promised. "You'll see."

The next afternoon, Megan said good-bye to Mrs. Leber, Princess, and the five newborn pups (two big black males, one big tan female, and two tiny black-and-white spotted females with pointy faces and oversized ears), then pulled her sack lunch and can of soda from the staff refrigerator. Dr. Duncan was holed up in his office, munching on a tuna sandwich between follow-up calls, so she knew she'd have a good half hour to eat and think in relative quiet.

The veterinary hospital bordered a community park, a quiet place for lunch, particularly in the humid heat of July. With her lunch bag and a book, Megan walked down the narrow path to her favorite bench, then spread her chips and sandwich on a paper towel. She hadn't felt like preparing much this morning, so her sandwich was peanut butter and jelly—not very creative, but filling.

The afternoon air was warm and sprinkled with sunlight that dropped through the dense canopy of oaks. Chewing on her sandwich, Megan turned away from the sight of a young couple sprawled on a blanket a few yards down the path. College students, from the looks of them, a young couple in love.

Insects filled the air with a continuous omnipresent *churr* as Megan hesitated and swallowed the thick peanut butter. Did that young couple dream of marriage and babies? Probably not. These days marriage seemed trivial to most people, and most career women regularly postponed motherhood until they had established their careers.

But Megan had wanted a baby almost immediately after her marriage. Two years of community college had resulted in a degree that enabled her to work as a certified veterinary technician, a job she'd hoped to keep until she married and had children. Dave was only two months shy of thirty on their wedding day, so a honeymoon baby would have been a surprise blessing. Megan knew she and Dave were in love, committed to their marriage and committed to God's plan for their lives. A baby would only have increased their joy.

A mosquito buzzed around her ear, and she swatted it away. How odd that some people conceived easily and others struggled for months. In the last two years she had often read the biblical stories of Hannah, who prayed for a child so fervently that the priest thought her drunk, and Rachel, who clung to her husband and cried, "Give me children or I will die!"

In her Sunday school days she hadn't been able to understand how the lack of children could darken a woman's soul. Now she knew that agony all too well.

Her gaze drifted to the edge of a sandbox, where a dark-haired woman sat with a blond, blue-eyed toddler in denim overalls. A boy.

As much as she wanted to look away, she couldn't. The sight of the child intoxicated her starved senses. Who was this woman who tended him, and what had brought them to the park? The woman could not be his mother—that fair-skinned child couldn't possibly have sprung from her genes. It was always possible that the boy's father was of Nordic descent, but it was far more likely that the woman was a nanny or baby-sitter.

Megan crinkled her nose in speculation. After working with so many canine breeds, her thoughts routinely wandered toward questions about bloodlines and heredity. If she had a nickel for every time someone brought in a pound pup and asked, "What do you think he is?" she could have retired two years ago. She'd grown adept at looking for the dark tongue of a chow, the pushed-in faces of pugs and Pekes, and soft, snubbed Labrador noses...

She looked again at the unlikely pair near the sandbox. Could the boy be adopted?

The memory of last night's conversation with Dave pricked at her nerves. He had been eager to embrace the idea of adoption, but he was thinking of adorable children like Daniella who needed homes. And she knew he didn't care for doctors and hospitals. It had taken nearly two years for him to agree to fertility testing.

But he shouldn't be so quick...because he didn't understand what he'd indirectly asked Megan to give up. For a man, the experience of pregnancy and childbirth was practically a moot point.

But he would never have to sit in a circle of women and remain silent as they swapped stories of back pains and labor and lactation…all the things that bound women together in a sorority of motherhood. He would never have to congratulate his friends on their impending arrivals when his own arms ached to protectively enclose a burgeoning belly; in a department store he would never walk the long way around in an effort to avoid the infant department.

Was she being selfish? Megan bit her lip. She didn't want to feel like a martyr, but she couldn't help it. In the past few months she had silently endured more hope and pain and agony than her friends and family would ever understand. Just last week her friend Shelia had stopped her in the church vestibule. With one hand on her own pregnant belly, Shelia had looked at Megan with sharp brown eyes and said, "No luck yet, honey? Maybe you and Dave just need to get away. You know—so you can relax."

Megan clenched her teeth at the memory. *Relax?* Shelia's comment had only wound her emotions tighter. She'd left church ready to scream, and things didn't get any easier when in the parking lot the pastor called out, "Good to see you, Dave and Megan." He then looked down at his wife, and, his voice booming, said, "Remember when we were young and not saddled with kids? Those two don't know how lucky they are!"

Megan felt about as lucky as a black cat.

The woman and baby were leaving now, piling a bucket and plastic shovel into a denim bag that overflowed with books and toys. Megan smoothed her features and took another bite of her sandwich, deliberately looking away, but a moment later she found herself staring straight into the boy's bright blue eyes.

"Excuse us for interrupting your lunch," the woman said, an apologetic smile on her face. She spoke with a slight trace of an accent, reinforcing Megan's belief that the pair could not be related. "But Andre wanted to give you something."

Surprised, Megan looked again at the boy, who wordlessly held up a dandelion between chubby little fingers.

"For me?" The words caught in Megan's throat.

The woman nodded. "He likes to give presents. And if I don't let him give it to you, he'll fight me all the way back to the car."

Megan leaned closer and held out her hands. "I would love a flower."

The wide blue eyes blinked once, then the boy edged forward and dropped the dandelion into Megan's cupped hands.

Megan couldn't stop a smile from stealing over her face. "Thank you, Andre."

The boy beamed for an instant, then tugged on the woman's hand and pointed to the dandelion-studded field beyond, eager to repeat his performance.

The woman sighed and released him. "All right, but just one more," she called as the boy toddled away.

Megan sat silently, watching him zigzag toward another dandelion.

"He's such a handful," the woman said, crossing her arms. "But I wouldn't trade him for anything."

"Your son?" Megan asked.

"Yes." The woman's voice softened. "Thank heaven."

Megan glanced up. A hint of wetness shone in the lady's eyes.

"Forgive my curiosity," Megan said, shifting her gaze to the boy again. "But I was wondering if his father is blond and blue eyed."

The woman let out a laugh. "He's Nigerian."

Shock flew through Megan. "African?"

The lady laughed again. "We are an international family. I am from Spain, my husband from Nigeria, and Andre is from Romania."

"Then—" Megan sat back, amazed. "You adopted him."

The woman held her head up in the hard light of the summer sun, and for the first time Megan realized that she was speaking to a woman well past prime childbearing years. "Obviously," she said, her voice soaked in politeness.

Megan bit her lip as a hundred questions bubbled to her lips. Could she ask? Or would she be prying personal information from a perfect stranger?

"My husband and I," she began, looking at her hands, "are thinking about adoption. But I'm not sure I'm ready to give up the idea of having a baby of my own."

"Your *own?*" A thread of reproach filled the woman's voice. "I hate to tell you this, dear, but no child is truly your own. Children may come from the wombs of women, but all of them spring from the hand of God. They are only placed in our safekeeping for a little while."

Megan nodded, reluctantly agreeing. "But you know what I mean—I wanted a natural child."

"Look at that boy there." The woman waited until Megan lifted her gaze. "Do you see anything *unnatural* about him?"

Again Megan felt the sting of rebuke. "That's not what I meant," she whispered, feeling as awkward as a baby taking his first tottering steps. "I wanted to be pregnant. To experience everything."

"Dear lady," the woman answered, her eyes darkening with emotion, "adoption is a life experience, just like childbirth. You'll have a time of waiting and a time of hard labor. You'll feel every pain and every joy. And when the child finally comes home, you'll call yourself blessed."

Andre came toddling forward now, his mouth spread in a gummy smile, a long-necked dandelion clenched in his fist. This flower he gave to his mother, who knelt and accepted it with a kiss, then drew him into a tight embrace.

As the woman made cooing sounds in the boy's ear, Megan lifted her head.

"May I ask what motivated you to adopt?"

The woman stopped cooing as the little boy laughed, then she released him and stood. Before leaving, she paused by Megan's bench and looked at her with eyes filled with compassion.

"Why did we adopt? Partly because of selfish reasons—my husband and I wanted a child to love. Partly because we knew there are children who need homes, and partly because we believe people ought to do more than talk about the ideals of racial reconciliation."

Her eyes softened. "But mostly because I realized that if I am faithful to teach and train, my children are the only earthly things I can take to heaven with me."

Those words remained with Megan long after the last of the dandelion fuzz blew away.

The house was dense with silence when Megan came home from work. Knowing that Dave must have stayed late to help a student, she moved into the kitchen, pulled a frozen dinner from the freezer, and put it in the microwave. After punching in the numbers, she leaned against the counter and stared at the cozy room—a space that should have been cluttered by a high chair, with baby bottles in the dish drainer and a bib hanging over the edge of the sink.

She had a choice—she could whimper and moan and mourn

her losses for another week or month or year, or she could move forward with her husband. After her encounter at the park, the former option seemed petty and selfish. Andre's mother was right—life was a cafeteria of rich experiences. Her tray would simply be filled with different choices than the average woman's.

She ran her hand over the spotless counter, then caught sight of Dave's photograph. He had snapped the picture as Daniella sat on Megan's lap at the child-sized book table. Their heads were a study in contrasts, one blond, one brunette, but the same joy lit their smiles.

After pulling a marker from the junk drawer, Megan wrote the date on the back. Then she rummaged for the tape dispenser, found it, and pulled off a piece. Carefully wrapping the tape into a sticky circle, she applied it to the back of the picture, then pressed the photograph to the refrigerator.

She was standing before the fridge when Dave came in and wrapped her in a bear hug. "Something smells good."

"Something looks good," she answered.

"Whaddya mean? You can't see me."

She pulled her arm free and pointed to the refrigerator. "I'm looking at that."

She felt his arms tighten around her when he realized the significance of her words. "Does this mean . . ." He let his voice fade away.

"Let's adopt one or two just like her." Turning, Megan slid her arms around his neck. "And if that goes well, we can try for three or four. Let's take as many as we can handle."

Dave looked at her, his eyes wide and questioning; then his mouth relaxed into a surprised smile. "Let's do it," he whispered, pushing a lock of hair away from her cheek. "I'm with you, Meg."

"And I'm with you, honey, no matter what." She waited until a sudden rise of emotion died down and she could control her wavering voice. "For as long as it takes, no matter what it takes. Let's wait on the Lord and see what He has in mind for this family."

Then she stood on tiptoe and pressed her lips to her husband's, hope and promise and acceptance all mingled in her kiss.

Three

wo months later, on an unseasonably warm afternoon in September, Megan clung to Dave's hand as they followed a winding sidewalk to a small brick building. A painted sign hung on the wall beside the glass door: Central Virginia Social Services.

A confusing rush of anticipation and dread whirled inside her as Dave opened the door. She'd made this appointment only a few days after their decision to pursue adoption, and during the intervening weeks she had read every book she could find on the process. She consoled her impatient heart with the knowledge that they were moving forward, and her reading had armed her with at least a cursory knowledge of what to expect in the process known as a home study. The Alta Vista social worker, Belinda Bishop, would investigate to determine whether she and Dave would be fit parents. And if she approved them, after completing her report she would place their names into a state database of waiting parents. When a child in Virginia became available, the database would be scanned for a possible match.

The process was simple and straightforward...and might possibly prove to be the most dreadful experience of her life.

The plain tile floor in the social services building was worn and dull, but clean. Fluorescent lights hummed overhead and shone upon glossy beige walls in the narrow corridor. Dave paused beside a door bearing a nameplate: Belinda Bishop. The door to the office stood open, and at the sound of his hesitant rap, the woman at the desk inside lifted her head.

Without being told, Megan might have guessed this woman was a social worker. Belinda Bishop had shoulder-length brown hair, wire-rimmed glasses, and wore a long skirt with a long-sleeved, full-cut blouse. The only trace of makeup upon her smooth face was a hint of lip gloss. The eyes that shone from behind the glasses were friendly and open.

"Mr. and Mrs. Wingfield?" She stepped out from behind the desk and offered her hand first to Megan, then to Dave. "I've been expecting you."

As Megan and Dave murmured brief "pleased to meet yous," Belinda picked up a folder, then gestured toward the hallway. "My office is really too cramped for meetings like this. There's a conference room down the hall."

They followed her to another room, still small, but unencumbered with heavy furniture. A sofa sat against the far wall, a faded wing chair faced it. A toy box sat off to the side, and above it, a bulletin board featured several black-and-white pictures of smiling children—all school age, Megan thought, noticing how many were missing their front teeth. First grade and up, from the looks of them.

Belinda gestured toward the sofa, and Megan and Dave sat down. Dave immediately reached for Megan's hand, and she didn't resist. Any physical display of marital harmony had to help their cause…or would Belinda think they were pretending in an attempt to aid their case?

"Well, now." Belinda sat in the wing chair, placed her hands together, and leaned forward in a position of earnestness. "I'm delighted you're interested in adoption. As I explained on the phone, this meeting will officially begin our home study process. I'll take six weeks to get to know you. I'll inspect your home, and we'll collect the necessary documents for your case file."

Dave's forehead creased. "What sort of paperwork is required?"

Megan felt a twinge of conscience. Knowing that Dave was preoccupied with the administrative details of a new school year, she hadn't shared everything she'd learned in her telephone conversation with Ms. Bishop. Would his question make this woman think they didn't communicate in their marriage?

The social worker smiled. "We'll need a complete financial statement from you," she said, her charm bracelet jingling as she clasped her hands. "You don't have to be wealthy to adopt, but we do have to be sure you can support a child. We'll also need a statement from your medical doctor to show that you are in good health and physically able to care for a child. We'll also ask for several letters of reference from your family and friends. We're not trying to pry, but we do try to make every effort to be sure our children are going to families who can provide healthy, stable homes."

"We understand, Ms. Bishop," Megan said.

"Please, call me Belinda." The warmth of the woman's smile echoed in her voice, and Megan felt warmed by the sound of it. "We're going to know each other well by the time this is finished, so we might as well be on a first name basis."

Dave nodded. "After the home study—what then? How long will the adoption take?"

Belinda sighed heavily, as if she'd answered the question many times before.

"I can't give you a definite answer, Dave. Once your home study is complete, you'll be waiting with many other couples in the state of Virginia. When a child is entered into the system and cleared for adoption, every couple is evaluated as to suitability. Sometimes a match is made quickly. Other couples wait longer, some for several years. It all depends upon the children's needs."

Her head lifted as she met Megan's gaze. "Please understand this—we're not here to find children for parents, though that is one happy byproduct of our work. We're here primarily to find homes for children. The kids are our first priority and concern. I'll be honest—most of our children come to us from families who either could not or would not take care of them. We don't often encounter pregnant girls who make adoption plans for their babies. Most of those young women make arrangements with private adoption agencies…if they carry their babies to term. With abortion these days—" she shrugged—"Well, there are fewer babies available for adoption than ever."

Dave tapped his thigh. "We understand. Megan's been reading a lot. We've investigated private adoption and international adoption, but we simply can't afford the fees. And we know about the kind of children you place. Megan has also read a lot about the adoption of an older child, and the adoption of a sibling group."

Megan winced inwardly. He said *she* was reading—would Belinda think Dave didn't care? Or that this was all Megan's idea? It wouldn't be good if the social worker thought their marriage was one-sided, or that Megan wanted the adoption more than Dave did…

Unruffled, Belinda smiled again. "It's good that you've thought about your options. The more open you are, the more likely we are to match you with a child. But we don't handle international adoption. Because we are a state government agency, most of our children come from Virginia. We can cooperate with other agencies, of course, but we don't have access to their children."

She paused a moment and searched their faces. "If you don't

have any other questions, let me explain how the home study works. We'll meet five more times—once a week, ideally, but I never know what my schedule is going to permit. In our next meeting we'll talk about your history as a couple. The next week, I'll meet with you, Dave, and the next week I'll want to meet with Megan alone. The fifth week we'll talk about the type of child you feel capable of parenting, and the sixth and final visit will take place in your home."

She pulled a sheaf of papers from her folder and extended them to Megan. "In the meantime, I'd like you to take this application with you. You can bring it back next week or mail it in, whichever you prefer. But I'll need the names and addresses of your references as soon as possible so I can send out a letter of inquiry. The sooner we get the paperwork started, the sooner we'll be finished."

Megan accepted the papers and gave them a quick glance. The application seemed fairly straightforward, followed by medical forms, a blank financial statement, and a page requesting the names and addresses of relatives and close friends.

Her fingers burned to reach for her pen. If given ten minutes, she could have most of these pages filled out…but she didn't want to appear overeager. Social workers probably frowned on prospective parents with no self-control.

"Thank you, Belinda," she said, folding the pages and slipping them into her purse. "I'm sure I'll be mailing them in. They don't look too complicated."

"That's good." Belinda clasped her hands together again, charms jangling on her wrist. "Any questions before you go?"

Megan looked at Dave, who merely shrugged.

"Next week?" Megan asked, breaking the silence. "Same time, same place?"

Belinda pulled out her appointment book, pulled a pencil from behind her ear, and frowned at the page. "I'm sorry, but I have to be at a conference next week. It looks like we'll have to settle for Monday of the week after next. Let's see—that'll be September 20."

Megan steeled herself to keep from grimacing. Now that they had committed themselves to the process of adoption, she wanted to get on with it, to keep the wheels in motion. She'd already had to wait two months for this initial meeting…but what else could she do?

She pasted on a smile that felt false. "We'll see you on September 20 then. And I'll mail in the list of references within the next day or two."

"That'll be great."

Belinda Bishop stood. Following her cue, Megan and Dave rose, too, and followed her out, walking with her as far as her office before sending her a departing smile.

As they walked from the building to the car, Megan felt as though her face were melting. Her stiff smile drooped along with her shoulders. "Well," she said, when Dave climbed in beside her, "that was…interesting."

"It went fine," Dave answered, turning the key. "Don't worry, honey."

Megan bit her lip and looked out the window. Easy for him to say. He wasn't second-guessing himself at every turn.

On Friday, Megan left the veterinary hospital and drove to Roberta's, a yuppie restaurant located two blocks from E. C. Glass High School. Ten minutes after twelve, a sparkling black Mustang zipped into the parking lot.

Megan glanced again at her watch. Melanie was late, as usual. Honestly, you'd think a high school senior could manage to be on time to *something*…

She frowned as her sister hopped out of the car, slung her purse over her shoulder, then jogged toward the bench where Megan waited. "Hey, Sis!"

"You're late." Megan shielded her eyes from the sun as her younger sister approached. Melanie was eighteen, just beginning her senior year, and the baby of the family. Five years Megan's junior, she was lean, leggy, and lovely. The striking combination of her dark hair and bright blue eyes rarely failed to turn masculine heads. Her smile could light up a marquee.

Megan's frown deepened as her sister drew nearer. The girl wore a tight sweater and a skirt that must have required a crowbar to enter and exit.

Breathless, Melanie dropped down onto the bench beside Megan. "I wasn't sure you'd remember."

Megan blew hair out of her eyes. "I'm not old enough to be senile."

Melanie grinned. "Yeah, but you said—"

"Never mind what I said. I disagree with senior skip day, but if you're going to skip school, that's your decision, not mine. And like I said, I have to eat."

Melanie grinned and pinched Megan's arm. "Loosen up, Miss Goody-goody. And let's go in. I'm starved."

Megan reluctantly followed her sister into the restaurant. They'd held senior skip day when she was in high school, too, but only the hoodlums observed it. Now, Melanie assured her, *everyone* celebrated it, and any seniors silly enough to go to school on senior skip day found themselves in an all-day study hall. Megan finally agreed to meet Mel for lunch when her sister assured her that their mother knew and approved of her plan. So now they sat in Roberta's, pondering the menu and trying to decide between fajitas and pita bread sandwiches....

"Megan Myers, I haven't seen you in *ages!*"

Megan glanced up when a familiar voice broke into her concentration. Debbie Jennings, a friend from Megan's high school days, stood at the edge of the booth...behind a swollen, terribly pregnant belly.

"Debbie!" Forcing a smile, Megan focused on her friend's eyes. "It's Megan Wingfield now. And how are you?"

"Fine—well, great with child, obviously." Debbie pressed her hand to the small of her back and leaned on the table. "Honestly, I can't wait for this kid to pop out. I was in labor with Bobby Junior for twenty-two hours, so I'm hoping this one will come quick."

Megan freshened her smile. "Your second?"

Debbie groaned. "Yes, and I don't know why I ever wanted to be pregnant. I haven't seen my toes in three months." She hesitated and tilted her head toward Megan. "You have kids yet?"

"Not yet." Megan looked toward the menu. "I'm working at Dr. Duncan's veterinary hospital, and my husband's an assistant principal at Valley View. We're pretty busy."

"You're lucky." Debbie shifted her weight. "Nearly everyone from our class is pregnant now—when I was in the gynecologist's office last week, I thought I'd wandered into a high school reunion! Laurie, Alma Joy, Diane, Susie, Donna, Kathy, and Gail are due in the next three months, and Ruth, Susan, Sharon, and Becky have new babies."

"Honey, I wondered where you went." Bobby Wilson, whom Megan dimly remembered as a high school football player, came up behind Debbie and tenderly laid a hand on her belly. "The car's waiting at the curb."

Debbie nodded at her husband, then twiddled her fingers at Megan. "I gotta go. But have fun with the puppies and kitties, okay?"

"Sure." Megan bit her lip as the Wilsons walked away, then turned her attention back to the menu. Beyond the expanse of plastic-coated paper, Melanie began to babble about her boyfriend, Todd.

Huddled over the menu, Megan slumped into morose musings. Was the entire *world* having babies? Was everyone her age pregnant or nursing? Yet it wasn't a pregnancy she wanted—she wanted to love a child.

Debbie Wilson had two children, one born and one about to be born, and she'd had the nerve to call Megan *lucky*. What did she know? Women like her got pregnant without half trying. She'd probably have a baby every year, and then gripe about stretch marks and the burdens of motherhood.

Megan would give anything for just one of those burdens. She'd gladly surrender her job, her time, her energy, even her identity, just for the honor of being called Mom.

"You're not listening, Megan!"

Blinking, Megan lifted her head. Across the table, Melanie's eyes were wide and her lips pursed in a petulant frown.

"I'm sorry. Were you talking to me?"

Melanie's blue eyes flashed. "And who else is in this booth? You haven't heard a word I've said, have you?"

Megan dropped her menu. "Sorry. I've had a few things on my mind."

"I was telling you about Todd. Mom and Dad don't like him."

Megan inhaled a deep breath, bracing herself for the inevitable. "So why do you keep going out with him?"

Melanie flipped her hair over her shoulder. "I dunno. Because he likes me. Because he makes me feel special. It's, like, all the other guys are so immature, but Todd's really cool."

As Melanie rattled on, Megan propped her elbow on the table and rested her chin in her hand. Time to play big sister. But it was okay—Melanie certainly wouldn't understand what Megan and Dave were going through.

"Tell me all about it," she said, smiling.

On a cold, windy October night, Megan lowered her head into her fur collar and followed Dave into the social services building. Belinda had suggested that they attend at least one meeting of an adoptive parents' support group, and, in an effort to prove how eager they were to do things properly, she and Dave had made plans to attend the first meeting after the commencement of their home study.

There were already a dozen people in the conference room when they entered, and by the way they were laughing around the coffeemaker, Megan guessed they knew each other pretty well. Their children, apparently, were in the care of baby-sitters or friends, for there were no children in the room.

Belinda greeted them with a smile, then glanced at her watch and clapped her hands for attention. "Welcome people," she called, her voice cutting through the congenial chatter. "I'd like to introduce our newcomers—Dave and Megan Wingfield, prospective adoptive parents. They are currently involved in the home study process."

Megan felt herself blushing as a dozen pairs of eyes turned in their direction. A few brows lifted, but most faces wore understanding smiles.

Belinda moved to the folding chairs. "If you'll all find a seat, we can begin. Tom, I think you are the moderator of this meeting. Why don't you get us started?"

Megan slipped out of her coat and took a seat next to Dave while the others left the coffeemaker and made their way to seats in the circle. Glancing around, Megan tried to find a common denominator that marked these people, but she could see nothing obvious. The men and women in the room represented every race and age. If clothing could be trusted as a guide, they also represented several different income levels.

Tom, a balding, middle-aged man in Gucci loafers, stood and rubbed his hands together. "All right. Who has an issue they'd like to bring before us?"

A heavy woman in a plaid sweater lifted her hand. "Something happened to me this week. My little Michael—" she paused as the others nodded, for apparently she'd discussed him before—"threw a temper tantrum in the grocery store. He was crying because I wouldn't buy him a bag of candy, but my mother-in-law, who has never really approved of our adoption, declared that he was crying because he missed his *real* mother!"

The woman slapped her hands on her blue-jeaned thighs. "Now how am I supposed to handle *that*? I wanted to slug her."

Megan sat, stunned and silent, while the other parents made suggestions. Then another couple announced that they and their child had just moved from the *honeymoon* to the *protest* stage.

"There are stages?" Dave whispered in her ear.

"I guess so," she whispered back. .

Tom, the moderator, scratched his chin as the conversation died down. "I think the thing that bothers me the most is the vocabulary people use with regard to adoption. People speak of birth mothers as *real* mothers or *natural* mothers, but adoptive mothers and fathers are the real psychological parents. And we speak of birth mothers who *give up* their babies, as if that's either really noble or pathetic. It's so much more accurate to say they *make an adoption plan* for their children."

"The one I can't stand," another woman inserted, "is when people meet my twins and then ask if I have kids *of my own*. As if these two don't belong to me!"

An African-American mother waved her hand. "You think that's bad? I have two, you know—LaShonda and Kareem—and the other day someone asked me if they were brother and sister. I said, 'They are now!'"

Belinda Bishop giggled. "I can top that. I have a friend who's recently adopted an infant from Korea. She was at the pediatrician's office the other day with her three-month-old, when a woman asked if the child spoke English! As if the baby could speak anything!"

As the group erupted in laughter, Megan caught Dave's eye. Like the rest of the world, she and Dave had undoubtedly been violating adoption taboos for years, as ignorant as anyone who had never explored the delicate art of grafting a branch onto a family tree.

She reached out and squeezed his hand. They had a lot to learn, but they were willing. And ready.

On the third Monday in November, over two months after beginning their home study, Megan stood in the middle of her small living room and regarded the area with a critical eye. The floors were freshly vacuumed, the sofa pillows plumped, and she'd spent most of Saturday washing and ironing the full muslin curtains. The room—the entire house, in fact—was as spotless as she could make it. Dave had tiptoed out this morning, afraid he'd make tracks in the rug or spill water droplets on her gleaming kitchen counters.

In less than a quarter hour, Belinda Bishop was to come for their final meeting, the home visit. She had assured Megan and Dave that this would be an informal time, more of a cursory check than a white glove inspection. The home visit was only required to be certain that the department of social services wasn't placing a child into a dangerous environment.

Despite Belinda's assurances, Megan had baked chewy chocolate chip cookies and prepared a pitcher of sweet tea—a Southern favorite. The pitcher and platter of cookies now sat on the kitchen table, a pretty spread that might appeal to Belinda's midafternoon appetite. Whether or not the social worker succumbed to the culinary treats, Megan couldn't imagine a less dangerous environment for a child. Throughout the house, she'd pulled up all the electrical cords, put rubber stoppers in the outlets, and screwed child-proof locks into all the cabinets.

She wiped the kitchen counter again, then folded the dish towel and hung it on the rod tucked beneath the sink. Then she moved through the house one last time, checking the bathroom, the master bedroom, and finally, the small bedroom meant for their child.

She'd begun to decorate it the week after they began their home study. Belinda's patient confidence and unflagging support encouraged Megan enough that she felt confident to buy paint and wallpaper, and each weekend she'd worked on one particular aspect of the room she intended to be their nursery. Dave had installed a chair rail, then Megan painted it with white enamel to match the tall dresser from her mother's house. Dazzling yellow paint covered the walls from the chair rail to the ceiling, and a bright rainbow wallpaper in primary colors decorated the space between the railing and the soft green carpeting.

The room looked large, bright, and empty. They hadn't bought a bed, not knowing the age of the child they would welcome home, and they'd chosen primary colors because they didn't know if they'd be getting a boy or a girl. Or both.

Megan leaned against the wall as her thoughts drifted back to last week's meeting with Belinda. At the outset she had warned them that she would ask difficult questions, and she'd been right. To her surprise, Megan had discovered that her willingness to parent had unexpected limits.

"Would you consider a child of rape?" she'd asked. Megan and Dave both nodded eagerly.

"Would you consider a sibling group?"

"The more the merrier," Dave answered, grinning. "I'm with kids all day, so more than one is no problem."

Belinda made a note on her pad and moved on. "Would you consider a child who is biracial or of another race? We try to discourage interracial adoption because we feel children should grow up with parents from the same background and culture, but sometimes it is in the child's best interest to make an exception."

Megan thought of Andre and his mother. "No problem."

"In some communities, a mixed family will encounter difficulties," Belinda said, a warning note in her voice. "You have to think about this."

"We'd never live any place our children wouldn't be welcome," Dave answered. Megan shot him a look of gratitude.

"Would you consider," Belinda consulted her list, "a child whose biological parent suffered from schizophrenia?"

Megan made a face. "I don't know much about mental illness. Are such things hereditary?"

Belinda tilted her head. "The evidence is not conclusive, but it suggests they can be."

Megan closed her eyes. Nothing in her lifetime had prepared her for dealing with mental illness—no one in her family had ever suffered from it. She felt certain God would give her grace and strength for anything that came her way, but would she be foolish to volunteer for a struggle He might not have intended to give her? Would answering negatively jeopardize their chances for receiving a child?

"I've had no experience with schizophrenia," she said slowly, looking at Dave. "I think we could handle anything that came our way after the child became part of our family—"

Dave picked up her thought. "But perhaps we shouldn't go on record as approving that choice," he said, his voice firm. "A mental illness like bipolar disorder would be difficult for us."

Belinda inclined her head in a matter-of-fact gesture. "Would you consider a child with a learning disability?"

"Yes," Dave answered without hesitation.

"Would you consider a child who needed elective surgery such as the correction of a cleft palate?"

Megan nodded. "Yes. We have good health insurance."

"Would you consider a child who needed braces? Orthodontia is not usually covered by health insurance."

Megan exhaled softly. She'd never dreamed she'd have to consider so many options. This experience was almost like choosing between options in a new car—but this was a *child*, not a clump of steel and fiberglass.

"Braces aren't a problem," Dave answered. "Somehow, we'll make it work."

"Now let's talk about age," Belinda said, adjusting her tone as she pulled out another sheet of paper. "You've stated your preference for an infant. Would you consider a child up to two years old?"

Megan smiled. "Yes."

"Up to three?"

"Of course. We've discussed it, and we'd be happy to accept any child of preschool age."

Belinda had glanced at her notes again. "Okay, what about a sibling group—one infant, one child school age?"

The sound of the front door's click snapped Megan out of her reverie. She glanced at her watch. Dave was ten minutes late, but she'd forgive him if he'd remembered to bring the fresh-cut flowers for the kitchen table.

She found him in the foyer, bouquet in hand.

"Thanks," she said, taking the bundle from his hand. "Let me put these in water. Did you have trouble getting away from school?"

"No, Dr. Comfort covered for me." He followed her into the kitchen. "And I brought home some work to do this evening…afterward."

Megan filled the vase with water, then snipped the stems from the long-stemmed daisies and placed them in the water. She barely had time to pull them into a pleasing shape before the doorbell rang.

Four

ave followed the women, his hands in his pockets and his thoughts wandering as he toured his own house. Despite Megan's casual demeanor, he could tell she felt nervous. She laughed more frequently than usual, and her voice sounded tight and strained.

Belinda, on the other hand, seemed as unflappable as always. She simply walked through the house and smiled as Megan pointed out the bathrooms, the two bedrooms, and the new wallpaper in the nursery.

He knew Megan would spend most of her time in the bright yellow room, so when they reached it, Dave leaned against the wall, crossed his arms in a posture of polite interest, and allowed his thoughts to roam. These days Meg thought of little but the adoption and the coming child, but his job forced him to think of other things. Now that Dr. Comfort had announced her impending retirement, he had hoped that the school board would notice that he'd been given more than an assistant principal's fair share of administrative duties. Dr. Comfort had purposefully arranged to gradually shift the mantle of responsibility from her shoulders to his, but so far the school board seemed unaware of her friendly maneuvering.

"Dave and I liked this rainbow wallpaper," Meg was saying,

playing Vanna White as she lifted her arms and gracefully gestured to the bright walls. "I read somewhere that primary colors
are more stimulating for babies than pastels—and for small children, too, of course."

Dave repressed a sigh. Meg was at it again, second-guessing
every word that slipped from her lips in Belinda's presence. She'd
added the bit about small children just so Belinda wouldn't think
their hearts were set upon an infant. Truthfully, they preferred a
baby, but so did almost every other waiting adoptive couple.
Healthy white infants were hard to find, especially if you couldn't
afford to pay for a private adoption arranged by people with con-
nections.

He didn't move in the circles of doctors and lawyers—his circle
included teachers and administrators and educational bureaucrats,
and lately that circle had done little but frustrate him. Instead of
noticing how so many students had *improved* over the course of
the Comfort/Wingfield administration, the school board had
focused on a recent series of standardized exams and whipped
itself into a frenzy. Because the exams indicated that Valley View
students were statistically average—*only* average—they'd commissioned a demographic study of the city and unearthed a series of
comparable student test scores. They bemoaned the fact that
Valley View students did not test as well as a similar group in
1985, and ignored the fact that mindless television, video games,
and absentee parents had undoubtedly taken their toll over the
years...

A month ago, he'd been confident he would be the next principal of Valley View Elementary. But if the school board's demographic study revealed a population shift to the outlying suburbs,
Valley View might not even *exist* next year.

He needed to discuss these things with Megan. She had a real gift for helping him calm down, put his emotions in order, and take the long view of things. But in the last few weeks she had thought of little but Belinda's home study, and tonight she'd be too tired to do more than whisper good night, crawl into bed, and sleep. She had exhausted herself with concerns about the adoption, and he didn't want to burden her with yet another uncertainty.

But she had to know. Like it or not, their future was anchored to the fate of Valley View Elementary School.

Standing on the concrete front porch, Megan waved a final cheery farewell to Belinda, then stepped back into the cool shade of the foyer. As Dave turned toward the kitchen, she closed the door and leaned against it, sighing in relief.

They were finished. Done with meetings, soul-searching questions, family histories, investigations, examinations, and confessions. Belinda now knew them better than anyone outside their families, and she'd peered into practically every corner of their house. Now all the social worker had to do was collect their letters of reference, write her report, and submit it to the state. If she was any kind of a friend, she'd do those things as quickly as she could.

Megan pulled herself off the door and moved toward the kitchen, where Dave was rummaging in the refrigerator. Poor man. In all the excitement, she hadn't even *thought* about dinner.

"Hey," she whispered, coming up behind him and slipping her arms about his waist, "you want to go out for a bite? Celebrate the end of the inquisition?"

Hunched inside the open door, he froze. "I'm afraid I don't really feel much like celebrating."

His flat tone caught her by surprise. She stepped to the side and peered at his face. "You sick or something?"

His skin color was normal, his eyes set and serious. "Things at school are in a bit of an upheaval."

Relieved, she waved the matter away. "Things at school will settle down; they always do." Suddenly thirsty, she moved to the cupboard and took out a glass. "That went well, don't you think? Belinda seemed to like the house."

Dave pulled a package of bologna from the fridge. "What's not to like?"

A little annoyed by his curt tone, Megan turned and studied him. Had the home study process taken a toll on him, too? She'd tried to relieve his stress by handling all the appointments and correspondence herself, but perhaps she'd underestimated the mental burden he carried.

A malicious little voice cackled from some obscure corner of her brain. *What* mental burden did he carry? Though she knew he wanted a child as much as she did, he'd come through the adoption process relatively unscathed. He had not had to endure the trial of knowing all his friends were pregnant. He hadn't spent more than twenty months playing pregnancy guessing games with his body and refusing to take medicine for a head cold on the chance that he *might* be pregnant. He had a job, an important career, to distract him from the waiting and the frustration, while puppies and kittens and birth and life surrounded her even at the office...

"Listen—" against her will, her voice trembled—"I think we've come through this pretty well, and it'd be nice if you could celebrate with me. I know things aren't always perfect at school, Dave, but school is only a job, and what we've been dealing with here is our entire *life*. Our family, our dreams for the future, who we are—all those things are wrapped up in this adoption. So I'd appreciate it if you could put the school out of your mind for a couple of hours and think about what's really important."

He turned to her, concern and confusion mixing in his eyes. "Meg, I've been with you every step of the way."

She lifted a hand. "Not quite. On the surface, sure, you've been great. But you don't know what I've been going through, Dave, not really. I haven't told you a lot of things because I didn't want to hurt you."

A sudden spasm of grief knit his brows. "You mean…because this is all my fault."

Wincing, Megan clutched the edge of the counter, drowning in waves of guilt. She'd promised herself never to bring this issue up. She had never wanted to shake her finger in his face or point to the reason why they couldn't have biological children…but maybe she'd been pointing all along and had been too engrossed to realize it.

"Honey," she closed her eyes, "I love you, and I know God put us together. I don't blame you for anything, and I know God has allowed this for a reason. It's the reason I can't understand. Of all the men I know, you're the one who would make the best father, and I've wanted to be a mother since I was old enough to dress my cat in baby clothes. I've been ready; I've been willing; and I haven't been able to understand why we weren't allowed to have kids like everybody else."

She turned from him and stared at the calendar hanging over the phone. "Remember last week when I went to Susan Michael's baby shower?"

His voice came out hoarse, as if forced through a tight throat. "I was surprised you went."

"I almost didn't, but I couldn't figure out how to get out of it, since Susan was my maid of honor and all. And I did pretty good through most of it—I sat and smiled while everybody oohed and ahhed over the gifts, and I played those silly shower games even though I felt like an automaton. But then Susan's mother came over and squeezed my shoulder, and I knew she knew what I was feeling—and something inside me snapped. I ran into the bathroom and stayed there the rest of the night. My eyes were so red from crying that I had to wait until everyone else left the party before I could even come out."

His voice faded to a whisper. "I'm sorry."

"It's not your fault." She lifted her gaze to the ceiling. "If anything, it's *my* fault. I'm just so tired. Tired of fighting a vicious battle against my own stubborn will and longings. Tired of trying to pretend I'm not hurting, tired of striving to be happy for other couples, tired of fighting to be patient and not explode in frustration, tired of struggling to speak of anything but the number one thought on my mind. I'm working to keep my faith, struggling to believe in God, fighting to live each day instead of willingly casting every day aside for just one tomorrow...."

She blinked when she felt a tear roll down her cheek. She wasn't crying, really, the tear resulted from overflowing emotion.

"I feel so alone, Dave. You are the only one who knows what I'm going through, and yet I don't know if you can know how it feels to be a woman and not a mother."

She bowed her head as Dave's arms slipped around her shoulders. "'To fight aloud is very brave,'" he said, in the hushed voice he often used when he whispered love poems into her ear. "'But gallanter, I know, who charge within the bosom the cavalry of Woe.'"

She lifted her gaze to meet his. "Walt Whitman?"

"Emily Dickinson." His hand cupped against her cheek and

held it gently. "You are the most gallant woman I know, Meg. And I know God is using this to prepare both of us…for something that lies ahead."

Megan groaned. "That's not a very comforting thought."

He laughed softly. "Then consider this—you don't have to fight anymore, honey. The hard work is done. Now we wait."

Megan laughed weakly. Dave, apparently, had no idea how tough waiting could be.

Dave watched as Megan swiped at her eyes and murmured something about needing to use the bathroom. She left the kitchen, leaving him in stunned silence.

In the three years of their marriage, he had never heard such an outpouring of raw emotion. Megan was usually calm and in control, confident in her faith and steady as a rock.

He had no idea she'd been weeping in bathrooms and doubting God.

He sat down at the table and pressed his hands to his right temple, trying to massage away the pain that threatened there. He loved the idea of a baby, he wanted children, but he loved Megan more than any person on earth. Would this as yet intangible and uncertain child drive them apart?

Pressing his face into his hands, he prayed for wisdom.

Five

hanksgiving and Christmas came and went. Optimistically predicting that this would be their last Christmas without a baby, Megan and Dave spent the holiday at the Peaks of Otter Lodge, a rustic retreat atop a mountain near Roanoke.

January brought snow; February, wind. March came in like the proverbial lion and went out like a lamb, leaving the Virginia mountains covered with the green-gold sheen of spring.

On a Saturday morning in April, Megan stubbed her toe as she hurried to catch the phone in the kitchen. "Helloooo," she moaned, massaging the injured digit as she settled the phone against her shoulder.

"Meg?" Her mother's voice seemed flatter than usual.

Megan's internal antennae snapped to attention. "What's wrong, Mom?"

She was hoping for a quick reassurance, but her mother sighed. "Have you spoken to Melanie lately?"

"Not in a while. Why?"

"She's pregnant."

Forgetting her throbbing toe, Megan slid down the wall and sat on the floor. "You're kidding."

"I wish I were. She told us last night, and she's already made her plans. She and Todd want to get married next month. The baby's due in November."

Megan's senses skittered in stunned disbelief. "She can't be pregnant; she's not the kind of girl who sleeps around. The last time I talked to her she said she and Todd were doing great, that he was a really nice guy—"

Realizing that she was babbling to cover her confusion, Megan snapped her mouth shut.

Her mother sighed audibly. "All kinds of girls get pregnant, Meg, and Todd does seem to be a nice guy. Your father and I were upset, of course, but we're beginning to think marriage is the best answer for them. That way the baby will have a home and a father—"

Megan's heart pumped outrage through her veins. "The baby will have a couple of *children* for parents! Melanie and Todd aren't ready to have a baby—why, they couldn't have survived the first *week* of our home study. They don't know each other, they have no financial security, and they don't know the first *thing* about raising a child!"

"All parents learn by trial and error, Meg."

"You sound like you're on their side!"

"Megan," her mother's voice flattened like chilled steel, "I'm on everybody's side. I want what's best for this baby, for Melanie, for Todd, and for you, honey. I know what you must be feeling."

Megan stiffened. "You could not possibly understand."

There was a short silence. "Maybe I can't," her mother finally answered, "but Melanie's situation has nothing to do with you, Meg. I only called because, well, you're her sister, and I thought you should know."

Megan bit her lip as desperation fortified her courage. "Maybe...if they really want what's best for the baby, they could give it to me and Dave. Maybe this has been the Lord's plan all along. We could adopt him, and he'd have two stable parents, but Melanie and Todd would know the baby was growing up in a good home, and Melanie could see him whenever she wanted—"

"Melanie wants this child, Meg. Somehow, believe it or not, this experience has been good for her. For the first time in months she's been focused on something other than herself. She's already been to the doctor; she's been taking her prenatal vitamins; she made sure everything was fine before she even told us the news."

Through her own regret, Megan heard the pain in her mother's voice. She drew a deep breath, realizing that the grief she felt had to be but a shadow of the anguish that had engulfed her parents. They had raised their daughters in a Christian home; they had taught their girls how to behave as examples of godly purity. One of those daughters had made a mistake.

Megan had made mistakes, too—but none so public.

She brought her hand to her forehead. "I'm sorry, Mom, about what I said before. I know this can't be easy for you or Dad. And I understand, I really do. If Melanie can love and raise this baby, then she should. It's just that—"

"You don't have to explain, Meg." Her mother hesitated a moment more, silence rolling over the telephone line, then added, "We'd appreciate your prayers. We're all going to need them."

"Okay, Mom." Megan blinked back tears and replaced the phone in its cradle.

Six

*I*n May, Melanie and Todd married in a quiet ceremony in the church chapel. Megan and Dave attended the wedding, then hosted a small reception in their home. The occasion marked the first time Megan had met Todd, and she later told Dave that her new brother-in-law seemed little more than a pimply faced adolescent. He certainly didn't look like father material…but she couldn't and wouldn't question their decision.

Melanie was in love—with Todd, her unborn baby, and the world. The newlyweds would live with Megan's parents until the baby came and Todd graduated from high school. Then he'd find a job and go to vocational school, and Melanie would go back to her job at the local grocery store. She had promised to get her GED and think about college. Together, Megan admitted, with help, they might make their marriage work.

The next two months passed with agonizing slowness. At work, Megan went about her duties as usual. In quiet lulls she stared at the big clock above the reception desk, noticing that the minute hand seemed to struggle to move from one black notch on the dial's perimeter to the next.

Belinda had urged her to call at least once a week. "Obviously, I won't have news, or I would certainly call you," she explained at the conclusion of their home study. "But I know how hard the waiting can be, and I love to hear from my prospective parents. So call me whenever you like, just to keep in touch."

Megan rationed herself to one call per week. She marked her calendar with "Call Belinda" every Monday and made the ritual contact during her lunch break. On Monday mornings the work seemed to go even slower than usual, the moment when she could call Belinda fluttering ahead of her like the tail of a kite. And each week, though Belinda had no concrete news to offer, that simple contact assured Megan that Belinda was alive and well, their names were percolating in the system, and the Virginia State Social Services computer was humming with good intentions to place waiting children with eager parents.

Spring melted into summer, and Megan struggled to look for the silver lining in the overhanging clouds. She and Dave took a few weekend trips to their favorite little hotels, romantic getaways that would be impossible once they had a baby to care for. They ate once a week in the town's nicest steakhouse, knowing such extravagances would be unwise once their family expanded. They stayed up late on Friday nights, slept late on Saturdays, and exploited the freedoms of childlessness. For soon, Megan told herself, this season would end.

Every day felt like a battle. Every hour was another yard gained on the field of conquest, every week a mile, every month a major victory. Months passed would never have to be relived again. Every day of waiting was one less she'd have to endure…if God was faithful and kept His promises.

In June, Belinda reported that she had placed one child and was working on another placement. Megan hung up the phone and breathed a sigh of relief. Maybe this activity signaled some sort of adoption baby boom, and they'd be called next.

In July, Megan was checking her makeup in the ladies room at church when a pregnant friend came in to wash her hands. "We felt the baby kick yesterday," she said, catching Megan's eye in the mirror. "Michael ran over to get the video camera, and we could actually see the little guy kicking."

Megan nodded. "That's nice."

The woman's gaze dropped to Megan's flat stomach, then her mouth wobbled in a poor imitation of a smile.

"So…have you adopted that baby yet?"

As if babies grew on trees! Megan bit back a caustic answer and shook her head. "No," she said, forcing a smile. "It takes a long time. We've been waiting nearly a year, and we might have to wait many months more."

The friend lifted her brow in surprise. "Really? Gosh, with all the people who don't want babies and abuse them, you'd think it'd be easy to get one."

The corner of Megan's mouth twisted. "It's not." Excusing herself, she left the ladies' room.

On July 13, Megan marked the one-year anniversary of their "we will have no babies day" with a glass of orange juice in her kitchen. She sat alone at the breakfast table, the newspaper at her left hand, a breakfast pastry at her right.

Another year of waiting lay beyond the horizon, and she steeled herself to face it. She had recently read a quote from Samuel Johnson. He called sorrow "a kind of rust of the soul" that could be "remedied by exercise and motion."

She knew exactly what he meant. The home study experience had been difficult, but she'd found pleasure in it, for she was doing something to bring her child home. Now she could do nothing but wait, and inactivity chafed at her rusty, sorrowful soul…as did guilt. She was a Christian, she was supposed to have joy and faith, but both seemed as elusive as quicksilver.

What did God want of her? Did He want her to quit her job to demonstrate faith that she'd soon be a mother? She'd quit in a minute, but it seemed foolish to sit home doing nothing when she could be earning money they'd need when they became a one-income family. And God was not the author of foolishness.

Sighing, she picked up her newspaper and shook it open. Nothing to do but wait.

Seven

The high-pitched warble of the bedside telephone shattered the predawn stillness. Megan sat up, as awake as if she'd been slapped from sleep by an invisible hand. She peered at the digital clock and read the glowing numerals: five forty-five.

No one ever called with good news at this hour.

The room shifted dizzily as she reached for the phone. "Hello?"

She had expected to hear her mother's voice, instead a man spoke her name over a weak connection.

"Yes," she said, strengthening her voice. "This is Megan Wingfield." Beside her, Dave stirred, then lifted his head.

"Megan, this is Joe Hogan."

Megan pushed a hank of hair out of her face and struggled to place the name. She had known a Joe Hogan in high school— they'd attended the same church; then he'd gone off to college and seminary. The last bit of news about Joe Hogan had him going overseas to be a missionary somewhere....

"Joe Hogan...from my church?" She tried to keep the disbelief from her voice.

Joe laughed. "Bet you didn't think you'd be hearing from me in the middle of the night, did you?"

Dave tugged on her arm. "Who's Joe?"

She gestured toward the lamp, feeling that somehow things might make sense if she weren't having this conversation in the dark. Light flooded the room as she asked, "Joe, why are you calling me?"

He laughed again. "This may sound crazy, Megan, but I'll come right to the point. You probably know my wife and I are missionaries in South Korea—"

She hadn't known, but she let him continue.

"—and yesterday someone left a baby on our doorstep. This happens fairly often, you know, but it's never happened to us. Some of the nationals here think all Americans are rich; therefore, life with a rich American has to be good. Anyway, Susan and I were praying about it, and your name popped into my head. I'm pretty sure the Lord put it there."

"You thought of me? For a baby?"

Megan stared at Dave. She needed a minute to orient herself— no, she needed an *hour*. This was too sudden, too unreal. There was no earthly reason why Joe Hogan, a man she hadn't spoken to or thought of in years, should wake her in the middle of the night with news of a baby.

Why her? Why now? And why that baby?

"Joe," confusion clotted her voice, "I'm not sure what you want me to do."

The line hissed with silence, then, "Don't you know?"

Megan hesitated, blinking with bafflement. What was she supposed to do? She and Dave had investigated international adoption, but the expense had been prohibitive. They couldn't afford to pursue international adoption last year, and they certainly couldn't afford it now.

"Don't you want a baby?" Joe's voice filled her ear, insistent and strong. "I'm sure you're the one I was supposed to call."

"Yes." She whispered the word. "Yes, but things are so complicated. We're already on a waiting list here in Alta Vista."

"I don't know about you," Joe went on, as cheerfully as if he were discussing the weather, "but I'm going to see what I have to do from this end to have this little girl declared adoptable. You do what you have to from your end and don't worry about a thing in the meantime. Susan and I will take care of her until things work out. We think she's about three months old, and she's a real sweetheart."

Megan nodded numbly into the phone. "Okay, Joe. We'll be in touch."

"What was that all about?" Dave asked as she hung up.

Megan gave him a bewildered smile. "Joe Hogan, a guy I went to church with years ago, is a missionary in Korea. He and his wife found a three-month-old on their doorstep. They seem to think we are supposed to adopt her."

Dave snorted softly as he lay back down and punched his pillow. "Was our name pinned onto the kid's diaper or something?"

"Something like that," Megan answered softly, reaching over him to switch off the lamp.

She returned to her pillow, but her whirling thoughts wouldn't let her sleep. Someone must have written the Hogans and mentioned that she and Dave were waiting to adopt. It was no secret—Megan had encouraged her friends to share the news because you never knew when someone might hear of a frightened pregnant girl who could not mother a child. Obviously the Hogans had heard the story, so when they found this baby they naturally thought of her and Dave.

But she'd had her hopes dashed too many times to pin them on a baby half a world away. A few weeks before, a pregnant girl who called herself Jillian had wandered into a local maternity home and applied for free care. While church members scurried to find her a place to live and a job with which she could support herself, the girl made all sorts of references to the kind of family she wanted to adopt her baby. She wanted Christian parents for her child, a couple who had been married at least three years, a family who loved animals and would let the child have a dog....

A friend called Megan, of course, and she'd let her hopes rise, even arranging to take Jillian to lunch for a friendly let's-get-to-know-each-other meeting. Two hours before the lunch, however, one of the girls from the church office called with devastating news. There would be no baby. Jillian's pregnancy was nothing more than a sweater tucked under her dress. They might never have known if one of the other ladies hadn't seen a cardigan fall onto the floor when Jillian entered a bathroom stall...and realized that Jillian hadn't been wearing a sweater in the summer heat.

Megan turned onto her side, pillowing her cheek on her hand. "Why now, God?" she whispered. "If this is from You, why today and not yesterday? Why is the baby in Korea and not Virginia? And why would You lead us away from a low-cost adoption to an expensive situation we can't possibly afford?"

She listened with her heart as well as her ears, but heard no answers in the soft gray twilight.

Belinda had no answers either. "I mentioned before that we don't do international adoptions," she said when Megan called from work. "But I'm pretty sure you can use the home study we've prepared. In most international adoptions, you work with two agencies—one in the child's country of origin and one licensed in the United States. You'll have to find out which area agency works with Korea, and you'll have to be sure the child is registered with a Korean agency who will work with the American agency. I can offer the home study I've written—which might save you time and money—and they may allow me to do the follow-up visits. But I can't handle any of the actual arrangements for this Korean child. It's not my jurisdiction."

More confused than ever, Megan hung up, then called her mother, who responded to the story with more enthusiasm than Megan felt. "God is working," her mother said, her voice filled with hope and a note of awe. "I knew He would. And He will take care of everything until that little baby is home with you."

"I'm just not sure, Mom." Megan stared at the veterinary office clock as she wrapped the phone cord around her wrist. "How do I know this is from the Lord? It could all fall apart tomorrow—"

"Ask Joe to send you pictures," her mother interrupted. "And start thinking of a name. This is a *real* little girl, Meg, and she's waiting. Stop looking at the obstacles and think of the child. She's alive. She's in Joe's house. And she needs a home."

Buoyed by her mother's confidence, Megan disconnected the call. A thrill shivered through her senses. Could this be the child they'd been waiting for?

Ignoring Laurie's curious glance, Megan picked up the phone book, then scribbled down the number for the church office. After speaking to the receptionist, she was transferred to the missions pastor, who gave her the Hogans' phone number in Korea.

"You should probably wait until early evening to call," the pastor reminded her. "The time difference, you know."

She laughed. "I know. And thanks."

The day dragged by with remarkable slowness. At four o'clock, Megan grabbed her purse and ran out the door. At five, with Dave sitting beside her, she placed the long distance call to Korea.

"Susan?" she asked when a woman answered. "This is Megan Wingfield."

"Megan!" Susan's voice was warm and compassionate. "I've been thinking about you." In the background, Megan could hear the sound of children laughing. Not *the* baby—she'd be too young. Susan and Joe must have other children.

"We're going to do whatever we must to make this adoption work," Megan said, smiling at Dave. "And we appreciate you taking care of the baby while we wait."

"We'll do whatever we can," Susan answered, a smile in her voice. "My boys love her. She's a little angel."

The sound of a baby's gurgle echoed over the phone line, and Megan's heart clenched at the sound of it. "Is that—"

"Yes," Susan answered softly. "She's right here on my shoulder."

Megan thought she might burst from the sudden swell of happiness that rose in her chest. "Will you—" she pushed the words out—"will you call her Danielle Li? And will you send pictures? I'll reimburse you for the postage and film—"

"There's no need for that," Susan interrupted. "Just do whatever you have to, and we'll do the same on this end. I have a feeling she'll be home very soon."

"Thank you." A hot, exultant tear trickled down Megan's cheek. "You'll never know what you've done for us."

Four days later, after a series of frantic calls, Megan and Dave sat in the lounge of the Washington, D.C., office of Welcome Home, an international adoption agency with official ties to South Korea. Though the office was nearly a four-hour drive from their house, the agency served Virginia, Maryland, and the District of Columbia.

Megan clutched the folder on her lap—it contained a letter from Belinda Bishop, a sealed copy of their home study report, their birth certificates, and a copy of their marriage license. In her purse, safely tucked away, she carried an application for a second mortgage on their home—a logical, practical answer to their financial dilemma. As soon as they knew how much the adoption would cost, they planned to apply for a loan.

Megan felt edgy after the four-hour drive from Alta Vista. The last thing she wanted to do was sit in a waiting room, but from this point every day counted. She was no longer waiting on a nebulous, chimerical child—she was working for a little girl living temporarily with the Hogans in Seoul, South Korea.

Megan ached to work the rust off her soul.

The door to the inner office finally opened. A tall, slender woman stepped out and shook their hands, introducing herself as Helen Gresham, a senior social worker for Welcome Home.

Megan nearly collapsed in relief at the sight of Helen's gentle demeanor and sparkling blue eyes. She hadn't realized how nervous she was until she sat before Helen's desk and the tension went out of her shoulders.

"I understand that you've done quite a bit of the work for us," Helen said, lowering herself into the worn leather chair behind her cluttered desk. "This is an unusual situation, but everything seems in order. I don't really foresee any problems, but I have to ask you a few questions." She smiled as she caught Megan's gaze. "You understand."

Megan nodded. "Of course." She felt as though she had been answering questions for the last year. She no longer had a private life, secrets, or untold confessions. She'd relay any detail of her past life if doing so would finally bring their baby home.

She reached for Dave's hand and held it as they again

answered questions about their families, their backgrounds, and their marriage. During the session the door to Helen's door opened, and an Asian woman entered, dropped a pile of mail on the social worker's desk, and slipped away.

Helen looked up and paused a moment to riffle through the mail. Her smile broadened as she picked up an envelope. "I had hoped this would come," she said, opening the letter. "Would you like to see a picture?"

Megan held her breath as Helen pulled a photograph free of its paper clip and passed it across the desk. Dave reached for the picture first, but he leaned over and held it in front of Megan's eyes.

The child was simply beautiful: Fair-skinned, with dark black hair that stood up like a Mohawk in the center of her head. Chubby and healthy looking, her little belly strained at the seams of a sleeveless sunsuit. Someone had propped her up in a little painted chair, and a place card beside her leg read *Danielle Li Wingfield*.

Megan swallowed hard and bit back tears.

"Your friends," Helen said, her eyes scanning the letter, "have listed the child with the Southern Child Welfare Agency, our partner in Seoul. They are serving as her foster parents, and the people at Southern are handling the child's paperwork. Everything seems to be in order."

Megan could scarcely tear her gaze from the picture. Never again would her imagination conjure up faceless images of infants; her child had a name and a beautiful, round-cheeked face!

She reached out and touched the photo. From across the miles, a little piece of her daughter had come home.

"If I were you," Helen said, glancing at her watch, "I'd head straight down to the Immigration office. The lines there can be terribly long, and we can't bring her over until you've done all the INS requires."

Megan clutched her folder to her chest. "We'll go now."

Helen smiled and held out her hand. "I'm sorry, but I need the photo for the file. Would you like me to make you a copy?"

Megan would have nodded, but Dave returned the picture and stood. "Thank you, Ms. Gresham, but our friends in Korea are sending a packet of pictures. They're probably waiting at home."

After thanking Helen and taking one last look at her daughter, Megan hurried after him.

They reached the INS office at one o'clock. Megan took one glance at the crowd occupying every available chair and bench, then took a number from the dispenser on the wall. Their number was 409. The digital readout above the main desk told her they were assisting whoever held number 335.

"I think we have time to get lunch," Dave said, his voice dry. "It's going to be a while."

Megan waved to catch the attention of a uniformed staffer walking by. "Is it always like this?"

The woman didn't bat an eye. "Immigration? We're the busiest office in the district."

Reluctantly, Megan agreed lunch was a good idea, but she insisted they go someplace with quick food. After walking about two blocks, they found a little mom-and-pop joint and ordered hamburgers and fries. After wolfing down one of the biggest burgers Megan had ever seen in her life, she took Dave's hand and dragged him back to the INS office. The clock said one-thirty; the digital counter had moved forward to number 350.

Torn between relief that they'd made it back in time and

consternation at the slow pace, Megan settled into a worn wooden chair. If she'd known the afternoon would turn into a marathon waiting session, she'd have brought a magazine or book. Then again, she thought, studying the assorted people in the waiting area, she probably would be too distracted to concentrate.

Amazing, the number and variety of people that came to America. Waiting with her were women in Indian saris, men in suits, babies tied in slings around their mother's necks. Like her, each of them clutched a folder of documents and the tiny rip-off number, a ticket to hope and the chance for a new life.

As the afternoon wore on, Megan found herself feeling rusty and frustrated again. She frowned as she glanced at the clock. She had no reason to rush back to Alta Vista, but surely the INS office closed at four-thirty or five. What would she and Dave do if they didn't see someone today? They had planned to drive home tonight, so they didn't have a hotel room or even a change of clothes…

At three-thirty, a uniformed woman stood at the main desk and called, "Four-oh-nine?"

Megan leapt to her feet, half pulling Dave with her. "That's us," she called, hurrying forward. The woman didn't crack a smile, but pointed them toward another caseworker at a desk.

Megan and Dave walked over, introduced themselves to the stern-faced woman working there, then Megan slid the folder with their paperwork across the desk. She briefly explained their situation, told the woman about the baby, and assured her that the adoption was proceeding without a hitch. "Of course, we understand that we have to clear her coming to the United States," Megan said, sinking slowly into the chair before the woman's desk. She gestured toward the folder. "So you'll find everything you need there. Our marriage license, birth certificates, copies of our drivers' licenses—"

The woman peered into the folder, flipped through the pages, then snapped it shut. "I'm sorry, but you've missed the fingerprint office. Immigration law requires us to run your fingerprints through the FBI database before you can apply for permission to bring an alien into the United States."

Megan felt her stomach drop. "We have to be *fingerprinted*? Before we can do anything else?"

The woman's mouth softened slightly. "If you hurry, you might be able to catch the guy across the street. He does fingerprints. For a fee."

Dave didn't hesitate. He was out of his chair before Megan could respond, so she stood and hurried after him, pausing long enough to retrieve their precious paperwork from the case-worker's hand.

The "guy across the street" turned out to be a gruff-voiced older fellow who listened to their frantic story with a gentle smile. Megan knew she was making little sense, but he seemed to listen intently as he pressed each of their fingers onto an inkpad, then expertly rolled them across a preprinted card.

When the cards were done, he pulled a stub of a cigar out of his mouth, then smiled and handed the forms to Megan. "Good luck," he said, grinning at Dave. "Now hurry back over there so you can bring that baby home."

Approaching the INS office, Megan felt her heart stop when she saw a rope stretched across the entrance to the INS waiting room. Had the office closed? As they hurried closer, however, she could see people in the reception area beyond. She could have fallen to her knees in gratitude when she realized they had merely stopped taking new arrivals in order to handle those who were still waiting.

The INS staffer at the main desk recognized them immediately.

"You won't have to wait again," she promised, glancing toward the caseworker who had spoken to them earlier. "Marcy's ready for you."

With an air of accomplishment, Megan strode over and returned her folder, now complete with fingerprint cards. The caseworker glanced at the documents, stamped their application, then looked up and smiled. "Glad you made it back," she said, standing. "Now if you will both raise your right hands and repeat after me."

Megan had never felt more solemn than in that unexpected moment. Together she and Dave took an oath to protect the child they had petitioned to bring into the United States, then the caseworker handed Megan a sheet of paper. "Go home, fill this in, and return it with a check for the application fee," she said, her tone cool and professional. But her eyes sparkled as she whispered, "And God bless you."

Megan's heart swelled with gratitude as she accepted the application. Everything was falling into place. Step by step, God was bringing them closer to their baby.

They found the first packet of photographs in the mailbox when they arrived home. Though she was dead tired from the trip to Washington, Megan tore open the envelope, then stared at the first picture with unabashed delight. The tiny black-and-white snapshot in Helen Gresham's office hadn't done Danielle justice—this baby was *adorable*.

Joe and Susan had taken and developed an entire roll of film—shots of the baby having a bath, wet haired and big eyed in the plastic tub; shots of her leaning out of a stroller; shots of her on Susan's hip. In one picture, Danielle had been propped against pillows and was falling over, her mouth open in what Megan was certain must have been a belly laugh. A deep dimple adorned her left cheek, a glorious smile lit her face, and, Megan realized as she memorized the photos, the robust baby was no frail infant.

Megan made a mental note to exchange some garments she'd bought earlier in a rush of excitement. This kid was growing like a weed.

"Come home soon," she whispered, pressing the photos to her chest. "Come home before you outgrow everything in your closet!"

After she and Dave studied every single picture, Megan separated several photos and slipped them into envelopes for Dave's sister, her mother, and her mother-in-law. She set one photo, her favorite, aside for the birth announcement. Tomorrow she'd take it to the drugstore and have a zillion reprints made.

"I cannot wait to hold her and love her," she whispered to Dave as they sat on the sofa and drank in the details of the remaining snapshots.

"This little doll will come soon enough," Dave answered, placing his hand on her hair. "All in God's time."

Eight

A strong sense of purpose carried Megan through the next few days. Before Joe Hogan's call, she had existed in a stagnant pool of possibilities; now she felt she and Dave had finally begun to make progress. Or, in the words of Samuel Johnson, their sorrow was being lessened by "exercise and motion."

The baby God intended for them was waiting in South Korea, and Megan was determined to do all she could to ensure that the time of waiting was as brief as possible.

With great regret on the first Monday in August she knocked on Dr. Duncan's door and gave her notice. She would quit work in two weeks, she told him, because her baby would soon be home. Though they didn't yet have an exact arrival date, they expected her to arrive in less than six weeks—by the end of September, at the latest.

"And I have so much to do," Megan explained, spreading her hands. "I have to shop, and there is paperwork yet to be done, and I've got a lot of reading to catch up on. My baby is three months old, and I need to know what to expect at this age."

The doctor's blue eyes twinkled behind his glasses. "I know I should offer my congratulations," he said, crossing his arms, "but it won't be easy to replace you. Are you sure I can't talk you into coming back to work after you've had some time to adjust?"

Megan shook her head. "Thank you, sir, but no. I've worked so hard to be a mother, and waited so long…I don't want to miss a minute of the experience. And my daughter will need me, so I want to be with her every minute I can."

Dr. Duncan's mouth drooped in a one-sided smile. "I think this is one lucky baby."

Megan shook off the compliment and returned to the desk, then pulled her pocket-sized calendar from her purse and marked off another day. It was August 1—little Danielle had been born on the ninth of April, so she was almost four months old.

Megan sighed. Infancy flew by so quickly! Susan had said Danielle was already a big baby, so if she didn't come home soon, Megan might never know what it felt like to hold an infant in her arms.…

She shook off the thought. She would harbor no regrets, for God had obviously brought this child to them in His timing and for His reasons.

Her eyes fell upon a calendar date marked with a red circle— the day for Helen Gresham's home visit. Korean regulations required the U.S. placement agency to visit the couple's home at least once, so Helen would have to fly to Alta Vista. Megan felt certain the visit would be uneventful—they liked Helen from the moment they met her, and Belinda Bishop had already approved their home. So this would be a perfunctory meeting.

Megan looked up and smiled as Mrs. Leber came through the veterinary clinic door, her arms filled with a wicker basket in which a new passel of puppies scrambled upward. "Mrs. Leber," she called, grinning. "Has that Chihuahua been visiting your yard again?"

Dave lowered himself to the sofa and bit his lip as he heard Megan singing in the kitchen. She'd been talkative and excited all through dinner, telling him about Dr. Duncan and what he'd said when she told him she planned to leave in two weeks. From that topic she bounced to the news that his sister in New Orleans had promised to send a box of baby clothes her daughter had outgrown. She'd mailed it a couple of days ago, and the package would arrive at any time.

"I think there are a lot of people who really feel involved with us," Megan had told him, her eyes shining. "Most of these people have been waiting and praying with us for years. I know it sounds silly, because nearly every baby is loved and anticipated, but I can't help feeling that ours has been more anticipated than most. Well—anticipated *longer* than most, in any case."

Dave had let her chatter and ramble, remembering to nod and smile in all the right places, but he breathed a sigh of relief when dinner ended and she rose to stack their plates and do the dishes. He emptied the garbage, fulfilling his part of the dinner deal, then moved to the living room and picked up the newspaper.

But he couldn't concentrate on the articles before his eyes. He couldn't think about anything but the trouble looming over his school.

He had chosen not to teach during this summer break for two reasons: He wanted to be free if they got a baby, and he wanted to be available if he was named to fill the vacancy created by Dr. Comfort's retirement. Though the start of the new school year was only three weeks away, the school board had not yet made any official appointments. They were meeting throughout the week, and things were supposed to be settled soon.

But how? The question nagged at him.

That afternoon he'd heard rumors that the recently commissioned demographic report indicated a shrinking elementary student population in the area zoned for Valley View, and every teacher on staff knew what that dire news could mean. Their school was one of the older campuses in the state, and the land was valuable and situated near a residential area. Even at this late date, the school board might shut Valley View down and send students elsewhere. If they did, over forty faculty members and administrators would be out of jobs.

He lowered the paper to his chest as he stared out the front window. Ordinarily, he'd have shared this news with Megan the moment he returned home, but he couldn't bring himself to cloud her happiness with dark possibilities. This was one of those 50/50 situations—the school board could close the school, or they could keep it open, and life would continue without a ripple. Why should he worry Megan with desperate situations that *might* be?

The phone rang, and Megan called from the kitchen. "Could you get that, hon? My hands are soapy."

With a sense of foreboding, Dave picked up the phone. "Hello?"

"Mr. Wingfield, this is Helen Gresham. I'm afraid I have a bit of bad news."

Dave sat silently, letting the words drop into his consciousness. Bad news on top of bad news meant more to keep from Megan.

"What is it?" he asked, his voice hoarse.

"It's a bit complicated, but I'll do my best to explain. In Korea, you see, a child cannot be declared abandoned if he or she has been entered into a family register—it's a bit like our birth certificates, only more involved. If a family claims a child, obviously, the child is not abandoned."

"But," Dave lowered his voice in case Megan was listening, "she was left on a doorstep. That's abandonment."

"Not necessarily. The extended family structure in Korea, you see, is more emphasized than in the U.S. And if this child is registered with a family, she is not legally available for adoption."

Dave's breath came raggedly. "But she's not with a Korean family. She's with my wife's friends."

"I know, Mr. Wingfield, but I'm telling you the facts. I'm still planning on visiting you, but I may bring news that you'll have to consider another child."

Helen Gresham's words echoed in his consciousness long after he hung up the phone. He sat on the sofa, trembling with frustration and fear, then flinched when Megan stepped into the room.

"Who was on the phone, hon?"

Dave looked at her, met her gaze, and saw her expression shift from curiosity to apprehension. He couldn't hide this from her— the baby, this *particular* baby, was all she thought about these days.

Drawing a deep breath, he relayed Helen's message as simply as he could. Megan sat on the sofa next to him, her face blank, her eyes expressionless as she stared into space.

"I have to believe this is only a test," she finally said, her voice vacant and hollow. "We have a choice—we can be distracted, disillusioned, and defeated, or we can press on in the faith that Joe and Susan are keeping *our* baby." She turned and looked at him. "Do you agree?"

Wordlessly, Dave nodded.

Standing, Megan squared her shoulders, then lifted her purse from the table by the door. "I'm going to that little secondhand furniture store by the church. I saw a crib there the other day, and I figure now's as good a time as any to buy it."

She pulled her keys from her handbag. "I'll stop by the hardware store, too, for some paint and a paintbrush. I think I'll paint everything white. It won't be beautiful furniture, but it'll look clean and nice. After all, she's a baby. It's not like she'll know the difference between secondhand and Ethan Allan."

With a little wave in his direction, Megan opened the door and stepped out into the night.

Dave felt his heart twist as he watched her go. In the face of overwhelming odds, his wife would fight the world with faith and a paintbrush.

At work the next morning, Megan greeted owners and handled patients with an almost robotlike precision. Laurie remained quiet and aloof, almost as if she sensed that something was wrong. Dr. Duncan spent most of the morning in surgery, so his thoughts remained elsewhere.

I will pray and trust, Megan told herself for the hundredth time as she checked the water bowls in the kennels. *God is in control of this situation, and He will walk me through it.*

But the moment she shifted her thoughts from that comforting mantra, she felt like Peter sinking into the sea. How could this latest problem possibly work itself out? Dave said that Helen thought they could get another child if Danielle didn't work out, but that option felt wrong somehow. At the INS office, they had applied for *Danielle's* visa; they had listed her name on the application; they had sworn, in their hearts at least, to protect and provide for *her*. How could they pop another child into that particular place in their hearts? They might as well forget about Korea and continue waiting on Belinda Bishop's computers....

That thought sent another realization zinging through Megan's brain. Last week, right after their return from Washington, they had gone to the bank and applied for a second mortgage. The banker had frowned at their completed application, particularly when Megan confessed that she would not be working when the baby arrived. The banker had said he'd see what they could do. This adoption would cost over seven thousand dollars—money they didn't have in cash, but they could borrow from the equity invested in their home. Most of that amount would go to the Korean agency to cover administrative fees and the baby's airfare; another portion would go to Welcome Home for expenses.

Megan checked the last kennel, then leaned against the wall and crossed her arms. What if they got the loan and couldn't get Danielle? She'd been so convinced Danielle was the child for them that she hadn't worried about getting the loan. After all, Dave had a good job, and they'd been living in their house for three years. The house had been a bargain when they bought it, and they'd made improvements, finishing a room in the basement and adding a back porch....

She closed her eyes, remembering how she had cringed at the thought of those adoption fees when they first investigated international adoption. Back then, she could not imagine how they could possibly consider such a notion. Now a second mortgage not only seemed wise, but practical. All they needed was the bank's approval, and money would no longer be an issue.

The phone rang, jangling her nerves. Megan's heart skipped a beat when Laurie answered, then put the caller on hold and held the receiver toward Megan. "It's for you," she said simply.

Megan felt her mouth go dry. Laurie knew Dave's voice and would have identified him. Megan's mother never called at work, so this *could* be Belinda Bishop....

She licked her dry lips, then took the phone. "Hello?"

"Megan?" Helen Gresham's dignified voice rang in her ears. "I have good news. First, I wanted to tell you that my plane will land at 10 A.M. on Monday, the fifteenth. I'm excited about our visit. Second, I wanted you to know that everything has been settled in Korea." She chuckled. "Your friend is something else. Apparently he personally carried the baby to the mayor's office in Seoul and made an impassioned plea on your behalf. I'm not certain of the details, but we've just heard from our Korean affiliate. The baby has been cleared. Danielle will be on her way home in about a month, as soon as her paperwork arrives."

Megan pressed her hand to her chest. This news came too suddenly; she couldn't take it in all at once.

She turned and grinned at Laurie. "That's wonderful news, Helen! Dave will be so happy to hear it!"

"I'm pleased it all worked out. So—you'll meet me at the airport on the fifteenth?"

"We'll be there." Megan exhaled a long sigh of relief. "You can count on us."

Nine

ave let the car door close with a heavy thud, then picked up his briefcase and trudged toward the door. Of all the moments in this long, exhausting day, the one he dreaded most still lay ahead. Megan had left him a message with the good news about the baby's paperwork, but now he had to counter that joyful announcement with news of his own.

The bad tidings had reached him an hour earlier: Valley View Elementary School would not operate in the next school year. Dave would not be a principal, and he'd be lucky to find an administrative opening in any of the other city schools. That meant he'd be back in the classroom, working for a teacher's salary, and starting over in a new school with new challenges.

Or...he and Megan could move. Roanoke, a good-sized city about an hour away, was growing, and he could commute until the house sold. And he'd heard that North Carolina school districts desperately needed experienced administrators on the elementary level. But if they left the state of Virginia, they'd be out of Belinda Bishop's jurisdiction...and Helen Gresham's. He and Megan would have to start the adoption process all over again.

He hesitated before the front door, his hand on the knob. How could he soften this blow? Megan had endured so much already;

it hardly seemed fair to ask her to roll with another punch. Any other woman would have already resorted to screaming fits, and many other wives would have thrown up their hands and walked out of the marriage.

He had married a strong woman…but even Megan's strength had limits. He wasn't sure she could handle this latest development, especially when he pointed out that it wasn't fair to ask Danielle to wait.

Father…give me wisdom, please.

That little girl deserved a home and loving parents. Joe and Susan Hogan had been the personification of Christian love and faithfulness, but they couldn't keep the child forever. Joe faced the demands of his ministry and family; Susan had her work and three children of her own.

He and Megan would have to let Danielle go to another couple. It should be a simple matter—she had been successfully entered into the system, both in Korea and in the United States. Helen Gresham had other waiting families; one of them, Dave knew, would be thrilled to love Danielle.

Because after the final school board meeting tomorrow morning, Dave would probably not have a job. And the bank would not grant a loan to a couple when neither of them worked, no matter how unique the circumstances.

Megan stepped back and surveyed her gleaming table. In honor of Helen's good news, she had slipped away from work early and prepared a glorious feast—baked chicken with cranberry sauce, broccoli and cheese, golden yeast rolls, and pumpkin pie. If it looked a little like a Thanksgiving dinner, well, tonight they had a lot to be thankful for.

She pulled the crystal candleholders from the china hutch and straightened the tall candle that leaned precariously to the right. After fumbling in the junk drawer for a moment, she found a book of matches and lit the elegant tapers.

She heard Dave's key in the door as she shook the flame off the match. She stepped back and dimmed the kitchen lights, loving the way the candles danced in the semidarkness. Dave might think she had lost her mind, and he'd be half right. She felt like a completely different person, as if she'd gone from being Megan Wingfield, wife, to Megan Wingfield, mother, in the space of a single afternoon.

She ducked behind a corner as she heard Dave's approaching footsteps. He seemed to hesitate in the kitchen doorway. "Meg?"

"Welcome home!" She peeked out from behind the corner and grinned, then stepped forward and wrapped her arms about his neck. Impulsively, she kissed him, then lowered her head to the space between his chest and chin. "Can you believe our good news?" she whispered, hearing his heartbeat beneath the soft cotton of his shirt.

"Meg." His hoarse voice was edged with a note of desolation. Alarmed, Megan pulled away and looked at him, reading the grief and despair on his face.

"What's wrong?"

He gestured toward the sparkling table. "Maybe we should sit down."

Moving woodenly, Megan slipped into her chair and sat erect as Dave stared at the burning candles. For a long moment neither said anything, then he drew a deep breath and reported on the latest school board decisions—Valley View would not open this month; the students would be transferred; there were few administrative openings in the city schools. At a meeting tomorrow the board would decide who would be transferred to what schools, and those for whom there were no jobs would have to find employment elsewhere.

Megan silently watched her husband, who seemed to be wearing his face like a mask. In a passionless voice he said he could look for work in Roanoke, which meant they'd have to sell the house, or he could find work in North Carolina. But if they moved out of state, there would be no adoption.

"Or—" his eyes finally met hers—"I could stay here and find work, any kind of work, that would pay the bills until after we get the baby. I don't know if the bank would give us the loan, and I don't know how we could raise thousands of dollars without a bank loan, but I'm willing to try anything. I could deliver newspapers in the morning, and maybe tutor kids in the evenings. I could stay home with the baby if you want to ask Dr. Duncan if he would let you keep your job. I'll do anything you want, but right now I'm too tired and too confused to know what we're *supposed* to do."

Megan stared, her mind and body benumbed, as a tear slowly found its way down her husband's cheek. Her own body quaked with repressed feeling, but she would not weep. Not now. They could not weep together; that would feel like surrender. One of them had to remain strong while the other weakened, one of them had to keep fighting…for Danielle.

"Honey—" her trembling hand reached out to cover his— "we'll know. Somehow, at some point, the Lord will show us what to do."

Dave swiped away the wetness on his cheek, then drew a deep breath. "As I see it, we have two immediate options."

"And they are?"

"Either stay where we are and pursue Danielle's adoption as far as we can, or we call Helen Gresham and tell her to give the baby to someone else. We can always wait on Belinda Bishop's list. As long as we remain in the state, we'll have a spot there."

His words hit Megan with the force of a physical blow. She closed her eyes. "I don't know what will happen with your job, but I can't lose Danielle. I *won't* lose her, Dave. I'll work, and you'll work, and we'll beg and borrow if we have to. But I can't give up my baby!"

They lay in bed that night without speaking, each of them tossing and turning until the clock struck two. When Dave finally settled and his breathing deepened, Megan sat up in the darkness and looked at his shadowy form.

Men dealt with emotions differently, she knew, yet she couldn't deny that Dave loved Danielle as much as she did. He would sacrifice everything he possessed if she were their daughter, and in that lay the problem—she *wasn't* their daughter, not yet.

Did God bring that little girl into their lives, or was her arrival mere happenstance? Was it God's will that they expend every effort to bring that particular child into their home, or were they pasting a "God's will" sign on coincidence and foolishly following an expensive dream?

Megan knew some folks in her church would frown on their bank loan. Oh, they wouldn't mind borrowing to buy a house or even a car, but they'd find a second mortgage unspiritual. "If God wanted you to have that baby," she could almost hear them saying, "He'd have provided the finances, too. You should walk away from any situation that will put you in debt."

But Megan felt God *had* supplied the finances—through the possibility of a second mortgage. After all, they were borrowing from the equity in their home, which God had generously provided.

She threw off the light blanket that covered her, then hugged her knees. How could she be certain she'd found God's will? As a child, she had relied heavily upon her parents for guidance, knowing that the biblical command "honor your father and mother" resulted in blessing. Even in college, when her parents tried to encourage her to make her own decisions, she had begged to know their preferences in difficult situations.

As a wife, she believed God often spoke through her husband. Dave trusted her to make most decisions regarding the household, but in important matters she always sought his opinion. In rare situations where they didn't agree, Megan always shared her feelings and convictions, knowing that Dave would respect them even if he decided to follow his own inclinations.

But how were they to decide what to do about Danielle? They had witnessed so many little miracles—Joe's unexpected and unsolicited phone call, the INS paperwork falling into place, and answered prayers regarding Danielle's family registry and availability. Surely the hand of God had manipulated those situations! So how could He now lead them away from this child?

Too burdened to sleep, she slipped out of bed and padded down the hall and into the baby's room. The freshly painted crib sat against the far wall, gleaming in the light from the streetlamp outside the windows. Her old bureau, also awash in a fresh coat of paint, stood next to the crib. Adjacent to that stood a bookcase she had discovered in another secondhand furniture store. With a new fabric cover and three inches of foam padding, the bookcase made a perfect changing table, with room for baby wipes and diapers on the shelves beneath.

Shivering in a draft from the air-conditioning, Megan rubbed her hands over her arms, then sank to the carpeted floor. She had planned to put a bentwood rocker in this corner. On many a recent night she had soothed her anxious heart to sleep by imagining herself rocking Danielle and reading the soothing cadences of nursery rhymes and *Goodnight, Moon*.

The thought now made her throat ache.

Rubbing her arms again, she glanced at the dark shape at her right hand, then recognized it—the box from Dave's sister, Vicki. Upon hearing the good news about Danielle, she had cleaned out her attic and boxed up all of her daughter's baby things.

Reluctantly, Megan lifted the cardboard flaps. A note lay on top, illegible in the semidarkness, so she dropped it to the floor. Then her fingers parted tissue paper and pulled out a beautiful smocked dress with lace at the hem and sleeves. The lovely little white dress seemed to glow in the silence of the empty room.

A new anguish seared her heart. What should she do with this box of beautiful things? Keep it in the hope that all would be well, or send it back with a thank-you note and regrets?

Her throat tightened, and it was only when she tasted the salt of tears did she realize she was weeping. "Lord," she whispered, her gaze lifting to the silent night outside the window. "What are You asking of me?"

The answer came, slowly and surely, on the wings of lessons learned in a lifetime of Sunday school: *Jesus asks us only to follow Him...to be obedient.* "Obedient?" she choked on the word. "I would obey, really I would, if I knew what You wanted me to do. I want this baby, and I think You want me to have her. If You want me to give her up, You're going to have to show me clearly." She lifted her chin. "It wouldn't be easy, but we could do it."

Follow me.

"Follow You *where?* Follow You *how?*"

As Megan battled her raging emotions in the silence, a realization began to take shape: In all the winding length of her life, God had never failed to guide her. She had accepted Jesus as a child, and, like a loving Friend, He had never left her alone or without direction. And when she wanted to turn inward and selfishly dwell on her own hurts, time after time He reminded her…that others were hurting, too.

Closing her eyes, she thought for the first time about the others who might be lifting prayers for wisdom at that same hour. Valley View Elementary had employed over forty faculty members, and tonight many of them were walking the floor, as fearful as she about what tomorrow might bring. In Korea, Joe and Susan were caring for *four* children and probably praying that Danielle's adoption would be finalized soon. And in the room next door a good man slumbered uneasily, burdened with guilt for bringing bad news home to the wife he loved.

"Forgive me, Father." Megan bowed her head as the enormity of her self-centeredness struck her. "I want what You want. I trust Your guiding hand. I praise You for Your goodness to me, even when that goodness takes the form of something I can't understand."

A praise song from church filled her heart, and she found herself paraphrasing the words in a broken whisper: "I will praise You, knowing that my praise will cost me every dream I have ever dreamed."

Danielle and the future and my motherhood. I said I would not lose her, Lord, but I will let her go, if that's what obedience requires.

"I will praise You with the joy that comes from knowing I have held nothing back."

Not these baby clothes, not this nursery, not my future.

"I will praise You, for I know nothing can harm me."

Everything comes to me through Your sheltering hand, so I know I can trust You.

"I will praise You for giving me this opportunity to realize how much I need You."

I need You for strength to face tomorrow and the day after that. I am at the end of myself, and I've nowhere to turn but to You, Lord.

"I will praise You for this opportunity to realize Your great provision and loving care."

You can and will provide…if not today, then tomorrow

"I will praise You for the plan You always reveal in Your time. I will praise You for giving me a husband who loves me. And I will praise You for knowing my mother's heart."

…and for designing it that way.

The next words hurt Megan's throat, but she forced them out into the quiet darkness of the nursery: "Though it costs me everything, I will offer up the sacrifice of praise."

Ten

Megan woke the next morning to the light touch of sunlight upon her cheek. Momentarily confused by her surroundings, she pushed herself off the carpet. She'd fallen asleep in the nursery, in the midst of baby clothes and the ashes of her dreams…desires which now lay in the hands of her heavenly Father.

She staggered into the hall bathroom and stared at her reflection. The nap of the carpet had mottled her cheek; the hair at the top of her head stood upright in some sort of Mohawk imitation, and her eyes were still red rimmed from weeping.

"Sleeping beauty, indeed," she murmured, turning the faucet. She splashed her face with several bracing handfuls of cold water, then reached for a thick towel on the rack. The singing of pipes in the walls assured her Dave was awake and in the shower. He could probably use a strong cup of coffee.

She walked to the kitchen, plugged in the coffeemaker, then cracked open the front door and shot a furtive glance up and down the street. When she was confident there were no neighbors about, she dashed out in her pajamas and picked up the newspaper, then took it to the kitchen.

Dave joined her a few moments later, his hair slicked back and shiny with wet. He wore a long-sleeved shirt, a dark blue tie, and matching navy pants. The conservative look, suitable for an educator eager to impress.

He lifted a brow when he saw her sitting at the table with a cup of coffee. "I saw that you were up already, but making coffee? What's gotten into you?"

She shrugged. "I just wanted to help get your day off to a good start. Figured a cup of coffee and the paper couldn't hurt."

He sat down beside her, sipped the coffee, and smiled in appreciation. "Perfect, Meg."

"Thanks." She nodded slowly. "That's what I wanted to tell you this morning. Whatever happens in your meeting today, I know things are going to be perfect. We want what God wants, and we're committed to Him. So I know things will work out."

He looked at her, a question in his eyes.

She lowered her coffee cup and met his gaze. "Last night I couldn't sleep, so I went into the baby's room to sort of argue my case before God. And I realized that what I said yesterday about not being able to give Danielle up—well, I was being stubborn. So, before I finally went to sleep, I gave her to the Lord. He loves that baby even more than I do, and I know He wants what's best for her. So whether she comes home to our house or someone else's, I'm okay. I want what God wants, no matter what that is."

Dave's eyes burned with the clear, deep blue that burns in the heart of a flame, then he reached out and gently stroked her cheek. "I love you," he whispered, gratitude gleaming in his eyes.

His hand pulled her forward until they met forehead-to-forehead. "Father, we are Yours," he prayed, his hand warm against the back of her neck. "Work Your will through us today, and we will give You the power, and honor, and glory for whatever comes. In the name of Jesus we ask these things."

When Megan lifted her head, Dave's eyes shone with confidence. She smiled, knowing that no matter what happened in the school board meeting, Mr. and Mrs. Dave Wingfield would be at peace.

Later that morning, Megan moved through her usual routines of attending patients, assisting Dr. Duncan, and helping Laurie at the desk. She functioned automatically, only half thinking about her actions, while her brain wrestled with the idea of revoking her resignation. She had another week and a half before her resignation at the clinic became final…but what if she'd made a terrible mistake?

If Dave lost his job, she certainly couldn't afford to leave hers. Dr. Duncan would almost certainly love to keep her, but he had already begun to interview prospective veterinary technicians. In fact, if Laurie's scribbled notation on the calendar could be trusted, Megan was fairly certain he had already asked someone to report next week to begin training for her position.

Begging to keep her job at this late date would be unfair to Dr. Duncan and to whomever he planned to hire. So she couldn't change her mind about leaving.

She bit her lip. If the news from today's school board meeting was as bad as they feared, she could always apply at another veterinary office in town, though that would seem disloyal to Dr. Duncan. Or she could set aside her training and investigate a new line of work—pet sitting, dog walking, or perhaps pet grooming. She knew nothing about how to give fancy haircuts to poodles and Malteses, but she could wash a dog as well as anyone. The world of dog shows had always interested her—she'd have to be trained, of course, but if she wormed her way into the circle of professional handlers who worked the dog show circuit, she could make a tidy sum working weekends and summers....

She shook those thoughts away. She wouldn't worry. She would take one day at a time and wait to see what God would do. He was in control; He owned the entire situation. Surrendering her dreams and her child had been the most difficult act of her life, but she had done it. Now she couldn't—*wouldn't*—take those things back.

Her thoughts filtered back to the day when they had first learned there would be no biological babies. Dr. Comfort had stood in her kitchen and given her a promise: "Hope deferred makes the heart sick, but when the desire comes, it is a tree of life."

When would her tree of life bloom?

"Hey, Meg," Laurie called from the reception desk. "Take a look at what's coming our way."

Megan stood from her chair behind the filing cabinet and looked out the glass door. Instead of the pet owner and patient she expected, she saw a man approaching, his arms overflowing with yellow roses.

The flowers drooped as the man struggled to free his arm and open the door, and that's when Megan saw his face. This was no florist or delivery person—it was her husband.

Without a word, Megan rounded the corner of the desk and flew to the door, nearly tripping over a weimaraner stretched out across the tile floor. "Dave," she cried, coming to an abrupt halt in front of him. Strangled by a sudden rise of hopes and fears, she could scarcely breathe. "What's happened?"

The yellow blossoms tilted to one side, and Dave's lopsided grin appeared. "You're looking at the new assistant principal of Pleasant Hill Elementary," he said, stepping forward to place the bundle of roses in her arms. "I received the appointment this morning. It's the same job I had at Valley View and at the same salary. It's not a promotion, but—"

"It's perfect!" Megan threw her free arm around his neck. As the people in the waiting room looked on in amusement, she planted a loud, smacky kiss on his smiling mouth.

"We're okay," he whispered, holding her close. "We still have a job."

We still have a baby.

"Thank You," she whispered, closing her eyes as her thoughts lifted to the One who had made it all possible. "Thank You, Jesus."

One month after their visit to Washington, Megan called the Welcome Home office in Washington to check on the progress of their case. Helen reported that Danielle's paperwork had not yet arrived from Korea, but they were confident the documents would arrive soon.

Megan hung up, simultaneously frustrated and relieved. The night before, she'd draped herself in hope and fortitude and attended a baby shower for her friend, Susie. Susie's baby, a beautiful little boy, sat in the center of the sofa, while another friend, Debbie, bounced her infant daughter on her lap. Not to be outdone, Megan passed pictures of Danielle around the circle. "I'm so sorry your baby isn't here yet," Susie whispered in a private moment, but the words didn't sting like they would have in a few months ago.

"I'm grateful to have pictures," Megan said, handing over a snapshot. "I thank the Lord for these."

On Monday of the next week, the bank called with more good news—the Wingfield's house had appraised for fifteen thousand dollars over the amount they owed on the mortgage, so they could pick up a check for the seven thousand dollars they needed whenever they could find the time to stop by.

Once the money had been safely deposited in their savings account, Megan paced in her empty house and stared at the calendar. She'd been unemployed for three weeks, and her soul was beginning to feel rusty again. School would begin in one week, so Dave had his hands full with preparation for his new students. She had hoped to be busy mothering her baby by this time, but it looked as though September would arrive without Danielle.

The days melted into weeks as September slid away in a blur of reds and golds. Near the end of the month, Helen Gresham called to ask for Danielle's airfare. "The check will be sent to Korea as soon as the baby's documents arrive here," Helen explained, "then she will be issued a Korean passport. While the passport is being finalized, you can finish filing with the Department of Immigration. Our babies usually arrive about four weeks after the paperwork."

Megan was delighted to have a task to exercise the rust away, so she hurried to the bank, ordered a certified check, and sent it to Washington by registered mail.

Unfortunately her task did not take long, and soon she found herself waiting again. Inactivity chafed upon her—like Martha of the New Testament, she had never been happy to sit when she could be working. She consoled herself with the thought that if the documents were due any day, and Danielle would arrive four weeks after her paperwork, she'd probably be arriving sometime in late October...perhaps in time for Dave's birthday on the twenty-first.

The days fell, like the autumn leaves on the oak outside her window, one after the other. Megan read books on childcare, visited her mother and sister, and tried not to be jealous of Melanie's progressing pregnancy. She did not covet Melanie's baby, but she did resent her sister's *security*. Mel knew where her baby was and approximately when it would be delivered. Megan had no assurances.

One day, when the tedium of waiting grew intolerable, Megan picked up the phone and called her mother. "It's so hard not to want her here now," she said, taking pleasure in the liberty of venting. "Danielle's five-month birthday is in two weeks, and I could go *crazy* if I think about missing these early months of her life. So I try not to think about it, but it's almost impossible—"

"I wasn't going to tell you this," her mother interrupted, her voice quiet and thoughtful, "but maybe it's something you need to know."

Megan's inner alarm bells rang. "What?"

"Your baby shower. Melanie and I are giving you a shower next week. We wanted it to be a surprise, but it sounds like you could use something to look forward to."

Megan could hardly sleep the night before the shower. And when the last party guest left her mother's house, Megan looked over the mounds of frilly dresses and diapers and books and crib sheets and marveled at the generosity and good wishes of her friends. Then, sighing, she prayed Danielle would have a chance to enjoy their gifts before she outgrew them.

On a gray afternoon, Megan sat in the living room window seat and stared out at the rain drizzling over the driveway. It was the eleventh of October, and they not only did not have their daughter, they still had not heard when she would arrive. Lately, Megan hated even to go to church—everyone she knew insisted upon asking when the baby was coming home. Each time she answered, "I don't know," she felt as if she were acknowledging a colossal defeat.

She was trying to be patient. Every day she struggled to silence her fears and doubts. God had done so many things for them— protected them during the job crisis, directed them to a special baby, provided money when they had no means to earn any—so why was He testing their patience? Megan had been waiting three years for a child, and every other expectant mother waited nine months. Why did she deserve such a long-term sentence?

"Sometimes," she told Samson as the cat jumped into her lap, "I think I'll still be sitting here a year from now. Danielle will have outgrown everything in the nursery, and you'll be the only one to play with her toys."

The cat purred, and Megan straightened at the sight of head-lights shining through the gray drizzle. The mail carrier had come early, probably in an effort to outrun the rain, and was placing what looked like a letter in her mailbox.

"Be back in a minute, Sam." She dumped the cat off her lap and hurried to the front door, then sprinted through the drizzle. Inside the mailbox, a blue airmail envelope sat atop the catalogs and bills. She pressed the precious packet to her chest in an effort to keep it dry, then ran back into the house.

This letter from Korea did not contain pictures, just an update from Susan. "Joe was hoping to come to Alta Vista and personally escort Danielle home," she had written, "but now it looks like he'll be unable to get away. Danielle is doing well, but she's so attached to me that she screams even when we leave her with a sitter to go to the market."

Megan felt a sharp twist of pain. Danielle should be *home*, attaching to *her*. She felt a sharp pang of jealousy, followed by regret for what Danielle would have to endure in the coming days. The baby would have to leave the loving foster home she'd known and come to America—a tremendous adjustment, even for an infant. Megan's heart ached to think of causing Danielle pain. Babies adapted quickly, the experts said, but how easily could a five-month-old adapt when she was taken from the home she had known half her life?

Desperate for comfort, she picked up her Bible and settled back into the window seat. Flipping through the thin pages, she read her favorite proverb again (not *if* the desire comes, but *when*), then idly turned a few pages back.

Another verse caught her eye, a psalm:

"You keep track of all my sorrows.
You have collected all my tears in your bottle.
You have recorded each one in your book."

As if the verse had called them forth, tears welled in her eyes. God was keeping track of every tear—and she seemed to be weeping buckets these days. She wept at the slightest provocation; even sentimental television commercials and sappy country songs could send her into a crying jag....

The ringing of the telephone broke into Megan's thoughts. She carried Susan's letter into the kitchen and stared at it through bleary eyes as she picked up the receiver.

Her heart jumped at the sound of a familiar voice. Helen Gresham was calling from Washington with good news: Danielle's legal documents had finally arrived from Korea, so the agency required only three more items: a letter of approval from the Department of Immigration, a letter from the Virginia state office in Richmond, and Danielle's passport from Korea.

Megan could hear a smile in the social worker's voice as she finished her report: "It should be two weeks at the shortest, three at the longest. She's nearly home."

Tears of joy blurred Megan's vision as she hung up the phone.

On October 26, Helen called again. Danielle was ready, another child was ready, but they were waiting on a third child to be cleared before they would book the children's flight. "Plan on next Tuesday," Helen said. "If there are any changes, I'll let you know. And as soon as I have her flight information, I'll call."

Megan hung up and sent a smile winging across the room. "Tuesday," she told her husband, knowing her smile explained everything. "Seven more days."

Megan filled the long week with busy work—she cleaned the baby's room, scoured out the kitchen cabinets, and organized the clothes in Danielle's closet—the tiny twelve-months' dresses on the right, followed by the eighteen months, then twenty-four months, and finally a couple of larger dresses she'd been unable to resist in a Polly Flinders outlet. One dress, a red-and-white concoction of tulle and ribbon, hung at the far left, size six. Megan looked at the huge dress and shrugged. Danielle would fit into it eventually. Her coming home was truly no longer a matter of *if*, but *when*.

On Saturday evening, Megan's mother called with breathless news. "Melanie just had her baby," she said, yelling to be heard over the commotion in the background. "A boy! She had him at the birthing center and barely had time to get there before the baby came."

"You should have called me," Megan said, frowning. "I would have liked to be there—and I could have handled it."

"There wasn't time, believe me." Her mother's voice was soothing. "Melanie had the baby quickly. I didn't get here until after it was all over."

"Wow." Megan smiled, drinking in the unexpected wonder. Melanie's due date was November 16, so this little guy had come early…and he'd managed to beat his older cousin home by at least three days.

"I'll be over to see her tomorrow," Megan promised, making a mental note to stop by the mall to pick up a gift for a baby boy.

She hung up, knowing she could be happy for her sister without reservation. After all, she was a mother, too, with a baby arriving in seventy-two hours.

On Monday morning, Helen called with concrete details—Danielle would be arriving with four other children, not on Tuesday, but on Friday evening. Megan swallowed her disappointment about the date and consoled herself with the realization that at last they knew a definite date and time: 5:59 P.M., November 4. Their little girl was finally coming home.

Megan spent the week in domestic activities—she planted tulips, raked the last bedraggled leaves from the lawn, and began a cross-stitched family portrait for her mother, complete with two new babies in the family. On Thursday night she boiled baby bottles, packed a diaper bag with disposables, and tucked in a new outfit, pink booties, and a soft yellow blanket. The car seat and baby stroller waited in the car.

After lunch on Friday, Dave and Megan got into the car and began to back out the driveway. Another vehicle screeched to a halt in the road behind them, and as Megan turned, she saw Dr. Stella Comfort leaning out the driver's window, waving. "I heard the good news!" she called, her eyes shining. "I'll be praying for you!"

The four-hour drive to Washington National Airport seemed to take forever, and not even the stark beauty of the autumnal countryside could take Megan's mind off her impending motherhood. Washington traffic had shifted into flee-for-the-weekend mode when they hit the Beltway, and after they finally found a parking place at the airport, they had to run and catch a shuttle to the terminal.

Breathless, Dave and Megan reached the gate at 5:30 P.M., where they learned that the children's flight had been delayed from 5:59 to 6:33. Helen Gresham stood there, soothing each of the four anxious couples with a calm and gracious smile. Megan wanted to camp out next to Helen's side but realized she shouldn't be possessive. Each woman in their small circle probably saw Helen as their personal rock of Gibraltar.

She suppressed a smile as she looked around the group. Each couple was as loaded down as she and Dave were, for each expected a child: one, a twenty-one-month-old girl, another a six-month-old boy, and the other a ten-month-old girl.

When at last the plane arrived, Megan stood on tiptoe and scanned each face as if by some miracle Danielle might walk herself off the plane. Every single passenger—a seemingly endless stream of them—entered the gate area before Helen and three other Welcome Home social workers boarded the plane to fetch the children. Finally the quartet reappeared and stepped into the blinding light of strobic camera flashes. Helen, the last woman off the plane, carried Danielle.

Megan stared in stupefaction when she recognized the smile she had memorized from precious photographs. Weeping silently, she took the baby from Helen for a brief hug, then handed her to Dave…her daddy.

Danielle grinned the entire time. As a few curious spectators drew near, she grinned even more…an active, curious little ham.

Megan wasn't sure what impulse guided her actions, but she opened the diaper bag, spread the yellow blanket on the carpet, and gently pulled off Danielle's pajamas and wet diaper. In no time at all she had dressed her baby in a clean diaper, fresh cotton booties, and a soft flannel sleeper.

And as she passed their precious daughter to Dave, she couldn't help noticing that the other families were changing their babies, too. Perhaps, she thought, watching them, the urge to dress these children came from practical considerations—after all, they'd been flying for nearly twenty-four hours. But Megan believed the urge sprang from deeper instincts. After waiting so long and working so hard, each family wanted to dress the child in clothes *they* had prepared and provided. Somehow, the simple act of placing clean clothes on a baby helped make him or her theirs.

The words from a long-ago afternoon returned on a tide of memory. In the park, Andre's mother had described the experience perfectly: Adoption was a time of waiting and a time of hard labor, complete with every pain and every joy. And now that their child had come home, Megan knew she had been blessed.

As Dave cooed and bounced the baby in his arms, Megan gathered the top and bottom of the orange pajamas Danielle had worn on the plane. She'd save these things for her daughter's memory box.

Then her gaze fell upon the crumpled yellow socks she'd peeled from those chubby little feet. They were unlike any booties she'd ever seen—longer than American baby socks, and embroidered with an image of a bumblebee hovering over a blossom.

She laughed softly as she smoothed out the wrinkles. She held a little bit of Korea, a small part of her baby's history, the essence of everything she had dreamed…and God had allowed. In the last three years she had been tested, tried, shaped, and hammered. At times she had borne the pain stoically; at other times she had whined and screamed and pounded the floor. But through it all she had been able to trace God's hand of provision. And that assurance of His abiding faithfulness would get them through the terrible twos, adolescence, dating…and the heartrending moment when they would watch their darling daughter walk into the arms of her future husband.

Megan's throat tightened at the thought.

No one had ever promised that adoption—or parenting—would be easy. Just worthwhile.

She swallowed the lump in her throat, then wrapped the yellow socks in the pajamas and placed the bundle into the diaper bag. "Come on, Dad and Daughter," she said, lifting the bag to her shoulder. "Let's go home."

The Story Jar

Beth lifted her face to Mrs. Halley's, and this time she smiled despite her watery eyes. How long had it been since she'd stopped to consider what gifts the Father had given her, what her life might have held if she'd never gotten the chance to mother Tommy and Mark?

When she had started off all those years ago, she never thought she'd be bringing up her two boys alone.

Megan Wingfield's story seemed to sing itself into the depth of Beth's very soul. The memory of that yellow sock, small enough for a doll, embroidered with a bumblebee and a tiny flower, would remain emblazoned in her heart forever.

Oh, to be able to learn to live with such faith in trying circumstances!

Oh, to be able to trust something that you couldn't see.

Beth had long since set her cleaning supplies aside. Mrs. Halley leaned toward her from the wing chair and took Beth's hands in her own. Her slender fingers felt cool and sensible, like soft leather. "I can tell how much you love your boys just from looking at you."

"I do." Beth nodded. She bit her bottom lip and sighed. "I've tried so hard."

Their eyes met and held. For a bit, silence enveloped the

pretty little sanctuary. That silence in itself spoke volumes. "Perhaps—" Mrs. Halley said at last—"the time has come for you to stop trying."

Tears welled in Beth's eyes. "I'm different than the women in those stories." Oh, dear, all the cleaning rags she'd brought with her, and not one Kleenex among them. "I guess I just don't have that much faith."

"None of us do, dear. I don't know if I've got the faith to say good-bye and walk out of this room in a few minutes, never to see it again. I don't know if I have the faith to climb out of bed tomorrow morning...." She faltered here, having to say the words. "To face the future without my John."

"I'm so sorry." Beth slipped her hands away. She rose and piled the spray can of polish and a bottle of glass cleaner into her pail. "I've said something that's made you sad."

"Faith is never something that we give to ourselves, Beth. Faith is something that the heavenly Father gives us, just when we need it the most. We have only to ask, and He will answer."

"It's been so long," Beth whispered. "I've even forgotten how to ask."

Even though Beth had noted the old woman's steps waver before, she saw her stand now with renewed strength, with the same confidence she'd had when she entered the room. "Would you like me to pray with you?"

Beth nodded. "Please."

"Come then. It will be my last time to pray for someone here. After so many." Together the two women walked to the simple pulpit. The sunlight against the ivory pews had lengthened to a rich, tranquil expanse of gold. Somewhere, in some place, it was the time when vespers would be sung. Everything in the sanctuary, the lectern, the piano, the rows of hymnals—perfectly aligned like soldiers—gleamed. In the gentle late-afternoon light, dust motes were suspended lightly in the air like swarms of glitter.

"Do you know the Lord as your personal savior, Beth?" Mrs. Halley asked.

Beth shook her head. "I don't think so. I've come to church sometimes but, no—"

"Would you like to?"

"Yes."

Together the two women prayed. For salvation. For faith. For healing. For rest.

At the beginning of the prayer, Beth felt afraid. What if Mrs. Halley expected her to say something? Wasn't it important to choose the right words when you were talking to somebody as big as God?

But halfway through the prayer, without even thinking of it, she found herself praying for Mrs. Halley, too. After the final *amen,* as their faces lifted and they smiled with sweet gratitude at one another, Beth thought of something she had never realized before.

Tommy and Mark belong to the Lord. They are more His children than they will ever be mine.

The thought staggered her. Overwhelmed her. And released her. She wasn't parenting alone; she never had been. Her boys had a heavenly Father to rely on.

And so did she.

"Well." Mrs. Halley lifted the jar, encircled it protectively with one arm, and made her way down the carpeted steps from the platform. "I've stayed longer than I planned. There wasn't anybody at home to hurry for."

When she tottered on the steps, Beth hastened to support the woman's elbow. "Thank you for sharing the story jar with me."

Beth gave her a grateful squeeze. "They're such wonderful stories. Perhaps now that you have a little more time, you could write some of them down."

She met Beth's gaze with a smile. "That's a nice thought. Perhaps someday I will."

Only when she reached the door did she turn back. For one last time, Beth saw her lift her gaze to the altar, to the pulpit, to all the love and sorrows, the joys and the memories, held before God in such an unadorned, simple place.

"Well," she breathed. That was all. Just one word: *Well.*

And then she was gone.

Beth stood watching after Mrs. Halley, her heart filled with stories from the jar. She realized that what seemed an ending for Mrs. Halley marked a beginning for her and her boys.

She'd be back here again. If not to clean, then to worship. It would be a good time to start attending a church. It pleased her, thinking of meeting the new pastor.

Oh yes. The organ. She'd almost forgotten that she hadn't finished with the dusting. Beth hurried forward and spritzed just a little more polish on the dust rag—the tang of lemon mixed with the faint perfume of carnations. As she began to buff the smudges from the instrument keys, she began to hum to herself.

A song of joy. And new beginnings.

Multnomah Publishers

The publisher and author would love to hear your comments about this book. *Please contact us at:* www.multnomah.net/thestoryjar

Tributes to Our Mothers

Heart to Heart

It was minutes before my college graduation party and time for reflection. Parties had been a regular part of my growing up as far back as I could remember, and always my mother was the planner, the catalyst. She would be so involved in the planning and baking and cleaning that she sometimes wasn't around to see hugs being exchanged or tearful sentiments being expressed. That was all right with her because she showed her love by serving others.

Tonight would be no different.

In the quiet before the storm I wondered about my mother and the memories we shared. As I did, a moment came to mind, the time when I was ten years old and showed her a poem I'd written. Wrought with emotion, the lyrical prose was beyond the imaginations of most children, and my mom studied it curiously, trying to recognize an insect she'd never seen before. "Hmm. I guess I just don't get it."

And for many of my teenage years I didn't think she did.

Instead I learned to appreciate my mother's knack for making our family laugh. There was the time a repairman came to the house to fix something in the backyard. Mom led him through the house, and he stopped short at the patio door, pointing nervously at our Siberian husky.

"Your dog okay?" He looked at my mom, waiting for the word that the dog wouldn't grab his leg the moment he walked outside.

My mom crouched down to the dog's level and stared at him, her face lined with concern. "I think so. He was okay this morning."

Those types of comments, time and again, earned her the reputation of being a "fun blonde," even though her hair couldn't have been darker if she dyed it.

The best example came during a family visit to the Santa Barbara Zoo. We had wandered around all day looking at exhibits and finally came to the giraffe compound. We stopped and looked at the majestic animals eating leaves and moving gracefully about.

Apparently in addition to the giraffes, there was a small duck-like animal that shared the area, but as is so often the case at the zoo, there were none of them to be seen. A sign facing the viewing area gave the scientific name for that creature with the simple headline, "Do they fly? Yes, they do!"

The look on my mother's face was priceless.

She parked herself in front of that sign and studied it, eyebrows lowered in confusion. My siblings and I watched as she looked from the sign—Do they fly? Yes, they do!—to the giraffes grazing nearby. Down at the sign, back up at the giraffes. Finally, she gave a slight shake of her head and said, "Huh. So they *do* fly."

At which point many of us pounced. "Mom! You don't actually think the giraffes—"

Her face grew red. "No, no. Of course not."

To this day I remember the look on her face, and the truth is—for just the slightest moment—she thought giraffes actually flew.

Of course there were other times, moments when we knew

she was probably smarter than the rest of the family combined. Like the time the stove shorted out before dinner and she took it apart and fixed it herself. Or days when her sales at work would be so far beyond that of her fellow employees that the entire family marveled at her talents.

These memories danced across the screen in my mind, and I sat at the old family piano waiting for my graduation party to begin. My fingers moved across the keys and the haunting refrains of "The Way We Were" filled the house as the first guests began to arrive.

Nostalgia gave way to loud greetings and ripples of "Congratulations!" and "I knew you could do it!" I was the eldest of my parents' five children, the first to earn my college diploma. Finally it was time to open gifts, and when everything had been acknowledged, from the back of the house came my mom and my sister, Tricia. "Surprise! Surprise!"

In their hands was a wall-size, framed collage of old photos representing my life and articles I'd written for my high school and university newspapers. There were Girl Scout badges, piano recital programs, and there in the middle of the poster was the poem.

The one I'd shown my mom so many years earlier.

I looked at her, tears in my eyes, and grinned, and she—eyes dry but sparkling—did the same. Though I know the idea might have been Tricia's, whose heart is emotionally driven like my own, the gathering of items, the placement of them, everything tactile about the gift had been from my mother.

Especially the poem.

I studied the gift again and gave my mom a hug I think we'll both remember for a lifetime. Because despite her busy practicality, for all the sentimental moments she missed doing dishes or hanging streamers, despite the times she came off as the one who actually believed a giraffe could fly, there was one thing I would never forget about my mom after that.

She did get it, after all. And deep inside her heart she always had.

KAREN KINGSBURY
MOTHER AND AUTHOR, *WHEN JOY CAME TO STAY*

One Brilliant Show

Flowers.

Mom has always had a passion for flowers. She believed they could brighten any drab room, liven any conversation, and change any dour mood. For twenty years, she took this vision each Sunday to the First Baptist Church. As the flower coordinator, she turned the plain wood altar at the front of the church into a dazzling display of God's creation.

A negligible budget only provoked my resourceful mother's creative mind. Every Saturday we searched the mountain countryside for willows and lilacs and wildflowers. Old dirt roads, creek beds—even abandoned graveyards were sources we would use. The cold winters limited our natural flower gathering, so Mom utilized her dried collections, pulled from boxes stacked high in the garage. Her delightful displays, no matter the season, were often the subject of talk after church—sometimes even more so than the sermons.

During the winter, Mom raised daffodils in pots that lined her kitchen window. Each day she watered, fed, and fertilized—all in preparation for one brilliant show on the church altar. Mom would always pick a spring day when the snow was deep, but the sun brilliant. With tender care she clipped the daffodils from her pots in the window. The shoots were full and ready to burst, their tops still wrapped tight in the leafy envelope.

She put the buds in a simple glass vase full of warm water, then placed it on the altar hours before anyone else arrived. I was perplexed that the buds were still tightly wound, yet mom's beguiling smile told me not to be concerned. As the time drew near, the church members traipsed through flowing gutters and slushy sidewalks and ducked streaming icicles from the roof edge as they entered.

The service began as had a hundred others, with the usual announcements and welcomes to visitors. Imperceptibly at first, then with amazing swiftness the buds began to open. By the time the service was over, the daffodils had exploded into a panoply of color. The miracle of flowers, generated by an eternal God who did not leave us in a drab, cold world, was on full display.

After all these years, I realized Mom treated her children much like those daffodils. There were many times my siblings and I thought we were overly protected, sheltered, and prevented from living normal "fun" lives like all of our friends. What we didn't realize is that she was really preparing us to bloom. Now that we have progressed to adulthood, her long labor of love is finally fulfilled. With dirt on her hands, this blessed woman places her children on the altar, an offering to her Maker.

DAVID RUPERT

NATIONAL CHAPLAIN FOR POSTMASTERS OF THE U.S.

Mom's Garden

The image of my mother's garden
Brings peace into my soul.
But only after I touched each plant
Did I sense my spirit's growth.
Each dawn beyond the cornfields,
A pink hue rises to meet the day.
God lifts the Lily to greet the sunshine,
Baby robins come out to play.
I smile as I watch these wonders,
Knowing there was a time I didn't care.
Now as I pull tomatoes from their vines,
I feel their beauty in a way I never dared.
Purring cats soak up each ray,
Stretching idly while lapping the sun's kiss.
Gently squeezing off a raspberry I think,
When I must go, it's not just Mom that I'll miss.
The day has passed, so I take one last look,
Knowing the sun is due to set.
I realize tomorrow's a brand-new day,
And God is not done with me yet.
Thank you, Mother, for your care,
And the garden you have grown.
Not just on this land you worked
But in this heart of mine that God now owns.

PEGGY M. WHITSON

What if I were asked to choose three items for a time capsule—things that would symbolize my mother's role in my life? What three significant symbols would I choose?

The first thing would be one of her flannel boards. A piece of cardboard covered with navy blue flannel and propped on an easel. That board came to life in our home and in the basement Sunday school rooms. My mother smoothed out a background of a lion's den over the flat flannel and then placed Daniel in jeopardy, facing hungry lions. She would tell of Daniel's faithfulness to serve and trust God no matter what the cost. She'd testify to God's faithful attentiveness to Daniel and to us—those listening to the story.

Mom's songbook comes next. *The Little Hymnal,* a soft cover, bright blue booklet traveled with us in Mom's purse. Rolling down the highway with Dad behind the wheel and her three, eventually four, daughters in the seat behind her, Mom would start the family sing-along. "Leaning on the Everlasting Arms," "Heavenly Sunshine, Heavenly Sunshine…," and "When the Roll Is Called up Yonder."

Mom was singing "The Lord is good, tell it wherever you go" over sudsy dishwater when Dad's captain on the California Highway Patrol rang our doorbell. Dad's patrol motorcycle had gone down with him on it. Four months later he was back on duty in a patrol car.

Twenty-three years later, with a lump of emotions caught in her throat, Mom sang "Turn Your Eyes upon Jesus" over Daddy's deathbed. The words from her songbook and their truth were imprinted on her heart, along with the tradition of singing hymns to pass and mark the time.

The third item? A strand of pearls known in our family as the wedding pearls. William Bert Gansberg, the man who would later become my father, bought the pearls in Adak, Alaska, at a Navy PX and presented them to his fiancée for Christmas in 1952. June 11, 1953, the white pearls shone with promise, adorning her neck as she walked down the aisle to become his bride.

Her granddaughters have begun a tradition of wearing the pearls in their weddings. My daughter, Amy, wore them down the aisle. My niece, Carolyn, will wear them in her upcoming wedding. The years have cast a shadow on the now golden patina pearls. But, like the family they encircle, they remain bound by a common thread.

Of course, there are many more things that could go into that time capsule to symbolize and summarize Mother's role in my life. But these have been instruments—training tools that stretched my sensibilities. Besides, Mom would say (or demonstrate it on her flannel board through the story of Moses and the parting of the Red Sea) that any ordinary thing placed in God's hands becomes extraordinary. Inanimate or human. And she should know.

MONA GANSBERG HODGSON

MOTHER AND AUTHOR

To Our Readers from Our Hearts...

Dear Reader,

Because this book is filled with wonderful stories about mothers, I can go no further without telling you about mine.

My mom stood beside me while I grew up, and she loved me enough to let me make my own mess out of things. She let me bake mud pies on the hot cement in our back driveway. She allowed me to catch pill bugs and carry them around in my purse. She kept boxes in the attic of all the bad poetry I wrote when I was in junior high.

The year I graduated from college, when I began to send out resumes to newspapers all over the Rocky Mountain West, she came into my room and, with sad eyes, asked, "You aren't applying for jobs anywhere nearby, are you?"

I shook my head. "No, Mom. I'm not." I wanted mountains. I wanted new lands, new places.

She hugged me that day, and it was the only time during my leave-taking that she let me see her cry.

When the job offer came for me to assume editorship of a weekly newspaper in Colorado, my mother helped me. It was a mad rush to garage sales for kitchen utensils, a wild search for just the right pots and pans, and a scavenger hunt for the "perfect" shower curtain. We drove across states together, and she helped me—with joy that was not her own, but the Lord's—to seek out my new mountain apartment a thousand miles from home.

Throughout my lifetime, I have watched my mother trust the Lord in beautiful, childlike ways. When she grieves, she is not ashamed to express it. When she rejoices, she is honest about that, too. The lesson that she taught me in childhood, I carry forth as I raise my own children and now, also, as a writer. Her credo: "In our Christian homes, when we put too many rules on what we think God can do, we are pulling God down to a size we can understand. It is only when we begin to trust a Father who is bigger than we can understand or comprehend that we begin to trust at all."

Once we'd driven to Colorado, I rented a downstairs basement apartment, complete with separate kitchen and—what I'd longed for—my own wood-burning stove. The woman upstairs, Mollie Bedford, helped me stock wood for the winter. She found out about a used mattress for sale in someone's barn, and together we went out, tied it to the roof of the car, and carted it home.

That first summer she taught me how to dig wildflowers and aspens in the forest and transplant them—very much the way I had been transplanted—in a garden beside my door. She became my best friend.

Then she introduced me to her son.

Poor shy Jack, who was moving back from a stint in the U.S. Coast Guard to find his old room made into an apartment and some strange girl living there. Mollie and I began inviting him to join us on our picnics and our afternoon "aspen hunting" excursions. Mollie took a picture of Jack and me heading off into the aspens together that day. We were engaged six short weeks later.

Now I have two precious mothers, one who was willing to let me go, and another who was willing to take me in. To the two of them, I owe a depth of gratitude.

Often we must be willing to give up what is good in our lives so we can arrive at the place where the Father waits with His very best.

This brings me to a second story of letting go.

After twelve years and twelve novels for Harlequin Superromance and HarperCollins, God has called me to embark on the same sort of journey yet again. He has called me to let go, to trust Him enough to let Him work a new career for me in Christian fiction. How can I express the joy, the freedom, the discovery that has come into my life as I finally release and turn over my writing, the very joy of my heart, to my heavenly Father?

"The Hair Ribbons" is largely based on a journal kept while we prayed for a Christian sister with cancer. It is the result of a new trust, a new vision that the Father has birthed in my life. So I share it with you. And I pray the Father will birth those precious fruits of Him into your life as well. To live in His presence, to understand His love, that is the definition of joy itself!

In Him all life and peace,

Deborah Bedford, "The Hair Ribbons"

Dear Reader:

Novelists are the world's best eavesdroppers, spies, and busy-bodies. Everything we hear, everything we see, everything we read, everything in life is grist for our imaginations, and much of it ends up in our books in one form or another. But some stories are a bit closer to a writer than most.

So it is with "Heart Rings."

Motherhood comes with no guarantees. But like centuries of women who have gone before, I plunged into the experience with joy. God blessed me with two beautiful daughters, Michaelyn and Jennifer. Over the years we've laughed together and cried together. We've fought and we've made up. And always we've been held close with bonds of love, even in the most difficult of times.

While Leah's and my stories are not identical, I understand the broken heart of this character. I understand because when Jennifer was sixteen, she ran away from home. Nose ring, tattoos, and blue hair followed. The pain went deep, and the lessons came hard, but God is good. He kept her safe and restored my precious child to me.

When I first got the idea for "Heart Rings," I called Jennifer, now a wife and mother herself, and I asked for permission to use our story for inspiration. But I didn't want to hurt her feelings in any way, so I left the final say to her. Her answer: "Sure, Mom. Hey, I'm a writer, too. I know you'll take creative license."

She was right, of course. I did take plenty of creative license, but the essence of what I learned from our journey as mother and daughter is what I most wanted to share in "Heart Rings." God taught me to look at the heart of my daughter, to see the inside of the cup, and to rejoice at what I see there.

I thank God for the blessing of my daughters, for entrusting them to me to raise. I thank Him for the privilege of being able to watch them grow into beautiful young women, for the joy of seeing them become mothers themselves. I thank Him for His patience as He taught me what's important and what isn't in my relationships with others and especially with my children. Most of all, I thank Him for drawing me into a deeper relationship with Him.

May you, dear reader, always see the inside of the cup.

In His grip,

Robin Lee Hatcher

www.robinleehatcher.com

PO Box 4722

Boise, ID 83711-4722

Dear Reader:

I set out to tell the story of a couple who adopt a child. By the time I'd finished, I realized I'd written a (thinly!) disguised account of my own family's journey. My wonderful husband and I are the parents of two children, a daughter and a son, adopted from South Korea.

Despite our family's unique beginning, we have grown and struggled and rejoiced like most families. As I write this, my children are sixteen and seventeen, so we've come a long way from those days when I wondered if I would ever be able to hold a baby in my arms.

But God has been faithful. He gave me a promise ("But when the desire cometh, it is a tree of life"), and He continues to be faithful in its fulfillment. My trees of life are growing beautifully and putting their mother and father through all the usual trials and tests of adolescence....

My prayer is that He will lead you in the perfect path He has planned for your family.

Always,

Angie Hunt, "The Yellow Sock"

How to Create Your Own Story Jar

After reading these tales of God's power and provision, and the accounts of real-life mothers and how they've blessed their children, you might be wondering how to go about creating your own story jars. It would actually be quite simple to do, whether individually, as a group of friends and neighbors, or as a church.

Scripture encourages us to remember all God has done for us, and there is no place more important to remember His provision and power than in the lives of our children. While we may not write the tales of God's goodness on our doorposts, we all have those special items, mementoes of places we've been, events we've experienced, miracles we've received from our loving Father.

You don't have to be a writer to enjoy a story jar. It can be a family's way of preserving memories. Consider having a family get-together where everybody brings an item to go into the jar, and as it drops in, they tell what it means to them, what it symbolizes. We can learn something new about our loved ones when we hear their memories in their own words.

A story jar can also be a tool for remembering all the wonderful things God has done in our lives. Mrs. Halley, the pastor's wife from our stories, was right. Not all of God's miracles are in the Bible. He is still performing them today in countless ways, changing lives, healing hearts.

Maybe you have your own ideas for creating a story jar. If so, we hope you'll share the ideas with others. And if you would like to write to Deborah, Angela, or Robin, please feel free to do so in care of Multnomah Publishers.

God bless you.

Deborah Bedford

Robin Lee Hatcher

Angela Elwell Hunt